MURDER MOST WITCHY
A WICKED WITCHES OF THE MIDWEST MYSTERY
BOOK 10

AMANDA M. LEE

WINCHESTERSHAW PUBLICATIONS

Copyright © 2017 by Amanda M. Lee

All rights reserved.

No part of this book may be reproduced in any form or by any electronic or mechanical means, including information storage and retrieval systems, without written permission from the author, except for the use of brief quotations in a book review.

❦ Created with Vellum

PROLOGUE

LATE SEPTEMBER

"I need to borrow a shovel."

Aunt Tillie, her face blank, didn't offer a greeting when I opened the guesthouse door and stared at her. In truth, I didn't expect her. My boyfriend Landon Michaels was due to arrive any second and I looked forward to spending a quiet night alone with him. I cooked and everything.

Okay, I ordered a pizza and baked cookies that originated from a cardboard tube from the grocery store, but that's the same as cooking. Either way, I knew Landon wouldn't complain. We rarely get to spend the night completely alone, an entire evening when we enjoy each other and don't worry about my family causing a scene or demanding time. He would've eaten cold cereal without complaint if it came down to it.

I knit my eyebrows and locked gazes with my great-aunt. "Why do you need a shovel? You didn't kill anyone, did you?"

Don't laugh. It's a fair question. My great-aunt may be elderly – although she claims she's only middle-aged – but she's responsible for a dead body or two. Sure, as far as I know those deaths have been in the name of self-defense (kind of), but I learned a long time ago not to rule anything out when dealing with the Winchester witches.

Oh, that's right. I'm a witch. My name is Bay Winchester and I come from a long line of witches who find more joy in causing toil and trouble than love and laughter. What can I say? Sometimes being naughty is more fun than being nice. That doesn't mean we're bad. It simply means we're prone to drama and hijinks.

"Do I get involved in your personal business?" Aunt Tillie asked, screwing her face into a dark expression. "I need a shovel. I don't need conversation about the shovel."

Instead of kowtowing to her demands, I crossed my arms over my chest and stared her down. "Why do you need a shovel? If you're going to dispose of a body I think you should find a river or lake instead. You need to dig deep if you don't want a body to be discovered, and that takes a lot more work than most people realize."

"Oh, well, that's what I like to hear my girlfriend talking about when I arrive for a weekend visit." Landon Michaels, his long hair brushing the tops of his shoulders, planted a kiss on my mouth as he edged around Aunt Tillie and into the guesthouse.

The guesthouse is essentially a small ranch house on the family property, within walking distance of the inn my mother and aunts run, but still far enough away that my cousin Thistle and I – we live in the guesthouse together – can pretend we have privacy. We don't, really, but it's always nice to live in a land of make believe when you're surrounded by busybodies.

"You're here." I couldn't help but be relieved as I watched Landon drop his duffel bag on the living room floor. "I was starting to worry."

Landon arched an eyebrow, amused. "You were starting to worry?" He shifted his eyes over his shoulder and focused on Aunt Tillie. "Why? What did she do?"

Aunt Tillie rolled her eyes, making a face only a family member could love – and from my perspective, she was pushing it. "What did I do? Why do you think I did anything? I'm an angel."

Landon remained unconvinced as the sky, visible through the open door, lit up with a bright flash of lightning. "The storm is almost here ... and it's going to be a big one."

"That's why I was worried."

Landon pursed his lips as he leaned closer and kissed the end of my nose. "I wouldn't have missed our weekend together for anything. You know that. Try not to get yourself worked up about things that will never happen."

"Like a sharknado?" I teased, grinning.

"Exactly."

"A sharknado is totally possible," Aunt Tillie countered, planting her hand in the middle of Landon's chest to stop him from getting too comfortable with me in her presence. "Before you two start smooching it up, I came here for a reason, and I'm not leaving until I have my shovel."

As an FBI agent, Landon is sworn to uphold the law, and he takes his job seriously. He barely batted an eyelash when Aunt Tillie demanded a shovel. He didn't outright dismiss the request either. "Why do you need a shovel?"

"Do I get involved in your private business?" Aunt Tillie challenged.

"Every single day I'm here."

"You're such an exaggerator," Aunt Tillie muttered, shaking her head. "I never get involved in your business. I'm the queen of minding my own business, in fact. You could learn a thing or two from me when it comes to staying out of other people's business."

Landon's reaction was blasé. "Okay, here's the situation," he said, pinning my great-aunt with an "I'm tired, but I can't let you bury a body without at least pretending to care" look. "Bay wants a private night with just the two of us. Thistle is spending the night with Marcus, and, from the looks of it, she's already gone. I like the sound of a private night, too, if I'm being truthful.

"You don't care about our private night, and the fact that you're down here looking for a shovel could be construed as a bad omen," he continued. "You tend to find mischief at the oddest of times."

"I'm pretty sure that was an insult." Aunt Tillie narrowed her eyes as she puffed out her chest. "I am a model citizen. I've never been arrested. I don't appreciate your tone."

"I arrested you myself a few weeks ago," Landon reminded her. He left out the part where he hated doing it and how it resulted in a sour stomach, but that didn't seem to be important given the circumstances, so I kept my lips zipped and opted to watch the show.

"Oh, right." Aunt Tillie tapped her bottom lip as she regarded him. They had a tempestuous relationship at best, but she respected him, which was something she would never admit unless desperate circumstances forced her hand. "I forgot about that. You're kind of a jerk, huh?"

Instead of being offended, Landon merely arched an eyebrow and smirked. He was used to Aunt Tillie's theatrics and sneaky behavior. He refused to be sidetracked. "Why do you want a shovel?"

"I'm going to garden." Aunt Tillie answered automatically, as if Landon asked a stupid question and she provided the only believable answer.

"Uh-huh." Landon shifted his eyes to me, unconvinced. "A storm is heading this way."

"So? I'm no wimp. I can garden in a storm. That's how we did it back in the day."

"Ah, the good old days." Landon's lips curved as he slipped an arm around my shoulders and tugged me closer. I got the feeling he was buying time as he decided how to respond. A responsible person would be worried about Aunt Tillie taking off in the middle of a storm with a shovel. The odds of her actually burying a body were fairly slim, so it ultimately came down to how much you wanted to know about her extracurricular activities. "Have you killed anyone?"

Aunt Tillie was understandably affronted by the question. "Not today ... but the day isn't over, and you're quickly worming your way to the top of my list."

Landon ignored the threat. "Are you going to kill anyone?"

"Probably not."

"Are you going to do anything illegal?"

Aunt Tillie didn't answer that question quite as quickly, instead shifting from one foot to the other. "Define illegal."

"Ugh." Landon made a disgusted sound in the back of his throat. "You give me heartburn. You know that, right?"

"I could make something else burn and really ruin your weekend if you're not careful," Aunt Tillie countered suggestively.

Landon shot me a worried look and I knew before he opened his mouth that Aunt Tillie had already won. "She can't do that, can she?"

I held my hands palms up and shrugged. "She can make me smell like bacon, which you consider a reward, so I guess she's given the idea of punishing you some thought as well," I pointed out. "That's the way she rolls."

"You're not wrong." Landon's eyes were thoughtful as he shifted them to Aunt Tillie. "Do you at least promise not to get caught?"

That was a new one. He usually made her lie, somehow preferring that she pretend she wasn't about to do something terrible so he had plausible deniability should things make the local news or come under the attention of regional law enforcement officials.

"I promise not to get caught." Aunt Tillie's smile was something right out of a horror movie. She clearly was going to do something terrible. "Does that mean I can borrow a shovel?"

"Last time I saw it, it was behind the guesthouse," Landon replied, quickly losing interest in the conversation as he shifted toward the couch. "It's probably still there."

Aunt Tillie looked at me for confirmation and I nodded. "Okay. That's good. Enjoy your night." She practically skipped out the front door, causing me to frown as I watched her go.

"Aren't you worried?" I asked, turning my head to Landon. "She's going out into a thunderstorm with no coat and a shovel. She doesn't even have her whistle in case she falls and breaks a hip. Doesn't that worry you?"

Landon shrugged. "I've decided to choose my battles today."

That sounded ominous. I shut the front door and shuffled in his direction, my eyes keen as I searched his face. "Why today?"

"What?" Landon seemed distracted, as if he was only half present. "What are you talking about?"

"What are you talking about?" I challenged, moving in front of him. My trouble detector was pinging in all directions and I hated the feeling settling in the pit of my stomach. "I ... is something wrong?"

Landon heaved out a sigh – which did nothing to dissuade my worry – and held out his hand. "Come here."

"No." The word was out of my mouth before I could think better about uttering it. Landon's eyebrows flew up his forehead as he locked gazes with me.

"No?"

"You're about to tell me something terrible. I know it."

"It's not terrible," Landon corrected, keeping his hand in the air and waiting for me to close the distance between us. "Bay, I have something to tell you. I was hoping to save it for the end of the weekend because I didn't want to ruin things, but that doesn't look to be an option."

My heart twisted at his downtrodden expression. "You're breaking up with me, aren't you?"

The muted weariness plaguing his features moments before shifted, a flash of anger causing me to jolt before Landon turned grim. "No, and I'm sick of you worrying about things like that." Landon's tone was cold as he dropped his hand to his knee. "Do you really think I'd come for the weekend, spend all of my time romancing you, and then dump you on my way out of town?"

Well, when he put it like that … . "No," I hedged. "It's just … you look serious."

"I am serious, but what I'm about to tell you is not the end of the world," Landon explained. "Will you please sit next to me?"

I remained dubious, but did as he asked, keeping my shoulders squared as I awkwardly rested my hands on my knees and stared straight forward.

"Oh, well, that looks comfortable," Landon muttered, shaking his head. "Bay, this won't ruin our lives. It's merely inconvenient."

I might believe that once he got the words out of his mouth. "So … what is it?"

"I got a new assignment."

My heart dropped to my stomach as the words washed over me. "Oh. You were transferred, weren't you?"

Landon shook his head and inhaled deeply – as if courting

patience – as my resignation smacked him in the face. "Bay ... ."

"You're moving." I pressed the heel of my hand to my forehead, distressed. "How soon?"

"Bay ... ."

I ignored his plaintive tone. "You're about to say that we can do the long-distance thing and somehow make it work, aren't you? We both know that's too hard over the long haul."

Landon opened his mouth to say something, words that I'm sure he thought would make me feel better, but I didn't give him the chance.

"When does your transfer go into effect?" I slid away from him a bit, keeping distance between our thighs. I feared I would burst into tears if I touched him ... and if I started crying, there was a possibility I'd never stop. "Maybe ... um ... maybe I can find a job wherever you move. Of course, you didn't invite me to go, so I guess I'm getting ahead of myself there."

Landon was quiet for a long time. When I finally found the courage to shift my eyes to him I saw anger reflected in the cool depths of his eyes.

"You don't want me to come." The realization hit me like a like a baseball bat to the face.

"You and I are going to have a big fight about this before the night is out, but I refuse to let you sit there and suffer," Landon said, choosing his words carefully. "I have not been transferred. I am not moving. I've simply been given an undercover assignment that could mean I will be away for a week or two."

"Oh." I let loose with a shaky sigh as relief washed over me. "Oh ... I ... oh. That's nowhere near as bad as I was expecting."

"Yes, well, you always jump to the absolute worst conclusion," Landon muttered, dragging a hand through his hair as frustration bubbled to the surface. "Bay, how could you possibly think that I would pick up and move without talking to you?"

"I ... ." Crap. He was going to turn this into a thing. I never think before I speak. It's a family trait, not one of the best Winchester offerings. "You looked upset," I noted.

"I am upset," Landon confirmed, scratching his cheek as he regarded me. "I'm not happy about being separated from you for a few weeks."

"Where will you be?" I hoped changing the subject would give him time to ease up on the anger.

"I can't tell you that," Landon replied, his voice soft. "It's against the rules. I won't be far if there's an emergency, though. I'll be able to call when I can … although it won't be as often as either of us would like."

"That's okay." I decided to be brave instead of whiny. After my earlier performance I figured he'd earned it. "I'm sorry I thought … ."

"Yeah, we're not done talking about that." Landon breathed heavily through his nose and then opened his arms, tugging me on top of him as he leaned back on the couch. "Bay, I have no intention of ever moving away from you. I can't believe you'd think that."

"I just … it's your job. They can transfer you without notice. You told me that."

"Yes, but I have a say if I want to move. I'd quit my job before leaving you."

"You would?" The admission made me feel better.

"I would," Landon confirmed, pushing my hair from my face. "I love you … although I'm not sure why when you doubt me like this."

"I didn't mean to doubt you," I argued. "I just … ."

"Love me," Landon finished, his expression softening. "Sweetie, I know you love me." He tightened his arms around my back and pressed a kiss to my forehead as I shifted to get comfortable. "I don't know if I should be agitated because you thought I'd leave you or flattered that you almost fell apart at the thought of losing me."

"I think you should be flattered."

"Because that means you won't be in trouble?"

"Yes … and I'm guessing this is going to be our last weekend together for a bit." I pressed my lips together, reality setting in. "You don't want to ruin our last weekend together, do you?"

"That right there is low and dirty." Landon wagged his finger in my face. "You're manipulating me."

"Is it working?"

Landon cracked a grin as he shook his head. "It's going to work because I refuse to fight with you. I'm not in a very good mood, in case you haven't noticed."

We'd first met when he was undercover. I always knew there was a possibility he'd have to disappear for another case, but this one seemed to have come out of nowhere and I couldn't help being thrown for a loop. "Because you'll miss me?"

Landon's expression softened. "I will miss you."

"I'll miss you, too."

"I know." Landon rubbed the back of my neck as he shifted lower, making sure my mouth was only inches from his as he stared into my eyes. "The good news is that by doing this job I should be able to surprise you with something really fun in a few weeks."

I brightened considerably. "What?"

"I can't tell you that either, because it's not set in stone yet," Landon replied. "Suffice it to say, though, I think you're going to be happy."

"I'm happy regardless where you're concerned."

"Except when you think I'm going to be transferred and leave you behind after nothing more than a weekend's notice."

I pursed my lips, rueful. "I said I was sorry."

"Only vaguely, and you didn't put a lot of effort into it." Landon stroked the back of my head. "Bay, I'll never leave you. I promise you that."

"I ... technically you're leaving now," I pointed out, my cheeks flushing. "You're leaving me to fend for myself. What happens if someone hits on me and you're not here to defend my honor?"

"Very cute." Landon shook his head, resigned to letting me off the hook. "Keep track of whoever hits on you and I'll pound them when I get back. Also, I'm not leaving you. If you need me, call my boss. I'll find a way to get in touch with you."

"I'm guessing that's only for emergencies, right? What if I simply can't sleep without you?"

"Then we're both going to be tired. I already know this is going to suck. You don't need to make it worse."

"I'll miss you." The words hurt coming out and I pressed my face to Landon's chest so he wouldn't see the threatening tears. Torturing him didn't seem fair. He had a job to do. I was an adult, for crying out loud. I lived the majority of my life without him, coming to rely on his presence only in the past year. This shouldn't be so devastating.

"I'll miss you, too." Landon tightened his arms around me. "I'll figure a way to contact you when I can. If we're lucky, this job shouldn't take too long. A week at the most."

He sounded upbeat at the prospect, but I could practically smell the lie. "What's the worst-case scenario?"

"I'll never visit again."

I jerked my head up and found Landon grinning. "That's not funny."

"After your dramatic meltdown I thought it was a little funny," Landon argued. "As for the question ... I don't know, sweetie. I'm hoping it won't be too long, but it could last a few weeks."

"Well, then we'll simply have to deal with it." I wrapped my arms around his neck and hugged him as tightly as possible, mentally binding myself to him. "I guess it's good that we have the weekend to get our fill of each other, huh?"

"Bay, I'll never get my fill of you." Landon returned the hug. "You will need to spoil me rotten before I go, though."

I mustered a rueful smile. "You're going to milk this, aren't you?"

"Oh, sweetie, you have no idea. Give me a kiss so we can get this show on the road. I've made a list of things I want to do this weekend, and each and every one starts with a kiss."

"Even gorging on bacon?"

"Funnily enough, bacon and kisses play heavily into my plans." Landon grinned as he smacked his lips against mine. "We're going to have a busy weekend, sweetie. You'd better prepare yourself for a whole lot of action."

Oh, well. I'd heard worse suggestions in my life. In the grand scheme of things, an undercover assignment was much easier to grapple with than my imagination.

I mean ... how hard could it be?

ONE

THREE WEEKS LATER

"My life sucks."

I stared at the small platter of bacon in the center of the dining room table and sighed. If Landon were around, the platter would be twice as big and his fingers would be greasy from shoveling slices into his mouth with both hands.

"Oh, here we go." My cousin Thistle, her hair a bright shade of orange in honor of the upcoming Halloween holiday, rolled her eyes. "Can't you choke yourself with that bacon so we don't have to listen to you whine any longer?"

I narrowed my eyes, anger coursing through me as I pinned Thistle with a dark gaze. "Was I talking to you?"

Thistle made a big show of glancing around the table. It was devoid of guests because it was a Monday. Last week's guests checked out the previous afternoon and this week's guests would arrive in dribs and drabs as the weekend approached. "If you weren't talking to me, who were you talking to?"

I answered automatically. "I was talking to my mother."

Mom merely rolled her eyes over the rim of her mug as she sipped her coffee. "I can see where I would be your best option given the fact that I have to love you because you share my genes, but I'm sick of your whining, too."

I opened my mouth to protest, but Mom cut me off with a firm headshake.

"Bay, we all understand that you miss Landon," Mom offered, adopting her best "I gave birth to you, so shut your mouth until I'm done talking" tone. "I happen to miss him, too. I didn't realize how much I would miss him until you started whining three weeks ago – and never stopped – but we all have to adjust to the real world and be adults from time to time."

"I don't." Aunt Tillie grinned from her spot at the head of the table and grabbed two slices of bacon, as if she knew it was a dagger to the heart because Landon wasn't around to complain. "I've decided that the real world is highly overrated," she said, dropping the bacon on her plate.

Mom scowled as she shook her head. "You're not helping."

"I didn't realize that's what we were supposed to be doing." Aunt Tillie flashed an innocent look. "I can do that, too." She turned to me, her face impassive. "Stop whining. You're embarrassing us. And it's completely annoying to listen to you carry on."

My mouth dropped open as Thistle snorted.

"I never thought I'd agree with Aunt Tillie – and that should tell you exactly how low you've fallen – but you're a big baby, and she's right," Thistle announced. "It's time to suck it up and shut your hole. Landon will be back when he's back."

I ran my tongue over my teeth, frustrated. In truth, I knew Thistle was right and that's what hurt worse than the insults. The Winchesters enjoy insulting one another. It's something of a pastime for all of us because we're not a very serious family ... unless the world might end due to magic or a pesky poltergeist. But in general we're gregarious and prone to humor rather than melancholy. Still, I couldn't wrap my head around the lack of sympathy.

"I need to find a new family," I announced, crossing my arms over my chest as I pushed back my chair. "I'm going through a terrible time. You'd think someone – perhaps my own mother – would feel bad for me."

"I do feel bad for you," Mom offered, her expression unreadable. "You're clearly miserable without Landon. I sympathize."

"We're miserable without Landon, too," Aunt Marnie offered, her dark head bobbing as she agreed with Mom. "We never realized how insufferable you were until he wasn't around to soak up all of your time."

"You're my least favorite aunt," I muttered.

"If that means you're going to start whining to me, then I want to claim that title," my aunt Twila interjected, shaking her head of bright red hair. "I can't listen to the woes of life without Landon for one more second. It's like a story to slit my wrists by."

I pressed the heel of my hand to my forehead, frustrated. "Fine! I won't mention Landon to you people ever again. Are you happy?"

"I am." Aunt Tillie beamed, crunching on a strip of bacon. "You know how I hate it when you bring up 'The Man' in the first place. Now at least we can get on with our lives. We can forget this sordid year and find a different boyfriend for you to obsess about. How do you feel about dating a farmer? I'd love access to fresh tomatoes."

I scalded Aunt Tillie with a dark look. "Landon is on a case. He's not dead."

"Don't ruin my fun," Aunt Tillie warned, wagging a finger. "Personally, I don't miss him at all. It seems all he was good for was eating half a pig every morning and shutting your mouth by placing his on top of it. I can find someone else to do both."

I slapped the table as I struggled to my feet. "I need a new family, not a new boyfriend."

"You need to get over yourself," Aunt Tillie shot back. "We're all sick of your grousing and griping."

I glanced at Mom, expecting her to admonish Aunt Tillie. When she didn't, I merely shook my head. "I'm going to run away from home. I hope you're all happy."

"If it means we don't have to listen to how much your life sucks, then I'm all for it," Mom countered. "Perhaps you should consider renting a room from your father. This might be a good time for the two of you to bond."

She must be getting desperate if she was seriously suggesting I spend time with my father. She didn't have a high opinion of the man – even though she married and procreated with him. Ever since he returned to Hemlock Cove and opened a competing inn with my uncles she'd been surprisingly quiet on the subject of my father.

"I might just do that," I warned, reaching into my pocket when my phone rang. "You'll miss me when I'm gone."

"I might need proof to back up that statement," Mom shot back.

I ignored her, furrowing my brow as I stared at the phone screen. I didn't recognize the number. Odds were it was a telemarketer, but it could be Landon. I hadn't heard from him in more than a week and I was starting to get antsy.

"Hello."

"Hi, sweetie."

My heart rolled when I heard his voice and I quickly moved out of the dining room, heading toward The Overlook's library so I could have some privacy. "Landon?"

Landon's chuckle was deep and throaty, and my stomach twisted as several emotions I couldn't quite name washed over me. "Did you forget the sound of my voice already?"

I swallowed hard to maintain my calm. "I ... no. How are you?"

Even though he couldn't see my face Landon recognized the hitch in my voice and knew I was close to tears. "Bay, don't cry. I'm sorry I haven't been in touch."

"I'm not going to cry." It was a lie. I was definitely going to cry. I had no idea why his absence affected me this way. I could only hope to stave off the tears until the end of the call. "How are you?"

"I'm fine, sweetie. I only have a few minutes, but I needed to hear your voice." Landon sounded pained. "How are you?"

"I'm at the inn. Everyone is sick of me. They want me to move into the Dragonfly because I'm whiny."

"Why are you whiny?"

"I ... ." I broke off, unsure how to answer. Guilting him about his absence seemed the wrong way to go. "I'm just crabby. It's fine. It will pass. How are you? Are you almost done?"

"I'm getting closer, but I don't know when this will be over," Landon admitted, causing my momentary flash of hope to fade.

"Oh, well, it's not your fault. I'm sure you're doing the best you can."

"Yes, well, that sounded convincing," Landon said dryly. "I'm going to try to figure out a way to see you, although I'm not sure when I'll be able to swing it. Even if it's just for an hour ... ."

My interest piqued. "Are you that close?"

"I'm close, sweetie, but I can't risk seeing you in case someone recognizes me," Landon replied. "I was hoping to be able to figure out a way to sneak to the guesthouse. I'm sorry."

"It's not your fault." I said the words automatically. "You're safe, right?" Some things were more important than the fact that I missed him. His safety was my top priority.

Landon seemed amused by the question. "I'm fine, Bay. I'm worried about you."

"Me?" That was fairly hilarious given the fact that I lived in Hemlock Cove. The town had only one stoplight, for crying out loud. "I'm fine. I've been working ... and apparently complaining to the point that no one wants to spend time with me."

"I desperately want to spend time with you," Landon supplied. "I miss you."

The tears were back, thickening my voice as I fought to maintain control. "I miss you, too."

"Oh, please don't cry." Landon sounded as if he was on the verge of tears, too. "I have to go in a few minutes. I have someplace to be, but I cannot hang up if you're crying."

I fought to regain control of my emotions. "I'm okay. I'm just ... tired."

"Haven't you been sleeping?"

That was a loaded question. Admitting I couldn't sleep without him beside me seemed immature and codependent rather than romantic and cute. "I'm fine."

"I can't sleep without you either," Landon said, instantly making me feel better. I could practically see his lips curling, and it lightened the load. "It's been almost exactly a year since we met."

"I know."

"We'll celebrate as soon as this case is done."

"Okay." I wanted to ask when that would be, but putting additional pressure on him didn't seem wise. "You're not in danger, right?"

"Bay, I'm fine." Landon cleared his throat. "I never seem to find danger unless I'm with you."

"That's true." The statement cheered me, though only marginally.

"You're not getting in any trouble, are you?" Landon's tone shifted from amused to serious. "I worry because I'm not there to keep you out of trouble."

I was fairly certain I should've been insulted, but I was so relieved to hear his voice. "What kind of trouble would I get in? I've mostly been working, and then I go home and read at night. Thistle spends all of her time with Marcus – they're moving in together as soon as his renovations are done at the stable. They're making plans with this cool interior design program she found for her laptop. I've been on my own. I can't get in trouble on my own."

"You've been alone?"

"I've been reading."

"Bay, I don't like the idea of you sitting around on your own," Landon grumbled. "I don't want you to be lonely."

"I'm a Winchester. We're always up in each other's business," I pointed out. "I can't possibly be lonely." That was an outright lie. I felt Landon's absence like a hole in the heart, and the reason I couldn't stop complaining was because of that simple fact. I tried to look at the bright side. "It's only for a little longer, right?"

"Bay, I'll get home to you as soon as I can," Landon promised. "I … miss you so much."

"I miss you, too." My voice was small as I fought tears yet again. "You need to stay safe. That's the most important thing."

"That's exactly how I feel about you." Landon was quiet for a beat. I could hear muffled voices behind him. When he spoke again he sounded resigned. "I have to go."

"Okay. Well … ."

"I love you, Bay." Landon's voice was rocky, almost strangled. "I will find a way to see you as soon as possible. I promise."

"Just finish your case." I didn't have the heart to tell him that a stolen hour would only make things worse if we had to say goodbye again. "I love you, too."

"Be good, sweetie."

I was reluctant to end the call, but I knew Landon hated being the first to disconnect. "I will. You, too. I … ." My voice broke.

"I love you so much. I'm sorry about all of this. I promise to make it up to you."

Landon's voice was stronger, so I forced myself to match his tone. "I'll have bacon waiting when you come back."

"I don't care about the bacon. I only want you."

"Oh, well, things must be dire."

Landon mustered a ragged laugh. "I'll call as soon as I can."

"I know. I love you."

"I love you, too."

I stared at the phone for what felt like forever. When I lifted my head I found Aunt Tillie standing in the open doorway.

"If you're going to give me grief, I don't want to hear it," I muttered, swiping at a tear on my cheek. "I know I'm being pathetic. I recognize it and would laugh and point if someone else in this family behaved in this manner."

Aunt Tillie scratched the side of her nose, her expression unreadable. "You're definitely a whiner."

"Thank you so much for your support."

"I don't know what you want me to say," Aunt Tillie admitted. "The boy has a job to do. You knew that when you took him on. He's doing the best that he can."

"I'm well aware of that."

"It doesn't help him to know that you're sitting around here pining for him," Aunt Tillie pointed out. "If he's worried about you he can't possibly focus on his job. He's probably in a dangerous situation, and you're only exacerbating things because you're such a crybaby."

I pressed the tip of my tongue to the back of my teeth as I fought to maintain my cool. I wanted to explode, tell her she was a terrible woman who gets off on making others miserable. But I knew she was right. Landon was in the middle of a serious situation, and I didn't want to make it worse.

"I don't mean to be a crybaby. I can't seem to help myself."

"That's because you and Landon are co-dependent." Aunt Tillie was blasé as she glanced at her fingernails. "He'll be back as soon as he can. You don't doubt that, do you?"

"No." I answered automatically. Even when at my worst I knew he loved me, wanted to be with me. He would show up as soon as possible. "He loves me. He's working as quickly as he can."

"Then perhaps you shouldn't push him to the point where he might make a mistake," Aunt Tillie suggested. "You need to keep it together. You're the even-tempered one in this family – which is saying absolutely nothing, because we're all crazy on some level – but we don't work well as a whole when you're off balance."

That was almost a compliment. I couldn't help but smirk when I met her gaze. "Thanks ... I think."

"You need to find something to distract you," Aunt Tillie said. "That's why you're spending the day with me."

All of the goodwill I'd been building up over the past few minutes died a quick death. "That sounds like a terrible idea."

Aunt Tillie puffed out her chest, insulted. "You don't even know where we're going."

"I'm pretty sure it doesn't matter."

Aunt Tillie ignored my tone. "I think it will be good for you. We'll spend the day together and you'll feel better about 'The Man' and his dangerous undercover assignment when we're done."

I had my doubts. "Am I being punished for whining?"

Aunt Tillie chuckled, amused. "You're a funny girl. We'll have a good time."

I was understandably dubious. "And where are we going?"

Aunt Tillie didn't immediately answer, instead drifting through the doorway and back toward the dining room. "You need to change your clothes if we're going out in public. I don't want to be embarrassed."

That was rich coming from a woman who wears combat boots and carries a whistle regularly. "Where are we going?"

"Don't worry about it. We'll have fun. Trust me."

TWO

I promised myself I would be a good sport for whatever Aunt Tillie had planned – as long as it wasn't illegal. My resolve lasted exactly thirty seconds before I realized where we were.

"Oh, man!"

Aunt Tillie pursed her lips but refrained from rolling her eyes as she stared at the bustling corn maze. "I think it's cool."

"The last corn maze we visited had a dead body in it," I reminded her, my mind traveling back to the previous year. That's how Landon and I had met. He'd been undercover with a biker gang trafficking in meth and other sundry activities. I'd been covering the opening of a new corn maze and discovered a body. Even though he was supposed to be undercover and talked a big game, I knew there was something different about Landon right from the start. "I've sworn off corn mazes."

"No one is asking you to write a story about this one." Aunt Tillie searched inside her large purse, her lips moving as she said something to herself that I had no interest in hearing. "Besides, this isn't just a corn maze. Look around."

I did as instructed, fiddling with the zipper on my hoodie as I scanned the large parcel of land. The farm – Barnaby Mill – was located between Hemlock Cove and Traverse City. It was just off the main highway, and the billboard touted fresh produce, fine antiques, naked furniture and the corn maze to end all corn mazes. Given the size of the crowd, the advertising offensive appeared to be working. "So … what? Are we here for fresh vegetables or something?"

"No, whinebox, we're here because I have my eye on a new plow and I'm supposed to meet the owner of the property so I can see his," Aunt Tillie replied. "This is a business trip. I thought it might do you some good to get out of Hemlock Cove, since all you do is sigh and moan because everything reminds you of Landon. You fancy yourself some tragic romantic heroine. All I hear is that you think you see him on every corner, which means you're probably crazy, not romantic."

I didn't bother to hide my scowl. "I hardly think I'm that bad."

"Put yourself in my place and then imagine I whined as much as you have over the past three weeks. Then say that again with a straight face."

I did my best to do just that, and when I did I realized she had a point – which was almost painful. "I don't mean to be such a whiner," I offered. "It's just … I miss him."

"I know you miss him." Aunt Tillie adopted a pragmatic tone. "I get it. You love him. He loves you. Everything is all bacon and roses when you're together. He's got a job to do, though. You knew that going in."

"I hate it when you're right," I muttered.

Aunt Tillie snickered as she patted my arm. "Probably as much as I hate it when you're right. While I hate to take the side of 'The Man,' in this case I think you're being unreasonable."

"I thought you hated taking the side of any man."

"You're not wrong." Aunt Tillie scanned the busy crowd. "Will you look at this place? I've never seen so many people at a corn maze."

I followed her gaze, my stomach unsettled, although I had no idea why. "I don't think anyone is all that interested in the maze," I pointed out after a beat. "No one is even going into the maze or wandering in that direction. I think the barn with the furniture and the farmer's market on the other side of the parking lot appear to be the big draws."

Aunt Tillie knit her eyebrows as she stared in the direction of the maze. "That's probably because there are hoodlums hanging out by the maze opening. Look at those ruffians. Someone needs to put a boot in their behinds."

I struggled to maintain a sense of calm as I stared at the individuals in question. They were dressed in denim and leather, motorcycles parked nearby in the adjacent parking lot. "I know you don't want to hear it, but this reminds me of when I first met Landon."

Aunt Tillie arched an annoyed eyebrow. "If you start crying I'll punch you."

"Most great-aunts would say nice things, like 'if you start crying I'll give you a hug,'" I pointed out. "If you were a good great-aunt you would buy me a cup of tea and a doughnut."

"If I were a good great-aunt I wouldn't be me."

"This is true."

"Besides, Landon was only pretending to be a ruffian," Aunt Tillie pointed out. "He wasn't a very good actor, either. You could tell he was a better man than the people he surrounded himself with. I watched him when he thought no one was looking – including you – and all he cared about was keeping you safe."

I'd almost forgotten the fact that Aunt Tillie was there when Landon and I met for the first time. She was doing something in the nearby barn she didn't want anyone to find out about. I didn't catch sight of her that day, only finding out about her presence when I inadvertently became trapped in her memories with Landon a few months ago.

"He didn't know me then," I reminded her. "He didn't care about keeping me safe. He cared that no one messed up his case."

"I don't know if you're telling yourself that because it will make you miss him less or if you actually believe it, but you're an idiot sometimes." Aunt Tillie gestured toward the barn. "Come on. The plow is supposed to be in there."

I followed her, irritation bubbling up. "You make it sound as if you believe Landon and I were destined to be together."

"I do believe that." Aunt Tillie was matter-of-fact. "You can't tell me you don't believe in fate."

I pursed my lips as I trailed behind her. She wasn't even five feet tall – a half-inch holding her back – but she packed a lot of attitude in such a diminutive frame. "I don't know that I've given it a lot of thought," I hedged. "Do you believe there's one person for everyone?"

Aunt Tillie shrugged. "I think that's too simplistic. I think it's more apt to say that you always find the person you're meant to find. I mean ... if there's only one person out there that you're meant to spend your life with that's leaving a lot up to chance.

"I happen to believe the universe steps in and makes sure you find your mate at the exact right time," she continued. "You found Landon at a time when you were looking for something else. Sure, you didn't know it. You thought you were going there for a boring story. You got a lot more, though, didn't you?"

I certainly did. Even after meeting Landon and recognizing the attraction I felt for him, that didn't mean things went smoothly. He was shot while protecting me, for crying out loud, and that was before he found out about the Winchester family's witchy secret. He left for a bit after that, returning only after he got his mind around things. He'd never faltered since, but I still couldn't help but wonder how things would've been different if I turned left instead of right in that maze the first day.

"Do you think he was looking for me?" The question popped out of my mouth even though I couldn't come up with an acceptable reason to ask it. Perhaps I needed validation because I was on such shaky emotional footing. I couldn't be sure, but I needed to hear something. I had a feeling Aunt Tillie would know what that was.

My elderly great-aunt shifted her eyes over her shoulder, pinning me with an unreadable look. "Don't you?"

"I ... don't know."

"I think you do know," Aunt Tillie countered. "I think at some point you felt the pieces that made up your heart slip into place, everything coming together at once as if it was always supposed to be that way."

"I think that's an incredibly schmaltzy thing to say, especially if you're the one saying it."

"What can I say? We're the schmaltz family sometimes. There's no sense arguing about it."

I bit the inside of my cheek to keep from laughing as I followed her, my eyes widening when I caught sight of the furniture offerings inside. "Oh, wow." I exhaled heavily when my gaze landed on a reclaimed wood bookshelf propped against the barn's west wall. "Did you know all of this was in here?"

"I knew they had furniture." Aunt Tillie works overtime to look unimpressed at most times, but even she seemed enamored with the shelf. "This stuff is neat."

"Definitely." I ran my fingers over the knotted wood. "This would look great on that big wall in the guesthouse."

"Are you considering changing things up when you're the only one left living there?" Aunt Tillie asked. In truth, I'd been giving my future living arrangements a lot of thought.

"It will be weird to live there alone," I admitted after a few moments of contemplation. "I moved to the guesthouse because I needed a place to stay when I came back to Hemlock Cove and I didn't have a lot of money. I've been saving since then."

Aunt Tillie snapped her head in my direction, surprised. "Are you going to buy your own place?"

I shrugged, unsure how to answer. "I'm considering maybe renting a place in Traverse City." It was the first time I admitted anything of the sort, and I expected Aunt Tillie to melt down ... or at least tell me I was stupid for throwing away a prime piece of property in Hemlock Cove, especially when I lived there for free. She did neither.

"Because you want to be closer to Landon."

I wanted to deny the charge, but it seemed like a waste of time. I didn't want to leave Hemlock Cove – after living in Detroit for several years, I realized how much I loved the small town – but being away from Landon became more and more difficult as time passed.

"He can't leave Traverse City because there's a residency requirement that goes along with his job," I explained. "I think he would like to live in Hemlock Cove, but it's not a possibility."

"So you want to uproot your life for him?" Aunt Tillie's tone was far from accusatory, but the way she phrased the question set my teeth on edge.

"I want to be with him."

"Have you talked to him about this?"

"I … no."

"Don't you think you should?"

"I don't want him to think that I'm pressuring him," I admitted. "If I bring it up, he might think that I'm trying to force his hand. If I get my own apartment in Traverse City it will hopefully be a happy surprise."

"And a complete and total waste of money," Aunt Tillie fired back. "If you're going to move to Traverse City, don't you think you two should talk about it so you can get a place big enough for the both of you?"

That had been my initial plan, but the more I thought about broaching the subject with Landon, the more uneasy I got. "Don't you think that's putting undue pressure on him?"

Aunt Tillie immediately started shaking her head. "I think you're an idiot."

I balked. "Tell me how you really feel."

"I feel as if you're an idiot." Aunt Tillie tugged a hand through her short-cropped hair. "I swear I don't know how I raised you three younger girls to be such morons sometimes. It's as if you don't think before you speak."

"That's ridiculous coming from you."

"And yet I'm not the one being an idiot," Aunt Tillie countered. "Bay, for crying out loud, do you really think Landon wants you to move to Traverse City and not share the same roof? For that matter, do you really think he wants you to move to Traverse City at all?"

That thought hadn't even occurred to me. Er, well, it had. I considered the fact that he might not want me living in the same town. I discarded it right away, though, because the idea made me sick to my stomach. "You think he likes the fact that we live in different towns."

Aunt Tillie made a "well, duh" face that would've caused me to laugh under different circumstances. "I think that he wants you to talk about things like this before you make a decision. This right here, young lady, would be an example of one of the things that drives him crazy."

I didn't bother to hide the fact that I was offended. "Excuse me?"

Aunt Tillie clearly wasn't bothered by my tone. "You heard me. It's just like when you freaked out because you thought he was going to move out of state without talking things over with you, that he got transferred and was simply going to break up with you and go on his merry way."

"How do you even know about that? Were you eavesdropping?"

Aunt Tillie ignored my question. "Bay, I know I say that Clove is the kvetch, but you're often the kvetch. I think the problem is that you're usually the easiest one to deal with and sometimes I forget that you can melt down with the best of them. You get that from me."

"You say that as if it's a good thing."

"It is a good thing, because you need a venting mechanism and this is yours," Aunt Tillie shot back. "You need to discuss your plan with Landon. I'm not saying he's the boss – for the record, the man is never the boss – but he should have a say in this before you do something stupid."

"What if he doesn't want me to move to Traverse City?"

"Then at least you'll know and won't waste money on something that's not going to work out," Aunt Tillie replied. "Do you know what your problem is?"

"No, but I have a feeling you're going to tell me."

"You've got that right. Your problem is that you can't see what's right in front of your face. I know part of that comes from the abandonment factor. Your father left when you were a kid, and now you're worried Landon will do the same.

"What you don't seem to understand is that Landon will never leave," Aunt Tillie continued. "He did it the one time because he was confused. You really can't blame the boy. He had no idea it was going to happen the way it happened, and he didn't so much as have an inkling about magic before meeting us. He needed time to think. He came back, though. I always knew he would."

"I hardly think … ."

Aunt Tillie cut me off with a shake of her head. "You're being a worrywart, Bay, and it's not attractive. You need to suck it up. Landon is doing his job. You're hardly alone, because you have us. You need to let it go."

I stared at her a moment, dumbfounded. "Believe it or not, I'm trying to be mature."

"And you're failing miserably." Aunt Tillie turned her attention back to the barn. "Now, look around and buy something frivolous. I don't care what it is, but it had better be something totally wasteful. They say that retail therapy is good for the soul … and you definitely need some sort of therapy. I'm going to see a man about a plow, and then I'll find you."

I pressed the heel of my hand to my forehead. "Fine."

"Great."

"Good."

Aunt Tillie's smirk was inescapable. "You hate it when I'm right, don't you?"

"I pretty much hate you regardless right now."

"I can live with that."

I tamped down my irritation as I wandered through the building, doing my best not to follow Aunt Tillie because I didn't want her to think I was pathetic and shadowing her for lack of anything better to do. I loitered next to the bookshelf for a long time, something wistful snapping off inside of me as I stared. I wanted it … badly. I couldn't guarantee I'd have room for it if I moved, though. I needed to be pragmatic.

Even though the barn was open and airy I felt smothered, so I headed back toward the parking lot. I figured I could get a cup of hot chocolate and wait for Aunt Tillie near the car. It was easier to breathe outside, though only marginally. I remembered seeing a hot chocolate stand when we pulled in, and I scanned the area to reacquaint myself with its location once I hit sunlight.

I wasn't outside long – only a few seconds, in fact – when I felt a heavy weight on my shoulders. The hair on the back of my neck stood on end and when I turned, I found myself staring into a familiar set of eyes.

He was across the parking lot, long legs clad in denim and a black leather jacket hanging off his shoulders. I would've recognized the long hair anywhere, the high ridge of his cheekbones as he laughed at something one of the biker dudes standing next to him uttered.

My mouth dropped open when Landon and I locked gazes, time ceasing its inevitable ticking forward. I felt as if I was walking on thin air as I tried to gain control of my faculties, my heart racing when I saw the blonde standing on Landon's right side lean in to whisper something to him.

My face flushed with color, my cheeks burning, and I grappled to keep from listing to the side as Aunt Tillie walked out of the barn and joined me.

"Well, this was a bust," she announced. "He wants more than I'm willing to pay, and he accused me of trying to rip him off when I offered him a lot less than he was asking. Can you believe that?"

There was a lot about this situation I couldn't wrap my head around. "I ... um ... ."

"He's a real idiot if he thinks I'm going to pay what he's asking," Aunt Tillie continued, apparently not noticing my discomfort. "He must think I'm new at this."

The words were enough to snap me back to reality. I grabbed her wrist, digging my fingernails into the soft flesh there. "We have to go, and we have to go right now. I don't want to hear one word of argument. Do you understand?"

THREE

"What's your deal?" Aunt Tillie looked nothing short of irritated as she glanced around.

"We have to leave right now," I stupidly repeated. I felt like a complete and total idiot – and not for the first time today – but I could think only of escape. I couldn't risk interacting with Landon. Things would completely fall apart if we came face to face.

"But … why?" Aunt Tillie knew something had happened, but she couldn't figure out what. "I haven't even gotten any food yet. We also haven't checked out the farmer's market."

"I'll take you to another farmer's market."

As if scenting blood in the water, Aunt Tillie circled like the shark in *Jaws*. She was about to gnaw my leg off, and I didn't have so much as a spear-gun to hold her off. "Why go to another farmer's market when this one is right here?"

"Because … ." Because why? I couldn't point out Landon, after all. She would insist on talking to him, and that wouldn't go well for anybody.

"Oh, hey, there's Landon."

She said it in a manner that indicated she was only mildly interested, but I could sense the shift in her demeanor. "Aunt Tillie ... ."

"What's he doing with that blonde?"

That was a very good question. I didn't want to know the answer. I had to get away. "We need to leave right now."

"Screw that." Aunt Tillie slapped my hand away. "I want to talk to him. He doesn't have time to visit you, but he can hang out with her? That chick's hair color came from a bottle. At least you're the real deal."

I couldn't help being flattered that Aunt Tillie would say something like that, yet I remained terrified of her intentions. I grabbed her arm, desperate to keep her from drawing attention to us. "Aunt Tillie, he's undercover."

"Oh, really? I never would've guessed that," she drawled, rolling her eyes. "Of course he's undercover. The boy can't carry off leather without looking like the Fonz. I'm not an idiot."

She didn't consider herself an idiot, but I certainly felt like one. "We need to go."

Aunt Tillie blinked several times, absorbing the statement, and then shook her head. "We have just as much of a right to be here as he does."

"Yes, but he's clearly with those ... people ... for a reason," I gritted out. "If we go up to him and act as if we know him we'll ruin his case."

The notion momentarily caused Aunt Tillie's eyes to fill with evil light. "That sounds fun."

"No, it doesn't." I gripped her wrist tighter. "He's been working hard for three weeks. You are not going to go over there and ruin it for him simply because you're in the mood to be a pain."

"Did I say I was going to ruin it for him?"

"No, but ... ."

"Did I say I wanted the bad guys to get away with whatever it is he's investigating?"

"No, but ... ."

"Do you have any faith in me at all?"

That was a loaded question. The way Aunt Tillie innocently batted her eyelashes made me believe she had mayhem on the brain. The woman almost always has mischief in mind.

"We're leaving." I kept my tone firm but undemanding. "Give me the keys. I'll drive."

Aunt Tillie snorted. She acted as if I suggested she join the circus rather than let me take control of her truck. "That's never going to happen. I'm driving."

"Fine. You can drive," I hissed. "But we need to leave right now."

"Okay, but I clearly didn't pass on my sense of whimsical fun to you, and that's a crying shame." Aunt Tillie fell into step next to me. I couldn't hide my relief as I slowly let go of her wrist. I didn't risk glancing at Landon again, instead staring at my feet to make sure I didn't inadvertently trip.

"Of course, I also apparently raised you to be a sucker, huh?" My reflexes were delayed as I realized what she was doing. Aunt Tillie hopped out of my reach and took a step toward the biker group. "I'm feeling a desperate need to wander around a corn maze. How about you?"

I felt a desperate need to find a hole in the ground to hide in, but that didn't look to be an option. "Aunt Tillie," I hissed, hoping I could stop her forward momentum with the mere power of my mind. "Come back here right now."

Aunt Tillie pretended she didn't hear me, her gaze intent as it roamed over the handful of bikers.

"Aunt Tillie!"

It was too late. I could either hide like a coward next to the truck or follow my great-aunt and lie about her mental prowess in an attempt to save Landon's case. I opted for the latter.

"Oh, look what we have here. How cute is she?"

The woman standing next to Landon – way too close for my comfort level, mind you – brightened when she saw Aunt Tillie approaching. I squared my shoulders, licking my lips as my mind zipped from one crazy lie to another. I needed to come up with something quick to head off whatever Aunt Tillie had in her mind to say.

"She's definitely cute." Landon uttered the words in a congenial manner, his eyes locked with mine instead of focusing on Aunt Tillie. I kept my face impassive as I increased my pace. "Are you here for the corn maze?"

"I do love a good corn maze," Aunt Tillie replied, her gaze bouncing between the rough bearded faces. Landon hadn't shaved in what looked to be weeks. I couldn't ever remember seeing him so scraggly. It wasn't a turn on. "I came to look at a plow, but the maze looks to be a nice diversion."

"A plow?" The man standing to Landon's left grinned as he took in Aunt Tillie's cargo pants and combat boots. "You came here for a plow?"

Aunt Tillie nodded without hesitation. "I like to plow things. You'd know all about that, wouldn't you, Skippy?"

Instead of reacting out of anger, the man merely smiled as he raised his eyebrows in Landon's direction. "Did you hear that, Landon? She thinks I like to plow things."

"Well, she's not wrong." Landon's tone reflected easy camaraderie. I knew him well enough to recognize the stiff set of his shoulders, though. "You do love a fresh field to plow."

Oh, well, that was delightful. "You'll have to excuse my aunt," I forced out, grabbing Aunt Tillie's shoulder as I caught up. "She tends to get distracted, and once she saw the corn maze I couldn't get her to turn around."

"Yes, well, she's old." The woman grinned as she leered at Aunt Tillie. "Did you get a day pass from the home today? Is your niece taking you on an outing? That sounds nice."

Aunt Tillie stilled, the woman's tone clearly agitating her. "And where is your mother? I'm doubtful you can cross the road without her help, so I'm certain she must be near."

The woman's smile slipped. "I ... excuse me?"

"It's not a big deal, Becky," Landon offered, resting against a hay bale wall. "Don't let it get to you."

"That's easy for you to say. She insulted me." The blonde – apparently her name was Becky – turned her glare to me instead of focusing on Aunt Tillie. "You should keep your aunt in check."

Despite my determination to grab Aunt Tillie and run, to keep Landon's case out of danger, I couldn't tamp down my agitation. "I'll take that under advisement." I yanked on Aunt Tillie's shoulder. "Come on. You've had your fun. I'll take you to another farmer's market."

"I don't want to go to another farmer's market," Aunt Tillie shot back, narrowing her eyes. She clearly disliked Becky. The feeling was mutual. "I want to check out the corn maze."

"No, you don't," I countered. "You came to check out a plow. You didn't buy a plow. Let's go home."

"I don't want to go home," Aunt Tillie argued. "Home is boring. It's full of whiny people feeling sorry for themselves." Her weighted gaze landed on me and I had to press my eyes shut to maintain control of my emotions. "If I have to hear one more complaint about how your life sucks I'm going to kill myself."

That sounded like a viable option right now. "I'll buy you hot chocolate and a doughnut back in Hemlock Cove if you leave with me right now." I wasn't above a good bribe, and that's all I could think of in the moment.

"Oh, now, don't be hasty." The man on Landon's other side gave me an appraising look as his eyes wandered up and down my body, causing me to clutch my hoodie tighter in the face of his predatory gaze. "What's your hurry, sweetheart? There's no need for you to run off."

"Oh, well ... ."

The man cut me off. "My friend here is busy with his girlfriend, but I'm open for offers." My stomach twisted when he inclined his head in Landon and Becky's direction. "I think you should make me an offer."

Landon shifted from one foot to the other although his expression remained flat. "Doug, there's really no need to mess with her."

Doug waved off Landon's concern. "I'm not messing with her. I wouldn't mind if she wanted to mess with me, though."

"I wouldn't take him up on that offer," Aunt Tillie suggested. "He looks like he has lice."

She wasn't wrong. Doug's gray hair looked as if it hadn't been washed in days. For that matter, Landon didn't look much better. "Aunt Tillie, we should really be going." I was starting to feel desperate. If I wasn't careful I'd burst into tears and make things that much worse. "We need to go home."

"You should listen to your niece," Becky suggested pointedly. "You're starting to bother me."

Aunt Tillie was never one to bow down to threats, even weak ones like Becky's proffered. "At least Doug here only has lice. I'm pretty sure you have crabs, Becky." She flicked her dangerous eyes to Landon. "You should watch out for creepy-crawly things when you climb into bed with her."

It took me a second to realize Aunt Tillie was talking to Landon. He met her steely gaze with a dark one of his own. I could practically see his mind working as he stared her down.

"Aunt Tillie, let's go," I urged, my voice cracking. I hated myself for the weakness, and steeled myself to gain control of my emotions. "There's nothing for us here. You said it yourself. You don't want the plow."

Aunt Tillie shifted her eyes to me, her expression unreadable. "What about the bookshelf? You loved the bookshelf."

"That was before. I ... it doesn't matter."

"Yeah, I'm guessing you're not interested in uprooting your life for a man any longer, are you?" Despite the surreal situation, Aunt Tillie shook her head. "Okay, we can go."

"Wait." The word escaped Landon's mouth as we moved to turn, catching both of us off guard. Landon looked equally surprised to find he'd said something when I leveled my gaze on him.

"What do you want them to wait for?" Becky asked, alleviating the weight of the world as it formed into a ball and landed in the pit of my stomach. "It's not as if they're the ones we're waiting for."

Oh, so they were waiting for someone. The information didn't mean much to me. In fact, the simple realization that Landon was doing exactly the same thing he did a year ago – a new blonde at his side – made me sick to my stomach.

"No, we're definitely not the ones you're waiting for." I tugged on Aunt Tillie's arm. "We should go. I have ... things to do."

Aunt Tillie pursed her lips as her gaze bounced between Becky, Landon and me. "Okay. But you need to buy me hot chocolate and a doughnut. You promised."

"Yeah, you promised," Becky taunted, haughty.

"I did promise." I nodded in silent thanks to Aunt Tillie. Even though I was annoyed – maybe even a little hurt – I didn't want all of Landon's hard work to be in vain. This was simply a misunderstanding, after all. I always overreacted. This was no different. That's what I kept telling myself, anyway. "I have things to do."

Aunt Tillie almost looked sympathetic as she fell into step next to me. That made matters worse. "Do you want to help me with curses when we get home?"

I could feel Landon's eyes on my back as we made the long, slow trek back to the truck. "Who are you going to curse?" I didn't care that Landon's new "friends" heard us. They would think we were crazy, but I was beyond worrying about something like that.

"I have an entire list of people I want to curse," Aunt Tillie replied. "Three just hopped to the top of my list."

I could guess who the three were. "Maybe. I might just want to drink myself into a stupor instead."

"That sounds like a solid plan, too."

I waited on the passenger side of the truck as Aunt Tillie climbed into the driver's seat before leaning across to unlock the door for me. I risked a final glance over my shoulder, my heart rolling at Landon's conflicted gaze as he stared after me. He was caught. We both knew it. Even if he wanted to follow me – which I hoped he did – he couldn't do it without risking his cover.

"Come on," Aunt Tillie prodded, drawing my eyes to her. "He can't do anything right now."

"I know." I forced a smile as I climbed into the passenger seat. "That will teach me to wish for something, huh?"

Aunt Tillie was understandably puzzled. "What do you mean?"

"I've been wishing to see him for three straight weeks," I replied. "I finally got to see him, and now I feel worse than I did before."

Aunt Tillie furrowed her brow. "I don't want to make excuses for his attitude, but he could hardly break cover. I shouldn't have gone over there. It wasn't fair to you. I thought it would be fun to mess with him. Breaking your heart was a byproduct I didn't see coming, although I should have."

The admission was enough to make me feel better, though only marginally. "It doesn't matter." I forced a smile even though my insides felt as if they were being shredded. "He's working. You said it yourself. There's nothing he can do."

"No, there's not." Aunt Tillie stuck the key in the ignition. "If it's any consolation, he looks as if he's ready to cry."

"That's some consolation."

Aunt Tillie snorted. "You still want to curse him, don't you?"

"I was thinking we could make any woman he comes in contact with smell like sauerkraut. He hates sauerkraut."

"Good to know."

"I ... ." I broke off as I glanced back at Landon one more time. He remained looking in our direction, even though his head was bent as he listened to Becky chatter in his ear. "Let's make sure the sauerkraut smells as if it spoiled three weeks ago, just to be on the safe side – and maybe curse him to smell badly, too."

"Now you're thinking."

I was definitely thinking. I was thinking that I wanted to crawl into bed, tune out the world and find out this had been a nightmare. Instead, I decided to embrace Aunt Tillie's plan.

"What else stinks?"

"Rotten eggs."

"Now you're thinking! Let's add that to the sauerkraut smell."

Aunt Tillie beamed. "I've created a monster ... and I couldn't be more proud."

FOUR

Four days later my nerves were no longer frazzled. I was simply numb.

The day I saw Landon at the corn maze I sat next to my cell phone the entire night, expecting him to call, even willing him to call at times. He never called. I told myself it was because he couldn't get away from his friends – who were very obviously criminals and quite possibly dangerous – and it was more important for him to be safe than to stroke my ego.

I somehow made it through the first night on faith alone. When he still didn't call by the following night I let rage take over and took every photograph I had of us and shoved them into a drawer so I wouldn't have to look at them.

By the third day I was manic, convinced he'd been hurt on the job and his boss was keeping it from me. The only reason I didn't call his boss and demand answers is because Thistle stole my phone and wouldn't allow me to do it.

By the fourth day, today, I was simply dead inside. I told myself that I didn't care, that he probably wouldn't even bother to call and break up with me because he figured it was already done. Everyone in the family said I was acting crazy and dramatic – which was rich coming from them, because I'm the calm one in the family – and then I climbed into myself and decided to be a martyr.

No, I can admit it. I fancied myself the most put-upon woman in the world as I walked around Hemlock Cove, going through the motions of putting together this week's edition of The Whistler, the weekly newspaper for which I was editor and sole reporter. It didn't take a lot of effort, and when I was finished I trudged to Hypnotic, the store Thistle and our cousin Clove ran, where I proceeded to throw myself on the couch and sigh dramatically.

Clove managed to muster a sympathetic half-smile, but Thistle simply looked annoyed.

"Knock it off," Thistle ordered, irate. "You're being pathetic. No one likes a pathetic woman, especially a man."

She had a point, and still … . "Landon doesn't even know I'm being pathetic because he can't bother to call."

Clove's dark eyebrows flew up her forehead. "Still?"

"He can't. He's undercover. He can't risk anyone overhearing him. Plus he has to buy a burner phone he can only use once before discarding it. He can't risk any of the people he's working with finding the phone and tracking the number." I was fairly listless while staring at my ragged fingernails. "I need a manicure … and pedicure. Heck, I'm thinking maybe an entire spa day would be the way to go."

"I could get behind that if I thought you weren't talking simply to hear yourself talk," Thistle snapped.

I ignored her and focused on Clove. She was easier to deal with when I was feeling down – mostly because she often went out of her way to cheer me up – and I was in desperate need of someone to dote on me. Even my own mother was sick of my crap, which should've told me how far I'd sunk. It wasn't that I was unaware of my mopey attitude and general wretchedness. I simply couldn't escape from my funk.

"Tell me about your wedding plans, Clove," I prodded. "Have you picked out a dress yet?" Clove and her boyfriend Sam Cornell became engaged several weeks ago and she hadn't stopped talking about it since the blessed day. The only thing getting more attention in the Winchester household was my depression.

"We haven't made plans yet," Clove replied, narrowing one eye and pursing her lips. "We're thinking of early summer. We want to have an outdoor ceremony."

"That sounds like a good idea."

"Yeah, we think so."

I didn't miss the look Clove and Thistle exchanged, but I refused to comment on it. "Have you been looking at dresses?"

"I thought that was something we could do together," Clove replied, lowering her voice. "Once all of this stuff is settled between you and Landon, that is."

"All of this stuff is settled between Landon and me," I countered. "It's done. We're ... done." Even saying the words was painful, and even as the statement escaped my lips my heart revolted.

Thistle took me by surprise with a derisive snort. "You're not done. Stop being a kvetch. I can't stand it. I'm used to it with this one, but you're supposed to be the cousin I can tolerate." Thistle jerked her thumb toward Clove for emphasis. "I'm used to this with her, but you're the strong one."

I didn't feel very strong. In fact, the only thing I could feel was sorry for myself. The realization was beyond frustrating. "He hasn't called." Surprisingly, my voice didn't break. I was all cried out. I held onto the tears until I was alone each night, and then cried until I fell asleep. "I don't think he's going to call again."

"Oh, you're so freaking dramatic," Thistle muttered, shaking her head. "He'll call. He's an FBI agent, for crying out loud. He probably can't call because it's dangerous. Do you want him to die just so you can talk to him on the phone?"

That was an interesting question. "Die? No. Right now I would be okay with him feeling some pain, though." I felt better admitting it, a bit more Winchester-like. How sad is that? "If he felt it in his naughty bits I'd be fine with that ... perhaps like a burning sensation he can't escape no matter how much cranberry juice he drinks."

Thistle chuckled, genuinely amused. "See, that sounds good. You're already feeling better."

I was. The simple act of admitting I was angry rather than wallowing in sadness was enough to elevate my spirits. "It feels unfair to blame him and yet ... I blame him."

"I blame him, too." Thistle was somber. "I don't care what's been going on. He should've been able to find five minutes to get a message to you."

"I'm really angry with him," Clove added, moving to sit next to me. "I want to kick him in the nuts. That's how angry I am."

She said it in such an innocent manner that I couldn't refrain from giggling. "We should form a line," I suggested. "I let Aunt Tillie put together the ingredients to make him and his new girlfriend smell like rotting sauerkraut that night when we got back from the corn maze. I stopped her before she could cast the spell, though. I realized it was juvenile."

Being an authentic witch isn't easy. Karma is a real thing, and cursing Landon to smell bad simply because I was angry with him didn't seem fair. That didn't stop me from seriously considering it, of course, but in the end common sense won out. If I punished Landon something worse would happen to me. Even though I wanted him to suffer a bit – I was certainly suffering enough for both of us, after all – I didn't want to hurt him. I couldn't take it.

"Do you honestly believe she didn't cast it?" Thistle asked the question with a doubtful lilt. "Seriously?"

"Of course. I ... ." Huh. Why did I believe Aunt Tillie when she immediately said she was okay with me putting the kibosh on the curse? "Crap. She waited until I left to cast it, didn't she?"

"I think being pathetic is also making you stupid," Thistle noted, grinning. "I wonder how Landon explained smelling like rotten sauerkraut to his new friends. I'm sure that was quite the conversation."

"You don't think that somehow blew his cover, do you?"

Thistle barked out a laugh, amused by the question. "I'm sure he explained it away by saying he rubbed himself in garbage or simply feigned ignorance. The point is that he knew why he smelled like rancid sauerkraut."

"Yeah." My smile slipped. "I'm sure he knew ... and still didn't call."

"Bay ... ." Sympathy washed over Clove's face, but she didn't finish the sentence. There was nothing she could say.

"It doesn't matter." I shook myself from my reverie. "There's nothing I can do about any of this. Driving myself crazy won't help anyone, especially me."

"On a normal day I'd agree with that," Thistle said. "Given what he's put you through, though, I can't help but think we should come up with another plan."

I didn't like the evil grin flitting across her face. "I don't even want to know what you're thinking."

"No, no." Thistle brightened as she warmed to whatever terrible plan was taking shape in her head. "I have an idea. You need to hear me out."

That was the last thing I needed. "I don't think whatever idea you're coming up with is a good one. In fact, I think we should forget all about Landon and go back to talking about Clove's wedding."

"I agree with that." Clove enthusiastically bobbed her head. She was always the least keen to embark on a potentially troublesome adventure. "Let's talk about my wedding. I love talking about my wedding. I was thinking of lilies for a bridal bouquet."

"Yes, that sounds lovely," Thistle deadpanned, rolling her eyes. "With your skin tone you should choose a pink lily. Let's get back to Bay. I think we should cast a spell."

"Did you listen to a thing I said about telling Aunt Tillie not to cast the smelling curse on Landon?" I challenged.

"I heard you, but that's not what kind of spell I'm talking about," Thistle argued. "I think we should perform a locator spell."

My eyebrows flew up my forehead. "And then what?"

"We'll follow him, watch him from the car until we get a few minutes alone, and then we'll approach him," Thistle offered. "Oh, we'll also do what Clove wants and kick him in the nuts before we go, but we'll find him first and give him five minutes to plead his case before we bring down the hammer and make him pay for breaking your heart."

Thistle's voice grew more and more excited the longer she talked. She clearly loved the idea. Sadly, I didn't hate the idea. The possibility of seeing Landon and kicking him where it hurt thrilled me. The notion of seeming even more pathetic in his eyes instantly diminished my temporary giddiness.

"My heart isn't broken."

Thistle cocked a challenging eyebrow.

"Okay, my heart isn't broken much," I clarified. "We can't find Landon and confront him. That will ruin his case."

"I said we would wait until he was alone," Thistle countered. "I meant it. I don't want to ruin his case. I simply want to kick him in the balls."

"Oh, well, that sounds mildly fun." I tilted my head to the side, considering. "Okay. We'll conduct the spell and see where it leads us. But if I decide it's a bad idea once we've found him I reserve the right to change my mind."

"That sounds like a plan." Thistle beamed as she moved to the store shelves to gather the appropriate ingredients. "I can't wait to see the look on his face when I kick him."

BIGFOOT IS LIVING in the woods behind the library."

Viola, a woman who had died in front of me months ago but remained behind in her ghostly form, popped into view thirty minutes later, causing me to jolt.

"What's wrong?" Clove asked, instantly alert. She can't see ghosts, but she can hear them if I talk to one long enough in her presence.

"Viola is here," I gritted out as I fought to refrain from exploding. "She says Bigfoot is living behind the library."

Thistle, unbothered by the announcement, dropped a pinch of ragweed into the cauldron to finish off the spell. "Ask her if he wears pants. I've always wanted to know if Bigfoot wears pants or just runs around commando."

"He goes commando," I shot back, not missing a beat. "He's a wild animal living in the forest. Where would he get clothes?"

Thistle shrugged. "Perhaps he steals clothing because he's modest."

"Or perhaps you're crazy," I muttered under my breath.

"I heard that."

"I meant for you to hear it." I fixed my attention on Viola. "What makes you think Bigfoot is living behind the library?"

"I've seen his tracks and heard noises in the forest," Viola replied. "It's clearly Bigfoot. I heard roaring, and we don't have lions in this area."

"Perhaps it was a bear," Clove suggested, Viola's voice becoming audible for her. "Supposedly we're attracting more bears in this area these days."

"Did you read that on a Yogi Bear campsite pamphlet?" Thistle challenged.

Clove ignored her. "It's true."

"I don't doubt it's true, but I seriously doubt that a bear or Bigfoot is hanging around behind the library," I pointed out. "There's nothing for them to do there. They'd be bored."

"Yes, that's the reason Bigfoot isn't hanging behind the library," Thistle drawled, rolling her neck until it cracked. "The spell is ready. We just need to give it a direction to follow."

"It would work better if we had some of Landon's hair," Clove noted. "It would anchor the spell."

"Oh, sadly I'm not pathetic enough to carry around a lock of his hair," I offered. "Next time I'll know better and steal huge hunks of it."

"Ooh. We should totally cut his hair as payback," Thistle enthused.

"I thought we were going to kick him in the balls." Clove looked disappointed. "I was looking forward to that."

"We can do both," Thistle said. "In fact, maybe we should think of a third thing to do to him so we can all enjoy the outing."

I'd heard worse ideas. "We'll make that decision when we get there," I said, inclining my chin toward the cauldron. "Let's do this. I'm dying to know where he is."

"You won't still feel that way if we find him in a hotel with that Becky woman," Clove argued.

"Yes, thank you for that." My heart rolled at the thought. "You don't think ... ."

Thistle cut me off before I could get up a full head of steam. "Of course he's not sharing a hotel room with Becky the skank. He would never do that to you. I don't care how angry I am with him, I will never believe that."

Deep down, I didn't believe it either. "That's good. I ... that's good." I let out a relieved breath. "We need to get moving. I want to get this over with before dark in case I need to hurry home and drink myself to sleep."

"Good plan." Thistle clapped her hands together, smiling as a blue ball of light popped into existence above the cauldron. We were capable of casting locator spells without using the cauldron, but they always worked better when we took the time to anchor them. "Okay. Find Landon Michaels," Thistle ordered. "Go!"

The light zipped through the front door of the store, taking me by surprise with its vigor. "Huh. That was quick." I grabbed my keys from the couch and moved toward the door. "Let's go. We'll take my car. I'm parked in the front."

"Okay. Let's do this."

Thistle and Clove followed me outside. The three of us pulled up short at the locator ball hovering in the middle of the street. It didn't move, nor give us so much as a hint as to which direction we should head.

"It's acting weird, right?" I tilted my head to the side as I stared at the bouncing light. "Maybe we did something wrong."

"We didn't do anything wrong," Thistle countered. "I followed all of the instructions. I wanted to make sure we found him, because I'm in the mood to punish someone for all of your whining and it seems mean to kick you while you're down. I ... don't understand."

"Maybe you should've sent it after Bigfoot," Viola suggested. I'd almost forgotten she was still hanging around. "That would be a better way to spend your time."

I ignored her. "Maybe it will start moving when we get in the car."

"Or maybe it's already found the person it's looking for," Clove suggested, inclining her chin toward the police station across the road.

I followed her gaze, my stomach twisting when I saw the open door. The man standing inside of the doorframe didn't look surprised to see me. He did look resigned, though.

"Landon," I said, exhaling heavily. "I ... he's here."

"Oh, man!" Thistle screwed up her face, outraged. "Now we're not going to get to kick him in the nuts. This day officially sucks."

FIVE

Landon, his face still covered with scruff, took a purposeful step toward me.

"I was just coming to find you."

I felt separate, as if somehow detached from my own body. All I could do was blankly stare for a moment. Then, when I finally found words, they were snarky. "Did you think I was in the police department?"

"No. I had to talk to Chief Terry first."

"So you were going to find Chief Terry and then eventually find me," I supplied. "That seems about right."

"You tell him," Clove muttered, narrowing her eyes.

"Ooh, is this going to go all *Dynasty* or something?" Viola asked, perking up.

Landon hesitated when he saw the look on my face. "Bay, we need to talk."

"Of course we do." My stomach twisted as I pressed my eyes shut. The manner in which he said the words immediately made my head go to a rotten place. I had no idea why, but it was frustrating. "This is unbelievable."

"What's unbelievable?" Landon took another step forward,

keeping one wary eye on Thistle as she glared at him. "What's with the ball of light? You probably shouldn't let that thing loose in downtown Hemlock Cove. Someone might see it and start asking questions."

"We were looking for you," Thistle offered, watching with grim satisfaction as the light briefly hummed before slamming into Landon's chest.

He jolted, as if expecting pain, but it dissipated instantly and he was left with nothing but a surprised look on his face. "You conjured that thing to find me?"

I didn't answer, but Clove nodded her head.

"Why?" Landon asked, his eyes clouding. "What were you going to do if you found me? That wasn't exactly a safe plan, Bay."

"It wasn't her plan," Thistle interjected, scorching Landon with the dirtiest look in her arsenal. She learned at Aunt Tillie's knee throughout the years, so she could muster a really nasty expression when the mood struck. "I suggested it."

"Oh, well, I guess I should be relieved about that," Landon shot back. "At least Bay hasn't completely lost her mind."

"Just mostly." The words were out of my mouth before I thought better about uttering them. Even after, though, I didn't regret saying them. The look on Landon's face was enough to give me some small measure of satisfaction. That should've filled me with guilt – or even modest shame – but I felt neither.

"Bay ... ." Landon looked pained. "Sweetie ... ."

"Don't call me that," I snapped, taking everyone by surprise with my vehemence.

"Okay." Landon held up his hands in mock surrender, his eyes going wide. "I see we have even more to talk about than I realized."

"Yes, well, it's been a long month."

"And I'm sorry for that," Landon started, whipping his head toward Thistle when he saw her forming fists and moving to cut off his avenue of approach. "What do you think you're doing?"

"I'm going to kick you in the nuts," Thistle replied, not missing a beat. "I've been dreaming about it for weeks."

"Hey," Clove protested. "I thought I was the one who gets to kick him in the nuts. You're going to cut his hair."

"We can both kick him in the nuts," Thistle shot back. "I think he's earned it."

"You don't think the hateful messages on my voice mail were enough?" Landon challenged. "What about making me smell like garbage for two days?"

I pressed the heel of my hand to my forehead, confused. "I ... ."

I didn't get a chance to ask the obvious question because Thistle was already crowing. "I told you that Aunt Tillie cursed him even though you told her not to. There's no way she would go through all of that trouble just to let you change your mind."

"It was supposed to be cathartic," I grumbled.

"Yes, well, I'm sure it was ... for her." Thistle's smile was wide, her eyes dangerous. "Maybe you should just go, Landon."

"I'm not leaving," Landon snapped, his temper flaring. "I'm here for Bay. This entire situation has nothing to do with you ... which is what I would've told you if I could've returned any of the fifty nasty calls you made to me. My voice mail was full of hate, by the way. I really appreciate that."

Thistle was unbothered by his tone. "I'm glad you got the message."

Something occurred to me. "Wait ... what?" I shifted my eyes to Thistle. "You called him? You're the one who told me not to call him."

"I know that." Thistle didn't bother denying her actions. "You calling him was pathetic – and you were already pathetic enough. Me calling him was not only allowed, it was encouraged. He needed to know that he was a hateful bastard."

"I see." I traced my bottom lip with my finger, my emotions jumbled. "I didn't know she called you." I found the strength to meet Landon's steady gaze again, although he appeared taken aback by my resolve. "I'm sorry. That was unfair."

"Do you feel the same way about making me smell like garbage?"

I shook my head. "No. You definitely had that coming."

Despite the serious nature of the situation, Landon forced out a laugh and shook his head. "There you are." The words were almost a whisper. He smiled for a moment before recovering. "Bay, will you please go for a ride with me so we can talk?"

Four days ago I would've jumped at the offer. Heck, I would've jumped him before showering his bearded face with kisses. Now I felt disconnected from him, separate from the relationship we were building, and I didn't fully understand how it happened. "I have things to do."

"Bay." Landon wet his lips, his eyes glassy. "I know you're upset, but ... ."

It took everything I had not to explode. The last thing I wanted was to cause a scene. I could see Mrs. Little, the town busybody, sticking her head out the door of her store and watching for potential fireworks. "I'm not even sure I'm upset," I admitted, choosing my words carefully. "Four days ago I was upset. Two days ago I was manic."

"I can vouch for that," Thistle muttered. "I didn't think you'd stop crying ... like ever."

Landon made a face as he tilted his head to the side. "Can't you please spare a few minutes to talk to me? I know this is payback for what I put you through, but we can't begin to move forward until you let me apologize."

"Is that what you want? To move forward, I mean."

Landon balked. "Of course. I ... what have you been thinking?"

I shrugged, noncommittal. "I've been thinking a lot of things."

"Yeah? Well, I've been missing you with everything I've got for a month." Landon held out his hand. "Come for a ride with me."

I stared at his hand a moment, torn. I kept thinking that this was the big moment I'd been fantasizing about and I should answer his lack of interest in my feelings with a dramatic scene, perhaps storming off and making him chase me. Deep down inside, hidden in a part of me I didn't want to admit existed, I worried he wouldn't follow me.

"I ... ."

"Bay, I need to spend some time with you," Landon prodded,

shaking his hand for emphasis. "Come on now. I think I've earned a few minutes alone with you."

I made my decision quickly, nodding as I skirted his hand and headed toward the Ford Explorer parked in front of the police station. "Fine. Five minutes."

Landon worked his jaw, his hand still stretched in my direction. Finally he dropped his hand and shifted his eyes to Thistle. "We're going to talk about those messages you left."

Thistle's derisive snort promised mayhem should Landon dare take her on. "You have bigger problems than my messages. You might want to pay attention to Bay instead of me. Of course … you're out of the habit of doing that, so it might take some time for you to remember."

"Oh, I remember how to do it," Landon shot back, annoyance bubbling to the surface. "I dreamed about it every night for the past month. Trust me. I could never forget."

LANDON WAS quiet during the ride to Hollow Creek. He knew about the location because we'd visited a time or two over our year together – twice solving cases on its uneven banks. Because it was October the area was vacant, the trees dropping leaves rapidly. I knew he didn't care about that, though. He simply wanted a place where he could be assured we wouldn't be interrupted.

"Bay."

I could feel his eyes on me as I stared out the passenger window. "I don't know what to say to you."

"I know, and that hurts." Landon reached over and grabbed my hand, refusing to let me yank it away from him. "I'm sorry."

My eyes burned, but I managed to hold back tears as I faced him. "What are you sorry for?"

Landon's eyes flashed, as if he thought it was a potential test, and he opened his mouth to answer before snapping it shut.

"It's not a trick question," I prodded. "I honestly want to know what you're sorry about."

"I'm sorry for being gone so long," Landon offered. "I know it was hard on you ... and unfair ... and painful. But I'm here to make things right."

"I see." I studied his face for a moment, the beard irritating me beyond belief. "Are you suddenly done with your assignment?"

"I ... don't ... know." Landon forced out the words. "I've turned over the information I gathered to my superiors. I'm not part of the current operation, which is supposed to be carried out this afternoon. That doesn't mean I won't get called back at a certain point, but if everything goes as planned my part in this is finished."

"Is that why you still have the beard?"

Landon grinned as he rubbed his cheek. "Not a fan, are you?"

"I almost didn't recognize you."

"That's the point of being undercover."

"Then you opened your mouth and I definitely didn't recognize you," I added.

"Bay, I'm sorry about that, but what did you expect me to do?" Landon's frustration bubbled over. "I wasn't expecting to see you there. I didn't handle things well – you have no idea how shocked I was when I saw you – but I was worried Aunt Tillie would say something stupid, and I panicked."

"Yeah, I worried she'd say something stupid, too," I admitted, snatching my hand back. I didn't miss the sad look on Landon's face when I put emotional distance between us. "I didn't even want to go there. Aunt Tillie insisted, though. She wanted to buy a new plow."

"It's a free world, Bay. You can go wherever you want. I'm not angry because you showed up. It's not as if you planned it. Now, if your plan to follow the spinning ball of light had worked and you ended up in the middle of my case, then I would've been angry."

"We were going to wait until you were alone."

"That still would've been too dangerous," Landon countered.

"Of course, I wasn't sure you'd ever be alone," I said. "I thought maybe your friend Becky was making sure you never felt lonely."

Landon's shoulders stiffened, his expression incredulous. "Excuse me?"

I ignored his tone. "You two seemed tight."

"Do you have something you want to ask me, Bay?" Landon's voice was chilly. "You can't possibly believe that I cheated on you with Becky, that something was going on between us."

"Only in my absolutely worst moments," I replied. "The problem is, I've had a lot of those over the past month. My entire family is sick of me. They think I'm a pathetic whiner. I'm starting to agree with them."

"Bay, it was a tense time," Landon pointed out. "We weren't expecting it and we didn't need to deal with it before because I hadn't been undercover in a year. But it's over. Can't we just go back to the way things were?"

Now it was my turn to be dumbfounded. "Are you serious?"

"Last time I checked."

"You just want to go back to the way things were?"

Something flitted through Landon's eyes, something I couldn't identify. For one brief moment I thought it was fear. He recovered quickly. "You don't?"

"I don't know what I want," I answered, my heart painfully twisting. "I sat by the phone that entire night waiting for you to call and … you didn't. I thought for sure you would find a way to call but … you didn't."

"I was undercover, Bay!" Landon exploded, causing me to jerk my shoulders as I sniffled. "Oh, sweetie, I'm sorry." He held up his hands immediately. "I promised myself I wasn't going to yell. I … you don't deserve that. This entire thing got out of hand."

He was right. Still, I couldn't help the growing hurt taking me over given his blasé attitude. "You didn't even consider calling me, did you?"

"That is not true," Landon countered. "I worked really hard to find a window to call you. I saw the look on your face, Bay, and I never want to be the person to put that expression there. I am sorry I hurt you.

"In case you didn't notice, Becky and Doug were suspicious of our interaction, and it only had a little to do with the fact that Aunt Tillie stared at me as if she was the parent and she already had the switch ready for my punishment," he continued. "They saw the way I looked at you, Bay. Both of them did, and they suspected something. I had to be extra careful."

I wanted to believe him, yet I wasn't sure I could. "They seemed normal to me. In fact, Becky seemed eager to spend time with you, allowing Doug plenty of room to put his grubby hands on me."

"And you don't think that was a test?" Landon's eyebrows rose. "Bay, they wanted to see how I'd react. Trust me. They were suspicious."

My stomach burned because I wanted to trust him so badly. Instead, all I could do was press my eyes shut and rub my hands over them.

"Bay, you have to know that I love you more than anything," Landon prodded. "I had to keep you safe. I couldn't risk contacting you when they were watching me so closely. Their attention to my actions is one of the reasons I got pulled out a day early."

I jerked my head in his direction, surprised. "I don't understand. What does that mean?"

"I can't tell you the specifics, sweetie. Suffice to say, Doug and Becky are not good people. I didn't want them focusing on you. I had to do my very best to keep them focused on me.

"But that didn't completely work, and Steve managed to pull me out while keeping my cover intact," Landon continued, referring to his boss Steve Newton. "I probably won't have to go back, but I don't want to make that promise in case the unthinkable happens."

"So ... what? You're home for good now?"

"I hope so."

"I see."

Landon scowled. "Is that not enough for you? Do you want me to beg or something?"

The idea held merit, but that was pretty far from what I wanted. "Actually, I simply want to feel important."

"You are important! You're the most important thing in my world."

"And yet you couldn't bother to call."

"Bay, you're killing me," Landon muttered, dragging his hand through his hair. "This is not the homecoming I dreamed about."

I stared at him a moment, frustrated. "Join the club. Now, if you would take me back to town, I have work to do."

Landon was incredulous. "Excuse me? We're not done here."

"I imagine we're not, but that doesn't change the fact that I have an interview scheduled," I said. "You were away for a month doing your job. Mine should take only an hour or two."

"This is a test or something," Landon muttered, putting the Explorer into reverse. "There can be no other explanation."

"You might try shaving while I'm working," I suggested, crossing my arms over my chest.

"I can't shave until I'm sure I won't have to go back," Landon snapped. "I'm sorry you don't like the beard, but … there's not a lot I can do about it."

"No, I guess not."

"I don't like your tone, Bay."

"Right back at you."

SIX

Thistle and Clove were waiting for me when Landon dropped me off at Hypnotic. We didn't speak during most of the ride back to town, but when I opened the door to hop out he finally found his voice.

"I'm going to make this right, Bay."

I swallowed the lump in my throat and kept my back to him. "I have work to do." My voice cracked, and I wanted to punch myself because of it. "I ... will talk to you later."

"You bet you will," Landon muttered, although he didn't put up a fight when I slammed shut the door.

I motioned for Thistle and Clove to head toward my car, and they did it without comment or complaint, Thistle shooting Landon a weighted look as he pulled away. My cousins were used to my moods, so they let me collect my thoughts before pressuring me for answers.

Finally I couldn't take the silence a second longer as I pulled onto the highway that led toward Traverse City. "I'm going back to that place Aunt Tillie and I visited the other day," I offered. "Barnaby Mill. You guys will like it. I have an interview with the owner. I thought it would make a nice article now that they've expanded their offerings. It's for next week's edition, but I want to get it out of the way."

"Okay." Clove rested her hands in her lap in the passenger seat. "It's not in Hemlock Cove but it's close enough to draw interest."

"That's what I was thinking. Besides, I'm running out of businesses in Hemlock Cove to highlight."

"What if Landon's undercover buddies are hanging out there?" Thistle asked from the back seat.

I shrugged. "Then we'll simply look like three people out for an afternoon of fun and shopping."

"I'm still looking for someone to kick in the nuts," Thistle pointed out. "If that Doug guy is here I can totally point my anger toward him."

"And I'll take Becky," Clove offered.

I didn't want to smile – it somehow seemed wrong given the circumstances – but I couldn't stop myself. "You guys always know how to make me feel better."

Clove sympathetically patted my hand. "That's what we're here for."

"Definitely." Thistle enthusiastically bobbed her head. "So, what did Landon say?"

"Thistle! We agreed to let Bay tell us when she was ready." Clove glanced over her shoulder and glared at our cousin. "Don't push her."

"You agreed to that," Thistle clarified. "I want to know what he said."

I couldn't blame her for being curious. If Marcus did the same thing I'd be all over him and ready to do battle on her behalf. I, however, merely felt drained.

"He said he was sorry but he couldn't get away to call because Becky and Doug were suspicious about our interaction."

"Do you believe him?"

I shrugged. "He's a trained observer. He probably sees things I don't. I was so flustered that day all I could focus on was my own feet because I was convinced I was going to trip over them."

"I can see that." Clove offered. "He looked upset when he dropped you off. I take it you guys didn't make up."

"No. I told him I had work to do and that I needed some time."

"Do you think that was wise?"

The question caught me off guard. "What do you mean?"

"You don't need to punish him, Bay," Clove prodded. "He looks as if he's punishing himself. He's clearly sorry."

"You don't know that," Thistle argued. "He may look sorry, but it could be an act."

"And you don't know that," Clove fired back. "I saw the way he looked at Bay. He was in pain. We both know Bay is in pain because she misses him so much. I think she should forgive him and get it over with."

I didn't admit it, but that's the way I was leaning. Of course, that was partly because it was simply easier to forgive him. The only reason I didn't is that a small, bitter portion of my heart honestly wanted to make him suffer like I did while he was away. I could never admit that to my cousins. Okay, I could admit it to Thistle. She would encourage it. Clove was another story.

"I think she should kick him a few times and see how many apologies fall out," Thistle countered. "She should treat him like a human piñata. When she's sure that he's really sorry and can't apologize one more time she can forgive him."

"That's not how karma is supposed to work."

"Oh, that's where I beg to differ," Thistle said. "Bay needs to serve up a big portion of karma to Landon so he knows how much he hurt her."

"If he doesn't already know that, then he's an idiot," Clove said, shifting her contemplative brown eyes to me. "Is he an idiot or does he know?"

That was a very good question and I wasn't sure how to answer. "He seemed to think we could just slip back into how things were a month ago without any comment or changes."

"Do you want changes?"

My mind flitted back to my conversation with Aunt Tillie regarding a potential move to Traverse City. I purposely kept that information to myself before spilling my guts to her, but if I admitted I'd been considering it to Clove and Thistle they would both melt down in different ways. I didn't think I could deal with that today.

"I want him to acknowledge that he did something wrong," I replied after a beat. "This can't all be on me. I mean ... I know that I acted like an idiot. I know I was immature and whiny. I know that I should've sucked it up and been a freaking adult. It still hurt, though, and he should've found a way to contact me after it happened."

"I don't think that's too much to ask," Clove agreed, twirling a strand of her dark hair around her finger. "I think he's probably beating himself up over it right now, if it's any consolation. The thing is, Bay, you're beating yourself up, too. You're as angry with yourself as you are with him. That can't be healthy."

"It sounds healthy to me." Thistle was blasé as she studied her fingernails. "If you want, I'll make Marcus beat him up. I think that might teach him a lesson."

Despite myself, I couldn't stop the snicker from escaping. "I'll keep that in mind."

"Or, even better," Thistle leaned forward as I pulled into the parking lot at Barnaby Mill, "we could all hide in the bushes and jump him when he's not looking."

"And then what?" Clove was horrified. "Are you suggesting we kill an FBI agent?"

Thistle scorched Clove with a "well, duh" look. "Yes, I was thinking we could all go to prison as our final act. Of course not, you idiot! I'm suggesting that we wrestle him down, make him eat some dirt, poke him until he apologizes and then give Aunt Tillie the okay to curse him until he cries."

I rubbed my chin as I turned in my seat to stare at her. "I can see you've given this some thought."

"I was bored last night between harassing calls to his voice mail."

I pursed my lips but couldn't stifle my smile. "I'm dying to know what you said in those messages, by the way. I get the feeling they were ugly."

"Oh, you have no idea." Thistle brightened at the memory. "Aunt Tillie would be so proud that I remembered some of the words she wanted me to forget she said when we were kids. I even remembered the Latin ones. I made a list and used them all."

"Well, that's something at least." I turned my attention to the corn maze. "At least Becky and Doug aren't here. I'm not sure I could get through the day if they were."

"Yeah, well, let's get moving." Thistle shoved open the door. "I wasn't keen on coming, but this place looks cool. I can't wait to check it out."

MY INTERVIEW with the owner took only about forty minutes and when I was done with the tour – making an extra-long stop by the bookcase I was so in love with – I realized I'd lost Thistle and Clove. I wasn't overly worried. The area wasn't that big and they were too old to wander off and get lost in the woods.

I made my way to the parking lot, stopping by the hot chocolate stand before conducting my search. I was lost in thought, worry about Landon and our relationship threatening to overwhelm me now that I didn't have anything to focus on, so I didn't immediately notice the figure moving in at my right until he was almost upon me.

I jolted at the familiar face, barely managing to keep from dumping my hot beverage on his well-pressed shirt as I sucked in a breath. "I didn't see you there, Chief Terry. You frightened me."

"I'm sorry, sweetheart." Chief Terry looked rueful as he tilted his head to the side and studied my face. "I called your name, but you didn't answer. I thought something might be wrong. So … what's wrong?"

I forced a smile for his benefit, shaking off the melancholy and hoping I looked relaxed rather than haunted. "I was just thinking. Nothing is wrong. Why do you think something is wrong? Did someone tell you something is wrong?"

Chief Terry chuckled, the sound low and warm as he pressed a hand to the back of my neck and guided me away from the crowd. "I might've had a visit from the FBI fairy. Wait, that came out a little more derogatory than I thought it would."

"I understand," I said dryly, leaning against Chief Terry's police cruiser as I sipped my hot chocolate. "Do you want some?"

"It looks good, but I'll get my own on my way out," Chief Terry replied. "I think you could use the sugar. I can't remember the last time I saw you this pale. Well, actually, that's not true. I know the last time – I believe you saw a woman die in front of you and were covered in her blood."

Viola. That's the death he was talking about. Chief Terry had been almost as shaken as Landon that day. Not quite, though. I didn't think it was possible for anyone to be more shaken than Landon. I'd witnessed the death, but he carried the bulk of the burden.

"I'm fine," I said, forcing myself to meet his steady gaze. "I'm just … tired."

"Yeah, you know I talked to Landon, right?"

My faux smile slipped. "Since when are you guys such good buddies?" I groused. "Don't you remember when you hated him and thought he was terrible for me?"

Chief Terry answered without hesitation. "Yes, and I was wrong."

"He … did something that I'm not exactly happy with," I explained. "I'm sure it will work itself out eventually. There's nothing to worry about."

"I'm sure it will, too," Chief Terry said. "You two are like magnets. You can't stay away from one another. It's actually kind of cute when it's not stomach-turning. He told me what happened."

"All of it?"

Chief Terry nodded. "He was so upset that day, Bay. You need to know that. He wanted to talk to you, but he couldn't risk anyone hearing him on the phone."

The thaw working its way through my innards stopped as realization washed over me. "You talked to him that day?"

As if sensing he'd stepped on a landmine Chief Terry took an inadvertent step back. "I'm part of the task force running the investigation."

That was news to me. "I see."

"Bay, what are you thinking?" Chief Terry was understandably alarmed. I never shut him out. He was there for me when I was a kid, always going out of his way to take care of me when I struggled because my father wasn't around. I was never angry with him. I never withheld emotion from him.

"It doesn't matter." My spine stiffened as I licked the chocolate from my lips. "I should probably find Clove and Thistle. We need to get going."

"Wait a second." Chief Terry grabbed my wrist, earning a glare for his efforts. "I said something that set you off. What is it?"

"It doesn't matter."

"It clearly matters to you," Chief Terry countered. "What did I say?"

"It's not a big deal."

"Bay." Chief Terry let loose with a low growl. "I can't make things better unless I know what's wrong. You need to tell me."

"You didn't do anything wrong," I said, briefly resting my fingers on top of his. "You didn't lie to me. You didn't tell me that your life was in danger and you couldn't risk getting away to make a phone call that day. The only thing you told me was that Landon managed to get away to call you, even though it was far too dangerous to call me."

Chief Terry's face drained of color as the ramifications dawned on him. "Bay, that's different," he chided. "He had a special phone hidden close to where he was staying and I was the only one that phone was authorized to call. The number was spoofed so if anyone checked they would think he was calling someone else."

"Oh, well, that's convenient." I feigned brightness. "The thing is, you live in the same town I do. If he was really worried – if he was really sorry about what happened and wanted to do something to make me feel better – all he had to do was ask you to get a message to me."

"Honey, that's easy to say, but a man doesn't want to ask another man to take care of his woman when he can't do it himself," Chief Terry argued. "It's especially hard in our situation."

"Because I think of you as a surrogate father?"

Chief Terry's expression softened. "Not just that, but thank you for saying it. That makes me feel all warm and gooey inside."

"That won't work." My tone was icy. "I'm still going to kill Landon."

Chief Terry's smile tipped upside down. "You won't be happy until this completely explodes, will you?"

"I won't be happy regardless," I shot back, tears filling my eyes. "Dammit!" I swiped haphazardly at my cheeks. "Why can't I stop crying? It's ridiculous. I don't want to cry."

"Well, that makes two of us," Chief Terry noted. "I don't ever want you to cry. If I had to guess, I'm thinking Landon doesn't want that either. Did you cry when you were with him earlier? Is that why he was so miserable?"

Something occurred to me. "Did he stop to see you again after our talk?"

"I … um … ." Chief Terry looked around the grounds, uncomfortable. "He most certainly did not if it's going to get him in more trouble."

"I'm not sure how much more trouble he could be in, but I'm just so … freaking tired." I almost yelled the final two words but managed to catch myself before drawing unwanted attention. "You don't need to worry about this. Everything will be … well … it'll work out how it's meant to work out."

"Yeah, I don't like the sound of that," Chief Terry muttered. "Bay, I know you're angry and I believe you have a right to your feelings. I always believe that, for the record. But Landon is miserable. He's blaming himself for hurting your feelings."

"Good."

"He didn't mean to do it," Chief Terry offered, ignoring my grim detachment. "He loves you, Bay. I wasn't sure if he was a good match for you at the beginning, but the boy loves you more than anything. Don't let this thing fester. Neither one of you deserve it."

"Can I ask you something?"

Chief Terry clearly wasn't expecting a question, but he held his palms turned out and shrugged. "Always."

"Did he send you here to make sure I was okay or because he

thought you might be able to soften me up and make things easier for him later tonight?"

"I ... think you need a nap or something," Chief Terry said, averting his gaze. "You're clearly exhausted."

"Yeah. That's what I thought." I spun on my heel, relieved to find Thistle and Clove approaching. "Let's go," I barked. "I have things to do and I don't have time to mess around here."

Thistle widened her eyes as she glanced between Chief Terry and me. "What did you do?"

"I have no idea, but I need to get back to Hemlock Cove and warn Landon," Chief Terry replied. "You might want to take the keys from her. She's not drunk, but she's running on rage and that's almost worse."

"I heard that," I snapped.

"I know you did." Chief Terry looked morose. "Sweetheart, I was only trying to help."

I wanted to say something to make him feel better – it wasn't his fault, after all – but my anger wouldn't let me. "I'm not sure anything will help right now."

"Don't say that." Chief Terry glanced at Clove for help. "Don't let her make things worse."

"I'm pretty sure that's inevitable at this point."

SEVEN

I dropped Thistle and Clove at Hypnotic before heading home. I gave them a terse rundown of my conversation with Chief Terry – something they wisely opted not to comment on – and then embraced the solitude as I drove out of town.

It's weird. The month Landon was gone I felt abandoned and hated being alone. Now that he was back and practically begging for forgiveness, the only thing I wanted was solitude.

I steered my car toward the guesthouse, although I recognized the inherent dangers in doing so. Landon would probably seek me out there. I wasn't sure how I wanted to handle our next interaction. I was angry enough to say things I might well regret at some point, and I needed to cool down. That meant I couldn't risk running into Landon.

I parked at the guesthouse, figuring Landon would attempt to approach me at The Whistler first. I told him I had an assignment, and that generally meant returning to the office to write my article before heading home. Once he realized I wasn't going to the office he'd head for the guesthouse and find my car. I wouldn't be there, though. No, I would be at The Overlook. He wouldn't dare look for me there, because he was afraid of the older generation of Winchester women.

The days were still warm enough that I didn't need more than my hoodie to stay warm during the walk to the inn. I was feeling better about things, stronger at least, when I let myself into the family living quarters at the back of The Overlook. I expected to find Aunt Tillie sitting on the couch watching her afternoon programs, but the room was vacant. That was fine. I wasn't in the mood to explain myself or expand on recent life upheavals. I avoided the kitchen, where I knew my mother and aunts were likely preparing meals for the guests, and instead used the back stairwell to cut through the second floor and descend again in the main part of the inn.

It was the weekend, and the inn was fairly well booked. Mom said they had one open room and expected it to be snatched up by a walk-in. That meant a steady stream of guests would wander in and out of the lobby. Landon knew better than to show up and pick a fight in the middle of my mother's place of business.

Er, well, I thought Landon knew better than that. I pulled up short when I shuffled into the small library off the main foyer and found him sitting in our favorite spot on the couch and staring at me.

"What are you doing here?"

Landon's smile was sly. "Well, I came to town to spend time with my girlfriend, but she doesn't seem keen to play nice. I thought it was probably wise to get a room to make sure I had a roof over my head tonight."

"That shows what you know," I shot back. "The inn is booked."

"No, they had one room available," Landon corrected. "I happened to arrive at a good time and secured the room in question."

My mouth dropped open as realization washed over me. "You can't be serious. You're going to keep my mother and aunts from making money on that room? That's ... not nice."

Landon snorted, genuinely amused. He seemed to have a bit of his swagger back. I wasn't sure how I felt about it. On one hand, I liked it when he was feeling good about himself. On the other, his ego tends to get out of control if someone doesn't take him in hand.

"This family is rarely nice," Landon said. "Besides, I'm paying for the room, so your mother isn't losing out on any money."

"I ... you're paying?"

"Yes."

"Is that because Mom wouldn't let you stay otherwise?"

Landon shifted on the couch, knitting his eyebrows. "That's not exactly how it went down. I'd be lying if I said our initial interaction was pleasant. It seems I've got to win over the entire family again. I guess it's good I'm up to the challenge."

"Are you? Up to the challenge, I mean."

"I'm not leaving this inn until we make up, Bay." Landon was earnest as he shifted the book he was perusing upon my arrival. "I'm not kidding. My heart hurts when I look at you."

I wanted to go weak in the knees and forgive him. Pride wouldn't allow me to take the coward's approach, though. "Yeah? Well, my heart hurt every time I thought about you for an entire month."

"I was doing my job, Bay."

"I have no problem with you doing your job," I shot back. "I knew when I fell in ... when I started dating you ... that you might have to go undercover. That was hard, but I could deal with it.

"Sure, if you listen to my family they'll say I was pathetic and whiny, but I was dealing with it," I continued. "My problem is with the fact that after you ran into me – and had another woman hanging all over you, for the record – that you couldn't be bothered to call me."

"I told you that wasn't an option." Landon extended a warning finger. "I'm also not happy that you cut yourself off before saying you fell in love with me. Are you saying you don't love me any longer?"

The question jolted me. "I ... no."

"That's good, because I would really prefer not crying in front of people," Landon muttered. "Bay, if there was any way I could have called you that night, don't you think I would've done it?"

"You found a way to call Chief Terry."

Landon's expression remained neutral, but I could almost feel the panic rolling off of him. "I ... what?"

"You heard me."

Landon worked his jaw, but no sound came out. I decided to help him out of his predicament.

"You talked to Chief Terry that night," I reminded him. "You managed to get a message to him. All you had to do was ask him to come to me – or hell, even text me – and apologize. All you had to do was ask him and he would've gotten me a message."

"Bay, I didn't even consider that," Landon admitted, his voice going weak. "I didn't want to have to use the man you consider your father as a proxy. That didn't seem fair ... or right."

"Oh, but letting me cry myself to sleep every night for the past four nights was right?"

"No. I ... did you really cry yourself to sleep?"

Admitting it a second time seemed too painful to consider. "No. I was absolutely fine. I didn't cry. I threw a freaking party."

"Bay." Landon struggled to his feet, a pleading expression on his face. "I am so sorry. You will never know how sorry I am. If I had to do it over again, I would swallow my pride and send Chief Terry to you. I didn't mean to hurt you."

"That doesn't matter now. You did hurt me."

"I didn't mean to do it, though," Landon protested. "Bay, I wouldn't hurt you for the world. You know that."

"I thought I knew that."

"No, you know that," Landon argued. "Deep down inside, in the part you're hiding because you're furious with me, you know I'd never purposely hurt you. In fact, I'd die before I did anything of the sort."

I stared at him a moment, the emotion washing over his handsome features tugging at me even as the anger refused to retreat. "That doesn't change the fact that I feel sick to my stomach and want to throw up when I look at you."

Landon pressed his lips together and forced a watery smile when two guests wandered past the library door. They peered inside, perhaps even considered entering, but the looks on our faces were enough to turn them away. Landon waited until he was sure they were out of earshot before continuing.

"I love you, Bay," Landon gritted out. "I am sorry for hurting you. I will do whatever it takes to make it up to you. I won't let your anger drive us apart."

"My completely justified anger," I muttered, crossing my arms over my chest.

"Your completely justified anger," Landon agreed, bobbing his head. "I'm not leaving until we make up. Period."

"What happens if you run out of money?"

"I'll sleep in my Explorer."

"What happens if I won't talk to you?"

"I'll follow you until you give in."

"That's the refrain of stalkers everywhere," I pointed out. "Is that a wise move for an FBI agent?"

"I haven't resorted to stalking yet," Landon said. "I won't rule it out, though. I can't be without you. I'm so sorry. You simply cannot understand the level of my regret, because I'm just that sorry. But I won't give up."

I stared at him for a long time. I wanted to give in. I wanted to throw my arms around his neck, wrestle him down so I could shave off that stupid beard, and then crawl into bed with him for a month. "It hurts to know that you didn't care enough to find a way to get me a message."

"Bay, I didn't realize the gravity of the situation from your perspective." Landon chose his words carefully. "I realize that was a mistake on my part, and I won't make it again. I was worried about what Becky and Doug would do. I didn't think about what had already been done to you, and I will be forever sorry for that. You can't punish me forever."

I let loose with a haughty laugh. "Oh, that shows what you know. I learned from the best. Aunt Tillie can come up with enough punishments to last forever."

Landon heaved out a sigh, resigned. "Fine. Bring it on. I'm ready."

"It will be worse than smelling like garbage for two days," I warned.

"Bay, I miss you so much I think it's going to swallow me whole," Landon supplied. "Nothing can be worse than that. I'll gladly smell like garbage for the rest of my life if you'll forgive me."

I met his gaze. "I'm not ready for that."

"Then we'll take it one day at a time."

"I guess we will."

Landon's lips curved as he regarded my obstinate stance. "Is the whole family going to punish me or just you? I hate to admit it, but I could get behind this deal if it were just you."

I didn't want to smile, but I couldn't help myself. "You're such a pervert."

"That's all I have to hold on to right now."

"Not all ... but mostly."

Landon smirked. "Come on. I'll get you a drink before dinner and then you can tell me about your day."

"I'm not talking to you," I reminded him.

"Oh, I wasn't thinking that you could tell Landon your boyfriend about your day," he clarified. "I thought you might want to tell the friendly inn guest about your day."

"Is the friendly inn guest a pervert, too?"

"Most definitely."

"Well ... I've had worse offers this month."

"WHAT ARE YOU DOING?"

Dinner wasn't nearly as bad as I envisioned. Landon took his usual seat next to me, although there was none of the playful banter or soft touches we usually engaged in during a family meal. He was polite and attentive, perhaps somehow guessing that's exactly what I needed, but otherwise he didn't force the issue.

Aunt Tillie delighted in treating him like dirt, but he didn't appear to care, instead focusing all of his energy on me. Mom started the meal throwing shade whenever the opportunity arose, but he was her favorite again by the end. She probably saw the obvious – that I would forgive him sooner rather than later – and embraced the inevitable. Still, I wasn't quite ready to let go of my anger.

I expected Marcus and Thistle to return to the guesthouse with me, which would make holding Landon off all the easier. Instead they offered a brief goodbye before heading to Marcus' apartment for the night.

That left me to walk to the guesthouse alone once dessert was over. Landon met me by the back door as I exited, though, taking me by surprise.

"I'm walking you back to the guesthouse," Landon replied, gesturing toward the well-worn pathway. "It's dark and you shouldn't be walking alone."

"I've been walking alone after dark for a month."

The muscle in Landon's jaw worked but he refrained from saying something snarky. "I'm sorry about that. But you're not alone tonight, so I'm walking you back."

"That doesn't mean you're staying the night with me," I warned, falling into step next to him.

"I wouldn't dream of it." Landon's grin was lopsided. "Besides, all of my stuff is unpacked in my room at The Overlook. I'm simply going to make sure you make it back to the guesthouse in one piece."

"Fine." The night air was cool and crisp, not altogether uncomfortable. "Are you going to shave your beard tonight?"

"This beard really bothers you, doesn't it?"

"You don't look like you."

Landon slowed his pace. "If I shave will you forgive me?"

"Oh, a negotiation."

"Sweetie, I'm ready to beg," Landon admitted. "If I thought it would work, I would get down on my hands and knees right here."

Even though the visual held some appeal, that wasn't what I wanted. "I don't want you to beg."

"I know you don't, but I'm desperate to give you whatever it is you do need to forgive me." Landon made a grab for my hand – it was second nature to him, after all – before he thought better of it and ceased his efforts. "I know you still love me. I'm not going to give up."

"Of course I still love you."

Landon's expression brightened. "Thank you for saying it."

"That doesn't mean I'm not upset."

"I know you are. I'll give you the space and time you need to get over it. I promise."

"It might take more than one night," I warned.

"I understand that." He didn't look happy with the prospect, but he didn't argue. In fact, the lines around his eyes were so pronounced that I couldn't help but wonder when he last had a good night's sleep.

"I just need a little time to think," I said, the guesthouse popping into view as we crested a hill.

"You'll have all of the time you need," Landon said. "Love doesn't go away just because of a disagreement, and mine isn't going anywhere."

"I guess that's good."

"Ever, Bay. My love isn't going anywhere ever."

I blinked back tears as I fumbled for the keys to the guesthouse. Landon ultimately grabbed my key ring, selected the right key and slipped it in the lock.

"Get some sleep, sweetie," Landon whispered. "I'll see you at breakfast." He pressed a surprise kiss to my forehead. "Lock the door once you're inside."

"Yes, sir."

Landon mustered a grin. "It's going to be okay. Have a little faith."

"I did have faith," I reminded him. "I think I lost it by a corn maze."

"It's a little ironic that you originally found that faith in a corn maze, isn't it?"

"Ironic or coincidental?"

"Does it matter?"

I shrugged. "I guess not. I'll see you in the morning."

"You definitely will." Landon stood in front of the guesthouse and watched until I locked the door. Then he offered a small wave before turning and trudging back to the inn. I considered stopping him, my hand on the door handle as I opened my mouth to call him back. Something to my right caught my attention, though, and when I swiveled I found I couldn't catch my breath thanks to a fast-moving shadow.

Someone was in the guesthouse. I was sure of it.

It wasn't a ghost. I would've recognized Viola's telltale presence. No, it was a human, and it was someone who wasn't supposed to be in my home.

"Who's there?" My voice was barely a whisper.

No answer.

"I know you're there," I narrowed my eyes and reached out with my heightened senses.

No answer again.

My inner danger alarm went into overdrive as I heard the unmistakable sound of shoes on the floor. I turned swiftly, opening my mouth to scream for Landon. I wasn't fast enough. A hand clamped over my mouth and dragged me from the door.

I fought against my assailant, briefly marveling at the strength I felt in the corded forearm muscles. I couldn't dwell on that for long, though, because the hands wrapped around my throat and cut off my air supply.

I slapped against the stranger's hands and clawed at his flesh, but it was fruitless. As my vision dimmed at the edges I found myself floating forward before slamming back into the wall next to the door, my head hitting with enough force to knock me for a loop.

I struggled to hold onto consciousness.

It was impossible. I slid into darkness as my body crumpled to the floor.

EIGHT

I woke in a slow roll instead of a pitched burst. Everything hurt. My neck ached, but nowhere near as badly as the back of my head. It took me a few minutes to get my bearings, and it was only after I registered the fact that I was wet – a cold rain pelting my face – that I finally managed to force open my eyes.

I rested over the threshold, my head on the front porch and my legs inside the guesthouse. It was dark, clouds obscuring the moon as the rain came down in a steady sheet. I was confused – go figure – and all I could wonder was when it had started raining. I vaguely remembered hearing a weather forecast earlier in the day, but I was certain it wasn't supposed to start storming until after midnight.

I rolled to a sitting position, realizing too late that I might not be alone. The events of the evening came back in bits and pieces, and that's when I remembered that someone had been inside of the guesthouse when I returned. That someone hadn't been happy.

Instinct told me to flee into the guesthouse and call for help. Fear kept me from doing that. What if my assailant was still inside? What if he was waiting to finish the job? I brushed off that thought almost immediately. If my attacker wanted to kill me he had plenty of time while I was unconscious. He must be gone.

Of course, I couldn't be completely certain it was a man. The strength in the hands, though, led me to believe that it couldn't have been a woman. Still ... .

Something caught my attention and I groaned as I shifted my head to the left. An odd lump stretched across the width of the pathway that led to the guesthouse from the driveway. It was a big lump, though I had trouble making out the shape.

I forced myself to stand, straggling in that direction as I furrowed my brow. I couldn't figure out what I stared at until I was almost on top of it ... er, I mean her. Yes, it was a her. I recognized the face even as I struggled for a name. I didn't realize I was standing in blood until the realization that I was looking at a dead body rolled over me.

I dug in my pocket for my cell phone, panic overtaking me. I hit number two on my speed dial and almost cried out in relief when a sleepy voice answered.

"Chief Terry?"

"Bay?" Chief Terry's voice went from muddled to alert in an instant. "What's wrong? Has something happened?"

"I need you to come to the guesthouse. I ... can you please come?"

"Of course, sweetheart. Bay, what's wrong?"

"Someone was here. I ... someone was here and I got thrown into the wall."

Chief Terry's voice turned gruff. "How bad are you hurt, honey?"

"I don't know, but ... someone's dead."

"What do you mean?"

"There's a body. There's a person. I ... can you please help me?"

"Sweetheart, are you safe? Is someone there who can hurt you?"

"I don't think so. I'm pretty sure he's gone." My teeth chattered as shock gave way to reality. "I need you to come now."

"I'm on my way, Bay. Don't move. I ... I will be right there."

I disconnected. For lack of anything better to do – including going inside – I moved back to the steps and sat. Then I stared into nothing, letting my mind float, and waited for help to arrive.

"BAY!"

Chief Terry's face was flushed as he bolted from his police cruiser a few minutes later and raced in my direction.

I recognized his voice and jerked my head in his direction, throwing off the remaining cobwebs as I climbed to shaky feet. "Thank you for coming." I threw my arms around his neck, letting his warmth center me as he rocked back and forth. When I pulled back I saw his gaze was already focused on the body.

"Are you sure she's dead?"

I nodded. "I didn't understand at first. I was confused."

"Stay here a second." Chief Terry left me in the middle of the walkway and moved toward the body. His expression was grim as he dropped to a knee. There was no reason to check for signs of life. Becky's eyes remained fixed and sightless, staring at something only she could see from the moment I discovered her. "She's dead."

"I already told you that."

Chief Terry mustered a horrific grin that was more a grimace than anything else as he moved back in my direction. "I called the state police because we're going to need some help. The medical examiner is on his way, too. I believed you when you told me what you found. I simply had to confirm it."

Mollified, I pressed my lips together. "I'm sorry."

"Don't apologize," Chief Terry chided. "I need you to tell me what happened."

"I'm not sure … ."

"I need you to try," Chief Terry pressed, resting his hands on my shoulders to center me. "Before the state boys get here and this is taken out of my hands, I need to know what happened."

It was only then that I realized I might be in more trouble than I initially envisioned. "Oh."

"Bay, focus on me," Chief Terry ordered, his voice commanding. "Tell me what happened."

I launched into the tale, never taking a misstep besides the few stops and starts I needed to keep things linear. When I was done, a cool rage cascaded over Chief Terry's face as he led me back to the step.

"I'm going to turn on the outside light, sweetheart," he said, reaching inside. "Hold still."

I did as instructed, blinking rapidly when the bright light flooded the porch and my head pounded with pain. "Ow."

"Yeah, I'm worried you might have a concussion," Chief Terry offered, his hands gentle as they swept over the back of my head. "You have a big knot back here. What time did all of this happen, Bay?"

"I'm not sure," I tried to retrieve my memory. "I ... it had to be around eight or so, I think."

"It was after midnight when you called me," Chief Terry noted. "That means you were unconscious for four hours."

That couldn't be right. Still, it felt later when I woke, like somehow my inner body clock marked time while I was out of it. "What happens now?"

"I'm not sure." Chief Terry tilted up my chin and frowned as he stared at my neck. "That's going to bruise badly."

"I don't care about that," I gritted out. "I need to know what she's doing here."

"Do you recognize her?"

I nodded, my heart sinking. "She's the woman who was with Landon at the corn maze the other day."

Chief Terry's face remained immovable, but I didn't miss his sharp intake of breath. "Are you sure?"

"I didn't recognize her when I called you. I mean ... I did. I knew I recognized the face. It wasn't until I sat down that it all came back."

"Well, that isn't good."

"You're a marvel with words."

This time the rueful grin Chief Terry mustered was real. "Honey, where is Landon? Why didn't you call him?"

Uh-oh. I didn't think it was possible to feel worse than I already did. I was wrong. "I forgot he was around when I first called. You were the first person who popped into my head. He's been gone for weeks."

"Well, that's flattering, but where is Landon? Did he go back to Traverse City because you were fighting?"

I shook my head. "He rented a room at the inn."

"Well, this is going to suck." Chief Terry tugged his phone out of his pocket at the same time the emergency vehicle lights pulled into the driveway. "I'll call him. You sit there and rest. Everything will be okay."

I wasn't sure I should believe him, but I really wanted to.

"BAY!"

Landon made it to the guesthouse in fifteen minutes. The property was already taped off and the state police were in the midst of questioning me when he made his appearance. He was disheveled, the beard giving him a tough quality as he flashed his badge to move past the trooper cutting him off.

"Are you okay?" Landon ignored the fact that we were in the middle of an argument and tugged me to him.

"Watch her head," Chief Terry instructed, exiting the guesthouse. The look he gave Landon was anything but friendly. "She took a blow, but refuses to go the hospital."

"I'm okay."

Landon's fingers were gentle as he carefully rubbed them over the back of my head. "That's some knot, sweetie."

"We need photographs of that." Trooper Rob Davis eyed Landon with speculative eyes. "I'll need to talk to you, too, Agent Michaels."

Landon arched an eyebrow, surprised. "Fine. I wasn't here when this happened, though. I'm still not sure what happened."

"Someone was inside the guesthouse when you dropped me off," I supplied. "I felt someone inside. I tried to call out for you, but … ." I broke off, swallowing hard.

"Whoever it was grabbed her around the throat and slammed her into a wall," Chief Terry finished, causing Landon to growl. "She was unconscious for about four hours. The emergency responders took some blood to see if she was drugged, because otherwise the fact that she was unconscious for so long is cause for concern."

"The fact that she was unconscious at all is cause for concern," Landon grumbled. "So ... who is it?" He shifted his eyes to the medical examiner toiling next to the prone form on the ground. "Is that the man who attacked you? If so, it was clearly self-defense."

Davis pursed his lips. "It's not a man."

Landon stilled. "What do you mean? That's not Thistle, is it?" He moved to stride toward the body, but Davis stopped him with a hand in the middle of his chest.

"It's not Thistle," Chief Terry said. He looked upset – even more upset than he had before Landon arrived – and I couldn't wrap my head around his attitude. "Her name is Becky Patterson. I believe you know her."

I didn't think it was possible for Landon to lose even more color from his face. He appeared almost chalky as he glanced between Chief Terry and the body. "Are you kidding?"

"Do you know her?" Davis asked.

"I do." Landon pressed the tip of his tongue to the back of his teeth as he idly ran his hand over my shoulder. "I need to call my boss. I became acquainted with Becky Patterson as part of an undercover operation."

"Chief Terry has already informed us of that," Davis volunteered. "He said he wasn't sure how deep the relationship ran. Were you having a sexual relationship with Ms. Patterson?"

Landon was affronted. "No! Bay is my girlfriend."

I considered arguing the point because I was grumpy, cold and wet, but now clearly wasn't the time.

"If she's your girlfriend, why are you staying at the inn instead of here with her?" Davis queried.

"Because ... ." Landon's eyes drifted to me, silently asking how much I'd shared with Trooper Davis.

I took pity on him. "I told him that we were arguing because I was feeling insecure about your time undercover. I included the fact that we ran into each other at Barnaby Mill – which he's quite familiar with because his uncle owns the property – and mentioned that was the only time I had met Becky."

"I don't think 'insecure' is the right word," Landon said dryly, brushing off the rest of my response.

"What word would you use?" Davis asked.

"Justifiably angry because I didn't take her feelings into consideration," Landon answered. "It was a tense situation, and things spiraled out of hand. I need to call my boss."

"That call has already been placed, sir," Davis said. "We have a meeting tomorrow morning."

"Well, how great for you," Landon deadpanned. "How did she die?"

"Someone cut her throat. We're searching the house for a murder weapon now."

"You're searching the house for a murder weapon?" Landon's eyebrows practically flew up his forehead as he glanced at the open door. "You can't possibly think that Bay did this. She was attacked when she arrived home. That woman had no business on her property. Bay was unconscious when it happened, for crying out loud."

"A home she shouldn't have been going into alone," Chief Terry muttered, veering off course.

Landon pinned him with a weighted look before focusing on Davis. "Bay is injured. She has a bump on the back of her head and contusions around her neck. She clearly didn't do this."

"No offense, Agent Michaels, but I'll be the judge of that," Davis replied, his tone resolute. "For the moment, it certainly seems that Ms. Winchester is the victim of mischief or foul play ... ."

"'It certainly seems,'" Landon snapped.

Davis ignored his tone. "We have to follow the evidence," he stressed. "Right now, she's a person of interest. We obviously have to investigate the matter before we can understand what unfolded here."

"So ... what?" I asked, rubbing my forehead. "I'm just supposed to go inside and get some sleep while you guys search my house and pack up the dead body on the front lawn?"

"For at least the next twenty-four hours, Ms. Winchester, your house is considered a crime scene," Davis replied. "You cannot stay here until we release it back to you."

I stilled. "But ... where am I supposed to stay? What am I supposed to wear? All of my stuff is in there."

"I'll pack clothes for you," Chief Terry offered. "Give me a list and I'll make sure you have everything. I'm sure you can stay at the inn until this is sorted out."

"But ... ."

"I know it's not ideal, Bay, but you can't stay here right now." Chief Terry was sympathetic but firm. "I'm sorry, sweetheart. I know this has been a terrible night for you – in more ways than one – but we can only tackle this one problem at a time." Chief Terry pegged Landon with a dark look. "I'm sure the FBI will be able to figure out why their suspect showed up dead at your house and you were almost killed."

"Do you have something you want to say to me?" Landon challenged.

"I have a lot I want to say to you, but now isn't the time," Chief Terry replied. "I'm going to go inside and pack some things. I'll grab some clothes and your lady stuff from the bathroom."

It was a serious situation, but I couldn't stop my lips from curving. "My lady stuff?"

"You know what I'm talking about." Chief Terry's tone was unnaturally gruff. "It'll be okay. I'll walk you up to the inn as soon as I'm done."

"I can't go to the inn." The realization hit me hard. "All of the rooms are full. There's nowhere for me to sleep unless I want to share a bed with Aunt Tillie ... and nobody wants that."

"I ... well ... ." Chief Terry glanced at the inn, which was barely visible in the foggy night air. "What about Clove? You could stay with her."

"Yes, the idea of living with my cousin who just got engaged and is doing it all over the lighthouse every chance she gets sounds delightful," I muttered.

"What about Thistle?"

"I'm not staying with her and Marcus either." I rolled my neck and glanced at my car. "I guess I can sleep in my car tonight and figure out something else tomorrow."

"You're not sleeping in your car," Landon countered, drawing my attention to him.

"Do you have another idea?"

"Yes. I have a room. You're staying with me."

The idea hadn't even occurred to me. "But ... I'm mad at you."

"I know you are, but you need sleep." Landon leaned closer and studied my bloodstained hands. "You also need a bath."

"I'm still mad at you." Even as I said the words I felt my resolve slipping.

"And I love you and I'm going to take care of you," Landon shot back. "Now, if you have no further questions, Trooper Davis, I believe I will take my girlfriend and put her to bed."

Davis' face was impassive. "That's all for tonight. I'll have more questions tomorrow."

"We're looking forward to it," Landon muttered, slipping his arm around my shoulders and guiding me toward The Overlook. "Don't show up until after breakfast. I've got a plate of bacon with my name on it, and Bay needs her rest."

"I'll take it under advisement."

NINE

"How are you feeling?"

Landon kept his voice low as he led me into his second-floor room at The Overlook. I'd visited the room plenty of times throughout the years, but it felt weird knowing that my boyfriend was essentially living under my mother's roof while we fought. I couldn't wrap my head around it.

"Numb." I answered honestly. "I feel numb."

Landon pressed his lips together as he nodded. "Yeah. That doesn't surprise me." He dropped the bag of clothing and toiletries Chief Terry collected for me before we left the guesthouse on the floor and gently lifted his finger to my face, rubbing his thumb over my cheek. "I'll bet you're exhausted."

I glanced down at my filthy clothes, the rust-colored stains on my hands giving me a jolt. It was Becky's blood. She died on my front walk. She'd been alive at some point a few hours before and then she died right next to me while I was passed out. "How well did you know her?"

Landon followed my gaze. "Not well, Bay. She was overtly sexual and flirted with everyone who crossed her path. She wasn't really interested in me. She simply didn't want anyone else to be interested in me."

"She seemed interested when I saw her."

"That's because she viewed every woman she ever met as competition. She didn't realize there was no competition because you'd won a long time ago."

I knew he was going out of his way to make me feel better and would say anything to achieve that goal, but I felt out of my element given our location and the events of the evening. "I'm in trouble, aren't I?"

"No, you're not." Landon rested his hands on my shoulders and turned me so I had no choice but to stare into his handsome face. "You didn't do anything wrong."

That's not how it felt. "And yet I'm being punished."

"No, I'm being punished," Landon corrected. "I screwed this up. I hurt you. This is coming back to bite me. You're simply the way the universe opted to do it."

"Oddly enough, that almost makes me feel better."

Landon forced a smile for my benefit and then shifted his eyes to my ruined clothes. "I know you're tired – heck, I can see the exhaustion on your face – but I think you'll feel better if you get cleaned up before bed."

He wasn't wrong. Still … . I flicked my eyes to the queen-sized bed in the middle of the room. "Where am I going to sleep?"

Landon looked pained by the question. "You're going to sleep in the bed."

"Where are you going to sleep?"

"I'm going to sleep with you."

"I'm still angry."

Landon heaved a sigh that almost sounded like a strangled chuckle more than anything else. "I know you are. In fact, I encourage you to remain angry until I've been flogged a bit more."

"You want me to flog you?" I was intrigued despite my weariness.

"If that will make you feel better."

I stared at him for a long time, the familiar angles of his face causing my heart to hurt. "I think you feel guilty because your undercover assignment keeps coming back to bite me. You want me to flog you because you can't punch yourself in the face."

Landon cracked a legitimate smile. "Even when you're exhausted you can read my mind, huh?"

"This isn't all your fault," I noted.

"No?"

"You didn't kill her, choke the crap out of me and then try to frame me for murder, did you?"

"No." Landon tilted my chin up and glared at the marks on my neck. They would be bright and ugly in the morning. "I'm going to kill whoever hurt you."

His tone sent a chill through me. "It's okay. I'm okay."

"No, you're not okay." Landon shook his head to dislodge whatever dark thoughts momentarily took him over. "You need to clean up." He leaned over, grabbing a bottle of shower gel from the bag Chief Terry packed before ushering me toward the bathroom. "Do you want a shower or bath? The shower would probably be quicker."

He wasn't wrong. Still, I couldn't stop myself from glancing toward the over-sized garden tub with longing. "Okay. A shower sounds good."

Landon followed my gaze. "A bath sounds better, though, doesn't it?"

"Yes."

"A bath it is." Landon dropped to his knees and started filling the tub, fiddling with the plug and making sure the water was hot – as I preferred it – before turning to me. "Let's get you undressed, huh?"

"That would've sounded a lot more fun a month ago," I groused, resting my hand on the bathroom counter to help me balance as I removed my boots.

"It's going to sound fun again, Bay," Landon said, his voice grave. "I promise."

"I hope so, because it's never going to be fun again if I go to prison for killing your girlfriend."

Landon fell silent and I realized I had taken things a step too far. I wasn't in the mood to apologize, though, so I focused on removing my filthy jeans and top without making a mess. When I finally risked a glance at Landon I found him staring at me with cloudy eyes.

"If you're going to yell … ."

Landon cut me off with a shake of his head. "I'm not going to yell. I've earned every hurtful thing you want to say to me."

"Yeah, but if you don't yell, it takes the fun out of kicking you while you're down."

"Well, you'll have to suffer through that tonight, because I refuse to yell at you for the foreseeable future. We'll see what happens when someone hasn't tried to kill you for a few weeks, okay?"

Landon prodded me toward the bathtub, and I let out a prolonged groan as I sank into the hot water. I figured he would leave me to my soak and refrain from pressing me on the big issues until I returned to the main room. Instead I jumped when he pushed me forward a bit so he could climb into the tub with me.

"What are you doing?" I wasn't embarrassed. He'd seen me naked so many times I'd lost count. Still, it seemed odd to share a tub with him given our fight.

"I'm going to wash your back," Landon replied.

"I'm still angry."

"I know, and I said I want you to stay angry with me until you decide I've earned forgiveness," Landon said. "I meant that."

He sounded so reasonable and innocent I couldn't help but snort. "How am I supposed to stay angry with you when you're naked in the bathtub with me?"

"Something tells me you'll manage." Landon grabbed the shower gel from the floor and opened the cap. "Now lean back and close your eyes."

I wasn't keen on being bossed around, but the second Landon pressed his fingers into my tense shoulder blades I let loose with a low moan and closed my eyes. "That feels … amazing."

"Good."

"I'm not kidding. You should win an award for that … or do it for a living or something."

Landon chuckled, the sound lightening the weight on both of our shoulders. "I'll keep it in mind if I need to find another career. As for you, just relax. I believe I have a month's worth of massages to make up for."

"That's sweet, but if you think you can do that in one night, you're crazy."

"Bay, I will gladly rub your back every moment of every day for the rest of our lives if it makes you feel better."

"That's big talk for a guy who is going to get carpal tunnel from all the massages I make him give me."

Landon snickered. "You sound a little better, sweetie."

"Yeah? I'm not sure I feel better."

"How does your head feel?"

"Sore. So does my neck. So does my hip from lying on the ground. The good news is that my shoulders are feeling better."

"That is good news." I felt his lips brush my cheek as he continued to rub my back. We lapsed into companionable silence, the only noise coming from the inn's furnace when it kicked on. Despite the fact that we were naked and in a tub together, there was nothing sexual about the interplay. Landon didn't even hint at taking the bath in another direction. There was still something intimate about the experience. The shared time together seemed to bridge a gap, even serve as a salve on festering wounds, as Landon busily moved his hands over my back.

I felt so much better ... and then he had to ruin things and open his mouth.

"Bay, I need to ask you a question."

"Oh, geez." I pinched the bridge of my nose as I moved to pull away from him.

"No, it's not the type of question that is meant to force your hand or lead to a bad place." Landon refused to let me move from my spot, his deft fingers remaining industrious. "I need to know, though. I feel ... sick."

Something terrible occurred to me. "I wasn't attacked ... that way."

"What? Oh, well, I'm glad to have that confirmed, but I asked the emergency responder when his partner was checking you that second time before we left to walk over here. If that happened to you I would be burning down the town to find whoever attacked you. It's bad enough that you were tossed around the way you were. If the other happened ... ."

He left it hanging, but I knew what he meant. "I'm okay."

"No, but I'm going to make sure you're okay again." Landon rested his chin on my shoulder. "That goes for everything. I'm going to make sure that we're okay again, Bay. I swear it."

"We're okay." I said the words, but put very little effort behind them. "I probably won't even be angry a little bit when I wake up in the morning." I knew sleeping close to him would eradicate much of my anger. There wasn't much I could do about it. The idea of sleeping separate from him tonight was almost too painful to fathom.

"We're not even close to okay, but that's what I want to talk to you about." Landon's hands stilled on my back. "I don't want to make things worse, but I need to know something."

I steeled myself for some sort of delayed meltdown. I had no idea if it would be him or me doing the melting, though. "Okay. What?"

"Why did you call Chief Terry instead of me after you woke up and found the body?"

Whatever I was expecting, that wasn't it. I risked a glance over my shoulder so I could meet his gaze, groaning as a jolt of pain shot through me. "Seriously?"

"On any other day you would've called me."

"Except I haven't been able to call you for a month."

"I know, but ... ."

"I don't think you do know," I corrected. "Every single time something stupid happened over the past thirty days, I've wanted to call and tell you. When Clove left her shoes in the middle of Hypnotic to dry and Thistle tripped over them and threatened to curse her with a spell that made it so she'd never fit in a wedding dress, I wanted to call you.

"When I had a bad day and wanted to curl up on your lap, you weren't here," I continued. "I couldn't even call you to talk for five minutes. You might think I'm spoiled, but I got used to having you in the same bed at least four nights a week, and when you weren't there … ."

"Sweetie, don't you think I missed you, too?" Landon's voice was ragged. "I didn't sleep more than a few hours a night without you. Sure, some of that was worry about the case, but most of it was worry about you.

"I didn't take this case to punish you, but I ended up punishing the crap out of both of us," he continued. "I didn't want to be away from you. When Steve offered it to me … I only agreed because we made a deal."

I stilled, surprised. Steve Newton, his immediate supervisor, was the big boss in Landon's office. I liked him a great deal – he was a nice guy – but the "deal" part of the conversation threw me for a loop. "I'm not sure what that means."

"It means that I told Steve I would do this one last undercover assignment because it was a big case and I was familiar with the ins and outs of meth from the last case, but then I wanted a few things to change around the office," Landon explained.

"Like what?"

"I wanted all of this to be a surprise when I was done," Landon muttered, his fingers returning to their previous task. "Once this case is over I'm going to get a promotion. Er, well, I was supposed to get a promotion … but that might not happen because of all this. The murder of one of my suspects probably will throw that off.

"Anyway, I agreed to the assignment even though it was taking me away from you because I thought it would be better for us in the long run," he continued. "The promotion doesn't involve a great deal of money, but it does allow me to choose my location."

"Oh." Realization washed over me, my freakout regarding the possibility of him being transferred pushing to the forefront of my brain. "You wouldn't have to move if you didn't want to move?"

"Bay, I'm not leaving you regardless," Landon replied. "I need you to know that. The promotion would simply be a way for me to make sure that they didn't even bother trying."

"Oh. Well, crap. That would've made me a bit easier to deal with if you told me that. You know that, right?"

Landon snorted. "I told you that I wanted it to be a surprise. I had a big weekend planned for us when this was done."

"And now it's nowhere near close to being done," I mused. "I suppose you can't tell me about the case, can you?"

"Not tonight, but I will tomorrow." Landon slid his hands around me, pulling my back to his chest. "I'm not supposed to talk about it, but you're in the middle of things now. I need to talk to Steve first, see where everything stands, and then move forward."

"And ask him if you can bring me in on the big secret?"

"No, sweetie, I'll be telling you everything whether he allows it or not," Landon answered. "I need sleep first."

"You're not the only one."

"Here, let me see your hands." Landon poured more shower gel into the palm of his hands and began working on my fingernails, determined to make sure none of Becky's blood remained behind. "You haven't answered my question, Bay. Why did you call Chief Terry instead of me?"

"When I woke up, I was confused," I admitted. "I felt as if I was caught in a nightmare or something. My head felt too big for my body, as if it might slide off at any second. When I saw her body ... when I saw her face ... I recognized her, but I couldn't remember a name. I'm not sure if that makes sense."

"I understand that part. It's just ... you called Chief Terry."

"Because I thought you were still out of town. I know that seems weird, but I kind of skipped past you because I had to constantly remind myself not to call you while you were gone. Eight times a day I would tell myself that you were undercover and I couldn't call. I guess it kind of stuck in my head."

"Why couldn't you call?"

"Because you were undercover."

"Yeah, and I didn't have my phone with me. I called in to check my messages every single day. I would've loved to hear your voice. You could've called."

"I'm fairly certain that would've made me even more pathetic than I already was."

"According to who?"

"Aunt Tillie."

"She doesn't count."

"Thistle."

"She doesn't count either."

"Even Clove thought I was whiny ... as did my mother ... and Marnie ... and Twila."

"I don't care about any of that," Landon argued. "I care about you and me. I missed you so much it hurt. I didn't think anything could hurt more than that until you called Chief Terry when you were in trouble."

"I didn't really think," I said. "I wanted you, and yet ... I simply kept telling myself that I couldn't have you."

"You have me forever." Landon tightened his arms around me to the point where I thought he would cut off circulation.

"What if you have to go back undercover now that this has happened?" I asked the question without thinking. "Is that a possibility?"

"No. Even if Steve asked me to do it – he won't, because it's far too dangerous now – I wouldn't do it. I'm not leaving you again, Bay. I promise. I swear it."

I pressed my eyes shut and rested my head against his shoulder. "Okay."

"Yeah, okay."

TWENTY MINUTES later Landon loaded me into a pair of his boxer shorts and one of his oversized T-shirts before piling into bed next to me. He turned off the light before slipping his arm under my waist and tugging me onto his chest, tucking the blankets in tightly before resting one hand on my back and the other on my hip, cocooning me in his muscled arms so I couldn't move ... or have the room to terrify myself in my sleep.

"What happens now?" I asked, my eyelids heavy as I rested my ear above his heartbeat.

"Now we both get the sleep we need. We'll tackle this together in the morning."

"What if I'm still angry?"

"Then I'll ask you to put a moratorium on the punishment until we get through this," Landon replied. "I'm not asking you to forgive me. I know I haven't earned it yet. We need to work together, though, Bay. It's important."

The edge in his voice told me he was much more worried than he wanted to let on. "Okay."

"Okay what?"

"I'm done being angry."

Landon chuckled. "I just said … ."

"I wanted to be done with the anger hours ago," I admitted, refusing to let him say something to derail my train of thought. "I had my hand on the door to stop you from walking away from the guesthouse when … well, when I felt someone behind me."

Landon's grip tightened to the point where I thought I might lose the ability to breathe. "I should've stayed. I shouldn't have left. But I didn't want to push things. I wanted you to be able to be as angry as you wanted to be. You deserved it."

"We both made mistakes."

"Yes, but … I won't hurt you like this again, Bay." I heard the crack in Landon's voice but refused to raise my head. If he cried I knew I would, and I already felt drained. "I won't do it again. I honestly was trying to make things better for us."

"I know." I rested my hand on his firm chest. "You should've told me about the deal."

"Then it wouldn't have been a surprise."

"I know. I … it's a mess."

"We'll fix it, Bay." Landon pressed a kiss to my forehead. "I'm so sorry. I'm so, so sorry."

"I'm sorry, too."

"Don't you dare apologize," Landon whispered, shifting a bit so he could tuck me in tighter. I was at the point where I couldn't move if I wanted to. "You didn't do anything. This is all on me. I'll fix it."

"I know you will."

"How?"

I shrugged. "I have faith."

Landon let out a relieved sigh as he rubbed his fingers over my back. "Thank you."

I knew he was crying before I felt a tear land on my cheek. Even though I thought my tear ducts were dry I realized quickly that I was wrong. "I love you." I sniffled as he rubbed his cheek against my forehead. "The beard has to go, though."

Despite our mingled tears, Landon let loose a guttural laugh that shook his entire body. "Your wish is my command."

"I thought you had to keep it until the case was completed."

"That was before the people who weren't supposed to know who I was went after the woman I love," Landon responded, serious. "Undercover time is over. This is war."

"Well, that sounds great. Aunt Tillie loves a good war."

"We might need her." Landon's breathing turned regular. "Now, go to sleep. You need to rest."

"I think you do, too."

"I simply need to hold you ... and love you ... and maybe eat some bacon in the morning. That's all I want."

"Then I think you're probably due to hit a streak of luck."

"Oh, sweetie. I've been riding that streak since I met you."

"You're being kind of schmaltzy," I pointed out. "Aunt Tillie won't like that."

"I don't care."

"Are you going to keep doing it?"

"Until I make us both want to puke."

The admission made me happy. "That sounds good. I think I can sleep now."

Landon didn't respond. He was already dead to the world. The simple sound of his steady breathing was enough to allow me to follow a few seconds later.

It felt good to have him back, even if I was now a murder suspect and a killer was out there somewhere … watching.

TEN

I woke in exactly the same position, my head resting on Landon's chest and his arms tightly wrapped around me. It took me a moment to get my bearings, and then the previous evening's events came flooding back, including the fact that Landon woke me with a kiss once an hour – as the emergency responder insisted – before asking me how handsome he was on a scale of one to ten, and then letting me fall back asleep.

"Morning," Landon murmured, his beard scratchy against my forehead. "How are you feeling?"

That was an interesting question. I wasn't sure. I decided to test my body by stretching my weary muscles, and immediately wished I did almost anything else. "Ugh."

"That good, huh?" Landon smoothed my hair and stared into my eyes. "How about we go to the clinic in Bellaire and have you checked out?"

That sounded like a terrible idea. "I'm fine."

"You're pretty far from fine, but I still feel guilty enough not to push you." Landon heaved a sigh before kissing my forehead three times in rapid succession. He couldn't seem to get enough of the tactile sensation. "How handsome am I on a scale of one to ten?"

It was the same question he asked each time he woke me. He was supposed to hold up fingers and ask me how many I saw, but we were both too exhausted to mess with the lamp on the nightstand.

"You're a five with the beard."

Landon scowled. "The beard is going today. I told you that."

"Then I can't answer the question until it's gone."

"You drive a hard bargain."

I thought Landon would immediately get up and retreat to the bathroom, but instead he kept me pressed tightly to his chest as he shifted to make sure we were both comfortable.

"It's morning," he murmured, focusing on the window.

"I noticed. The sunlight coming in through the window was a dead giveaway."

"I see your smart mouth is back." Landon poked my side. "We need to talk about a few things."

"Are you considering becoming a woman?"

Landon was somber, but the question caused his lips to curve. "I'm thinking that I would like nothing better than to pack you up and go away for a month. Just you, me, a hotel on the beach and room service. How does that sound?"

"Nice, but impractical. I'm a murder suspect."

"You're not a suspect." Landon said the words, but he didn't put a lot of effort behind them. I knew he was worried about Davis' attitude.

"If you didn't know me and I called in what happened last night, wouldn't you think I was a suspect?"

Landon immediately started shaking his head. "No, sweetie, I wouldn't. You would have to be an idiot to set a scene that way if you really expected to frame someone for a murder they didn't commit."

"How so?"

"Well, for starters, you're injured," Landon supplied. "You have visible injuries on your neck, a knot on the back of your head and your eyes make me want to cry."

The last part jolted me. "What's wrong with my eyes?" I instinctively reached up to touch them. "I still have two of them, right?"

"You do and they're beautiful. They're also really red from blood rushing to the surface."

"Oh, well, great," I muttered. "People will think I'm stoned."

Landon snorted out a laugh, relaxing a bit. "I think that's the least of our worries. I haven't seen the autopsy report yet, but from what I saw, whoever killed Becky did it with brutal force. You're not strong enough to murder someone in that fashion."

"So ... why kill her on my front walk? Why knock me out and leave me in the doorway?"

Landon wrinkled his nose as he traced his fingers over mine. "To send me a message."

That hadn't occurred to me, yet it fit. "I ... huh."

"Yeah. Someone clearly figured out that I was an FBI agent. They wanted to send a message."

"Do you think they figured it out before or after we ran into each other at the corn maze?"

"That's a good question," Landon answered. "I thought I'd managed to play it off even though they were watching me closely. I got the distinct feeling that Becky somehow felt something when I saw you."

"I thought you played it pretty cool. I barely recognized you."

"Yes, but when I first saw you, that moment when I saw you walk through the doors of the barn, I kind of ... jerked ... a little bit," Landon explained. "I almost called out to you I was so excited to see you. Then reality set in."

"Seeing me was the worst possible thing, huh?"

"Seeing you was the best thing that happened to me in almost a month," Landon clarified. "I didn't realize how much I needed to see you until you were standing in front of me. Aunt Tillie was ... well ... Aunt Tillie. Becky thought she acted odd during our brief conversation, but Doug thought she was funny and pointed out that she was old and possibly senile."

"You probably should leave that part out when Aunt Tillie hears this story."

"Yeah." Landon was grim. "I was desperate for them not to focus on you. I wanted to punch Doug in the face when he looked at you. He didn't say a lot … but I could tell what he was thinking. I wanted to kill him."

"Well, Doug would be the obvious choice for a murder suspect because only the three of you were there that day," I pointed out, opting to be pragmatic rather than letting him wallow in negative emotions. "If you were the target and Becky was the victim, that leaves only Doug. Maybe he figured out you were an agent and wanted to make sure Becky couldn't rat on him."

"Whoever it was wanted to maim me," Landon said. "Hurting you is the best way to do that. You could've easily been killed. That means someone is playing with us."

"I'm kind of glad I wasn't killed." I offered him a rueful smile. "I don't think I could make you my massage slave if I were dead."

Landon's expression softened. "I think we're both glad you're not dead. I wouldn't be here if that were the case."

"Where would you be?"

"Finding you."

"I … what?" I narrowed my eyes as I propped myself on an elbow, ignoring the way my body screamed in protest. "Are you saying you'd kill yourself?"

Landon averted his gaze. "I never considered myself the type, but … now that I know there's something on the other side, that you'd be on the other side … ."

"That I'd be ticked and kicking you in the rear end on the other side," I clarified. "Landon, you can't think things like that."

"I don't want to talk about it." Landon licked his lips and gently supported me as we sat. "You're okay. I'm going to keep you that way if it kills me. We need to figure out who did this and then find them. That's the only way we'll get our lives back."

"I guess we need to start by filling in the rest of the family on what happened. They were asleep. They don't know."

"I'm guessing Chief Terry filled them in this morning." Landon tugged a hand through his tousled hair. "It's later than you realize."

"What time is it?"

"Almost noon."

The answer floored me. "But ... I can't believe I slept that long."

"You needed it."

"I can't believe you slept that long."

"I needed it, too."

"Yeah, but you missed your bacon." It felt odd to worry about something that trivial, but Landon's laugh was worth the general awkwardness.

"I much prefer being with you to eating bacon," Landon said, grinning. "I know it boggles the mind, but it's true."

"Still, I'm hungry." As if on cue, my stomach growled. "I also need to talk to my family. We have a crime scene on the property. It's not the inn, but they're still affected."

"I'm already their least favorite person these days. I can't think this will help matters."

I sympathetically patted his arm. "They'll get over it. I did."

"You're not over it yet. I'm hopeful you will be soon, but you're still upset, and I don't blame you. I suppose we should get cleaned up and face the cursing squad."

Now it was my turn to laugh. "It'll be okay."

"I'm pretty sure that should be my line."

WE SHOWERED TOGETHER, and although it was nothing like our normal playful showers I enjoyed the sense of familiarity and returning to our former rhythm. I especially liked watching from the counter as Landon lathered his face and shaved off the unsightly facial hair.

"I can't believe you don't like my beard," he teased, catching my eye in the mirror. "I have it on good authority that women like scruffy-looking men."

I returned his smile. "I like it when you have stubble in the morning. That's sexy. But you look like one of the guys from *Duck Dynasty*. That's the opposite of sexy."

Landon rolled his eyes. "I don't look like one of the guys from *Duck Dynasty*."

"You know what? Even if I had no choice but to live with the beard forever I'd find a way to live with it. That's how much I love you."

Landon's expression softened. "Right back at you." He dropped a kiss on my upturned mouth before wiping away the stray shaving cream that landed on my chin. "I know you don't mean that over the long haul, though. You'd wear me down on the beard."

"I'm just glad it's going away."

Landon smirked. "Give me five minutes."

I dressed in simple jeans and a T-shirt – Chief Terry didn't get fancy when packing for me, and I was thankful for that – and my hair was still wet when I returned to the bedroom. I spent five minutes running my fingers over Landon's smooth face, "oohing" and "aahing" about how handsome he was before reluctantly tearing myself away from him. I was keen to spend time with that freshly-shaven face, but I was absolutely starving.

I pulled up short when I realized we were no longer alone, my mother and Aunt Tillie holding trays in the open doorway.

"What … ?"

"Good morning." Mom's tone was warm and friendly, and she managed to muster a smile for Landon as he walked into the room behind me. "You look much better without the beard."

"So I've been told." Landon arched an eyebrow as he stared at the trays. "What's that?"

"Breakfast."

"Really?" My stomach growled as I shifted closer. "Is there poison in it? Did you hear what happened last night?"

Mom made a face as she carried the tray to the small table at the edge of the room. "Like I would poison my own food. I don't spend hours a day slaving over the stove so I can poison you."

"That wasn't really an answer to my question." I sat in the chair, doing my best to keep from groaning at the pain, and then sighed when I lifted the cover from the plate. "You made me an omelet."

"It's your favorite." Mom's smile was gentle. "Ham. Onions. Mushrooms. Tomatoes. There's also hash browns and fresh toast. Do you want coffee or juice? I can bring up either."

"You don't have to wait on me," I said, grabbing the napkin from the tray. "I'm starving. We were on our way down. We had no idea how long we slept."

Landon accepted the tray from Aunt Tillie, giving her a dubious look as he sat down across from me. "Did you spit in it?"

"I wanted to, but Winnie wouldn't stop watching me," Aunt Tillie replied, moving to the bed and flopping down at the end. "I'm not rolling in sex cooties, am I?"

Landon shot her a dirty look as he lifted the cover on his plate, the corners of his mouth tipping up when he saw the French toast. It was offset by a huge mound of bacon. "I can't believe you did this given … well … given everything."

"I happen to believe most of this isn't your fault," Mom said.

"Thank you."

"That doesn't mean a lot of this isn't your fault," Mom pointed out. "Terry came for breakfast. He told us most of it, by the way. He's not happy."

"I figured that out myself last night." Landon bit into a slice of bacon and moaned. "Oh, it's as good as I remember."

"What? You didn't have bacon when you were undercover?" I asked, cutting into my omelet with gusto. "I'm so hungry I could eat your bacon."

Landon flipped several slices of bacon from his plate to mine. "Eat up. You need your strength. As for having bacon while I was away, I used it as a psychological tool. I thought I would get things in order faster if I didn't have my two favorite things in the world."

"What else didn't you have beside bacon?" I asked, genuinely curious.

Landon answered without hesitation. "You."

"Oh, that's kind of sweet." Mom cuffed the back of Landon's head. "You're still an idiot. I can't believe you didn't call after running into Aunt Tillie and Bay at that corn maze."

"Yes, my idiocy has been well established," Landon noted. "I'm prepared to grovel for the rest of my life to make up for it."

"That's well and good for Bay, but I might need something more," Aunt Tillie said. "I'll make a list for when things are back to normal. For now we have to focus on the dead person."

"Becky," I supplied. "It was the woman we met at the maze that day."

"Yeah, that's what Terry said." Aunt Tillie looked serious. "How does your case stand now?"

"I thought it was done," Landon replied. "I gave the information I gathered to my superiors. The Prosecutor's Office issued warrants for various arrests. I was not around for those arrests because I headed straight here the moment I was free."

"So, as far as you know, everyone should've been in custody," I mused.

"Yes, except Becky clearly wasn't in custody, and neither was the person who killed her," Landon supplied. "I need to find out what's going on. We can't move forward until we see where we stand."

"And then what?" I asked, my stomach flipping as something occurred to me. "What happens if I'm arrested for murder and go to jail?"

"That won't happen," Landon replied, his tone gruff. "I won't let it happen."

"I won't either," Aunt Tillie offered. "I've already got a plan ready to get you out of the country. Don't worry about it."

Landon shot her a warning look. "Don't be cute."

"Who's being cute?" Aunt Tillie challenged. "If you think I'm letting one of my girls go to prison for something she didn't do – heck, I wouldn't let it happen for something she did do – then you're crazy. I won't simply sit back and let someone hurt Bay."

"Then you can join my club," Landon suggested, handing me another slice of bacon as he kept his eyes on Aunt Tillie's serious face. "I won't let anyone hurt her, either. I promise."

Aunt Tillie wasn't ready to back down. "What if you can't stop it?"

"Then I'll be with her when you get her out of the country,"

Landon replied. "I won't let Bay pay for something she didn't do, and I won't live without her. For now, though, we're nowhere near that point of no return. We have to find out what's going on and then adjust our planning from there. Can you live with that?"

Aunt Tillie's face was hard to read as she perched on the end of the bed and blinked. Finally she was stirred to movement. "I can live with it for the time being, but I can't promise what will happen down the line. If I feel this thing is going in a direction I don't like, I'll start handling things myself."

"That's a terrifying thought," Landon muttered. "I won't let anyone take Bay from this family. More importantly, I won't let anyone take her from me."

"How is that more important?" Mom asked, confused.

"Because I love her more than anything," Landon answered, refusing to back down. "We're going to figure this out. I need everyone to work as a team to do it. Okay?"

Aunt Tillie furrowed her brow. "Okay, but I'm still going to curse the dickens out of you when this is over. You hurt her feelings."

"I know, and I'm sorry." Landon flashed me a reassuring smile. "She's going to punish me later, too."

"Oh, please," Aunt Tillie scoffed. "Kisses aren't punishment. You'll be crying when I'm done with you."

"I'm looking forward to it."

"You won't be when I'm done. I can promise you that."

ELEVEN

"Where is your coat?"

Landon looked me over once we hit the front lobby after finishing breakfast. He placed a call to his boss while I talked things over with my mother and aunts in the kitchen before rejoining him. I thought for sure he'd put up a fight when I said I wanted to go with him – wherever he planned to start the investigation – but he opted for the opposite tack.

"I ... don't know." That was a good question. I racked my brain about the night before and frowned. "Someone took it."

"What do you mean?" Landon was confused. "You were wearing it when I dropped you off at the guesthouse."

"And I was wearing it when I got attacked," I said. "I wasn't wearing it when I woke up. I didn't take it off so ... maybe it's in the guesthouse. Chief Terry probably didn't think to grab it. I can borrow a hoodie from Aunt Tillie. She has a bunch of them."

"I'm fine with that – although try to grab something that won't draw too much attention when we're questioning people at the corn maze. I don't understand how someone got your hoodie off while you were unconscious."

That was a good point. "Maybe they wanted it for something."

"What?"

"I don't know." I ran my hand over the back of my neck. In the bright light of day my neck and head hurt the most, although my hip didn't feel great either. "I didn't even notice it was missing until you asked about it."

Landon absentmindedly moved my fingers from my neck so he could rub the area. "I don't like that. It's weird. Call Chief Terry and ask him if he saw your hoodie inside the guesthouse. I'd like to go over there and check out the scene myself, but I don't want to run into the state troopers. I'm guessing they're over there again today."

"Why don't you call him? And that feels really good."

Landon smirked, although the expression hung around for only a few seconds. "Chief Terry isn't accepting calls from me right now. I think he's angry."

"Why? You didn't choke me."

"No, but I left you to walk into that guesthouse alone and this is happening because of me," Landon pointed out. "He's angry, and he has a right to be. You're his favorite, after all. I'll talk to him when I get a chance."

"I'll call him on the way. Let me grab a hoodie from Aunt Tillie and we'll get going."

"That sounds like a plan."

LANDON DROVE by the guesthouse on our way out, his eyes narrowing as he studied the cars in front of the structure. He didn't look happy, but refrained from commenting.

"Chief Terry has no idea what happened to my hoodie. He doesn't think it was inside when he packed for me," I volunteered once I disconnected the call. "He's definitely angry with you."

Landon didn't look surprised at the tidbit. "What did he say?"

"That he's worried about what happened to my hoodie, the same as you."

"Not that." Landon made an exasperated face. "What did he say about me? Wait ... don't tell me. No, I want to know. Tell me."

"He didn't say much." I averted my gaze and stared out the window as Landon pulled on to the highway. "It's not important. He'll get over it."

"You're a terrible liar. You know that, right?"

"It's not a lie." Technically it wasn't. Chief Terry said very little about Landon. His tone was a different story. I could feel the fury over the call, and he wasn't happy when I mentioned that Landon and I planned to spend the day investigating. I decided to change the subject. "What did Steve say?"

"He said the entire thing is a mess and he doesn't know how Becky evaded arrest," Landon replied, apparently opting to let the Chief Terry kerfuffle go for the time being. "They had eyes on her before serving the warrants, but when they entered her place she was gone."

"Did anyone else evade arrest?"

"Doug."

"It's him." I was certain. "I told you it was him."

"Yes, well, I would like a little more proof before settling on him as the only suspect." Landon reached across the center console in his Explorer and gathered my hand. "If he ran, there's no telling where he'll end up. Part of me hopes he's already left the area."

"And the other part?"

"I hope he's close, because I'm going to beat the living snot out of him if he touched you."

Landon sounded so bloodthirsty my mouth went a bit dry. "I'm okay," I reminded him. "I'm right here."

"No thanks to me."

"Oh, geez." I rubbed my forehead as I leaned back in the seat, being careful to keep the hard seatback from pressing against the knot on my head. "Are you going to go into martyr mode? If so, I'm really not in the mood."

"I'm not being a martyr."

"That's exactly what you're being," I countered, refusing to back down. "You were doing your job. Things got out of hand."

"And you're paying the price. That's on me."

"Oh, yeah? How many times have things gotten out of hand with my family? How many times have you covered for us? How many times have you paid the price for something I did?"

"I ... ." Landon broke off, uncertain how to answer. "I don't think that's even remotely the same thing," he said after a beat. "I brought someone to your door who almost killed you."

"And you've been shot protecting me."

"I was doing my job."

"And you've risked yourself to save me other times," I reminded him. "You've jumped off tankers with me because we were being chased by mean ghosts. You've saved me more times than I can count. Should we keep a running tally to make sure things are equal?"

"I hate it when you use that tone," Landon muttered, refusing to meet my gaze.

"And I hate it when you use that tone," I shot back. "We can't go back in time and change what happened. We can only move forward ... if you want to move forward, I mean. You acted like an ass when you didn't call me, but I don't believe you did it out of malice. That's what I'm angry about, by the way. I'm not angry because the people from your undercover operation came after me."

"Which shows you have skewed priorities." Landon lifted an eyebrow as his eyes drifted to me. "Bay, the fact that you got hurt because of me makes me sick."

"And the fact that you didn't bother to call after we ran into each other at the corn maze makes me sick," I shot back. "The thing is, I've decided to let it go. You made a mistake. You apologized. I'm going to make you into my personal masseuse for at least the next month. I'm pretty sure things worked out in my favor."

"Except for the pesky fact that you're now a murder suspect."

"Yes, well, that bites the big one, but there's nothing we can do about that until we delve further into this investigation," I conceded. "You blamed yourself for a long time after I fell off the horse even though it had nothing to do with you. That drove me crazy. This has the potential to drive me even crazier. Do you want to drive me crazy?"

Even though I could tell he was determined to remain serious, I didn't miss the way Landon's lips quirked. "I'm pretty sure you're already crazy. In case you've forgotten, when I found you on the street yesterday, you and your cousins were using a magic ball of light to find me … even though I could've been in the middle of a very dangerous situation."

"And up until now you've wisely pretended that didn't happen."

"Wisely?"

I nodded. "That's my freebie. I went crazy and it ended before something terrible happened. You can't bring it up again. It's not fair."

"Ah! Well, what can I bring up again?"

"How much you love me is always a crowd pleaser."

Landon choked out a laugh as he rolled his eyes. "I would complain about the way you look at the world, but I'm so relieved to have you sitting next to me that I can't do it."

"See, it's my freebie."

"I guess it is." Landon squeezed my hand. "I'm going to make all of this up to you. I promise."

"You don't have to make up for anything other than the fact that you made me crazy when you didn't call. You didn't do this, Landon. You didn't kill that woman and dump her on my walkway. You didn't choke me. You didn't steal my hoodie."

"Yeah, I'm still agitated about that," Landon muttered. "For now, we're going to table the guilt discussion. Once this is all settled, though, I'll want you to punish me severely."

"You make it sound dirty."

"If you can manage to make the punishment dirty, it will be an added bonus."

"I'll keep that in mind."

LANDON WAS out of the Explorer and opening my door to help me out of the vehicle before I had time to register his movement. He extended a hand, putting his other on the small of my back to make sure I didn't jolt myself when I hit the ground.

"Since when are you so gallant?"

"What?" Landon cocked an eyebrow as he met my gaze. "What do you mean?"

"I'm kind of sore, but I'm more than capable of getting out of the truck without help."

"Have you ever considered I'm a gallant guy?" Landon challenged.

"More often than you're probably comfortable with," I replied. "Still, I won't break."

"Bay, I just spent a month away from you, came home to a big fight and then found out you were choked and someone is trying to frame you for murder," Landon argued. "If I want to help you out of the truck, I'm going to help you out of the truck."

The admission squeezed my heart, mostly because he was so earnest. "You're going to want to rub my back later, just for the record."

Landon smiled as he shut the door and linked his fingers with mine. "I'll keep that in mind."

I fell into step with him, letting him lead me toward the barn. He seemed to have a specific destination in mind. "How often were you here while you were undercover?"

Landon shrugged. "Only twice. But Becky spent a lot of time here. She hung out with several of the girls who worked the sales counter."

I eyed him speculatively. "You seem to know a lot about Becky."

"Only because she wouldn't stop talking about herself." Landon pinned me with a hard gaze, slowing his pace. "Bay, if you need to talk about this, we should do it now. If you need me to reassure you ... ."

I shook my head to cut him off. "I don't need that."

"Then why did you say it?"

"Because it's the Winchester way. Sometimes the snark overtakes me ... like a smelling curse that leaves me flustered and reeking of bacon."

Landon's smirk eased some of the tension building between my shoulder blades. "I can guarantee it's better than smelling like garbage."

"Why do you keep saying that? We made it so you smelled like rotten sauerkraut and eggs. We didn't just decide to make you smell like garbage. And, for the record, I told Aunt Tillie not to cast the spell, but she went against my wishes."

Landon snorted. "I think you knew she would do whatever she wanted despite what you told her. But that's hardly important now. As for the rest, I recognized the sauerkraut, but I honestly thought you made me smell like garbage because you wanted me to feel like garbage."

"Oh." Realization dawned. "That would've made sense. You're giving us far too much credit for forward thinking. We simply wanted you to smell, and those were the two smelliest things we could think of."

Landon shook his head as he shifted me so I was in front of him, narrowing his eyes as he scanned the various booths looking for someone specific. "Over there. That's Cindy."

I followed his gaze, frowning when I caught sight of the buxom brunette. "And how well do you know her?"

Landon let loose a weary sigh. "How long are we going to play this game?"

"I don't know. It hasn't even been a day yet."

"It somehow feels longer."

"That's because you're intent on being a martyr." I grinned as I dragged him forward. "Come on. She's working next to that cool bookshelf. I freaking love that bookshelf."

Landon followed me to the bookshelf, smiling as he ran his free hand over the wood. "It's really beautiful."

"It is. I considered getting it for the guesthouse, but ... well ... I don't think I should be making any big purchases in case I get locked up for twenty to life."

Landon sobered. "I won't let that happen, Bay."

"I know." I believed him. "Let's see what Cindy has to say, shall we? She probably won't recognize you without the beard."

"I would prefer that."

Landon and I patiently waited while Cindy – she of the huge boobs and peak-a-boo bra that showed through her low-cut tank top – finished helping a customer. Cindy was blasé when first turning to us, but her gaze narrowed as recognition flashed over her face.

"It's ... you."

"It's me," Landon agreed, keeping one hand firmly on my back as he flashed his badge with the other. "I need to ask you a few questions."

Cindy gaped at the badge, dumbfounded. "You're with the FBI?"

"I am."

"But ... how?"

"I don't really have time to discuss my work habits," Landon replied smoothly. "I need to ask a few questions about Becky."

"Oh." Cindy nodded knowingly. "You arrested her, didn't you? That's why she missed our meet-up at the bar last night. I thought maybe she was hooking up with you – she was determined to get you even though you were fairly clear that you weren't interested. I didn't bother calling her to find out why she missed bar night. For the record, I thought you were gay. I think it was the beard. Any-who ... did you arrest her for drugs, prostitution or running over that guy with her car?"

I bit the inside of my cheek to keep from laughing and risked a glance at Landon. He seemed neither surprised nor worked up by Cindy's nonstop chatter.

"I didn't arrest her, although I was mostly interested in the drugs," Landon replied easily. "Thanks for the tip on the beard. I've found most everyone hates it, although I'm hoping not for the same reason." He cast a weighted look in my direction, but I wisely remained quiet. "As for why Becky didn't make your chick date, she's dead. Someone stabbed her to death last night."

Cindy stilled. "Did you kill her?"

"No, but I would've happily done it, given certain circumstances," Landon replied. "She died in Hemlock Cove. Do you know why she would've been over there?"

"Hemlock Cove?" Cindy wrinkled her nose in concentration. "I never heard her mention Hemlock Cove. Most people think that place is crazy – you know, the folks over there pretend to be witches and stuff – so I don't know why she would've been there."

"What about Doug?"

"I'm not sure who that is," Cindy admitted. "Is that the guy who was here with you the other day?"

Landon nodded.

"That's the first and last time I've ever seen him," Cindy supplied. "I can't even remember Becky ever mentioning him. Of course, we weren't good friends or nothing. I'm tight with her sister, but I hardly knew Becky."

I swallowed at mention of family. That hadn't even entered my mind. Sure, I disliked Becky with the fire of a hundred curses, but I didn't wish ill on the woman. Okay, I kind of wished she'd trip and accidentally lodge her head in a dirty toilet, but I didn't want her to die. I certainly didn't want her family to go through something so terrible.

"Does she have a lot of family around here?" I asked.

Cindy flicked her eyes to me. "Who are you?"

"She's with me," Landon interjected. "Did Becky have a lot of family around here?"

"Not as far as I know," Cindy replied, quickly losing interest in me as she flashed a flirty smile for Landon's benefit. "You know, you're a lot hotter without the beard. You also don't look gay. Do you ... I don't know ... want to get a drink when I'm done with my shift?"

"I'm spoken for." Landon snapped his fingers to keep Cindy on task when her eyes darkened and floated in my direction. "Tell me about Becky's family."

"Are you dating this one?" Cindy ignored his command. "She looks as if she likes it rough."

"Don't worry about her," Landon ordered. "Focus on me."

"I'm trying, but you're standing so close to her I can't help wondering where your hand is at."

"It's on my butt," I supplied.

Landon hurriedly looked down, checking to see if his fingers had slipped when he wasn't looking, and scowled. "Keep it up. This is all cutting into your massage time."

I didn't like the sound of that at all. "So ... Becky's family? Who exactly is local?"

Cindy shrugged, noncommittal. "I only know about her sister, Rhonda. She works at the Bayside Diner in Acme."

"I know that place." Landon nodded as he moved his hand from my back to my neck and absently rubbed at the sore spot. "What about her mother? I thought I heard her complaining about having to meet her sister and mother for dinner."

"I don't know her name, but she owns that bed and breakfast about four doors down from the Bayside Diner," Cindy replied, her eyes latching on to Landon's busy fingers. "Rhonda lives there, too. She works at the diner because it's so close."

"Okay." Landon forced a smile as he tugged me in front of him. "Thanks for your time."

"Wait." Cindy narrowed her eyes. "Is this your girlfriend? She looks so ... normal ... except for the bruises on her neck."

"She's my everything," Landon replied. "And don't believe everything you see. Sometimes people aren't who they appear to be."

"I guess if anyone would know that, it would be you."

Landon pushed me toward the door as he slid a business card on the counter. "You've got that right. If you see or hear anything about Doug, give me a call. Don't approach him yourself. He's dangerous."

"Yeah, okay. I ... good luck."

I waved goodbye, silently hoping that we wouldn't need a lot of luck to get through this. I wasn't sure how much longer mine would last.

TWELVE

"How do you want to handle this?"

Landon helped me down from the Explorer, dropping an impulsive kiss on my cheek as he tugged Aunt Tillie's hoodie tighter around my waist.

"I thought we would play it by ear." Landon glanced at the beach-themed restaurant, his face unreadable. The parking lot was mostly empty – normal for this time of year – but that meant Rhonda Patterson might have more time to spend with us.

"Are you considering going by another name?"

Landon shifted his eyes to me, surprised. "Why would you ask that?"

I shrugged. "Because it sounds as if Becky liked to talk about you, and Landon isn't a very common name. Wait ... did she know your real last name?"

Landon slipped a strand of my hair behind my ear and shook his head. The wind close to the lake was fierce, sending my hair in a hundred different directions. "That's not how it works. I kept my real first name because there's less chance of screwing up, but you never use your real last name."

"Did you pick your new last name?"

"I did."

"Ooh, I kind of want to guess what you picked."

Landon chuckled as he rested his hand on the small of my back and prodded me toward the restaurant. He made a face at the back of the hoodie – Aunt Tillie didn't own very many normal clothing items, but I took the one with the witch that said "Croak and Haggard" because it was close to Halloween and wouldn't stand out. He whispered something I didn't quite catch as I strode toward the restaurant's door.

"Did you just say that I would never guess?" I asked.

"I did."

Oh, well, that sounded like a challenge. "Bacon. Sir Landon Bacon."

Landon snorted as he held open the door so I could enter. "No."

"Aniston? You do think Jennifer Aniston is hot."

"I think you're hotter." Landon glanced at the "Please seat yourself" sign and directed me toward a table near the window.

Now it was my turn to snort. "You think I'm hotter than Jennifer Aniston? I think you need to take a step back from the groveling because it's starting to get a bit unbelievable."

"I said it and I meant it." Landon shifted his eyes to the woman walking in our direction. She wore a simple black uniform and carried menus. While her hair was darker than her sister's bottle blonde tresses, I could tell Landon recognized the woman's face right away. She looked exactly like Becky. In fact, they could be twins. "Be careful about what you say." He kept his voice low, but that didn't stop me from rolling my eyes.

"I'm not a rookie." I flashed a smile for the waitress's benefit and let my gaze linger on her nametag for a moment before focusing on her face. The darker hair made her features much prettier. "Good afternoon."

"Good afternoon." Rhonda beamed. "Can I start you off with something to drink?"

"That would be great," I answered. "Is your iced tea sweetened or unsweetened?"

"Unsweetened."

"I'll have a large glass of that."

"Make it two." Landon remained unnaturally still, going out of his way not to draw attention to himself.

"I'll be right back with your drinks."

I waited until Rhonda disappeared to lift a challenging eyebrow. "Did you really think I was going to scream your name, hop to my feet and do a cartwheel in the middle of the room and then finish off with a little dance to make sure I really got her attention?"

Landon shrugged, although his smirk was obvious. "I didn't give it much thought. I've never seen you do a cartwheel, though. Can you really do one?"

"I ... ."

"I've seen you do a little dance numerous times," he continued. "I love your little dances."

"Yes, well, I have negative rhythm, and you're a man in love," I shot back. "You're apparently blind to how stupid I look when I dance."

"I'm often blind drunk when you dance, so that's a definite possibility," Landon conceded. "I still think you're adorable."

"Okay, you're starting to lay it on a bit too thick," I admonished. "I've forgiven you. There's no reason to keep groveling."

"I'm nowhere near done groveling, but we'll table that for the time being." Landon rested his hand on top of mine, curling his fingers around the edge of my palm before shifting his attention to Rhonda. She worked behind the counter, chatting with the cook. "She doesn't seem like a woman in mourning, does she?"

"I was thinking the same thing," I admitted. "Is there a possibility she doesn't know?"

"I ... don't know," Landon hedged, flicking his eyes to me. "They should've made notification last night. Even if they waited a bit, it should've happened first thing this morning."

"Maybe they went to the bed and breakfast to tell the mother, but she wasn't there," I suggested.

"Maybe." Landon's expression was thoughtful. "I don't want to be the one to tell her."

"I don't blame you. What do you want to do?"

"Well ... ." Landon licked his lips and flashed a flirty grin. "How would you feel about a night away from it all?"

It took me a moment to realize what he was suggesting. "You want to stay at the bed and breakfast?"

"It probably won't be full," Landon replied. "This area doesn't have the Halloween traffic that Hemlock Cove does. We should be able to skate right in. It will allow us a chance to interact with the mother. She might spill information about Becky."

It was an interesting suggestion. "Yeah, but ... we don't have any clothes or luggage," I pointed out. "Won't the mother think it strange if we check in without luggage?"

"Good point." Landon's grin was lazy as he leaned back in his chair. "Do you want to go shopping with me?"

That had to be a trick question. "Are you buying?"

"Whatever your heart desires."

"A pony?"

Landon's smile slipped. "You know how I feel about you and horses."

"Yes, you're almost as thrilled by the notion as you are with the idea of me being the lone woman at a biker bar," I drawled, causing his smile to return. "Well, it's not as if we can stay at the guesthouse and sleep in our own bed yet, so there's really no harm in staying here. We might as well try it."

"I'm going to get you home to our bed," Landon promised, his smile slipping. "I promise."

"Until then, we've never been on vacation with one another," I pointed out. "This could be fun. We'll be undercover, right?"

Landon nodded. "We will."

"Does that mean I can come up with our back stories?"

"I'm almost afraid to give you that much power, but ... why not. How bad could it possibly be?"

Oh, he would regret jinxing himself like that. I could already feel it.

"WHERE DO YOU WANT TO START?" I scanned the thankfully slow

Target store with a mixture of excitement and worry. "Should we get duffel bags or something?"

"We'll each get a small suitcase with rollers," Landon countered, turning his attention to the women's clothes. "We'll tackle the store in order. You can pick out a few things to wear first … maybe get a new hoodie."

I followed his gaze. "I don't need new clothes. I can wear these clothes tomorrow. I don't want you wasting your money."

"I'm going to be reimbursed for all of this so there's no harm in picking out a few things," Landon said, pushing the cart as he kept his eyes on me. "You're not getting stuck in the same clothes, so don't bother being a martyr."

"You're the martyr," I muttered.

"Perhaps we're both martyrs."

Landon helped me pick out a pair of jeans and several plain shirts before stopping in front of the intimates section. "You'll need underwear."

I'd already considered it, but it seemed a bit odd to be shopping for underwear in front of him. "I'll just grab a pair of these." I snagged a pair of purple boy shorts from the closest rack and shoved them in the cart.

Landon, apparently oblivious to my shift in mood, picked up a pair of Wonder Woman briefs and smiled. "I think you should get these."

I stared at them a moment, dumbfounded. "Why?"

"Because you're my Wonder Woman."

"But … ."

"I'll love you forever if you wear these," Landon offered, not waiting for an answer before dropping the panties in the cart.

I pulled them back out, scowling. "How big do you think my butt is?"

"What?" Landon stared at the panties, his eyes traveling to the colored tag at the top. He realized his mistake. "Oh, well … they looked small. Just like your butt."

"Such a smooth talker," I muttered, switching out the Wonder

Woman panties for the right size. "Okay, the men's section is over there."

"Don't forget a hoodie." Landon pointed toward a rack. "Pick out whatever you want."

"I can wear Aunt Tillie's hoodie."

"Pick out a new one," Landon ordered, his voice hardening. "I'm officially bothered by the missing hoodie. I want you to have one of your own. It's getting cold."

"Okay. Okay. You're so freaking bossy sometimes." I moved to the rack and grabbed a simple black hoodie.

"And don't you forget it." Landon kissed my cheek before wandering toward the men's clothing section. "By the way, I have something to bring up, and I'm a bit nervous."

Uh-oh. That didn't sound good. "Are you going to ask me to put on the Wonder Woman panties – and wear nothing else – and then twirl really fast when we hit the hotel?"

Landon snorted, amused. "No, but I'll take that under advisement. It's just ... I'll need you to use your credit card to check into the room."

Oh, well, that certainly wasn't what I was expecting. "Okay."

"Okay?" Landon cocked a challenging eyebrow. "Don't you want to know why?"

"I trust you."

Landon took me by surprise when he framed my face and planted a loud, smacking kiss against my lips. "Thank you. I'm going to tell you anyway. While I didn't use my real last name, as you mentioned earlier, Landon isn't something you hear every day. There's always a chance the mother could be suspicious.

"I also don't have my government credit card with me," he continued. "They'll reimburse everything, but we don't have time to get the credit card, and I don't want to risk the mother asking me about my name."

It made sense. "In case Becky was bragging about her new boyfriend, right?"

Landon gripped my hand so tightly I almost yelped. "Bay, I never flirted with that woman. Not even in an undercover capacity. I was there for Doug. We were most interested in him."

"I was just joking." I tried to yank my arm away, but Landon kept a firm hold on my wrist. "I didn't mean to upset you."

"I don't care about you upsetting me," Landon replied. "I care about you being upset. I spent the entire time I was away from you thinking about you."

"Oh, geez." I couldn't hold back the eye roll. "You have got to stop doing that. It's starting to make me feel uncomfortable."

"Yes, but I'm not in the mood to lie to you," Landon countered. "I missed you. I pined for you."

"Oh, come on!"

Landon smirked as he released my wrist and poked my side. "I missed you terribly."

"I missed you, too," I conceded. "You still could've called."

"Yeah, you'll never let that go, will you?" Landon tossed several pairs of boxer shorts into the cart. "I need to grab a T-shirt."

I followed him to a rack, tilting my head to the side. "I'm fine with using my credit card."

"I'll make sure you're paid back right away, before the bill is due, in fact."

"I have the money to pay for a night at a hotel," I reminded him. "I live in the guesthouse for free. While I'll never get rich working at The Whistler, I've managed to put a decent amount of money away."

"You'll still get your money," Landon said. "I simply don't feel comfortable using my credit card in case Becky ever mentioned my name to her mother or sister. We'll be checking in before the sister's shift is done, but ... you never know."

"You definitely never know." I tapped my bottom lip as I tilted my head. "We got sidetracked at the restaurant, and I didn't hear the last name you picked. All I know is that it wasn't Aniston or Bacon."

I couldn't be certain, but I was almost positive that Landon's cheeks reddened as he pointed toward the main aisle. "We'll get suitcases and then hit the toiletries section."

Much like Aunt Tillie when she realized she was about to make someone really uncomfortable, I couldn't stop myself from grinning. "Wait a second." I grabbed his arm before he could shuffle too far. "What last name did you pick? By the way, if you tell me it was 'Bay' I really will never stop laughing ... or believe you."

"It was not Bay," Landon shot back, pressing the heel of his hand to his forehead. "It was, however, inspired by you."

"Oh, that's entertaining." I searched my head for possibilities. "Landon Whistler?"

"No."

"Landon Blonde?"

"No."

"I'm out of guesses," I admitted. "Tell me."

"I don't want to tell you." Landon made a big show of turning away from me, but I wedged myself between the cart and him, batting my eyelashes.

"Please."

"No."

"Puh-leez!" I was so dramatic we earned a few odd gazes in our direction.

"Fine." Landon shook his head as he stared into my eyes. "Winchester. I said my last name was Winchester."

I couldn't help being flabbergasted. "But ... our name is well known in this area."

"As a group of crazy women," Landon clarified. "Winchester itself is a fairly common name and ... I wanted to feel close to you."

"And my name did that?"

Landon shrugged. "Every time I said the name I thought of you. That's what I wanted."

"Oh, man. You're hard to make fun of when you're being earnest."

"That won't stop you, though." Landon planted a kiss on my lips. "Do you want a book or something? We might be stuck in the room for a few hours before we can look around tonight."

"I'll get some trashy gossip magazines at the checkout counter," I replied, watching his back. "Does that mean, if we ever get married, you'll be Mr. Bay Winchester?"

Landon made a disgusted face. "No."

"Can I buy you a Mr. Winchester apron?"

"No."

"Can I give you a hug because I think it's incredibly cute that you did that?"

Landon stilled. "Yes … but I want you to grope me a bit when you do it, because then I'll feel like your personal property and my humiliation will be complete."

"Done." I threw my arms around his neck, holding him close for a minute before letting my hands drop to his rear end and giving it a good squeeze.

Landon jolted when I did it, chuckling as he shook his head. "That was meant as a joke, but it was so enjoyable that I'm not sorry you did it."

"Just wait until I put on the Wonder Woman panties," I teased. "Then I'll have super powers when I do it, Mr. Winchester."

Landon snagged me around the waist before I could scamper away. "You already have super powers, Bay. You're magic. You always have been."

I studied his serious face. "You're magic, too, Mr. Winchester. In fact, we should probably pick up some lotion so your magic fingers can rub me while we're waiting to explore tonight."

Landon grinned. "I love the way your mind works."

"Right back at you."

"We should get snacks, too," Landon said, grabbing my hand as we moved through the store. "Do they make bacon-flavored potato chips? I'm feeling an urge."

He wasn't the only one.

THIRTEEN

Wanda Patterson was pleasant as she checked us in to the Bayside Bed and Breakfast. She had dark hair – like Rhonda – but her features were round and soft. She seemed to be in a good mood when we walked through the front door with our newly purchased belongings.

I zipped my new hoodie up as far as it would go to cover my neck, and because Landon agreed I could make up the story for our visit, I did most of the talking.

"We just wanted a night or two away," I explained, handing over my credit card. "Hemlock Cove is madness at this time of year."

"Oh, I love Hemlock Cove," Wanda enthused, taking the credit card and beaming. "This is actually our slow season until the spring. We're always completely booked from April through September, but then we slow down. You pretty much have the run of the place."

"We're just looking for a romantic night to ourselves," I said. "We'll probably spend most of the time in our room. Isn't that right, pooky?"

It took Landon a moment to realize I was talking to him. He lifted his eyebrow a fraction of an inch before responding. "Yes, honey pot, we're really looking forward to spending time in our room."

I ignored his poor pet name selection. "We won't be any bother," I promised Wanda, signing the sheet she pushed in my direction. "We never cause any trouble."

"**YOU LAID** it on a bit thick, don't you think?"

Landon double-checked the hallway before closing and locking the door. He gave the room a dubious look – it had an ocean theme with seashells decorating almost every horizontal surface – and he launched himself onto the bed next to me as I struggled to remove my boots.

"I'll have you know that I'm a very good actress," I sniffed, grunting as I freed my foot. "That woman believes we're young, in love and interested in spending an entire night messing around. That's what we wanted, right?"

"If you had to fake the fact that you love me, we have bigger problems than your ability to spin a believable yarn."

I yanked off my second boot and threw it on the floor before rolling to rest my head on Landon's chest. "I wasn't faking that part."

"Oh, really?" Landon smirked as he inched lower on the mattress. "I thought maybe you were trying to make me suffer, honey pot."

"That's a stupid nickname, by the way."

"No more than so than pooky." Landon made a face. "Out of curiosity, what made you go with that one?"

"You're my pooky. It seemed natural."

"You've never called me that."

"I guess I haven't," I conceded.

"You don't really have a nickname for me."

I pursed my lips, considering. "Do you want a nickname?"

"Not if you choose pooky." Landon was diffident as he picked up one of the gossip rags I tossed on the bed while shifting through my small suitcase. "If you want to call me 'King Landon,' well, that's another story."

"Oh, your majesty, that sounds like a divine idea," I teased, giggling when Landon abandoned the magazine and tickled my ribs, rolling so I was on my back and he leaned over me.

He sobered once he caught sight of my neck. "How are you feeling?"

"I'd feel better if you'd stop hovering." I considered rolling off the bed, but putting distance between us wasn't high on my to-do list. "What do you think of Wanda?"

"I think she doesn't know that her daughter is dead yet," Landon replied. "I have no idea why, but I'm not keen on being the one to tell her."

"Is that because you spent the better part of the last month lying to Becky while working against her in an undercover capacity?"

"It's because ... well ... she seems like a nice woman," Landon hedged. "Rhonda, too. They're normal people, at least on the surface. I think that Becky's death is going to hurt them very badly."

"Do you think they know what she was doing in her free time? Of course, technically I don't even know what she was doing in her free time."

"We haven't really talked about that in depth, have we?" Landon ran his index finger down my cheek. "How much do you want to know?"

"How much did your boss say you could tell me?"

"That doesn't matter. I'll tell you anything you need to hear."

"Oh, well, in that case ... I think you should tell me that you're my love slave and no other woman will ever fill the Bay-sized hole I've carved into your heart."

Landon's smile was slow and seductive. "That's true."

"I like the way you're sucking up, but it's starting to make me uncomfortable."

"I'm not sucking up. I do have a Bay-sized spot in my heart. It's not a hole, though. You're in it ... all of the time."

"Oh, you're so cute." I tapped the end of his nose. "Give me the basics on Becky."

"Okay." Landon rolled his neck, returning to business. "I thought she was Doug's girlfriend when I first started hanging around the group. Undercover work isn't nearly as entertaining as you probably imagine. You can't force yourself on people who make their living by doing illegal things. They're naturally paranoid and suspicious.

"So I got a tricked-out motorcycle and an apartment in Doug's building," he continued. "It was a hellhole and I'm fairly certain everyone inside was a criminal. I think that was by design.

"I spent the first day 'moving in' to my new apartment. I carried boxes up and down the stairs until I wanted to crawl into bed and die. I made sure Doug saw my motorcycle – the requisitions department seized it a few months ago. It was a nice bike. Otherwise I acted as if I didn't want to talk to anyone."

"That was by design, right?" I asked, feathering my fingers through his silky hair. "You wanted them to think you had something to hide."

"Exactly. I spent the night in my apartment, made sure I was seen outside having what looked to be a tense conversation on my phone the following morning, and then conveniently ran into Doug when I was leaving the building," Landon said. "He wasn't overly friendly, but I could tell he was intrigued. Becky interrupted us right away. Even though they weren't affectionate with one another, I got a vibe off them. I thought they were sleeping together."

"Obviously not, huh?"

"No, but I didn't find that out until later," Landon replied, rolling to his back. "The next few days involved a lot of pretending to be on the phone and taking off at frequent intervals. I wanted them to think I was constantly on the move and cutting deals."

"And this was for meth?"

Landon nodded. "Even though Hemlock Cove seems immune because it's a tourist trap, it's an epidemic up here these days," he answered. "It's harder to cook meth in cities because people can smell it. Up here they can find houses that are literally falling apart and that have no neighbors. They get the houses for cheap and no one bothers them while they're cooking."

"How big was the operation?"

"Big enough that I grew nervous when I saw how many people Doug had working for him," Landon replied. "I wasn't really worried for myself. I knew that Steve would send in a team right away if something happened. I was more worried about you."

"Me?"

Landon nodded. "My biggest fear when Steve told me how close I would be to Hemlock Cove was running into you. Sure, I wanted it really badly because I missed you so much, but there was something about Doug that made me feel cold all over.

"I really felt it that day at the corn maze," he continued. "I couldn't stop thinking about you because we'd met at a corn maze and it was almost exactly a year ago."

"Was it like when people see Jesus in their toast?" I asked, hoping to lighten the mood. "Did you see my face in the corn?"

Landon smirked. "I felt you. At first I thought it was the corn, but now I think I really felt you when you arrived. I think that's what Doug sensed. He saw me look at you and I couldn't hide my surprise. I tipped him off ... and put you in danger in the process."

"Landon ... ."

Landon held up his hands and shook off whatever I was about to say. "Becky sensed it, too. She'd been trying to flirt with me for days, maybe even weeks. I don't think she really wanted me as much as she wanted me to want her, if that makes sense."

I nodded. "I know what you're saying."

"All I was supposed to do was find the route," Landon explained. "I needed to know where they cooked the stuff and how they transported it. We were sure they used boats because of proximity to the bay – perhaps they even used this place, for all we know – but all I had to find was the house and the route."

"Did you?"

"The day after I saw you Doug all of a sudden invited me to the cook house," Landon replied. "I should've been suspicious, but I was so relieved because it meant I would soon be going home to you now that I knew the location. I didn't pay close enough attention to what was really happening."

"And what was really happening?"

"I've been giving it a lot of thought since last night, but I think

Doug knew I was undercover and wanted me to take down the people he was working with," Landon supplied. "We took out his crew, but he wasn't there for the bust. He and Becky escaped with a load of money. All of the money I saw at the house when I was there disappeared when Doug did."

That was interesting. "But ... what about Becky? Why go to Hemlock Cove if you did what he wanted?"

"Because I betrayed him all the same and he wanted me to know he wasn't going to forget it," Landon said. "He recognized in that moment when I couldn't mask my emotions upon seeing you that I had a weak spot. He wanted to make sure I understood that he could get to you when he wanted."

"Do you think he wanted Becky to escape the initial run?"

"I don't think he ever had any intention of taking Becky with him, but I don't know if he saved her to teach me a lesson after the fact or it was merely a coincidence."

"Okay, well ... I know you're bothered by this, but you seem to forget that we have an ace in the hole."

Landon shifted his eyes to me, amused. "Oh, yeah? What's that?"

I answered without hesitation. "Aunt Tillie."

Landon arched an eyebrow. "How is she our ace in the hole? That's an expression I've never understood, by the way."

"Aunt Tillie can find Doug if we need her to. She casts a solid locator spell. We can always find him and then call in his location to the police. You don't need to worry about that. He's not going to get away."

Landon appeared intrigued by the suggestion. "I hadn't considered that."

"We'll find him. I promise."

"We will." Landon grabbed my hand and gave it a good squeeze. "The problem is that we don't know that he's the one who killed Becky. Can you think back to that night and be sure that he's the one who hurt you?"

In my heart, I wanted to answer immediately. It was too dark, though. I had trouble remembering the attack. "I don't know. All I really remember is trying to scream for you. It was too late. I couldn't make any noise, and you were already gone."

"Sweetie ... ."

I shook my head and blinked back tears. "I kept thinking that I was going to die and you wouldn't know that I forgave you. I wasn't really angry. I mean ... I was. I was hurt more than anything, though.

"When I picture it – this is in the thirty seconds I tried to fight and thought I wouldn't be able to escape – I thought you would come back to the guesthouse and find me dead," I continued. "I thought you'd blame yourself and I hoped I would be able to hang around as a ghost long enough to tell Aunt Tillie that it wasn't your fault. I thought maybe she'd be able to help you."

A muscle worked in Landon's jaw. "Bay, I don't want to hear you talk like that. I ... will need to punch someone if you do."

"I'm not saying it to hurt you," I offered. "I'm simply saying it so you know that you were all I could think about."

"That doesn't make me feel better. I should've stayed with you."

"Even though I told you I didn't want it? That sounds a bit creepy and stalkerish."

"Which is why I left," Landon admitted. "I had every intention of buying as many flowers as I could find in Hemlock Cove and returning at dawn to woo you."

I didn't want to laugh. It was a serious moment. "Woo me?"

"You heard me." Landon made a face. "I needed you to forgive me, but I didn't want to push you before you were ready. It didn't seem fair."

"And now?"

"Now all I want is to keep you close and safe," Landon answered. "Part of me doesn't want you involved because I don't think it's safe, but the other part can't bear to be separated from you one minute longer."

"Look at it this way, at least you'll be able to make sure I don't get into trouble if I'm with you."

Landon laughed, the sound taking me by surprise as he rubbed his forehead. "I love you so much, Bay. You have no idea how happy I am to be back with you. I know it seems weird given the fact that you were attacked last night, but ... I can't stand being away from you."

"Some people might call that co-dependence," I pointed out.

"I don't care what other people think. I only care what you think."

"Yeah?"

"Yeah."

"Well, I think you should come over here and give me a kiss." I patted the spot next to my thigh. "I'm ready to make up all the way, if you know what I mean."

Landon snickered, his shoulders shaking. "I know what you mean. Are you sure that's a good idea? You are recovering?"

"I think you're hurting my feelings because you don't want me."

"I always want you, Bay."

"You don't seem to now."

Landon heaved a dramatic sigh and stared at the ceiling. "You need to come over and kiss me if this is going to work."

I was understandably confused. "Why?"

"Because if you climb on me and start the kissing I can always claim it was your idea and I was simply too weak to stop you."

I bit the inside of my cheek to keep from laughing. "Oh, well, that's very pragmatic."

"It is," Landon agreed. "I need you. A lot. I don't want to be the jerk who rolls on top of you when you're hurt, though."

"That makes perfect sense." I rolled to my left, taking him by surprise when I planted myself on top of him. "Are you ready to do my bidding, Mr. Winchester?"

Landon nodded, pushing my hair from my face so he could stare into my eyes. "Yes. Just one thing, though."

I tamped down my impatience. I was antsy to finish making up. I think we both needed it to right our world completely. "What?"

"I love you, honey pot."

I gave his flank a vicious pinch. "That's Queen Honey Pot to you." I planted a firm kiss on his lips. "No more talking. It's time for action."

"You read my mind."

FOURTEEN

"Why don't you stay here," Landon suggested a few hours later, the room completely dark except for the power light of the television. He trailed his fingers lightly over my bare back as he kept his lips close to my ear. "I'll take a look around and come back as soon as possible."

It was an intriguing suggestion – mostly because I felt limp and boneless after our intense makeup session – but I had no intention of letting him do anything alone. "No. I want to be with you."

"You are with me," Landon pointed out. "I feel as if we're so close right now that we might be the same person."

"Oh, that's definitely codependence. Aunt Tillie would punch you in the nuts if she heard you say that."

Landon snorted out a laugh. "Yes, well, that's how I feel."

"I feel kind of hungry," I admitted, trailing my fingers down his lean stomach. "We haven't eaten since lunch."

"That's because you're a complete and total pervert, honey pot."

"And here I thought that was you." I kissed his chin, feeling the weight of the past month simply melt away. We were back in sync, and I couldn't be happier. Impulsively I wrapped my arms around him and buried my face in his neck. "I missed you."

"I missed you, too." Landon kissed my forehead. "You cannot understand how much I missed you."

"I'm pretty sure I missed you more."

"It's not a contest."

"Of course it isn't. I already won."

"Ha, ha." Landon patted my naked bottom. "It's dark, but it's not late enough to start wandering around the bed and breakfast without worrying that Wanda will catch us. We have at least two hours until we can do that. What do you want to do in the meantime?"

I couldn't see much of Landon's face in the darkness but the way his lips curved told me he had a very specific idea.

"Seriously? I won't be able to walk if you're not careful. I'm already hobbled."

Landon's smile slipped. "Are you in pain?"

"Just the pain of hunger."

Landon grinned as he slipped out from under me and moved to his suitcase at the end of the bed. I could see the moonlight filtering in through the window bouncing off the hard muscles of his body. "I thought of that and bought snacks at Target."

"Oh, score!" I couldn't move my eyes from his back. "You're thinner."

"What? Oh." Landon shrugged as he carried armfuls of junk food to the bed, letting me hold up the blanket so he could slide underneath before spreading out his bounty. "I wasn't much in the mood to eat while I was gone."

"Because the beard zapped your appetite?"

"Because I got spoiled eating food at the inn and nothing holds up to it in the real world," Landon replied. "All I could think of when I was eating greasy fast food burgers was that your mother probably made pot roast ... or chicken ... or homemade mashed potatoes ... or red velvet cake."

"Yeah, I can see that."

"Or kebabs ... or prime rib ... or those awesome prawn things she made that one time."

"Uh-huh."

"Or how about her pancakes ... and omelets ... and bacon ... and French toast ... and croissants ... and that pork loin she made that time she was experimenting with that honey glaze. I still dream about that loin."

"Everyone loves a good loin," I deadpanned.

"Funny girl." Landon tickled my side before handing me a box of doughnuts. "We're going to have a huge sugar rush when we're done with all of this food. I should've taken you out to dinner, but all I could think about was ... making up."

"That's because you're a pervert."

"Hey, you were the one who suggested it," Landon reminded me. "I was willing to forego the experience because you're hurt."

"Yeah, you put up a tremendous fight."

Landon grinned as he opened a bag of potato chips. "So, tell me what you did while I was away."

The change in subject matter threw me for a loop. "What do you mean?"

"I want to know every single thing you did while I was away," Landon prodded. "You said you were upset because we couldn't talk about that stuff. I want to know all of it."

"You want to know how my family spent weeks calling me pathetic and whiny?"

"If that's what happened, then yes."

"Oh, geez. Well ... ." I licked my lips. "Viola is convinced that Bigfoot is hanging around behind the library."

"Why does she think that?"

"You know, I didn't really give her a chance to tell me why," I admitted. "That was the day we decided to use the locator spell to find you and instead ran into you on the street."

"That remains a rather stupid idea," Landon pointed out. "I'm going to let it go because you didn't follow a magical blue light into danger and potential death. If you had, we'd probably still be fighting."

I didn't believe that for a second. "You would've given it to me as a freebie even if it had led to danger – kind of like the whining and crying – because you felt guilty about abandoning me. I don't know who you think you're kidding, but I don't believe that for a second."

Landon opened his mouth to argue and then snapped it shut. "You're such a know-it-all. It drives me crazy."

"It's genetic. You can't hate me for genetics."

"I can't hate you for anything," Landon argued. "As you've reminded me all day – nonstop, I might add – I'm completely whipped where you're concerned. I'm codependent. I would've spent the last three weeks whining about missing you if I weren't undercover. In fact, I did spend those weeks being just as pathetic. I simply had to do it in my head."

"Yeah? Is it wrong that I'm happy about your misery?"

Landon smirked as he grabbed the package of Oreos. "No."

"Are you only saying that because you intend to spoil me rotten until this thing is settled?"

"Maybe."

I wrinkled my nose and grabbed an Oreo, twisting it and handing Landon the side with the filling. "I'll tell you about my month if you tell me about your month."

"I already told you about my month. It was ninety percent boring and ten percent worrying. It was also a hundred percent internally whining while everything else was going on."

"I still want to hear about it."

"Fine. You first." Landon licked the filling before pressing his mouth to mine and causing me to giggle. "I want to know everything. I don't care how mundane you think it is. I want to know it all."

"Okay, but I don't think you're going to find the discussion about Aunt Tillie's potential hemorrhoids and her obsession with shovels nearly as entertaining as I did at the time."

"Let me be the judge of that."

"You're on."

WE SPENT two hours eating junk and chatting, catching up on anything and everything. Even though twenty-four hours earlier I'd worried nothing would ever be the same between us we had no problem slipping into a happy rhythm that erased the dull ache that plagued me for weeks.

I told him about my mother making me feel bad, Thistle torturing me for being weak while apparently phone stalking him at the same time, and Clove's excitement about getting married. I finished with Aunt Tillie's determination to drag me out of my funk.

"That's how we ended up at the corn maze." I hopped into a pair of yoga pants and tugged my hair back into a ponytail. "What are we going to say we're doing if Wanda catches us searching the main floor, by the way?"

"We'll say we're hungry and looking for food," Landon answered, not missing a beat. "If we do our job correctly, she won't know we're out of our room."

"She must really think we're perverts."

"Just you. She thinks I'm completely normal."

"Says the guy who asked if we could take a bath with the Oreos and potato chips and not get them soggy while engaging the jets," I groused, shaking my head.

Landon grinned as he pressed his hand to the small of my back and ushered me out of the room, pocketing our key before pressing a finger to his lips and glancing back and forth down the darkened hallway.

We'd had our pick of rooms. He had opted for one in the middle of the hallway, explaining he didn't want to get caught in an area of the building where we had no business being. Of course, we were sneaking around an almost-vacant bed and breakfast in the middle of the night. Everything on the first floor was an example of an area we had no business visiting.

Landon dug out the small flashlight he bought at Target and pointed it at the stairs as we descended. Once we hit the main floor, I shot him a questioning look and he gestured toward the door behind the front desk. It was a small office. Wanda had been sitting in the office when we had checked in, and I caught sight of a froufrou lamp and a nature painting that looked as if it came straight out of a "how to buy bland art for a boring office setting" book.

The office was locked, causing Landon to mutter something under his breath as he dug in his pocket. I watched him, curious. It took me a few seconds to recognize he had a lock pick set in his hands when he reached for the door handle a second time.

"What are you doing?" I whispered, grabbing his wrist.

"I'm opening the door."

"I know, but ... why are you doing it that way?"

"Because I don't want to kick it in," Landon answered, his patience apparently endless because we both were riding high after our makeup session. "I'm pretty sure that would alert Wanda to our presence."

"Yeah, well, I wasn't suggesting you do that either," I said dryly.

"Sweetie, I love you more than anything, but I could already be in that office right now," Landon pointed out. "I'm not trying to be difficult, but ... how do you think I should get in the office?"

I narrowed my eyes and turned back to the door, annoyance flaring for the first time in almost twenty-four hours. "I love you more than anything," I mimicked his voice to perfection, raising my hand. "That's why I talk to you like you're twelve and I'm stuck babysitting for the night."

I muttered a spell under my breath, a brief flash of light sparking against the jamb before the door popped open.

Landon arched an eyebrow, impressed. "I forgot you could do that."

"Yes, well, I'm a witch of all trades."

"You're my witch of all trades." Landon leaned over to kiss me. "I don't sound like that, though."

"You sound exactly like that."

"Whatever." Landon cast another glance over his shoulder before following me into the office. He shut the door before flicking on the light, grabbing a blanket from the small couch in the corner and dropping it on the floor next to the door crack before moving toward the desk.

AMANDA M. LEE

"What's that for?" I asked, confused.

"In case Wanda comes downstairs," Landon replied, keeping his voice low. "Nothing will keep her from discovering us if she comes in here, but the blanket will make it look as if the room is still dark from the other side of the door."

"Huh." I hated to admit it, but that was fairly genius. "You're smarter than you look."

"I'm going to show you how smart I am as soon as we're done here," Landon muttered, sitting in the desk chair and opening the top drawer. "I'm going to have you chanting my name because I'm so freaking smart."

"I'm looking forward to the attempt." I moved toward a crate in the corner of the room and bent over. "Hey, Landon?"

"What?" He was engrossed in a stack of letters he found in the desk.

"There's box of stuff over here and the envelope on top has a stamp from the state police on it."

Landon slowly shifted his attention in my direction. "Hold it up."

I did as instructed, causing Landon to frown. "The state police must've made notification while we were locked in our room."

"I feel a bit guilty that we were so wrapped up in each other we didn't even notice that Wanda got the worst news of her life."

"Yeah? I feel relieved because if we would've wandered down here and Davis was the one notifying her our cover would've been blown and we would've looked like the worst jerks in the history of jerks."

"Even more jerky than a Kardashian when a television camera is around?"

"Even more." Landon stared at the envelope. "I don't suppose that's open?"

I shook my head. "No. It feels as if there's a book inside, or maybe a journal."

"Oh, well, great." Landon ran his tongue over his teeth. "I don't suppose you know a cute little spell that will allow us to open mail and then reseal it without anyone being the wiser, do you?"

"No, but Aunt Tillie knows how to steam an envelope with an iron and she's really good at faking innocence when caught steaming my mother's mail."

"Bay, how does that help this situation?"

"It was simply an interesting tidbit."

"I still love you more than anything." Landon turned back to his task. "You can't open that. I'm sorry."

"Okay." I kept the envelope in my hand as I searched through the rest of the crate. "It's family photographs and stuff. Maybe the troopers collected it at Becky's place and brought it to her mother."

"Does it look as if Wanda went through it?"

"No. I'm betting she was so upset she shoved it in here and didn't even look inside. She probably didn't even see this envelope."

Landon shot me a quelling look. "Bay ... ."

"Whatever." I rolled my eyes. "You're no fun at all."

"Yes, well, I will show you a mountain of fun as soon as we're back in our room."

"You have a very high opinion of yourself."

"I didn't hear you complaining when the Oreo bath went so well," Landon pointed out. "I ... ." He broke off, an odd look washing over his features.

"What's wrong?" I asked, instantly alert.

Landon raised a finger and shushed me before killing the light. I couldn't see what he was doing, but the sounds led me to believe that he was removing the blanket from the bottom of the door.

I remained rooted to my spot as he cracked the door, cocking his head to the side before snapping his fingers in quick succession to get me to his side.

"We're going to talk about you snapping your fingers as if I'm a dog later," I whispered, annoyance bubbling up.

Landon didn't respond, instead pressing a hot kiss to my mouth before dragging me out of the office and toward the stairs. The bed and breakfast was quiet – too quiet for a woman who grew up in a house where Aunt Tillie was always sneaking around in the middle of the night. I didn't say anything until Landon had me at the top of the stairs with our bedroom door open.

"What … ?"

I didn't get a chance to finish, because Landon shoved me inside, being extra careful as he shut the door and locked it before turning his full attention to me. "I think it would be best for all concerned if you stripped."

He was so serious I couldn't help but laugh. "I see."

"You probably need to do it quickly, because … well … I'm feeling the urge to make up again." I emptied my hand of the item I carried without paying much attention to it and reached for the hem of my shirt.

"You'd better hope I'm not exhausted tomorrow. If I am … it's entirely your fault."

Landon didn't wait for me to finish undressing, instead crushing his mouth to mine as he pulled me into his arms. "I can live with that."

I could, too.

FIFTEEN

I woke on my stomach, my hair plastered to one side of my face and drool pooling on the sheets below my mouth. Landon rested on top of me, his head on my shoulder. The bulk of his weight was on his own hip, which thankfully didn't hold me down, but his body was large enough to keep mine warm despite the lack of covers.

"Holy crap!"

"Yes, and thank the Goddess while you're at it," Landon murmured, pressing a kiss to my shoulder as he rubbed his hand up and down my back. "What time is it?"

"I don't know. I can't see the clock."

"I guess it's not important." Landon stretched a bit, but didn't move his head from my back. He seemed to be lost in the lazy morning, as if he didn't remember where we were. I understood the inclination but not his reticence to move ... especially when I was in desperate need of a bathroom visit.

"Landon?"

"Hmm."

"I'm going to wet the bed if you don't get off me."

"Oh, sorry!" Landon rolled to his back, relieving the immediate worry as I sucked in a breath. "Sweetie, how do you feel?"

And just like that he jolted back to reality.

"Landon, other than the fact that you woke me up three times to … um … make up, I'm fine." I groaned as I shifted over the side of the bed, my eyes falling on a familiar item as I moved past the clothes I'd dropped on the floor once we returned to the room the previous night. Crap! I forgot all about that. I needed a distraction. "If you ask me how I'm feeling one more time I'll cut you off again."

That sounded plausible, right? It's better to pick a fight that I don't want rather than admit what I accidentally did.

"I don't believe that for a second," Landon said, studying his fingernails. "You enjoyed that just as much as I did."

He wasn't wrong. To give myself time, I disappeared into the bathroom and made sure to lock the door behind me. After quickly completing my business, I brushed my teeth while struggling over the conundrum facing me.

I could lie. That was always a possibility. I could shove the item in my bag, pretend I was unaware of its existence and dump it the second I got free of Landon's watchful eye. That didn't seem like a great way to celebrate the resurgence of our relationship.

I finished brushing my teeth, combing my fingers through my hair and splashing water on my face before returning to the bedroom. Landon remained in his spot on the bed, seemingly lost in his own world. When he dragged his eyes to me he flashed a smile, sobering almost instantly when he read the tilt of my shoulders.

"Sweetie, what's wrong?" Landon scrambled toward the edge of the bed. "Are you sick? Did you eat too much sugar last night?"

"No. Well, yes," I conceded. "I felt sick at one point, but then you distracted me with that thing you did with the big licorice rope and I worked through my stomachache."

"Oh, well, no one can say you're not dedicated." Landon relaxed, though only marginally. He cupped the back of my neck as he forced my eyes to him. "Tell me what's wrong. You're scaring me."

"Don't be afraid." I ran my fingers up and down the arm that held me in place. "I accidentally did something ... and it's bad. It's not end-of-the-world bad or anything, but it's not good. I'm afraid you're going to be really upset, and that's the last thing I want."

Landon pressed his lips together and exhaled heavily through his nose. I couldn't decide if he was calming himself because he wanted to make sure he didn't blow up at me or because he thought he might claw at the curtains in frustration when I admitted what happened.

"Should I tell you or lie?"

Landon arched an eyebrow. He looked amused, but that seemed unlikely. "I want you to tell me. No lies, sweetie. I thought we agreed about that."

"We did, but I don't want to fight."

"We're not going to fight."

"You don't know that," I countered. "We could fight. This is definitely something we would fight about if we weren't getting over the biggest fight in the world."

Landon ran his tongue over his lips as he regarded me. "We won't fight. I won't let it happen. I don't care what you did. Heck, I've been with you for a good thirty-six hours straight now. You couldn't have done anything big."

"Oh, yeah? What if I forgot to take my birth control pills or something?" I decided to frighten him with something truly terrible so that what I really did would pale in comparison.

Instead of reacting with terror or anger, Landon merely shrugged. "We'll deal with it. I'm guessing it will be a little girl, huh?" He cracked his fingers as he leaned back. "There are no boys in your family, are there?"

I was flabbergasted. "Are you serious?"

"Last time I checked."

"You wouldn't be upset if I forgot my birth control pill?"

"No. It sounds like you're upset about it, though."

"I'm not upset about it because it didn't happen," I shot back, my temper ramping up. "Cripes! We're not ready for a kid. We just spent a month apart when I whined and complained and you couldn't be bothered to pick up a phone. You can't do either of those things if you have a baby."

Landon extended a warning finger. "I won't make the mistake of not calling again. In fact, I'm going to start calling five times a day. I'm going to start calling so much you'll complain about that for a change."

"Oh, well, that will fix everything."

Landon ignored my sarcasm. "We could handle a baby. I know that you're trying to wind me up because you did something else and you thought that would send me over the edge, so I'm not particularly worried about crossing that baby bridge right now. Tell me what you did."

I heaved out a sigh and leaned down, picking up the envelope that housed Becky's mysterious book. I'd forgotten to return it to the crate before fleeing the office last night and now there was no way to return it without drawing attention.

"I ... didn't mean to steal it. I forgot."

"Oh." Landon chuckled, the sound low and warm. "It's not a big deal."

"I stole evidence. I'm a ... stealer."

"I think thief is a better word, but you're neither," Landon corrected. "It was an accident."

"But ... what are we going to do?" I felt strangely helpless.

"Well, we can put it with the two letters I accidentally stole so it won't be lonely." Landon's smile was wry as he leaned over the other side of the bed and returned with the items in question. "I panicked when I heard someone in the lobby, too."

"Oh." Relief washed over me as I leaned forward. "Thank you."

Landon snickered. "What are you thanking me for?"

"I hate being the only one to screw up. It's so much better when you do it, too."

Landon opened his arms so I could lean in for a hug. "Yes, and I'm a trained professional. That's so much worse than what you did." He kissed the top of my head. "Do you feel better?"

"So much better."

"Good."

We lapsed into silence a moment before the obvious question bubbled up.

"So, do we keep the stuff we stole or own up to what we did?" I asked.

"Oh, we take it," Landon replied. "There's no way to put it back, and I refuse to risk getting caught."

"I like the way you think."

"Right back at you, sweetie."

LANDON DROPPED me at The Whistler when we got back to Hemlock Cove, but only after I promised I'd need only a few minutes to collect what I needed to work from The Overlook for the rest of the week. He was resigned to what he had to do next, which was talk to Chief Terry, and I think he wanted to make the first attempt on his own.

We considered staying at the Bayside Bed and Breakfast another night, but there was a strange woman behind the counter when we ventured downstairs. Landon was fairly certain Wanda wouldn't be back anytime soon. He wasn't ruling out questioning her, but he wasn't comfortable doing it today. I didn't blame him. We could always return after Wanda had time to absorb the news.

Landon walked me to the front door of the office, leaving his Explorer in the parking lot and trudging in the direction of the police department. I realized Chief Terry was angry with him, even understanding it a bit deep down inside. I offered to talk to Chief Terry first, but Landon said it was his responsibility. He promised to pick me up at the newspaper office as soon as possible. Given Chief Terry's mood, that could be as soon as five minutes.

Brian Kelly, the owner of The Whistler, was in the office. I knew that because his vehicle was in the parking lot. Thankfully his office was located down a separate hallway from mine. I opted to tread lightly as I headed toward my private space.

I unlocked my office, moving to the desk so I could grab a few files and my laptop. I hoped I could make it out of the building before running into Brian, planning to wait in the Explorer for Landon to return, but the second I heard a throat clearing at my open doorway I knew I was trapped.

"Hello, Brian." I forced a smile as I met his smarmy gaze. I couldn't stand him. There was no sense pretending otherwise. I was ridiculously fond of his grandfather William, who hired me when I returned to Hemlock Cove after a few years in the Detroit area. William was always nice and sweet, allowing me the freedom to run the news side of the business as I saw fit. Brian was exactly the opposite.

"Hello, Bay." Brian seemed sunny and happy, but I could practically feel the underlying tension rolling off of him. "I wasn't sure you still worked here."

I summoned my limited patience to keep from flying off the handle. That wouldn't help anyone. "I've been a bit distracted, but you don't have to worry about this week's edition. I have everything under control."

"I'm not worried about this week's edition."

"Oh, really?" Somehow I had my doubts. "Would you like to know what I have planned?" I didn't have anything planned because I hadn't even thought about what story to focus on. I had the story about the corn maze, but that was hardly lead story material, even for a weekly. Still, I could make something up on the fly if I had to.

"No, because I don't really care what you have planned," Brian replied, his mouth going grim. "I've brought in someone else to handle the news side of things."

The words were matter-of-fact but they hit me like an iron fist to the stomach. "Excuse me?"

"You're a murder suspect, Ms. Winchester. I can hardly let you handle the coverage on the murder you committed at your own house."

The fact that he was calling me "Ms. Winchester" didn't bode well, but I couldn't focus on innuendo when I had his words to fuel me. "You don't have the authority to take decisions on news coverage away from me."

"I think you'll find you're wrong on that front."

"Your grandfather ...."

"My grandfather gave you free rein over the newsroom when things were going well," Brian said, cutting me off. "There are stipulations in his instructions for when things go badly."

That was news to me. "You can't fire me."

"I'm not firing you," Brian countered. "I'm merely ... asking you to take a step back for the good of The Whistler. You can't cover a murder investigation that's focused on you. It's unethical, and no reader would ever trust us again."

"People don't read The Whistler for murder coverage," I pointed out. "They'll watch the evening news if they want updates on what happened. Besides, I didn't kill Becky Patterson. I was attacked in my own home, and someone else killed her."

"That's a convenient excuse, but that's not what the state police trooper who stopped by to interview me related during our discussion," Brian supplied. "He seems to think you'll be arrested ... and soon."

I doubted very much that Davis said anything of the sort to Brian. He was extrapolating for his own needs. Sadly, there wasn't much I could do about it. "I know what this is."

"It's an executive decision," Brian supplied. "If you're cleared ...."

He left it hanging. I figured that was for plausible deniability. He'd wanted to wrest control of the newspaper from me since the day he took charge.

"You're a real son of a bitch," I snapped. "I know what you're trying to do. If you think I'm going to let you do it, you're crazy."

"And yet you have no say in the matter."

I shook my head, pressing my tongue into my cheek as I gathered my laptop. "Fine. Do whatever you want. I'll be at the inn. Quite frankly, you're the least of my worries right now."

"I believe that's company property," Brian said, his tone chilly as he inclined his head toward the laptop.

He wasn't wrong. It burned to have it tossed in my face, though. "Fine." I left the laptop where it was and moved past him, purposely slamming my shoulder into his because he refused to move. "You'll be sorry you did this. I promise you that."

"I sincerely doubt it."

I pulled up short when I saw Landon standing in the hallway, his eyes dark as he glanced between Brian and me.

"What's going on?"

I sucked in a breath to calm myself. "Brian has relieved me of my position."

Landon's eyebrows flew up his forehead. "He fired you?"

"I temporarily suspended her because she's a murder suspect," Brian corrected, his eyes wary as he took in Landon's aggressive reaction to the news.

Landon pretended he didn't hear Brian's clarification, or the tone in which it was delivered. "Can he do that?"

"It appears so." I extended my hand, mostly because I needed an anchor point so I wouldn't burst into tears. "We should get back to the inn."

Landon grabbed my hand and squeezed it, his fury obvious as he flicked his eyes to Brian. "You're going to be sorry."

"I don't believe, as an FBI agent and all, that you have the right to threaten me. I'll call your superior to find out, though. Just to be on the safe side, of course."

Landon didn't back down. "His name is Steve Newton. I'm sure he'd love to hear from you. As for threats, that wasn't a threat." Landon kept my hand in his as he stood toe to toe with Brian. He was much taller and stronger, and Brian had the smarts to look fearful as he swallowed hard. "This is the part where I threaten you."

"You can't ... ."

Landon shook his head to cut off Brian. "I'm not going after you. You're right. I don't have cause. I don't think I can hit you where it hurts anyway, so it would be a wasted effort."

Brian straightened, smoothing his polo shirt. "I guess that means you can go."

"We're going," Landon said. "By the way, just because it would be a wasted effort for me, that doesn't mean it will be a wasted effort for Aunt Tillie."

The change in Brian's demeanor was overt. He was terrified of Aunt Tillie. Apparently he hadn't taken her potential rage into consideration when deciding to oust me. "I hardly think ... ."

"No, you didn't think," Landon agreed. "You will now. Aunt Tillie will love it when Winnie unsnaps the leash she's had around her aunt's neck since you arrived in town. Oh, you didn't know that? Yes, Aunt Tillie was warned about moving against you."

That wasn't exactly true, but Brian didn't need to know that.

"Now you'll get to deal with Aunt Tillie on her terms," Landon added, directing me toward the door. "She's going to enjoy this ... and I'm going to enjoy watching it. May the Goddess have mercy on your poor, wretched soul."

Brian didn't bother to hide his gulp. "I'm sure ... ."

"Shh." Landon pressed a finger to his lips. "If I were you, I'd start running now."

With those words Landon wrapped his arm around my shoulders and led me out of The Whistler. I could only wonder if it would be the last time I set foot in the building.

SIXTEEN

"Bay...."

Landon's face was a mixture of worry and fury as we walked to his Explorer.

"It's fine," I said hurriedly. The last thing he needed was to feel guilty about this on top of everything else. "William left stipulations in his will. I'm sure I can hire a lawyer or something."

"Yeah, but...."

I ignored him. "Who knows. Maybe I won't even go back to the newspaper. Maybe I'll get a new job."

The possibility seemed to surprise Landon. "What would you do?"

"I ... don't know." That was the truth. All I'd ever wanted to do was be a reporter. I thought that would entail gruesome murders, bribery trials and late-night fires. Sure, I got to cover some of those things, but the pace in Hemlock Cove was much slower. I spent most of my time writing what could loosely be described as advertorials for area businesses. "Maybe I could open my own shop."

"That's an idea." Landon followed me to the passenger side of the vehicle so he could open the door and help me in. "What kind of store would you like? Right off the bat, I'm thinking you should do something with bacon."

I stared at him a moment, unblinking. "If I did that, every man in the neighborhood would be all over me. They might try to lick my face, like someone else I know."

Landon's enthusiasm waned. "I hadn't thought about that. I'll think of something else, although ... you're not going to lose your job. I won't let it happen."

I met his steady gaze, unsure how to respond. He was wallowing in guilt due to everything that happened. This simply compounded the issue. "You might not have a say in this one. You know that, right?"

"I won't let him hurt you."

Landon was determined, but so was I. He needed to understand that this wasn't his fault. "Landon, this isn't because of you." I grabbed his hand so he couldn't walk away. "Brian has been plotting to get rid of me from the beginning."

Landon's eyes flashed. "What do you mean?"

"I've been expecting it from him for some time," I explained. "He never really wanted the newspaper for what it was. It makes a profit, you see, but for someone like Brian who wants a buttload of money, it doesn't make enough profit.

"I could easily live off the profits of the newspaper and be comfortable and happy," I continued. "To him it's not enough, though. I know he wanted to sell the newspaper to someone else at one point, but he couldn't ... because of me."

Landon tipped his head to the side, considering. "I know some of this, but I think you need to refresh my memory."

"William always liked me," I explained. "He thought I had good instincts. That's what he said, at least. He used to work for one of the big daily newspapers in Detroit. He genuinely loved breaking news stories and political corruption.

"I started interning for free in high school," I continued. "My mother was fine with it, because she thought it would keep me out of trouble. She only had a problem when she realized that my interest in the news business would ultimately take me out of Hemlock Cove, or I guess it was Walkerville at the time."

"You didn't like being away from the town," Landon prodded. "You told me that. I saw that when we were trapped in Aunt Tillie's memories."

"No, I didn't like being away from the town," I conceded. "I liked some of the news stories, though. I liked that things were always hopping. Anyway, when I came back, I thought I would be working for my mother and aunts. I had no marketable job skills, after all. At least none for this area.

"Instead, William approached me about serving as the lone reporter and head of the newsroom," I continued. "That basically meant I was doing all of the work alone. Still, the idea of being able to do what I wanted was fun. And, let's face it, Hemlock Cove has its share of weird stories. So, three weeks out of every month, I'm bored with my work. The fourth is always fun, though."

Landon tucked a strand of my flyaway hair behind my ear. "It sounds as if you really liked William."

"He was a great guy, and he took care of me even after his death," I replied. "He stipulated in his will that as long as I was with The Whistler, Brian couldn't sell the newspaper. He also made sure that Brian couldn't fire me."

Landon shifted his eyes back to the building. "If that's true then ... ."

"Brian claimed his grandfather has some line in the will about being convicted of a crime or something," I explained. "He's not wrong about me not being able to cover a story in which I'm the prime murder suspect."

Landon balked. "You cannot be serious. He's going to publish that story?"

"He doesn't have a choice but to publish the story," I answered. "I am a suspect. A murder happened in front of my home. He can't ignore that. That's not how the news business works."

"No, but ... ." Landon dragged a hand through his hair. "As long as you're not convicted, Brian can't do anything, right?"

I held my palms out and shrugged. "I'm not sure. I need to look at a copy of the will. I have it back at the guesthouse, but I'm not sure we can get in so I can snag it."

"I'll find a way for you to get it," Landon said, rubbing his hands over my shoulders. "I won't let him do this to you, Bay."

"It might already be done." I opted to be pragmatic instead of emotional. "Still, let's not freak out until I read the will, okay? Brian could be talking out of his ass."

"Brian is going to be getting my foot in his butt if he's not careful," Landon muttered, dropping a kiss on my upturned mouth. "We'll figure this out. I don't want you to worry about this."

"I'm not worried." That was true. I was more numb than anything else.

"Okay. Fasten your seatbelt and we'll head straight to the inn. I think we both need some food to bolster us."

He wasn't wrong.

By the time Landon moved to the other side of the Explorer and opened the door, I had enough time to collect my thoughts and shift my attack plan.

"I'm going to rip his hair out and feed it to him," I muttered, rubbing my hands together in front of the heating vents as Landon fired up the engine and spared me a glance. "I'm going to make all of his body hair fall out and let Aunt Tillie curse him to smell like cabbage."

Instead of reacting out of worry, Landon grinned. "There's my sweetie."

I didn't as much as look in his direction. "Brian Kelly will be sorry he ever met me."

"He's going to be sorry he ever met both of us," Landon muttered, pulling toward Main Street. "I can't wait until we let Aunt Tillie off her leash. She'll terrorize him to the point of no return."

Hmm. That was a fun thought.

THE LOBBY WAS empty when we entered the inn. Landon and I headed straight for the dining room. It was after breakfast but before lunch, so I found my mother and aunts exactly where I expected them to be, sipping coffee and hanging around the dining room table gossiping.

"We have a problem," I announced.

"Oh, well, I wasn't sure you were still alive," Mom drawled, ignoring my call to action. "We cleaned the room yesterday – and you guys had clearly been inside – but when we cleaned this morning we found that you hadn't slept in the bed."

"I'm sorry," Landon offered. "We got caught up and stayed at the Bayside Bed and Breakfast."

"A competing inn?" A horrified Twila clapped a hand over her mouth.

"The dead woman's mother owns it. We had hoped to find some information," Landon explained.

"Did you?" Marnie asked.

"Well, I technically stole mail and Bay stole some sort of book in an envelope that we still haven't looked at, so I can't answer that just yet," Landon replied. "The day is still young, though."

"And yet I feel old," Mom muttered, never moving her gaze from my face. "Why didn't you call?"

"I … ." Crap. This was the last thing I needed. My plate was already overflowing – and with mostly my least favorite foods. We're talking cooked carrots, guacamole and hummus here.

"It's not her fault." Landon immediately jumped to my defense. "We made the decision to stay there on the fly. We ran to Target to pick up new things. If you want to blame someone, blame me."

"Oh, I blame you for quite a lot these days," Mom shot back. "I just … I'm not really happy with you right now Landon."

"Mom … ."

Landon held up a hand to quiet whatever I was about to say. "Your mother has a right to let me know how she feels."

"Oh, well, thank you for your permission, Landon," Mom deadpanned, her eyes flashing. "Do you have any idea what you put us through when you decided to go undercover and left Bay floundering for a month?"

"I didn't mean to hurt her," Landon offered, keeping his voice low and even. "That was the last thing I wanted. I missed her so much ... but my boss and I came to an understanding that if I did this job I would probably get a promotion and be taken out of the running for other undercover operations."

Mom stilled, the admission clearly surprising her. "Oh. I ... did you tell Bay?"

"No, and that was a mistake," Landon said. "I wanted to surprise her. I wanted to make a big deal out of it."

"That's kind of sweet." Twila sighed as she topped off her coffee. "I knew you couldn't be the tool Aunt Tillie kept accusing you of being."

"That's possibly very flattering," Landon said, although he kept his gaze on Mom. "Winnie, you know I wouldn't hurt Bay for anything, right? I didn't mean for this to spiral so far out of control. This wasn't what I had planned."

"Oh, well, of course it wasn't." Mom reached across the table and patted Landon's arm, offering him the solace he so desperately needed. "This isn't your fault. You tried to do a good thing for Bay and it blew up in your face."

Landon risked a sidelong look in my direction. "Yeah, and it keeps blowing up."

"What is that supposed to mean?" Marnie looked wary. "Has something else happened?"

"It's not a big deal," I answered automatically.

Landon shook his head as he squeezed my hand. "It is a big deal. We stopped at The Whistler on our way out here. Brian Kelly has ... relieved ... Bay of her position at the newspaper."

There was an immediate intake of breath, but no one spoke. I did hear the unmistakable sound of a growl and when I turned to the swinging door that separated the dining room and kitchen, I found Aunt Tillie standing there. The look on her face was chilling.

"How much did you hear?" I asked.

"Enough to know that Brian Kelly will be trying to bring body casts back into style in the foreseeable future," Aunt Tillie answered, striding into the room. "What exactly did that little turd say?"

I balked at the fire in her eyes. Aunt Tillie was the master of payback, and she looked to be ready to earn whatever belts they doled out for revenge in karate school. "Aunt Tillie … ."

Landon looked thrilled to see Aunt Tillie's attitude directed at Brian rather than himself. "He used some language from William Kelly's will that said that he could fire Bay if she's convicted of a crime."

"She's pretty far from being convicted of a crime," Mom pointed out.

"And she's going to stay that far away," Landon said. "Bay says she has a copy of the will at the guesthouse. We're going to try to get it after lunch – we're starving, by the way – and go from there."

"Why didn't you eat lunch at this fancy new inn you stayed at?" Mom sniffed, crossing her arms over her chest.

"Who cares about that?" Aunt Tillie challenged, scorching Mom with a dark look. "It's not the time to get your knickers in a twist because Bay is in her twenties and didn't bother to call before spending the night at a nearby inn with her boyfriend. I mean … come on. Grow up, Winnie."

Mom had the grace to look abashed as Aunt Tillie circled the table, sitting in the open spot next to me instead of her regular position at the head of the table.

"What are you going to do to Brian?" I asked. I could see Aunt Tillie's mind working from here – and it was a terrifying visual. Whatever she had planned for Brian Kelly, it wasn't good.

"Don't worry about that flaming pile of cow manure," Aunt Tillie answered, taking me by surprise as she rested her hand on my wrist. She'd never been overly demonstrative with her affection, so the maneuver caught me off guard. "I'll handle Brian Kelly. You guys need to focus on the dead girl."

"That's the plan," Landon said, leaning back in his chair. "When the warrants were issued for the bust after my assignment, two people evaded capture. Becky Patterson was one of them. Doug Lockwood was the other."

"That means Doug is probably the killer, right?" Mom asked.

It was a reasonable assumption, and I wholeheartedly agreed with her. "That's what I believe. Landon isn't so sure."

"I didn't say that I thought he was innocent," Landon clarified, drawing my attention to him. "I think it's very possible he's guilty. What I said was that we didn't know for a fact that Doug is the guilty party, and I would hate to focus all of our attention on him only to find out we missed someone."

"He has a point, Bay." Mom primly folded her hands in front of her. She was clearly renewing her membership in Landon's fan club. "You shouldn't rule anyone out until you have more information."

"Thank you so much, Nancy Drew," I deadpanned, earning a stern glare from Landon and cuff at the back of the head from Aunt Tillie. She conveniently missed the knot on my head.

"Don't talk to your mother that way," Aunt Tillie admonished. "She deserves far more than that. She gave birth to you, after all. You should thank your lucky stars every day that she even brought you into this world. I wanted to trade you for a new tractor."

Landon snorted as I scowled.

"You're so funny," I drawled. "How did you get to be so funny?"

"It's a gift." Aunt Tillie rubbed her chin. "I have a few ideas for dealing with your problem regarding the dead girl, but I want to put my plan in motion for Brian Kelly first. You know … priorities."

"Yes, it's much more important that you make Brian Kelly's butt itch than find the person who choked Bay." Landon's sarcasm was on full display. "Good choice."

"Butt itch?" Aunt Tillie cocked her head. "That's interesting."

"Just out of curiosity, what do you plan to do to him?" I pressed.

Aunt Tillie's smile was so big it threatened to swallow her entire face. "Oh, don't worry about it, dear," she said, her eyes sparkling. "I'm simply going to declare war on Mr. Kelly. Then I'm going to ask him if he'd prefer the bayonet through his eye or in his butt."

"Hey, that could work well if you plan on making his butt itch," Landon noted. "There's nothing worse for guys than an itchy butt."

"I like the way you think," Aunt Tillie said, wagging a finger. "We'll talk strategy later. For now ... I want to conduct some reconnaissance."

"What does that mean?" I asked, worried.

"That's for me to know and Brian Kelly to find out," Aunt Tillie said, hopping to her feet. "That boy is going to wish he'd never met me."

Landon's grin was impish as he slid it in my direction. "That's exactly what we were hoping for."

SEVENTEEN

Mom filled us with comfort food for lunch – homemade chili and grilled cheese sandwiches – and then Landon and I headed toward the guesthouse. We crossed paths with Aunt Tillie again in the family living quarters. She muttered something about needing her shovel and a dress that could fit a man but otherwise ignored us.

I slipped my hand in Landon's as we walked the pathway that stretched between the inn and the guesthouse, the idea of returning to my home both exciting and a little terrifying when I thought of the attack. That's when I realized I'd flaked out and forgotten to ask about Landon's task from earlier.

"Did you talk to Chief Terry?"

"His secretary said he was otherwise engaged," Landon replied, choosing his words carefully. "I could see him in his office, but he was on the phone. I thought about waiting, but … ."

"You chickened out," I finished.

"I'm not fond of that expression, but … yeah. I chickened out."

I shot him a rueful smile. "Chief Terry likes you. He won't stay angry forever."

"Chief Terry likes me now," Landon clarified. "He hated me when I first showed up."

"That's because you were undercover in his town. He worried you'd drag me into danger." I hoped he wouldn't take Chief Terry's fury to heart. "He didn't realize that I would be the one dragging you into danger more often than not."

"I know what you're trying to do and I appreciate it," Landon offered. "I don't want you worrying about Chief Terry. We'll figure things out. We always do."

"You can't spend all of your time worrying about what I'm worrying about. That's going to cause us to run in a circle, which puts us behind when trying to figure out what's going on. Right now Chief Terry is involved with the state police, so that's good for us. He'll get over being angry."

Landon didn't look convinced. "He blames me for leaving you at the guesthouse by yourself the other night. I blame myself for that. If I'd stayed ... ."

"I told you to go."

"I could've ignored you," Landon pointed out. "I felt that chilly wall you built up melting. I knew I could push you into at least pretending to forgive me if I'd stayed."

That was news to me. "Why didn't you?"

"Because that wasn't fair to you," Landon replied. "You earned the right to be angry. You're very rarely unreasonable when it comes to punishing me, or at least making me think about my actions and how they affect you. I also needed to be held accountable for my actions. I didn't want to take anything away from you, and I wanted to earn my forgiveness."

That was an interesting way of looking at things. "Landon, I'm not sure everything I felt while you were gone was reasonable. I knew darned well that you were an FBI agent when I fell in love with you. Potential undercover assignments were part of that deal."

"Yeah, but ... ."

"Let me finish," I prodded, scratching the side of my nose. "I let insecurity get the better of me. I went into the entire thing with a martyr complex, which was wrong. I told myself that I was going to be strong and keep it together because I wanted you to be proud."

"I'm always proud of you, Bay. Being strong while I was undercover has nothing to do with that. In truth, I liked that you missed me. I'd be lying if I said otherwise. Deep down inside, it meant that I was important to you, and I needed to at least feel important. That's how I got through everything."

"Of course you're important to me," I scoffed, amused. "How could you think otherwise?"

"I didn't really think it," Landon clarified. "I simply missed you so much I let rational thought out for recess and then forgot to ring the bell to call the class back inside."

"I think we both did that," I admitted, releasing his hand and linking my arm with his. "I wanted to believe I was above it all. I was obsessed with what you were doing ... and eating ... and whether or not you were in danger. I was fixated on the people you were probably hanging out with. Aunt Tillie made me watch some movie in which an undercover agent slept with one of the people he was going to arrest and fell in love with her. Even though I knew it was ridiculous, I started wondering if that would happen to you."

"It couldn't, but that's hardly the point. As for Aunt Tillie, if she wasn't the front line of our offensive against Brian Kelly I would totally yell at her. I'm going to let it pass because I want her focused on him."

"That's probably a solid plan." We rounded the final corner that led to the guesthouse and I pulled up short when I saw the multitude of vehicles in front of my home. There were five state police cruisers and another unmarked vehicle in the driveway. A bevy of police officers and evidence technicians walked in and out through the open front door. "I ... what the ... what is going on?"

"I don't know." Landon slipped his hand to the small of my back and prodded me forward as he licked his lips. "I thought they would be done here by now and we could slip in and find your copy of the will, but ... this is something else entirely."

I increased my pace when I saw Chief Terry scurrying in our

direction. Landon slowed a bit, but didn't allow too much distance between us. Chief Terry's face reflected profound sadness when we locked gazes.

"I'm so sorry, sweetheart."

"About what?" I stopped in front of him. "What's going on?"

"I've been completely removed from the case other than in an advisory capacity," Chief Terry explained, sparing a glance for Landon over my shoulder before fixing his full attention on me. "The state police were willing to work in conjunction with me up until this morning."

"What happened this morning?" Landon asked, joining us.

"He happened this morning." Chief Terry pointed for emphasis, and when I followed his finger I found myself staring at Agent Noah Glenn, Landon's co-worker and a general tool. I'd hoped to never see the little ferret again after he threatened to throw Aunt Tillie and me behind bars for murder several months ago. Apparently the only luck I had these days was of the bad variety.

"What is he doing here?" Landon was furious as he clenched his fists at his sides. "Why is he here?"

"That's a very good question." Chief Terry's eyes were contemplative as he pinned Landon with a hard gaze. "He says that your boss sent him because you and I can't be trusted to follow the evidence where Bay is concerned. A conflict of interest, he said."

Landon was flabbergasted. "There's no way that Steve said anything of the sort."

"I happen to agree with you," Chief Terry said. "That doesn't mean he won't be trouble. He managed to worm his way into the investigation and form a partnership with a state trooper who came into this situation with a definite chip on his shoulder."

"What does that mean?" I asked, confused.

"I think that Trooper Davis has already convinced himself that you're guilty," Chief Terry replied. "He's also convinced that Landon and I are dirty enough to cover up a murder for you. It doesn't help that your drug test came back negative, so it looks suspicious that you were knocked out for so long that night."

My stomach twisted. "But ... ."

"Don't worry about it," Chief Terry ordered, gruff. "I won't let them railroad you."

"We won't let them railroad you," Landon clarified pointedly. "I stopped in to see you earlier. I wanted to talk about a few things. Your secretary said you were busy, and then I got sidetracked by Brian Kelly."

Chief Terry's eyebrows rose. "Brian Kelly? What is he up to?"

"He fired Bay."

"What?" Chief Terry was beside himself. "That little rabid ferret better start running now."

I couldn't stop myself from chuckling. "You've spent so much time with us that you're starting to sound like a Winchester," I noted.

"That's a terrifying thought," Chief Terry muttered. "What are you going to do about it?"

"We came here because Bay has a copy of William Kelly's will in her filing cabinet," Landon replied. "We need, it but ... I'm guessing we can't get it until these guys release the guesthouse back to her."

"I'll get it," Chief Terry growled. "Don't worry about that. Do you need anything else from inside?"

"Maybe some more clothes."

"I'll grab those, too." Chief Terry rested his hand on my shoulder. "Everything is going to be okay, sweetheart. Please don't worry too much about this."

I forced a smile for his benefit. "I'm not worried. I have you and Landon, right? I'll be fine."

The look Chief Terry shot Landon wasn't full of friendship and loyalty. "Yes, well ... ."

I decided to ignore his obvious evasion. "So they're going to search the guesthouse again? What do they hope to find?"

"I have no idea, but that's not all of it," Chief Terry replied. "They're going to search the family living quarters at The Overlook, too. That's their next stop."

The information knocked the wind out of me. As I decided how to answer – and whether or not I should warn my mother and aunts –

Landon took everyone by surprise when he burst into hysterical laughter.

"You can't be serious," he sputtered.

"I'm damn serious." Chief Terry cocked a dubious eyebrow. "How is this funny?"

"Oh, it's not funny." Landon sobered, although the corners of his mouth remained curved. "It's going to get funny when Aunt Tillie finds out the state police and Agent Glenn are searching her property."

Something occurred to me. "The greenhouse!"

Aunt Tillie's greenhouse was her private space, where she grew marijuana and a variety of herbs for spells. Landon suddenly sobered.

"Oh, crud on toast," he muttered.

"It's late in the season," Chief Terry pointed out. "No plants could survive out there this time of year."

"That's true," I conceded. "What about seeds, though?"

Chief Terry shrugged. "I'm not sure what to tell you, but … I guess we're about to find out." He inclined his chin in Davis' direction. "Here comes trouble … and I'm guessing the next stop will be The Overlook."

Things just kept getting worse.

AN HOUR LATER we were back at The Overlook and the family living quarters were under siege as the state police moved furniture and went through every drawer in search of … well, I wasn't exactly sure what they thought they would find.

Chief Terry and Landon watched their every move to make sure they didn't break or destroy anything, Chief Terry going so far as to threaten one of the troopers when he moved to drop a vase on the floor.

I felt sick to my stomach for causing this, anger threatening to overwhelm me. This was hardly my fault, yet my family was paying because I was now a murder suspect. It wasn't fair … or right.

"How long do you think this will last?"

Landon shifted his eyes to me. "Not long, sweetie. The good news is that the search warrant covers only the family living space. The inn itself – and the outer buildings, for that matter – are free from the search."

I wasn't sure how that was good news, but I kept the thought to myself. "Have you seen my mother?"

"Last time I saw her she was in the kitchen with Noah," Landon answered. "He was trying to get bossy, and she was having none of it."

That made me feel better, if only marginally. "What about Aunt Tillie?"

Landon swallowed hard. Aunt Tillie was here when we hurried back to warn everyone about the search, but she disappeared not long after. I had no idea what she was doing – and whether or not it would get us in more trouble than we were already in, if that was even possible – but I was starting to grow fearful.

"Have you counted the number of troopers present?" I asked after a beat. "They're not disappearing, like in a horror movie, right?"

Despite the serious nature of the situation, Landon chuckled. "I don't think, so but that would be kind of funny."

I didn't get a chance to explain exactly why that wasn't funny – or that it was a distinct possibility because Aunt Tillie watched the original *Predator* movie a few days ago and commented that she really identified with the alien – because the sound of raised voices drew me to the kitchen.

I hurried in that direction, my eyes widening when I slid through the door and found Davis squaring off with a wall of Winchesters.

My mother and aunts stood in front of the door that led to the dining room, arms crossed over their chests and defiant as Davis moved to walk around them.

"I believe you're overstepping your bounds," Mom announced, planting her hand in the middle of Davis' chest as he tried to bully her into stepping aside. "The warrant says you have the jurisdiction to search the family residence. What's on the other side of this door is not part of the family residence."

Instead of apologizing or responding with sheepish retreat, Davis merely cocked an eyebrow. "Are you telling me where I can and can't go?"

"I believe the warrant has laid that out for you," Landon interjected, causing Davis to jump.

Davis turned and locked gazes with Landon. "You have no part in this investigation."

"That's true," Landon conceded, keeping me close to his side. "That doesn't mean I can't report what I see to the judge who issued the warrant. I can have the entire search rendered invalid if you walk through that door."

"And why would you do that?" Davis challenged. "What are they hiding?"

"Nothing," Landon replied, refusing to let Davis' tone unnerve him. "The answers aren't here. The answers are with Doug Lockwood. I know it, and you do, too. The problem is that you can't find Doug so you've opted to focus on Bay, because this is the highest profile case that's ever crossed your desk.

"Oh, yeah, I looked into your background," he continued, chuckling. "I know you're hoping to make a name for yourself with this case. You're a small-town boy – from one town over – and you happened to land at the state police post closest to home. You're all about making a name for yourself. You won't be making it on Bay, though. I promise you that."

"I'm merely following the evidence." Davis' expression didn't soften, but he wisely stepped away from the Winchester clan blocking the door. "Your girlfriend is the obvious suspect."

"Really? How did she knock herself out? How did she choke herself?"

"Perhaps one of her family members did it," he said, jerking a thumb at the women behind him.

Landon rolled his eyes. "Yes, the Winchester women often run around choking each other into unconsciousness. Good grief."

Landon's tone was dismissive, expressing exactly what he thought of that theory. Of course, that was the moment Aunt Tillie showed up to claim her rightful place as ringmaster of the circus. She breezed through the door, her eyes busy as they bounced between faces, and then plastered a serene smile on her face.

"This won't be good," Landon muttered, shaking his head. He clearly suffered from the same sense of worry invading my stomach.

"No one panic," Aunt Tillie ordered, lobbing a pointed look in her nieces' direction. "I've got everything under control."

"What is that supposed to mean?" Davis asked, genuinely curious.

"It means that I'm ready to fight to the death for my right to protect my liberty, happiness and – most importantly – freedom." Aunt Tillie delivered the line as if she were on a stage in front of an audience. I almost wanted to applaud ... and then laugh.

Davis wasn't nearly as impressed. "What is that supposed to mean?"

"It means that I found my shovel," Aunt Tillie replied, not missing a beat. "Let the games begin."

Uh-oh. I had no idea what she was referring to, but it couldn't be good. Yeah, scratch that. The look on her face told me things were about to turn downright awful.

EIGHTEEN

"Why do you need a shovel?"

Davis was obviously confused regarding Aunt Tillie's sudden appearance. Either Noah hadn't filled him in on my great-aunt's quirks or he didn't believe the rumors were true. If it were the latter, that would prove a fateful mistake.

"I need to dig a bunch of holes," Aunt Tillie replied. She'd managed to find her combat helmet and change into camouflage pants. "Speaking of that, how tall are you?"

"I ... what?" Davis furrowed his brow.

I expected Landon to insert himself in the argument, but instead he moved to the counter and hopped on one of the stools. "Are there any cookies?"

Mom didn't respond verbally, instead grabbing a plate from the counter next to the refrigerator and shoving it in Landon's direction.

"Ooh, chocolate chip." Landon removed the plastic wrap and grabbed a cookie. "What's for dessert tonight, by the way? I've got a hankering for cake."

Davis rolled his eyes so hard I thought he would topple to the side before pinning Landon with a dangerous look. "Do you really think you should be here, Agent Michaels? You have no standing in this investigation."

"No, but I have rented a room and I'm a guest," Landon shot back.

"He's also a member of the family and can come and go in the family living quarters however he likes," Mom added. Whatever anger and resentment she harbored for Landon during his long sojourn was apparently gone.

"Except he can't go into my room," Aunt Tillie volunteered. "I'll have to dig another hole if he tries."

Davis snorted, seemingly amused by Aunt Tillie's bravado. "I've heard stories about you."

I wasn't sure what Davis was insinuating – or what he ultimately hoped to accomplish – but the idea that his statement would dissuade Aunt Tillie was laughable. Instead of interjecting myself into the conversation, I sat next to Landon and smiled as he handed me a cookie.

"I should hope you've heard stories about me," Aunt Tillie fired back. "I haven't spent decades cultivating the perfect public persona only to have the Hemlock Cove rumor mill implode at the wrong time. What have you heard?"

Davis shrugged. "I've heard a lot of things. We've been interviewing people around town about Ms. Winchester's habits. Your name came up quite frequently."

"Well, that's a little disappointing," Aunt Tillie sniffed. "I've done a lot more entertaining things when Bay wasn't around, because she's kind of a kvetch when it comes to following the rules. No one told you about that stuff?"

"That's not true," I protested. "I broke the rules with you all of the time when I was a kid."

"That doesn't count." Aunt Tillie made a derisive sound, as if she was clearing her throat of phlegm so she'd have something to spit in Davis' direction. "I always tricked you guys when you were younger so you thought that breaking the rules was preferred to being boring. You still grew up to be boring."

"Don't listen to her, sweetie," Landon said. "You're not boring."

"Says the guy whose wildest dream is rolling around naked on giant slabs of bacon," Aunt Tillie muttered, shaking her head. "You're boring, too."

"I don't have the energy to argue with you, so I guess I'll be boring for the day," Landon countered. "Is there more chili? I could use another serving of lunch."

"Is that what you do with your time here?" Davis asked, incredulous. "Do you simply sit around eating?"

Landon wasn't bothered by the accusation. "You haven't tasted their food. I dreamed about eating here every night for a month straight. I might as well take advantage of it while I'm sleeping under the big roof."

"I'll heat up some chili," Twila offered, shuffling toward the refrigerator. "Bay, do you want some?"

I wasn't hungry until Landon mentioned the chili. "I could eat," I said after a beat. "Thank you."

Davis merely shook his head and turned back to Aunt Tillie. "Are we done here?"

Aunt Tillie snorted. "Not even close. I want to know what other stories you've heard about me."

"They're varied and entertaining," Davis replied. "I think you're kind of like an urban legend around this town. People blame you for everything short of controlling the weather."

That was mildly interesting because Aunt Tillie could actually control the weather. I'd watched her bring down lightning storms on no less than two enemies, and she made it snow one Christmas when I was depressed about the possibility of a green holiday.

"Whoever you're getting your information from is clearly falling down on the job," Aunt Tillie supplied. "You might want to pay a visit to Margaret Little. She'll fill your ears with more of the truth."

"I've talked to Mrs. Little," Davis said. "She's the lady with all of the unicorns, right?"

"Yes." Aunt Tillie nodded, brightening. "You would think she'd realize after all these years that the phallic nature of the unicorn says a little something about her, but she hasn't caught on yet."

Davis snorted. "And what do the unicorns say about her?"

"That she needs to get some because she's clearly craving horns," Aunt Tillie replied, not missing a beat. "I should think that'd be obvious. You need to learn to keep up. You're not very intuitive for a fed, are you?"

For the first time, Davis' façade cracked a bit. It was obvious he thought he could bully Aunt Tillie with minimal effort, but she'd brought down bigger foes – and probably this week.

"Well, I guess everyone is entitled to their opinion," Davis said carefully. "The residents of this town have varied opinions about you, of course. They think you're mean, crotchety, theatrical and a little too interested in other people's business."

Aunt Tillie was blasé. "You forgot suspicious by nature, good with a gun, not bothered about the prospect of hiding a body and utterly terrifying."

I risked a glance at Landon, fear momentarily overtaking me as I wondered if Davis would take her into custody for threatening him. Landon didn't look worried in the least.

"Was that a threat?" Davis asked.

"When I threaten you, you'll know it," Aunt Tillie replied. "I don't have time to threaten you at this point, because I have someone else to focus on. I don't want you getting too comfortable, though, because I'll make time if it becomes necessary."

"I don't know what to say to that," Davis hedged.

"I don't expect you to say anything to it," Aunt Tillie said. "I honestly don't give two sprigs of dogwood about what you think or feel. You're barking up the wrong tree with Bay. You won't find anything here. The sad thing is that I believe you know that but you're too stubborn to realize you're looking in the wrong place.

"Now, I'm not surprised that you're lazy and refuse to do actual work to solve this thing," she continued. "I have a severe dislike for 'The Man,' and I've always known that 'The Man' is lazy. Chief Terry and Landon confused me for a bit because neither one of them is lazy. This one is gluttonous, but he's hardly lazy." Aunt Tillie jerked a thumb in Landon's direction as Twila placed a fresh bowl of chili in front of him.

"Thank you so much for the vote of confidence." Landon winked at Aunt Tillie as he broke a breadstick and gave me half to dunk in the bowl Twila delivered to me. "I love you, too."

Aunt Tillie didn't respond, but it was impossible to miss the way her lips quirked. "As I was saying, you're lazy and you're not going to do anything to solve this case. I'm not stupid enough to believe otherwise."

"I'm not sure what the point of that little diatribe was, but … ."

Aunt Tillie cut off Davis with the shake of her head. "The point is that I don't trust you. You won't do your job. I need to make sure you don't get in the way when we do your job for you."

"If you insert yourself in this investigation I will arrest you," Davis warned.

Aunt Tillie didn't appear intimidated in the least. "Oh, please. You don't frighten me. I've squashed turds bigger than you without even realizing I had dung stuck to the bottom of my shoe. I only need you to know that I'll be watching you … and if you stick your nose too far into my business I'll find a way to fix the situation that won't sit well with you."

It wasn't a violent threat, but it was the closest she'd uttered since popping into the kitchen.

"Thank you for the warning." Davis was purposely calm, although I could tell that Aunt Tillie's refusal to capitulate grated. "Do you have anything you want to add to this conversation, Michaels, or are you okay letting the old lady do all of the heavy lifting?"

Landon shrugged at the challenge. "I think she said what we're all thinking. Besides, she's far more terrifying than I am."

"You've got that right," Aunt Tillie muttered, crossing her arms over her chest.

"Well, I guess I'll return to the search." Davis moved toward the door that led to the family living quarters. "I thought the people in this town were exaggerating when they said you were all loopy, but I'm starting to think they were right."

It was meant to be a parting insult, the last word. Davis didn't know that Aunt Tillie always gets the last word.

"They're not even close to knowing everything," Aunt Tillie called to his back. "You never did say how tall you are."

"I'm six feet tall," Davis barked.

Aunt Tillie snorted. "In your dreams. You're like five-foot-seven, right?" Aunt Tillie did the math in her head. "Yeah. You've got Little Man's Syndrome written all over you."

Davis paused near the door. "Why do you want to know how tall I am? Are you going to kill me, perhaps bury me in the backyard?"

Aunt Tillie rolled her eyes. "You don't bury a body in the yard, moron. That's how you get caught."

"Oh, well, at least you've thought it out." Davis was almost through the door before Aunt Tillie spoke again. They were both determined to get the last word, but Aunt Tillie had much more practice.

"You don't bury anyone in your yard," she repeated. "I have a blender and a garden, though. I'm always looking for new fertilizer."

"**ARE YOU** ready for your bedtime story?"

Annie, the daughter of an inn worker, appeared in the library doorway after dinner. She had a book in her hand and a smile on her face. Landon and I had retired to the small library for a drink and some privacy after stuffing ourselves with manicotti and fresh bread, a delectable chocolate cake capping the meal.

The search team scoured the living quarters for hours, but left without seizing anything. Davis looked grim as he stood on the back patio talking to Noah. They seemed deep in conversation, but Landon remained convinced they were posturing. Aunt Tillie hid behind the small wall on the east side to listen. She'd reported the only thing they talked about was how they could never find anything worth covering up in their pants.

The rest of the day passed in relative quiet, although I couldn't quite shake the underlying feeling of doom resting on my shoulders. As if seeing it himself, Landon attacked my tense muscles with gusto once we were alone, not stopping until I was ready to fall asleep in the middle of the floor. We were ready to head upstairs for bed when Annie found us.

"You're going to read us a story?" Landon flashed a smile as Annie shuffled closer. "That sounds fun." We were both exhausted, but there was no way he'd deter Annie from spending time with us. She spent months being afraid of Landon because he was 'The Man' and Aunt Tillie had a tendency to run off at the mouth. Annie's hero worship of Aunt Tillie caused her to fear Landon, something that had pained him greatly. "What story did you pick?"

"*Aunt Tillie's Wonderful World of Stories to Make Little Girls Shut Up*," Annie replied, not missing a beat. "It's new. Aunt Tillie gave it to me a couple of days ago."

Landon and I exchanged a knowing look as he grabbed Annie around the waist and tugged her to the spot on the couch between us. "I believe I'm familiar with that book." He wasn't happy about being reminded. Aunt Tillie had cursed us into the book so she could illegally sell her wine during the summer. "I'm not sure I'm up for hearing one of those stories, though."

"Aunt Tillie says you need a bedtime story or you won't sleep well," Annie argued. "I promised to read you one."

Landon pursed his lips. "And Aunt Tillie is always right, huh?"

"Always." Annie nodded earnestly. "She's the smartest woman in the world, only we can't tell anyone because the government will try to grab her and do experiments on her."

"Yes, and that would be terrible," Landon said dryly, rolling his eyes as he grabbed the book. "Do any of these stories not have something terrible happen in them?"

Annie tilted her head to the side, doing a great impression of Thistle when she was thinking hard, and tapped her bottom lip. "No. All of them involve little girls who have something bad happen because they didn't mind their own business."

"And that's a lovely message to send," Landon said. "Okay, if you want to read us a story, I'm ready to listen. Pick whichever one you want."

Instead of doing as instructed, Annie flicked her eyes to me. "Aunt Tillie said you should pick."

"Me?" That was surprising. "Why me?"

"She said you needed something to remind you that Winchesters always win in the end."

That sounded exactly like Aunt Tillie. "How about the one about Thistle being in Witchland? I always liked that one."

Landon made a face. "Witchland?"

I nodded. "Wonderland is boring. Witchland is something to behold."

"Ah, well, as long as there's a reason for it." He sank lower on the couch, making sure Annie was comfortable between us before reaching over to snag my hand. "Did you pick this one because something bad will happen to Thistle?"

He knew me too well. "And it's not overly long," I added. "The author of this particular book has a tendency to go off on tangents."

Landon feigned shock. "You don't say!"

Annie giggled at his wide eyes. "I like this story, too. I especially like it when the Mad Witch drowns the whiny unicorn in the river of melted chocolate."

Landon's smile tipped upside down. "That sounds freaky for a children's book."

"All children's books are kind of freaky," I supplied. "Even the stories Aunt Tillie didn't write to scare us have horrible things happen to children. I don't think Aunt Tillie was the first to realize that stories could control the small-sized masses."

"Ah, well ... ." Landon broke off, smiling as Annie found the place in the book she wanted and tightening his grip on my hand. "I know you were joking earlier, but eventually – and I'm talking down the road, so there's no reason to panic – but eventually, this is what I want."

I couldn't help being confused. "You want to go to Witchland? I'm going to be honest, there aren't a lot of men there. I think Aunt Tillie was feeling particularly nasty about the male gender when she wrote that one."

"Not that." Landon made a face. "This." He inclined his head toward Annie. "I want a couch of our own ... a kid of our own, even if I know she'll be mouthy and love Aunt Tillie more than me ... and I want this book on a fall night. You asked me if I was sure about what I wanted the other day. I'm sure this is what I want."

My heart rolled at the admission. "I ... want it, too."

"I know you do. That's why I jumped at the chance to make sure I wouldn't have to go undercover again. I know I caused this, Bay, but I honestly thought I was doing the right thing for both of us."

Sympathy washed over me. "It's okay. We'll figure it out."

"We will." Landon gave my hand a reassuring squeeze and then smiled for Annie's benefit. "Lay it on me, kid. Make sure you don't stop until we get to the happy ending."

"That's a myth," Annie said, sounding older than her years. That's how I knew she was parroting Aunt Tillie.

"What's a myth?"

"A happy ending," Annie replied. "Life doesn't end. You simply move on to a different part of life. People are always living their happy endings, because nothing ever stops."

Instead of being agitated with the answer, Landon grinned. "Right you are. Still, I want to hear the entire story. I don't want to miss a thing."

"You won't." Annie sounded sure as she began to read. "Once upon a time, there was a little girl with blond hair and a mean smile, and she hated doing housework so much she decided to run away from home. Because she was a terrible girl who thought only about herself, she spent all of her time looking forward instead of down, and she didn't see the big hole – even though it had teeth and was bigger than a horse's butt – until she was already falling inside of it."

"I can already tell this is going to be a great story," Landon murmured.

"They're all great stories," I said. "I simply forgot that the destination isn't as important as the adventure."

NINETEEN

"Wakey, wakey."

It took me a moment to remember where I was, confusion reigning as I stared at the unfamiliar ceiling fan circling overhead. Landon's body was warm next to mine, but something odd sat on my foot.

I tipped up my chin and stared at the end of the bed, my morning-muddled mind briefly wondering if my mother got a cat without telling anyone. She'd been threatening to for years because she said that a cat's disdain was more comfortable than Aunt Tillie's, but I didn't put much stock in the threat. Cats are self-sufficient, but someone still needs to clean the litter box, and I couldn't imagine my mother doing it.

I found something much worse than an odd cat staring back at me.

"Aunt Tillie!" I grabbed at the covers, glancing beneath and letting loose with a relieved sigh when I realized I wasn't naked. I'd been so exhausted the night before I stayed in my T-shirt and merely crawled under the covers, curled up next to Landon and immediately dropped off.

"What the … ?" Landon narrowed his eyes as he realized we weren't alone. "Someone needs to get you a bell."

I swallowed the urge to laugh because I'd just been thinking that a cat was sitting on my feet seconds before. I maintained an air of annoyance as I ran a hand through my tousled hair. "What are you doing in here? I know for a fact that you're not allowed to wander around and let yourself into the guests' rooms when they're sleeping."

"You are not normal guests."

"There's nothing normal in this house," Landon complained, readjusting his pillow so he could prop himself up, and glaring. "Did you ever consider knocking?"

Aunt Tillie was blasé. "Why would I knock? This is my property. Technically you're under my roof. You're part of the family. I have no intention of knocking."

"Well, at least you're honest," Landon muttered, shifting his eyes to me. "How is your head and neck?"

Even an unwelcome visit from the wakeup witch couldn't derail Landon's one-track mind. "I'm fine," I yawned, rubbing the sleep from my eyes. "You need to stop hovering."

"When we catch the guy who throttled my girlfriend, I'll stop hovering. Until then, you need to suck it up."

"Wow. He's strict." Aunt Tillie made a face that couldn't be misconstrued for anything but annoyance and turned her attention to me. "He snores and you drool. You're a good match."

"That's not what you said when you cursed him to smell like rotten sauerkraut," I reminded her. "Speaking of that, I told you not to cast the spell, but you did it anyway. What's the deal with that?"

Aunt Tillie snorted, brushing off my middling outrage with an austere wave of her hand. "Oh, please," she scoffed. "You said you didn't want me to cast it, but you were near tears the entire time. He had it coming."

I risked a glance at Landon. "I honestly told her not to cast it."

"I don't care about that," Landon countered. "She's right. I did have it coming. I actually found the entire thing funny. Doug and Becky thought they smelled bad."

"They did," Aunt Tillie said. "I cursed all three of you."

"Well, that explains that." Landon tilted his head, picking up my hand from on top of the covers and flipping it over so he could trace the lines in my palm with his index finger. "I actually enjoyed it. I thought about you the entire day."

I wasn't sure how to take that. "You smelled like rotten sauerkraut and thought of me? Should I bathe more often?"

Landon grinned. "I just thought of you guys working together to cast the curse, and it made me happy. I knew you were safe and – well, not happy – but busy. I knew you were out there thinking of me. I liked it."

"You're an odd duck." Aunt Tillie made a quacking sound before shifting. "So, we have a lot to talk about, and you guys need to come down to breakfast so we can plan out everything."

That sounded a bit worrisome. "What about the guests? We can hardly plot in front of the other guests."

"They're conveniently distracted with a trip to the corn maze," Aunt Tillie replied. "Marcus arranged a bus and is acting as a guide. Thistle volunteered him for the job. Plus, well, Winnie didn't think you would want the guests staring at you after the search."

"Why would they stare at me?" I questioned. "They didn't see the troopers."

"No, but word has spread thanks to Margaret Little and her big, fat mouth," Aunt Tillie grumbled. "She's telling anyone who will listen that you're a murder suspect and we're hiding bodies on the property."

"I wouldn't put much stock in what Mrs. Little says," Landon argued. "Everyone knows she's a bitter hag."

"Yes, but the tourists can't pick one small iota of truth out of the huge web of lies we weave in this town on a daily basis," Aunt Tillie pointed out. "It's a town where real witches are pretending to be normal humans pretending to be fake witches. For all the guests know, this is part of an elaborate play. Still, it makes some people uncomfortable."

"I didn't even think of that," I mused, rolling my neck. "Maybe we should stay someplace else."

"I'm not necessarily against that – if only to keep Aunt Tillie from peeping – but where do you suggest we go?" Landon challenged.

"Like I want to see you naked," Aunt Tillie scoffed. "All cops have small junk. That's a universal fact."

Landon narrowed his eyes to dangerous slits. "You're on my list."

"Yeah? I've got a buttload of people ahead of you on my list," Aunt Tillie said. "Thistle is excited because this is the first time she hasn't been on top of it in weeks. She has some breathing room."

"Well, great," Landon muttered.

"We'll shower and be downstairs in twenty minutes," I said, hoping to head off a larger argument. "I'm pretty hungry."

"That universal truth of yours isn't true," Landon added.

"Oh, whatever." Aunt Tillie smiled as she stood, clearly happy to have gotten under Landon's skin with minimal effort. "We all know that's why detectives carry around magnifying glasses. Don't dilly-dally, by the way. I'm hungry, but Winnie says we can't eat until you guys are downstairs."

"Maybe I'll take my time just to torture you," Landon called to her back. "How would you like that?"

"Winnie made a double load of bacon."

Landon's face was so adorable I had to force myself to keep from kissing it.

"We'll be down in fifteen minutes," Landon said, resigned. He waited until Aunt Tillie shut the door to turn his full attention to me. "I hate the fact that she knows exactly how to irritate me. It's like her superpower."

I grinned. "She has many superpowers."

"Which is why I'm glad she's on our side." Landon kissed the corner of my mouth before bolting out of bed. "Now, hurry up. Breakfast awaits, and I've been dreaming of bacon, eggs and hash browns for a month. It's going to take me days to catch up."

"What kind of foods didn't you dream about while you were gone?" I was genuinely curious.

Landon answered without hesitation. "Sauerkraut."

"Good to know."

THE TABLE WAS PACKED with expectant faces, Chief Terry, Clove, Sam and Thistle joining the regular players. I flashed a grateful smile and kissed Chief Terry on the cheek before sitting.

"Are you okay?" He'd been completely miffed at the state police's gall while searching the family living quarters. We finally had to force him to leave because I feared he'd have a heart attack if he didn't calm down. "Everything turned out all right, so there's no reason to worry."

"Everything is hardly all right," Chief Terry said gruffly, although he patted my hand. "I heard all about how they didn't find anything. They ate dinner at the diner and complained very loudly to one another about it."

I lifted an eyebrow, surprised. "Who told you that?"

"I have spies everywhere, missy." Chief Terry tapped the end of my nose before pouring me a glass of tomato juice. He knew it was my favorite, and appeared to be in doting mode. "You look better. Did you get a good night's sleep?"

"I did," I confirmed, bobbing my head. "I think I slept a full ten hours."

"That means you needed it," Mom said, handing Landon the platter of bacon and shaking her head when he grabbed a fistful. "We have tongs."

"I'm simply streamlining the process," Landon said, unbothered by the fact that his eating habits caused Mom to make faces. "Other than the fact that they didn't find anything – and really, what did they expect to find here? – did you hear any other gossip?"

Chief Terry stared at Landon for a long moment. I could practically see the internal debate flitting through his eyes. I decided to finally put an end to this problem.

"Chief Terry, you can't be angry at Landon," I scolded. "He didn't do anything wrong. This isn't his fault."

"He didn't call when he should have," Clove reminded me. "That was wrong."

"Yes, and we've talked about that," I said. "He couldn't get away and he didn't want to ask Chief Terry to act as a gopher given ... well, given the fact that Chief Terry is like a father to me."

I knew it was emotionally manipulative, but Chief Terry went positively gooey whenever I referred to him as my father figure. I was hopeful that today would be no different. I really needed him to forgive Landon. Apparently it worked.

"Oh, geez." Chief Terry pinched the bridge of his nose. "You think I don't know what you're doing, but I do."

I feigned ignorance. "What are you talking about? Do you not want me to think of you that way?"

"Oh, and here are the wide eyes," Chief Terry muttered. "I hate those wide eyes. All three of you used them when you were kids – Clove often added tears. You know I'm a sucker for the wide eyes."

"I do." I gripped his hand before he could grab his fork. "It's not Landon's fault. None of this is."

Chief Terry licked his lips as he stared at his coffee mug. "I know that, Bay," he said finally. "You could've died in that guesthouse, though. The only reason you're alive is because someone decided to play a game rather than hit Landon where it really hurt.

"Have you considered that this individual only went after you because Landon was undercover and they wanted to teach him a lesson?" he continued. "Have you considered that he could've killed you – or done something almost as bad – when you were unconscious?"

I had considered both of those scenarios. "Yes. I was lucky."

"You don't seem all that lucky when I look at the bruises around your throat."

"It doesn't feel lucky to me either," Landon interjected. "Bay, you had a right to be angry with me because of what happened. We've talked about this. Chief Terry has the same right. You can't act as mediator for everything."

"I'm not acting as mediator," I countered, my temper flaring. "We have enough going on without you two at odds. I want you to make up."

"Well, maybe Chief Terry isn't ready to make up," Landon suggested. "It doesn't seem fair to force him, does it?"

Probably not, but that wouldn't stop me. "Please make up?" I pressed my hands together in a reflection of prayer. "Please. Pretty please with sugar on top. Puh-leez."

Chief Terry was laughing by the time I finished, shaking his head as he leaned back in his chair. "Okay, Bay. I forgive Landon. All is right with the world again ... except the fact that you're a murder suspect and in danger of losing your job." His eyes darkened at the last part.

"Yeah, well, Brian Kelly is low on my list right now," I said, sobering. "I need to get a copy of that will, by the way. You said you would look for it once the state police were off the property."

"You don't need to worry about Brian Kelly," Chief Terry stressed. "I will handle Brian Kelly."

His vehemence caught me off guard. "What do you mean?"

"Don't worry about it," Chief Terry said. "I had a meeting with a few local business owners yesterday afternoon. Brian Kelly is not going to be an issue."

That sounded ominous. Apparently Aunt Tillie thought so, too.

"Do you need to borrow my shovel?" Aunt Tillie asked, perking up. "I found it, by the way. Someone keeps hiding it, but I have it now. I was thinking we could put him at Hollow Creek. It smells as bad as he does, so he'd fit right in."

"I don't think that will be necessary," Chief Terry said.

"What do you mean?" I pressed, curious. "Who did you meet with?"

Chief Terry waved off the question. "That doesn't matter now. What matters is that we keep you safe and find a killer."

"It also matters that the state police seem fixated on Bay to the detriment of investigating anything or anyone else," Landon added, licking his finger after finishing his last slice of bacon. "They're not going to look for the real culprit because Davis is trying to rise through the ranks. I talked to a guy I know in the state police yesterday. Davis thinks solving a high-profile murder is his ticket to early promotion. He's not interested in looking beyond Bay."

"That means we have to," Chief Terry said. "Don't worry. I've got people watching the troopers and Agent Glenn."

And the surprises simply kept rolling in. "You have people watching the cops and an FBI agent? Where are you getting these people?"

"I know people." Chief Terry offered a wink. "Davis and Glenn got rooms in town last night. They're staying at the same inn, which means they're working in lock-step on every avenue of this investigation."

"You've got to be kidding." Landon's temper flared. "That's just ... freaking annoying. What inn?"

"I'll give you two guesses," Chief Terry replied. "You'll only need one, though."

Things clicked into place fairly quickly. "The Dragonfly," I muttered, exhaling heavily. "Of course it would be the Dragonfly. They want to question Dad about me, and that's the easiest way to do it."

After years away, my father and uncles had returned to town several months ago and opened their own inn. The Dragonfly was popular and getting good word of mouth, but it was nowhere near as popular as The Overlook – which was exactly how my mother and aunts liked things.

"This sucks," I complained. "I haven't even bothered to tell Dad I'm a murder suspect and they're already out there questioning him."

"Yeah, but they're not staying." Landon's voice was cold as he grabbed more bacon from the platter. "I won't allow it."

"You can't force my father to kick them out," I argued.

"I wouldn't bet on that," Landon muttered. "Eat your breakfast, sweetie. Make sure you fuel up. As soon as we're done here we're heading out there."

"And what?" I didn't want to cause a scene. "My father isn't going to just do what you want because you ask nicely – or more likely yell."

"We won't know until we try," Landon said. "Eat your breakfast. I'm not joking about needing your strength."

I wanted to argue further, but it seemed pointless. I mashed my eggs and hash browns together, and forked up a huge hunk of the mixture.

"This day is going to blow, isn't it?"

"I wouldn't say that," Aunt Tillie answered. "I found my shovel and my list is full. From where I'm sitting, it's going to be a good day."

"Maybe we should switch seats."

"Then I wouldn't be having a good day, and we both know it's all about me."

Well, she wasn't wrong.

TWENTY

"How do you want to handle this?" Chief Terry insisted on driving to the Dragonfly with us. I had a feeling he worried Landon would fly off the broom handle and beat Noah until he was a bloody stump, but I was happy for his presence. The fourth member of our hunting party was another story.

"I think you should walk up behind him and drag his hands behind his head, like so," Aunt Tillie answered from the passenger seat, demonstrating to the best of her ability as Landon pressed his lips together to keep from laughing. "Then, when you've got him so he can't move, I'll take over."

Chief Terry returned Aunt Tillie's calm stare. "And what will you do when you take over?"

"I will kick him in the nuts, rip out all of his body hair with the hottest wax I can find and pull out his nose hairs with tweezers," Aunt Tillie replied. "I considered using the tweezers for all of the hair stuff, but that will take forever. We must be practical."

"That's exactly what I was thinking," Chief Terry drawled. "Okay, I like this plan. I'll give you a signal right before I get into position."

I didn't for a second believe that Chief Terry would give in to Aunt

Tillie's demands. She probably didn't either, but she's the type of person who continuously pushes someone until they crumble and admit defeat.

"No, I'll give you a signal," Aunt Tillie corrected. "Oh, and just so you know, this constitutes a binding verbal contract – I saw that on television the other day and I'm really looking forward to taking advantage of it – and if you don't grab Agent Asshat by the arms I will sue you for breach of contract."

Chief Terry remained immovable. "We both know you won't sue me, and I haven't ruled out grabbing that moron by the arms so you can carry out your dastardly plan. I don't, however, need added pressure to make up my mind."

Aunt Tillie snorted. "You won't let me beat him up. I know you. You're too *Law and Order* when you need to embrace *The Wire*."

Chief Terry flicked his confused eyes to me. "Did she just explain something?"

"We've been watching a lot of Netflix this month," I supplied. "She lives her life by what television shows her is possible."

"Ah."

"Yes, and now that you have your love monkey back, I'm assuming I will have control of the remote control again." Aunt Tillie puffed out her chest, haughty. "I can't wait to go back to watching porn."

Chief Terry's mouth dropped open as Landon chuckled. "You watch porn?"

"Not since Bay has been bored and spending so much time with me," Aunt Tillie replied. "She's a prude who won't watch porn. I find I've really missed it. The last time I ordered a pizza I didn't even wonder for a second if the delivery boy was going to strip down and show me his sausage."

I pressed the heel of my hand to my forehead, my cheeks burning. "I don't even know what to say to that."

"I don't either, but now I totally want to deliver a pizza to you," Landon said, directing me toward the Dragonfly's front door as we hopped out of Chief Terry's vehicle.

"Does someone want to explain to me why we brought Tillie with us again?" Chief Terry prodded. "I know you told me at The Overlook, but the reason has escaped me between there and here."

"Because Noah is terrified of her," Landon answered easily. "He prides himself on only believing what he can see, yet he knows that Aunt Tillie will essentially skin him alive if given the chance. I want him to know that we're going to give her a chance."

"And you think that's a good idea?" Chief Terry clearly wasn't convinced. "What if Tillie turns him into a frog or something?"

"I never bow to clichés," Aunt Tillie countered. "If I turn him into an animal it's going to be something fun ... like a dung beetle. Or what kind of monkeys have their butts hanging out? The ones with the red behinds? I like them."

"Baboons," Landon automatically answered.

"Don't encourage her," I chided.

"Yes, please don't encourage her," Chief Terry echoed.

"Oh, I'm going to encourage her," Landon muttered. "I can't get away with punching Noah in the face without losing my job, but Aunt Tillie is a master at doing that with words and threats. I can't wait to see what she comes up with."

Aunt Tillie stilled near the Dragonfly's front door, her eyes going wide and glassy as she leaned forward and wrapped her arms around Landon's waist. I was surprised by the gesture – Aunt Tillie isn't much of a hugger – but the look on Landon's face told me he was ready to find a cave to hide in if the expression of affection didn't immediately cease.

"I think that's the nicest thing you've ever said to me," Aunt Tillie sniffed, dabbing at her eyes. "You're officially my favorite FBI agent ever."

Landon awkwardly patted her shoulder. "I ... well ... thank you. Is that saying much, though? Do you like any other FBI agents?"

"Of course not." Aunt Tillie recovered quickly and pulled back. "You know I hate 'The Man.' Now ... let me at this one. Wait, maybe we should go back and get my shovel. I can't believe I forgot it."

"THIS IS A SURPRISE."

Dad's eyebrows settled near his hairline as he opened the door and ushered our group inside. While Landon and I visited regularly – okay, we try to visit once a month and usually only on those rare occasions because Clove makes us – Chief Terry and Aunt Tillie aren't exactly what I would call regulars at the Dragonfly.

"Yes, well, we were in the neighborhood." I knew the comment sounded lame, but I have an odd aversion to talking to my father as if he's the parent and I'm a grown-up who doesn't need his approval. He left when I was a kid – visiting every once in a while and calling once a month or so – but we didn't have the easiest of relationships. He was desperate to make it better, and I was fine keeping a bit of distance and the peace between his and Mom's sides of the family. Our mission today wouldn't improve family relations.

"You were in the neighborhood?" Dad's gaze bounced between faces. "You were in the neighborhood with Landon, Terry and Tillie first thing in the morning?"

Well, when he said it like that it sounded implausible. "Um … ."

Landon rested his hand on my shoulder as a show of unity and fixed Dad with a calm expression. I didn't even know he had that one in his repertoire. The fact that he could pull it out when he wanted to do serious bodily harm to Noah was impressive.

"Actually, we need to see two of your guests," Landon said, keeping his voice even.

"Is this official police business?" Dad looked confused.

"Yes," Landon answered without hesitation.

"No, it's not," Chief Terry corrected, lobbing eye daggers at Landon as he shook his head. "Technically Landon and I have been cut out of the investigation that the two individuals staying here are heading. We simply need to talk to them for a moment."

"Uh-huh." Dad rubbed his chin as he glanced between Landon and Chief Terry before focusing on me. "Do you want to tell me what's going on?"

That was an interesting question. "Not really." I decided opting for the truth was in my best interests. "No matter how I explain it, I'll end up looking bad."

"She's not wrong," Aunt Tillie said, glancing around. "This place is a hole, by the way, Jack. You should condemn it and leave town again."

Dad was used to Aunt Tillie's attitude, often blaming her for his decision to leave when I was younger. I would never pretend that living with Aunt Tillie was easy. I also refused to make excuses for a father who let my great-aunt bully him out of my life.

"The Dragonfly is fine," I snapped. "That's not why we're here."

"And why are you here?" Dad pressed. "I'm confused, but it's fairly obvious that something big is going on."

"I'm pretty sure I can answer that question."

I internally cringed when Davis and Noah landed at the bottom of the staircase, the duo exchanging amused glances before focusing on our small group.

"Are these the people you're here to see?" Dad asked, shifting from one foot to the other as a chill dropped over the room.

"They are," Chief Terry confirmed, narrowing his eyes. "These are the people investigating Bay for murder."

Whatever he expected Chief Terry to say, that wasn't it. Dad's mouth dropped open as his gaze bounced between faces. "You can't be serious."

"How have you not heard about this?" Landon challenged, pinning Noah with a warning look before turning to Dad. "It's been all over the television and radio."

"I heard that a body had been found on The Overlook grounds," Dad replied, clasping his hands together in front of him. "I didn't know Bay was a suspect."

"The body was found right in front of the guesthouse," I explained. "I woke up right next to it."

"You woke up?" Dad scratched his cheek. "I'm not sure I understand ... and what happened to your neck?"

"Someone broke into the guesthouse," Landon supplied. "Someone grabbed her around the throat in her own home, squeezed until she thought she was going to suffocate and then slammed her head into a wall. Whoever it was hurt her … and then left her to wake up next to a body."

"Landon was on an undercover case," Chief Terry offered, taking pity on my shaken father. "Two people escaped arrest when the warrants were served. One of those people ended up dead in front of Bay's house. The other is still missing. We believe he's responsible, but … ." He broke off, casting a helpless look in Davis' direction. "Other people think Bay's to blame and are treating her abysmally."

"I see." The last part of the statement seemed to shake Dad out of the confused fog invading his head. "And these two individuals are treating her poorly?"

"They searched the inn yesterday," Aunt Tillie said, taking a menacing step in Noah's direction and grinning when he inadvertently reacted to the movement by taking a step back. "They didn't find anything, of course. I'm a rule follower and would never break the law."

"Of course," Dad said dryly, shaking his head. "I guess I'm confused about this."

"There's nothing to be confused about, sir," Davis said, adopting a smarmy tone. "We're simply investigating a brutal murder that happened to occur at your daughter's domicile. We're certainly not fixating on her to the detriment of other suspects."

"Oh, he talks all fancy and stuff 'cause he wants to confuse us," Aunt Tillie shouted, mimicking a stereotypical country bumpkin as she danced in her spot. "Aw, shucks. I think he believes he's bamboozled us."

"I think you're right," Landon said. "As for the rest, if you weren't focused on Bay you wouldn't have searched the family home. You would take one look at the evidence – the fact that she was terribly hurt and left outside in the elements – and realize that she's not the one putting others in danger. She's in danger herself."

"What do you mean by that?" Dad was beside himself. "And you, young lady, why didn't you call to tell me you'd been attacked? It seems to me that's something a daughter should tell her father."

"Oh, well … ."

"Don't yell at her," Chief Terry and Landon barked in unison, squaring their shoulders as they faced off with Dad.

"It's okay," I said, holding up my hand. "I should've called. I just … that night was a mess. I was confused when I woke up."

"And why weren't you with her?" Dad asked, his voice full of unbridled accusation as he glared at Landon. "You two are usually joined at the lips and hips. Why weren't you there to protect her?"

"Well … ." Landon looked caught. "The thing is … um … we were kind of fighting at the time."

"Really?" Davis leaned forward, intrigued. "Is that because you had a sexual relationship with the victim? I know you've denied it, but I don't believe you."

"Of course you don't," Landon gritted out, his temper getting the better of him. "You don't believe anything that's not handed to you on a silver platter. I didn't have a sexual relationship with Becky Patterson. I have a sexual relationship with my girlfriend. It's a very nice relationship."

One look at Chief Terry's dark expression and the uncomfortable way Dad stared at nothing on the wall told me Landon had gone too far. "That was probably an overshare," I whispered.

"Yeah, I heard it the second I said it," Landon conceded. "It was already too late to take it back. Just pretend I didn't say anything and eventually they'll get over it."

I wasn't so sure, but I opted to let it go. "I didn't kill Becky. I mean … I didn't even know her last name. How would I find her to get her to show up at the guesthouse?"

"I'm thinking that she showed up to stake her claim to Agent Michaels and you responded out of jealousy," Davis replied. "You killed her in a fit of rage and then decided you needed to cover it up."

That didn't make much sense. "So … what? I strangled myself, slammed my own head against the wall in the foyer and then somehow floated to the spot in the doorway after I was unconscious?"

"You said you woke up in the doorway," Davis clarified. "We don't have proof of that. No one saw you at the time and can testify to the fact that you were ever unconscious."

Landon slipped his arm around my waist and jerked me closer, as if he wanted to protect me from Davis' innuendo even though it was obviously too late. "I know what you're doing, Davis. I know why you're doing it. I'm not an idiot."

"I would never suggest anything of the sort," Davis said, outwardly congenial even though his eyes flashed with annoyance.

"You shouldn't fool yourself into believing that your boss doesn't know what you're doing," Chief Terry offered, taking me by surprise with the edge tinging his voice. "We had a long talk yesterday. I understand why I can't investigate the case. My relationship with Bay's family creates a conflict of interest. You don't have carte blanche to do whatever you want, though. Your own superiors are concerned that you're so fixated on Bay."

The words were enough to knock Davis off his stride, though only marginally. "I don't believe you."

"I don't care," Chief Terry said. "I'm not the type to get my feelings hurt because you call me a liar."

"Then why are you here?"

"Because I've had enough," Chief Terry replied without hesitation. "You two are only here because you hope Jack offers dirt on Bay. That's why you selected this inn. Don't bother denying it, Agent Glenn. I'm well aware that you know who Jack is, thanks to your previous stay in town.

"Bay has been through enough over the past few weeks. I won't idly sit back and watch you mess up her world even further," he continued. "I'm tired of you. I'm tired of Brian Kelly. I'm also tired of trouble finding Bay even though she's a good girl."

"You've got him fooled," Landon teased, slinging an arm over my shoulders. By all outward appearances he was calm and collected. I knew he was ready to pounce should Noah insert himself into the conversation. Like all cowards, though, Noah appeared comfortable hiding behind someone else.

"What else has Bay been through?" Dad asked, focusing on Landon. "What else is happening?"

"Well, we're living in The Overlook, and Brian Kelly is trying to oust Bay from the newspaper," Landon replied. "Bay and I were separated for almost a month. We're over that, though. Right now, our biggest concerns are these two idiots and Brian Kelly, because they think she's a murderer and Kelly is trying to steal her job."

"Brian Kelly is trying to fire Bay?" Dad's expression was thoughtful as he turned to Chief Terry. "That's why you've been approaching area businesses and asking them to turn on Kelly?"

The question was like a punch to the stomach. "What?"

"Don't worry about it, Bay," Chief Terry supplied. "I told you I would fix the Brian Kelly situation and I meant it."

"You're trying to rally the area businesses to choose Bay over Brian," Landon noted, his lips curving. "You're going to force his hand."

"I'm going to do what's right."

"You and I should talk," Aunt Tillie said, grinning. "I'm kind of planning to do that myself, although I'm going to use a dress, clown makeup, tweezers and lighter fluid before getting my shovel to finish things off."

"What is it with you and your shovel?" Davis asked, annoyed. "You're not strong enough to bury a body."

Everyone familiar with Aunt Tillie's wrath sucked in a breath and waited for her to explode. Instead she chuckled, the sound low and eerie. "I'm going to enjoy ramming those words down your throat. As for the lodging arrangements, it's time for you to grow a pair, Jack. These men are trying to hurt your daughter. They're trying to use you to do it.

"Now, I know you like to whine and complain about your relationship with Bay and how you think it's lacking," she continued. "I'm not going to try and stop you. Your relationship is lacking. You're still her father. You need to act like it."

Dad stared at her a moment, unblinking. I recognized the moment he made his decision.

"Trooper Davis and Agent Glenn, I'm sure you understand that this arrangement is no longer going to work," Dad said. "I'll have your bills ready so you can square up once you pack your bags. We've appreciated your patronage at the Dragonfly but it is no longer wanted or appreciated."

Aunt Tillie crossed her arms over her chest and grinned. "And that's how it's done."

TWENTY-ONE

Chief Terry and Landon called in enough markers within the state police hierarchy that I was allowed to reclaim the guesthouse after lunch. Landon accompanied me to the house, but cautioned me not to be too excited about sleeping under my own roof. The sinking feeling in my stomach told me he was right when I surveyed the mess.

"I don't understand why they did this."

The guesthouse had been trashed. The couch had been upended, the cushions scattered about. All of the cupboards in the kitchen were empty, the sheets stripped from the mattress in the bedroom, and all of my clothes tossed on the floor. Then, after making a mess, the state troopers walked over everything for two days.

"I'm sorry, sweetie." Landon's earlier anger had dissipated over soup and BLTs for lunch. It was back with a vengeance. "We'll clean it up."

"Yeah." Cleaning it up wasn't the problem. I felt violated – by the cops more than the guy who jumped me – and I couldn't wrap my head around the mess. "I only wanted to come home."

Landon looked as if I'd shoved his heart in a vise and started squeezing. "You're coming home tonight. I'll make sure of it." That was the exact opposite of what he'd told me during the walk from the inn.

"How? Look at this. It'll take me a full day just to do the laundry."

"You're not alone," Landon reminded me. "There are a lot of people willing to help."

"I can't bother them with this." I didn't want to take my frustration out on Landon, but he was the only one present. "They have their own lives, their own responsibilities. This is my responsibility."

"You didn't do this, Bay," Landon argued. "You don't have to shoulder everything yourself. You think I'm a martyr, but I know you're one. If we ask for help ... ."

"I'm not asking for help." I was firm, but I forced a smile for his benefit. "You don't have to be here. You should go back to the inn. I bet Twila will make you cookies if you ask nicely."

Landon stared at me for a long time, silent. Finally he licked his lips and opened his mouth. "I'm going to run up to the inn for cookies because now that's all I can think about. I also think you need a few minutes to decompress, and you don't want to do it in front of me for some reason. I respect that, but I will be back ... and soon."

I heaved a sigh, amused. "Thank you."

"You're welcome." Landon cupped the back of my neck and thoroughly kissed me, allowing me to lose myself in him for a bit before separating. "Lock the door while I'm gone. I'm not joking about being away for only a few minutes. Until this is over, I don't want you here by yourself for an extended amount of time."

"I'll miss you terribly during your absence."

I jolted when Landon unleashed a playful swat on my rear end before wagging a finger as he trudged toward the door. "I'll let the sarcasm go because you're obviously upset ... and I don't blame you. This is not acceptable. I'll be lodging a complaint with the state police and FBI regulation committee."

"What good will that do?" I challenged.

"It won't do anything for us today," Landon conceded. "It will earn Noah a black mark on his record, though, and he's a guy who obsesses about his record."

AMANDA M. LEE

"Oh. So you're saying it's sort of insidious. It's like that time we locked Clove out of the guesthouse and told her Bigfoot was in the area, and then asked Martin Henderson to walk his really big dog past the property."

Landon pursed his lips to keep from laughing. "It's exactly like that."

"Okay. I'll see you in a little bit."

"You'll see me very soon," Landon corrected. "I'm only grabbing cleaning supplies and cookies from The Overlook, and then I'll be right back."

I knit my eyebrows, confused. "Cleaning supplies?"

"Please. I know you don't have any here. You guys don't clean. You trust that maid gnome thing you made up to cover that fact."

He wasn't wrong. "We need garbage bags, too."

"I'm on it."

"And maybe some caffeine."

Landon paused near the door to study the lock. "We need to switch out the front and back locks. I won't feel comfortable until we upgrade the security here."

"I'll be here when you get back."

"You'd better be." Landon's tone was no-nonsense. "I can't take another bout of fear where you're concerned. It would break my heart."

"Oh, now you're playing dirty."

"I use what I have to use," Landon said. "I'll be back. Just ... be careful."

"I'm always careful."

"Be ten times more careful than that."

I SPENT the next twenty minutes gathering laundry into a big pile. When someone knocked at the door I opened it without checking, expecting Landon and his cookies. Instead I found a furious Chief Terry.

"You don't look through the peephole before you open the door?"

he barked, causing me to take a step back. "You were attacked in this place a few days ago. I'd think you'd have more sense."

I stared at him, blinking rapidly, and then surprised myself when I burst into tears. Chief Terry instantly relaxed. "I take it back. Do whatever you want to do."

For some reason, simply seeing his familiar face was enough for me to give in and allow the past few days to wash over me. "Everything is such a mess." I threw myself at him, burying my face in his chest as he hugged me. "What am I going to do?"

"Oh, sweetheart, everything will be fine. I promise." I couldn't ever remember Chief Terry crying, but his voice cracked now, forcing me to lift my flooded eyes and search his face. "It'll be okay, Bay. We'll fix all of this."

I wanted to believe him. Everything inside of me screamed to give in and let him baby me. I worried that if I fell down – even for a moment – I would never get back up. "I'm sorry."

"Don't apologize."

"I cried on your shirt." I wiped at the smudge my mascara left on his pocket. "Have you really been trying to pressure the business owners to turn on Brian?"

Chief Terry shrugged. "I don't like him. It wasn't exactly a hard decision."

"Are they going for it?"

"Most of them are," Chief Terry replied. "I know you don't believe it, Bay, but people like you."

"Mrs. Little?"

"She's working with Brian."

I stilled. "Seriously?"

"I can't prove it in a court of law, but I saw her going into the newspaper office last night after dark," Chief Terry replied. "She runs the same ad every week, so … I don't think it's much of a leap to believe she and Brian are in cahoots."

I smirked. "I'm not sure how I feel about you using the word 'cahoots.'"

"And I'm not sure how I feel about the tears." Chief Terry used his

AMANDA M. LEE

thumb to wipe my cheek. "Bay, you're a good person. I know it seems that bad things are stacking up on you right now, but everything will get better. I firmly believe you're going to get everything you want and deserve."

"It doesn't feel that way," I admitted, gesturing toward the mess. "All I could think about was coming home. I don't hate staying at the inn, but I want to sleep in my own bed. I know it sounds whiny, but … there it is."

"It doesn't sound whiny," Chief Terry countered. "I guarantee you'll sleep in your own bed tonight."

"How?"

"I didn't come empty handed." Chief Terry held up the brown bag I missed upon initial inspection when he first walked through the door.

"What's that?"

"New handles and deadbolts so we can change out every lock in this place."

"But … how did you know?" I asked, confused. "Landon said we needed to do it a few minutes ago, but he's up at the inn getting cookies."

Chief Terry smirked. "Do you really think the boy is getting cookies right after he saw this mess?"

"I … no." Things clicked into place. "He's getting people to help us clean."

"There you go." Chief Terry tapped the spot between my eyebrows. "Now you're thinking. I worried you forgot how to reason things out there for a second."

"You know, I wanted to say something to you at the Dragonfly, but I didn't feel it was appropriate in front of Dad."

"What's that?"

"I have two fathers," I choked out, the tears returning for an entirely different reason. "You're always there for me. I don't know that I can ever thank you, but … thank you."

"Oh, please don't cry." Chief Terry looked as if he wanted to find a closet to hide in. "I hate it when you cry."

"Well, good news for you then," Aunt Tillie announced, barreling through the open door with a broom in her hand. "I make the world a better place with my mere presence. She'll be smiling in seconds."

Chief Terry offered me a stiff pat on the shoulder before facing off with my great-aunt. "I'm surprised you even know what a broom looks like, let alone what it does."

"Oh, ye of little of faith," Aunt Tillie shot back. "Brooms are for riding."

"Ugh. This family makes me tired sometimes," Chief Terry muttered. "I'm going to start with the locks. You two do … whatever it is you plan to do."

"We plan to turn this endeavor into a movie," Aunt Tillie supplied.

"A movie?' Chief Terry furrowed his brow. "What … like *Mrs. Doubtfire*?"

"You're showing your age, Terry." Aunt Tillie made a clucking sound in the back of her throat as she studied the destroyed room. "Have you ever seen a little movie called *Fantasia*? It's a cartoon, so it really can't be dated."

It took me a moment to get what she was insinuating. "You wouldn't dare."

"You'd be surprised what I'd dare to do," Aunt Tillie said. "Now … step back. I'll have this place put back together in five minutes. Time me. Oh, and I need you to find my shovel. I thought I left it by the back door, but it's missing again."

"What's with you and the shovel?"

"I like to bury things. Sue me."

IT TOOK LONGER than five minutes – and Aunt Tillie's efforts were more *Home Alone* than *Fantasia* at times – but by the time Clove, Sam, Thistle, Marcus, Mom, Marnie and Twila showed up we had the makings of a productive day.

Mom and Twila carried the bulk of the laundry to The Overlook. They had multiple sets of washers and dryers and could tear through the loads quickly. Someone had to stay at the inn and help the guests if necessary, but they did their share.

Marnie, who's something of a workhorse, stayed behind. She tackled the kitchen with little preamble, slapping it together in less than two hours, while Thistle and I set our bedrooms right and everyone else took on the bathroom and living room. By the time we were done the guesthouse looked as good as new. Sure, I still felt a bit of trepidation when I glanced at the hallway where I was attacked, but the new locks went a long way toward making me feel safe.

By nightfall, only Thistle, Marcus, Sam and Clove remained. Thistle technically still lived in the guesthouse even though she spent half her nights at Marcus' apartment, and Clove decided that she and Sam would join us for martinis and spend the night so we could have something akin to a sleepover. Thistle promptly rolled her eyes at the suggestion, but I liked it. The fuller the guesthouse felt the less likely I was to panic at a moving shadow.

As if sensing my potential distress later in the night, Landon moved to the floor next to me on one side of the coffee table and topped off my chocolate martini before grabbing a deck of cards.

"Who wants to play a game?"

"Seriously? We're going to play card games?" Thistle didn't look thrilled with the notion. "I think we should play Twister or something."

"That sounds weird; we're adults," Landon argued.

"It's only weird because we have no clothes – and that includes underwear, mind you – to change in to tomorrow morning, so it's like we'd be playing Twister in our pajamas."

"That reminds me, I gave your mother the key to the Explorer," Landon told me. "They're putting all of the laundry in the hatchback. We can drive it back to the guesthouse after breakfast tomorrow, so we'll have to wear the same clothes up to the inn tomorrow morning. They also dropped off a bag of pajamas for everyone at the front door the last time they were down here. It's not much, but it's something."

"That sounds good." I rested my head against his shoulder, listening to the wind howl outside. "Sounds like a big storm is brewing."

"Yeah, we're supposed to get a series of them throughout the week," Thistle said. "That's going to put a real damper on the Halloween festivities, but if we're lucky they'll still get the trick-or-treating in on Friday."

"That would be nice." I moved Landon's hand from the cards and flipped it over, tracing his lifeline as I stared. "Thank you for getting everyone to help even though I expressly forbade you to do it."

"Oh, that was a backhanded compliment if I ever heard one," Thistle teased, amused. "That's like 'thank you for the chlamydia even though I told you not to screw around.'"

Marcus barked out a laugh, genuinely amused. "That was a lovely sentiment, honey."

"I try."

"What's going to happen now?" Sam asked, sobering. "The state police can't possibly think you killed that woman, can they?"

"I don't think they believe Bay did it," Landon answered for me. "I am, however, worried they'll try to prove she did it."

Clove made a strange sound as she swallowed. "You think they might try to frame her?"

"I think I don't like or trust Davis," Landon replied, choosing his words carefully. "I also think Noah has a vendetta regarding this family."

"So what do we do?" Thistle asked. "Do we pack up and head for Canada?"

Landon cocked an eyebrow, amused. "Are you going to run with Bay if it comes to it?"

"She's not going to run alone."

"No, she's not," Landon agreed. "If it comes time to run, I'll go with her. We'll contact all of you when we get settled."

The matter-of-fact way he delivered the words was like a punch in the gut. "Landon, you can't be serious."

"I have faith in the system, and I'm going to work within it," Landon said. "That doesn't mean I'll give you up … or let you go to prison for something you didn't do. If it comes to a choice of letting them take you or running, we're going to run."

I was dumbfounded. "What about your job?"

"I care about you more than the job. This past month taught me that."

"It should've taught you to call when you're in public and pretend you don't know your girlfriend," Thistle muttered, averting her gaze.

"Thank you, Thistle." Landon's eyes flashed. "I made a mistake. We're trying to move on from it. We can't do that if you keep bringing it up."

"Fine." Thistle blew out a sigh. "What about that Doug guy? Are there any leads on him?"

"He's in the wind," Landon answered, turning toward the window when the bush outside brushed against the glass. "We might have to use alternative means to find him."

I knew exactly what he meant by that. "A locator spell?"

Landon nodded. "I don't want to resort to that, but we might not have a choice. I need to give it some serious thought before agreeing to it, though."

"When do you want to do it?"

"We'll talk about it over breakfast tomorrow," he replied, rolling to his knees and leveling a pointed gaze on me. "If we're not going to play cards, I'm going to bed. I don't think getting super drunk will help us. Besides, there's another game I want to play once we're alone."

"Such a smooth talker," Marcus teased, grinning.

Landon ignored him. "Let's go to sleep, sweetie."

"I want nothing more than to sleep in our bed," I said, grabbing his hand. "It's good to be home again."

Landon merely smiled, serene. "You have no idea."

TWENTY-TWO

I felt twinges of panic several times throughout the day, usually at obscure moments when I felt isolated (even though someone was always close as we cleaned the guesthouse). I had no intention of telling anyone about my feelings. I figured it was something I would have to work through on my own.

Landon was having none of that. He seemed to sense my distress before I could register it myself.

"Here." He handed me flannel pajama pants and a T-shirt, items he collected from the bag by the door before following me into the bedroom. "I'll grab you some socks."

I watched him a moment, dumbfounded. "I thought you would want to ... you know."

Landon smirked. "We're both exhausted. I think you need sleep more than anything else. We'll discuss ... you know ... in the morning."

I bit the inside of my cheek, unsure. "Are you angry?"

Landon's expressive face flooded with surprise. "Why would I be angry?"

"I don't know. It's just ... I feel the need to apologize and I can't explain it."

Landon planted his hands on his narrow hips. "I feel odd making demands given the situation."

"I've never heard you demand sex," I pointed out.

"Not that." Landon made a face that bordered on hilarious, which eased a bit of the tension in the room. "I'm talking about the fact that you keep apologizing. Bay, you didn't do anything wrong. You need to stop saying 'I'm sorry' whenever you turn around. You're only supposed to apologize when you've done something to truly be sorry for. That doesn't apply to you in this situation."

"Because you should've called that day after we ran into each other at the corn maze and now you're the one who should be apologizing?" I was going for levity. I knew Landon was treading very close to the edge when it came to jokes about his behavior that day. He'd yet to fly off the handle – he was holding tightly to his anger and I had a feeling it was because he didn't want to make things worse for me – but it was coming.

"You're funny." Landon tapped the end of my nose. "It bothers me when you apologize for anything that has happened here. I'm not going to lie. You've done things on occasion that you needed to apologize for and thought you didn't do anything wrong. That's not what's happening here. You didn't do this."

"You didn't either."

Landon cocked a dubious eyebrow. "No? None of this would've happened if I hadn't been undercover."

"That's your job."

"But it's not your problem to worry about."

I balked at his tone. "I thought you said we were a team. My pain is your pain, right? Your trouble is my trouble and all that other crap."

Landon pursed his lips to keep from laughing. "You have such a way with words, Bay. It's like loving a poet."

I ignored his sarcasm. "You didn't cause this and it bothers me when you blame yourself."

"I did cause some of this," Landon argued. "I refuse to fight about it, though. This is our first night back together under this roof. We both need sleep. It's been a long day, and I think we're going to have another long one tomorrow. All that taken into consideration, I've decided to simply agree with you because I'm too tired to fight."

Winchesters like to win arguments, but it wasn't much of a resounding victory. I was too exhausted to press him on the issue. I was also too stubborn to completely let it go. "Intentions mean as much as actions, and you were trying to give me a gift by not going undercover any longer. That's the most important part."

Landon's expression softened. "The gift was for me as much as you. When I first joined the bureau I thought I'd always want to be undercover. It sounded exciting, and I loved a good adventure. That's not what I find exciting any longer."

"Is this story going to a dirty level, or is it all going to be about bacon?"

Landon snickered. "It's going to a mushy place," he replied. "I find that the things that drew me to undercover assignments no longer exist. I still have nonstop adventures, don't get me wrong. These days they're with you."

I tried to swallow the lump in my throat without falling to pieces. "You're kind of charming when you want to be. You know that, right?"

"I do." Landon bobbed his head in confirmation and then pointed toward the bed. "Change into your pajamas and get in. We'll handle the romance end of things in the morning."

"Oh, that was less charming," I teased, although I did as he instructed. I wasn't sure I'd be able to sleep out of fear, but I'd imbibed just enough that I knew sleep wouldn't elude me. "You did it on purpose," I mused. "You had me drink just enough that I'll pass out, but not enough that I'll be hungover tomorrow."

Landon averted his gaze. "I have no idea what you're talking about."

"It's true," I countered, amused. "You handled me, and I didn't even realize it was happening."

"I thought it would be good for both of us," Landon conceded. "I don't want you afraid in your home. That will kill me. Still, it wouldn't be unusual for you – or someone in the same position as you – to be nervous about spending the night here. You haven't been back since it happened. Once you get this first night behind you, things will be better."

"Even when it was happening, I wasn't afraid." I tugged the fresh T-shirt over my head and met his gaze, hair sticking out in a hundred different directions. "I was worried about you finding me dead, but I wasn't afraid."

"Don't ever say that." Landon extended a warning finger. "I don't want you to be afraid, but ... I need you to have a healthy fear of death. I plan to spend a lot more time with you before everything. You need to be alive to enjoy it."

"Duly noted." I climbed into my pajama pants before slipping under the covers. Landon waited until I was settled before killing the light and climbing in next to me. I rolled so I could rest my head on his chest and he tugged me close as we sighed in unison.

"This feels right, doesn't it?"

Landon grunted in agreement. "It's what I dreamed about while I was gone. Er, well, I added bacon to the mix."

I snorted. "You never know. Once this is settled, maybe your dream will come true."

"And that right there is why I love you."

"Right back at you."

I SLEPT hard and woke slowly, taking a long time to gauge my surroundings. I'd been away from my bed for several nights, but the comfort of familiarity returned right away and I knew I was home. Darkness told me it was late.

I glanced to my left, finding Landon dead to the world. His chest rose and fell in a steady rhythm, his breathing even and soothing. I put my fingers in front of his lips. Even though it was obvious he slept without issue, I found the need to reassure myself with his hot breath on my knuckles. He was fine. He was with me, safe. That's not what woke me.

I linked my fingers and rested them on my stomach, staring at the ceiling as I listened to the sounds of the guesthouse. For years it was just Thistle, Clove and me inside these walls. We lived together, played together. We laughed together and talked about love together. That love was always far off and distant when we chatted over flavored martinis. We considered ourselves too young to settle down. Our mothers settled down young, after all, and we didn't want our husbands to run screaming from us at the first sign of trouble.

Landon had seen more trouble than most men would tolerate. Marcus and Sam, too, but especially Landon. He considered himself a good agent – and he definitely was – but he didn't hesitate when it came to lying for us. He was keen to protect our secret, keener than me at times, which defied reason. At first I thought it was because Landon was embarrassed and didn't want anyone to know he dated a real witch. Loyalty and genuine emotion dissuaded me from that theory at some point.

Landon loved me. No matter how improbable I found the situation, he loved with his whole heart, and I had no doubt we would somehow survive everything thrown at us. Landon was not my father. He would not run when the going got tough, and he would stay by my side forever. Doubting that did nothing but drive him insane. It didn't make me feel better. Waiting for something to happen, for him to leave, was an exercise in futility.

Landon wasn't going anywhere. I wasn't going anywhere. Our future wasn't exactly fixed, but we were committed to facing it together. Could I ask for more? Not really. So how did I manage to completely lose my mind when he was out of town? How did I convince myself that being apart for a few weeks could somehow change everything?

I shifted my eyes to the window when a shadow moved on the other side of the blinds. I wasn't particularly worried – a lilac bush resided on that side of the house, and while it was no longer in bloom, its branches swayed with the wind. As if on cue, a bolt of lightning flashed and illuminated the room, causing me to jerk to a sitting position.

Landon didn't so much as shift, even when the thunder roared loud enough to rattle the windows. I stared at the window, convinced

I imagined the shape outside, and waited for another flash of lighting. When it came, I let loose with a relieved sigh. This time it was clearly nothing more than the bush.

I tried to get comfortable again, pressing my eyes shut and listening to the storm. I wanted it to lull me. I generally love a good storm, and this could very well be the last storm I got to enjoy until the spring. My head refused to let go of that first flash, though, and before I realized what I was doing I was on my feet.

I was quiet when I twisted the door handle, silently escaping the bedroom and leaving Landon to sleep. He didn't need to be a part of my paranoia. The living room was dark, although the small light over the kitchen sink provided minor illumination. Clove and Thistle had straightened up before retiring. I knew Clove and Sam were sleeping on an air mattress in her old bedroom. Thistle and I spent months arguing about the space – I wanted to turn it into an office and she wanted to turn it into a crafts room – but it remained empty because we couldn't agree. It didn't matter now. Thistle would move in with Marcus once construction on his new stable and barn complex was finished – he was converting an old barn into a beautiful home right near the town square – and then I would have the guesthouse to myself. I'd considered abandoning it and moving closer to Landon, the idea of being away from him three nights a week becoming more and more depressing, but now wasn't the time to talk about something that big. We needed to put this behind us first.

Lightning flashed again and I found myself staring at the front window to see if I could catch movement, inching along the wall as I did. I was so focused on the window I didn't notice Thistle's door open until she was already moving through the opening. We smacked into each other, jolting, and sucked in calming breaths before locking gazes. Without hesitation, we both slapped each other across the shoulder and arm respectively and spoke at the same time.

"You scared me."

"You're an idiot."

I rolled my neck until it cracked, working overtime to tamp down my anxiety as I regained control of my fear.

"What are you doing out here?" Thistle asked, breaking the silence first. "You better than anyone should know the dangers of sneaking around the guesthouse in the middle of the night."

"Oh, whatever," I muttered. "You're sneaking around, too."

"That's because I thought I saw something."

I stilled. "What?"

"I ... you'll laugh."

"I won't." I was being truthful. "I thought I saw something outside of my window. I ... it looked like a man."

"That's what I saw, too!" Thistle slapped my arm for emphasis. "Do you think that means someone is outside?"

"Ow ... and yes." I slapped her a second time, but only because I wanted to make sure we were even. "I thought I was imagining it. I didn't want to wake Landon and have him worry that I was losing my mind."

"He wouldn't think that," Thistle shot back. "No one would, given what happened. You're allowed to be freaked out about this. It's only your first night back. Take a pill and chill. You're making things worse by being a martyr."

I narrowed my eyes. "Have you been talking to Landon?"

"Yes, we had an enlightening conversation regarding the texture of bacon yesterday," Thistle drawled. "He told me not to tell you because he doesn't want you to think he's cheating with conversation regarding his chosen breakfast food."

I hit her again, frustrated. "You're such a pain."

"You're a bigger pain," Thistle shot back, pinching my flank for good measure. "Don't hit me again. It makes me want to punch you, and you've already had one head injury this week."

"Oh, please," I scoffed, rolling my eyes. "If you pinch me again, by the way, I'm going to kick you in your naughty bits."

"You only want to do that because you never got to kick Landon. He feels so guilty now that everyone would think you're meaner than Aunt Tillie if you gave in to your baser urges."

I tilted my head to the side, considering. "No, I really want to kick you. I think it's your attitude."

"What's wrong with my attitude?"

"It bites the big one."

"I'll have you know that people around the globe would love to have my attitude," Thistle argued. "I could win the attitude Olympics. Heck, if there was a job about having attitude, I could totally do it and be the highest paid person ever."

"Yes, you could totally do it professionally," I deadpanned. "You get more and more like Aunt Tillie every single day. You know that, right?"

Thistle's mouth dropped open. "That's the meanest thing you've ever said to me."

"You'll live."

We both jerked our shoulders at the sound of another door opening. For a wild second I thought someone was entering through the front door. I stared in that direction even though nothing moved. It took me a moment to realize it was Clove's door that opened. The expression on her face when she found us standing in the middle of the living room was almost comical.

"I think I saw someone through the window," Clove hissed. "I'm pretty sure it's the murderer."

"You're so dramatic," Thistle scoffed. "You probably imagined it."

I cast her a sidelong look, incredulous. "That's why we're out here."

"Yes, but we're not prone to histrionics," Thistle pointed out. "She is. She probably thinks it's Bigfoot. She's now convinced he's hanging around behind the library. Did I tell you that?"

"I do not," Clove snapped, adopting a whiny tone. "I simply said that there was a small chance that Viola isn't crazy. That's not the same thing at all."

"It's close enough."

I rubbed my chin and glanced between faces. "I think we can rule Bigfoot out tonight. Can we table that discussion until next week or something? What should we do about the guy outside?"

"I think we should wake Landon," Clove answered promptly.

"I think we should look ourselves so we don't come across as idiots first," Thistle replied.

"What do you think, Bay?" Clove's dark eyes were expectant as they locked with mine.

"I . . . ."

"She's caught in the middle," Thistle supplied. "She doesn't want to look like a kvetch, but she's genuinely scared."

Those were fighting words in the Winchester household. "I am not a kvetch."

"Sucks to be looked at that way, doesn't it?" Clove muttered.

I ignored her. "I think we should look for ourselves."

"Great." Thistle beamed as she squared her shoulders. "What door do you want to use?"

She said the words in the form of a dare. I knew exactly what she was doing, yet I couldn't back down. "The back one," I answered automatically. "It's darker back there, and we can find immediate cover in the bushes if someone attacks."

"Awesome." Thistle swished her hips as she strode in that direction. Clove's stride was decidedly heavier.

"I think this is a terrible idea, for the record," Clove whispered. "We have three men sleeping in this house. We should wake them and send them outside."

"Oh, that's just pathetic," Thistle complained. "Every Winchester woman ever born is standing up in her grave and screaming because that was the lamest thing ever."

Clove's mouth dropped open as she shifted her eyes to me. "Tell her to take it back."

"I would . . . but she's not wrong." I moved past Thistle and grabbed the door handle, staring for a long moment.

"I still think we should get the guys," Clove volunteered.

Thistle, perhaps sensing my worry, took me by surprise and nodded. "We'll get the guys. We don't need to do this ourselves."

When I considered that option, I knew it was the smartest way to go. The Winchester women aren't cautious, though. They were never cautious.

"We'll just look," I said, keeping my voice low. "Once we see no one is out there, we'll be fine. If we see something, we'll scream."

Thistle stared at me a moment, her expression unreadable. "Okay," she said finally. "We'll do it. We'll open the door, give it a good look, and then come right back inside. I think all of us are letting our imaginations run wild."

"I don't," Clove countered. "I think we should wake Landon."

Thistle and I ignored her.

"Let's do this." I inhaled heavily and then breathed out through my nose, sucking in another big breath before throwing open the door. Thistle and I jumped through the opening, prepared to act in case someone attacked. Clove loitered a bit behind. I knew she would scream if we were attacked. This was about me, not her, after all.

"Anything?" Thistle asked nervously.

I shook my head. "I don't see ... no."

"There!" Thistle yelled loud enough to cause Clove to take a step back and slam into the doorframe. She screamed without catching a glimpse of what Thistle indicated, and I knew the guys would be joining us soon. I pushed that out of my mind as I followed Thistle's finger. Sure enough, a dark shadow detached from the trees and began running.

"What should we do?" Clove asked, regaining her composure, though only marginally. "Should we run and hide? Maybe we should get a truck and run him over."

"Or maybe we can do this," Thistle said, grabbing a shovel from beside the house. Someone had left it there, resting against the siding, and Thistle heaved it with everything she had in the direction of the fleeing figure. It moved faster and farther than it should've, as if propelled by more than Thistle's attitude and fury.

Something made a noise in the woods and I was certain the shovel made contact. I couldn't help but be impressed. "That was a nice shot."

"Thank you." Thistle puffed out her chest as Landon, Marcus and Sam barreled through the back door.

"What is it?" Sam asked, breathless.

"Thistle and Bay made me come outside," Clove automatically answered. "It wasn't my idea."

Thistle made a disgusted sound in the back of her throat. "You wimp."

Landon ignored the burgeoning argument. "Did you see anything?"

"Over there." I pointed toward the thick trees. "We saw someone run, and then Thistle threw a shovel at him. At least I think it was a him. It was really too dark to tell."

"Did she hit him?"

I nodded. "I heard someone groan."

"Stay here." Landon moved in the direction of the trees. He was halfway there before I realized he wasn't armed.

"Wait ... ." My voice wasn't loud enough to carry, but Landon was already at the site, his sharp eyes searching the area. After a few minutes, he returned to us.

"If someone was there they're not any longer," he said. "The shovel is definitely there. I don't want to tramp all over the area until morning because I won't be able to see anything until it's light out and I might accidentally ruin evidence."

"Do you believe me?"

Landon nodded without hesitation. "I do. I believe someone was out here."

"Oh, well, good."

"Yes, good." Landon didn't sound happy. "Now we're going to discuss what possessed the three of you to come out here without waking us."

"I told you." Clove was full of herself as she crossed her arms over her chest. "Now we're going to get yelled at, and it's your fault."

"He's not going to yell," I said.

"Oh, I'm going to yell." Landon's expression was grim. "You are in so much trouble they're going to have to invent another word for trouble."

Uh-oh. That didn't sound good. Although, it did remind me of how he usually sounded when we found danger.

"Okay, but I'm going to want hot chocolate before you start yelling," I said. "I'm cold and it's wet out here."

"Fine." Landon pressed his hand to the small of my back to prod me inside. "No marshmallows, though. You're being punished."

TWENTY-THREE

"Get up."

As far as wakeup calls go, it was pretty much the worst I'd faced in quite some time. I opened one eye and stared at Landon as he leaned over me.

"If you want to do it, go ahead," I said, moving my hands so they rested on either side of me. "You have to do all of the work, though. Also, I'm too tired to strip, so you'll have to do that, too."

Landon's expression waffled between amused and annoyed. "Yeah, if that's what I wanted I would already have you begging."

I snorted. "I don't beg."

"I could make you."

"You have a mighty high opinion of yourself."

"I have one of you, too." Landon wrapped his hand around my wrist and tugged me to a sitting position. "You need to get dressed."

That was the exact opposite of what I thought he had in mind. "I thought you were going to romance me." That sounded a lot less whiny in my head, but it was too late to adjust my tone. "Are you punishing me because of what happened last night?"

Landon didn't immediately answer, instead cocking an eyebrow.

He licked his lips and made a sound I couldn't identify before finally speaking. "Do you think you deserve punishment?"

That was an interesting question. "Are you going to punish me with kisses?"

Landon's lips curved before he remembered we were in the middle of a serious conversation. "I might do that later. As for the rest ... I believe we discussed that last night. Do you need me to remind you of how stupid your actions were?"

That discussion lasted far longer than it should have, mostly because Thistle insisted on taking on the role of chief instigator and acting as poker to stoke the fire whenever she sensed that Landon was close to winding down. "Definitely not."

Landon flashed his world-famous grin. "I don't want you to get up because I'm determined to romance or punish you. Although, to be fair, I do have romantic plans I'm hoping to work in before the end of the day. We don't have time for that now."

"Oh, well ... ." I straightened my shoulders. "What are we doing now? I can't seem to remember making plans or anything."

"We didn't. Noah is on his way."

That was the last thing I expected. "Why?" This time I knew I sounded whiny, but I didn't care. "He's not going to trash the house again, is he?"

"He's not coming into this house." Landon was firm. "I had to tell him what you guys saw last night, though. I know it doesn't seem like it right now, but I believe the system will work for you. He needs to know, and I told him what happened. He's on his way out here to search the scene."

I pressed the heel of my hand to my forehead, dragging it upward along a slow path until it touched my hair. "The system hasn't really been helping me this week. In fact, the system and I aren't on the best of terms because the system took you away for a month. I think it's fair to say that the system and I are on a break."

Landon snorted. "I know that, sweetie. If I feel things are going south, I'll get you out of here. You have to know that."

"I do know that." I honestly did. "I guess I should get in the shower, huh? I'd hate for Agent Give-me-a-headache to see me with bedhead."

Landon pressed a kiss to my forehead. "I happen to be a big fan of the bedhead. But yes, I think you would prefer being put together when he gets here."

He wasn't wrong.

LANDON WAS ALREADY outside standing next to the spot where the shovel landed when I exited the bathroom. I caught a glimpse of him through the window as I trudged into the living room. Clove and Sam had returned to the Dandridge for breakfast and showers, but Thistle and Marcus sipped coffee in the kitchen as I passed through the room.

"Have you seen Agent Gasbag?"

Thistle snorted. "I saw him when he knocked on the door," she replied. "Landon answered it and they shook hands all prim and proper like. Instead of inviting him inside of the house to cut through to the back door, though, Landon followed him outside and they walked to the back on the east side of the house."

Hmm. That sounded like a mild power play to me. "Landon is trying to show him who's boss."

"I'm the boss," Thistle said, not missing a beat. "No one should ever forget that. I'm the boss ... the big, big boss."

"You're a pain in the butt is what you are," I shot back. "Do you think I should go out there or stay in here?"

"I guess that depends what sort of message you want to send," Thistle replied. "If you go out there you're kind of giving him the power to make you go to him. Of course, you don't want him in the house, and if you go out there you can be as mean as you want because he's got it coming."

That was an interesting way to look at it. "I think I'll go out there."

Thistle slapped a fresh mug of coffee into my hand before topping off her mug. "I think I'll go with you."

Marcus, completely silent since I joined them, arched a questioning eyebrow.

"If I'm mean to him I'll get it out of my system," Thistle explained to his unasked question. "I won't feel the need to explode all over you if I do it all over him."

Marcus offered Thistle an enthusiastic thumbs-up. "My day is already looking up."

"Just wait until I'm riding high on adrenalin and sarcasm fumes," Thistle said, kissing his cheek before following me toward the door. "Your day will be freaking outstanding then."

"Perhaps I should invite Agent Glenn to hang out more often," Marcus suggested.

Thistle narrowed her eyes in warning. "Don't ruin it."

"Have fun terrorizing the FBI agent," Marcus called out. "Wow. There's something I never thought I'd say."

"Welcome to the Winchester world." I winked for good measure before walking through the back door. I immediately glanced to the left and found Landon standing next to Noah as they discussed something near the area where I was certain Thistle managed to nail our intruder with the shovel.

"I'm not saying I don't believe you," Noah said, impatience bubbling up. "Why do you assume that I'm your enemy in this? All I'm saying is that this scenario doesn't sound likely."

"You are my enemy in all of this," Landon shot back, his cheeks flushed with color. I was fairly certain the brisk morning air didn't cause that flush.

"What's going on?" I asked, drawing two sets of eyes to me.

"Agent Glenn thinks I'm lying," Landon answered.

"I didn't say that," Noah protested. "I merely said that there's nothing here to indicate that anyone was slinking around the house last night. You said yourself that you didn't see anyone – that you couldn't tell if it was a man or a woman because you were inside – so that means that all we have to go on is the word of ... these two."

Landon's eyebrows arched. "What is that supposed to mean?"

"It means he thinks we're liars," Thistle supplied. "Keep up."

Landon's glower grew more pronounced. "Really? Do you think I didn't get that myself?"

"You asked," Thistle reminded him. "It's not my fault you're slow."

"We'll talk about this later," Landon warned.

"Now that I know your form of punishment involves withholding marshmallows from hot chocolate, somehow I think I'll survive."

"I did that for her," Landon said, jerking his thumb in my direction. "I won't do that for you."

"You really know how to suck the fun out of life, don't you?" Thistle's tone was mild, playful even, but Landon's expression told me he wasn't in the mood to play games.

"Okay, I think we're getting off on a tangent here," I said, holding my hands up as I stepped between them. "What part of the story do you have trouble with?"

"The part where you woke up in the middle of the night for no apparent reason," Noah replied. "What woke you?"

"I'm not sure," I admitted, tucking a strand of hair behind my ear. "I was down for the count, but something caused me to bolt awake."

Landon's expression was thoughtful. "Did you hear something?"

I shook my head. "I don't think so. It was storming. Maybe I sensed something, but … I'm fairly certain I didn't hear anything."

"You sensed something?" Noah didn't look convinced. "Like … magic?"

I stilled. I didn't like the way he used the word, as if it was somehow toxic or I was a huge joke. "More like my inner danger alarm either heard or registered something outside the house," I clarified. "Or maybe it was the fact that I was attacked here a few days ago and I was already edgy because I feared someone would climb through the window and try to choke me to death again."

Noah had the grace to look abashed. "I wasn't accusing you of anything."

"That's exactly what you were doing," Thistle countered. "Why would we make up the fact that we saw someone outside? What could we possibly gain from that?"

"Help in your attempt to convince law enforcement that Bay isn't a murderer," Noah answered. "You would do anything to protect her.

Fabricating a shadow in the middle of the night hardly seems like a lot of work."

"Oh, I'm so going to enjoy being mean to you," Thistle muttered, her temper flaring. "When was the last time a woman made you cry? Wait ... it doesn't matter. After today you'll have to start counting all over again."

"I'm guessing that it happened the last time he had sex with someone," I offered. "He probably stripped naked and she laughed. Before you know it ... tears."

Thistle snorted. "That makes perfect sense."

"That's not true," Noah protested. He was young and could be baited with relative ease. "I'm great in bed."

"I'm not going to believe it until I have independent confirmation – and your sister doesn't count," Thistle said. "Or your mother, for that matter."

"Don't talk about my mother!" Noah exploded, extending a finger. "My mother is a saint."

"Oh, geez." I exhaled heavily, fluttering my bangs. "What is it about boys and their mothers?"

"I guess some people simply never want to grow up," Thistle replied. "What were we talking about again?"

"The fact that Noah thinks that we're liars," I answered.

"That's not what I said," Noah barked. "There are no footprints out here. There are no broken bush branches. The only people who saw this supposed intruder all happen to be related to you. There's nothing out here but a shovel." Noah kicked the shovel for emphasis. "Does anyone want to explain why the shovel is here?"

"I threw it when I saw the shadow run for the woods," Thistle replied. "I'm pretty sure I hit him, too."

"Him?" Noah cocked an eyebrow. "Can you verify it was a man?"

"Well ... ." Thistle broke off, shifting her eyes to me. "Actually I can't. It was too dark. All I saw was movement. I threw at the movement, but ... I can't absolutely say it was a man or woman. It was dark."

"And you?" Noah turned to me.

"I can't say what it was either," I admitted. "I know it was a man in my house the other day. I don't know about last night, though."

Noah chewed his bottom lip as he nodded. "Okay, well ... there's still nothing we can do. There's no proof anyone was out here. If there were footprints or something else to go on that would be a different story. All you have here is innuendo ... and a shovel."

I wasn't expecting more from Noah, so I couldn't muster much outrage at his words. Landon was another story.

"You suck," Landon hissed, taking me by surprise with his vehemence.

I put my hand on his arm to calm him. "There's no sense getting worked up. We knew it would go this way. You had to tell him. You did. Let it go. I mean ... it's okay."

"No, it's not okay." Landon's hand was gentle as it landed on top of mine. "I've been telling you to trust in the system because it works. I've always believed that. Bu this system is rigged against you.

"Davis is so focused on getting ahead at work that he refuses to look anywhere else. And this guy ... well, this guy ... he wants you to be guilty because he was convinced last go around that you were guilty and somehow got away with it," he continued. "They're both so fixated on their own agendas that they'll never look past you."

That was hardly news. "That's not your fault."

"It feels like my fault," Landon said, his voice low. "I brought this into your life. I was supposed to keep you safe, protect you and make you happy. Instead, you were attacked, and this idiot won't even look for the guy who did it."

"If you don't stop insulting me I'm going to ... ." Noah broke off, unsure how to continue.

"What?" Landon challenged, his eyes flashing.

"He's going to tattle on you to your boss," Thistle supplied. "That's what mama's boys do."

"I'm not a mama's boy!" Noah exploded, gesturing wildly.

Instead of shrinking back in the face of his rage, Thistle smirked and drained the rest of her coffee. "I think my work here is done."

"Aunt Tillie trained you well," I said, grinning.

Noah shook his head, our repertoire serving to annoy rather than amuse. "You think you're funny, don't you?"

"Most of the time," Thistle replied. "We value comedy above all else. Er, well, actually we value sarcasm above all else. Comedy is a close second, though."

"And how about you?" Noah asked, shifting his attention to Landon. "Do you think they're funny?"

Landon shrugged. "Most of the time. I wasn't particularly thrilled when they went snooping around in the dark last night, but I got over it."

"Yes, he punished by withholding marshmallows," Thistle supplied, snickering.

Noah ignored her. "When I first started at the office I was in awe of you," he said, keeping Landon pinned in his gaze. "I wanted to be just like you because you closed every case that crossed your desk and you were diligent."

"Are you telling me this for a reason?" Landon challenged.

"I'm telling you this because my opinion of you has changed," Noah replied. "Everyone laughs behind your back now. They say you gave up your place on the fast track for a woman. I didn't believe them at first, but I've seen it with my own eyes. You've lost your focus. You picked a woman over the work."

Landon didn't appear bothered by the statement. In fact, he seemed amused. "I got the better end of that deal. You're too young to see it, perhaps too blind to what's right in front of you. Either way, I don't care.

"What I do care about is that you're making Bay miserable and you're doing it for a reason I can't quite fathom," he continued. "I'm done trying to reason with you."

"What does that mean?"

"It means that I'm done trying to reason with you," Landon repeated. "I'm going to solve this one on my own. You might not be willing to delve deeper, but I am. I won't quit until I have all of the answers."

"You're not to get involved in this investigation," Noah reminded him.

"Well, you just said it yourself, Agent Glenn," Landon said, extending his hand for me to take. "I'll do anything for my woman. That includes clearing her of murder. Now, if you don't mind, we have work to do."

Noah's mouth worked, but no sound came out.

"In case you're confused, he basically told you to get off our property," Thistle said, grinning. "By the way, he's a lot nicer than I am. I'm done trying to reason with you, too. I'm simply going to go all Aunt Tillie on your ass instead of being reasonable."

"I ... don't know what that means." Noah was clearly flustered.

"It means you should go," I called out, letting Landon lead me toward the door. "We don't need you to solve this. We never did."

TWENTY-FOUR

"So what's next?" Landon ran his tongue over his teeth as he regarded me from a stool in the kitchen twenty minutes later. I gave him a bit of time to sulk – although not a lot, because I didn't feel as if we could risk it now that Landon was essentially ready to go to war with Davis and Noah. He had drawn the line in the sand and we needed to make a plan.

"I don't know," Landon admitted, taking me by surprise. "I've never been the one going around the law before."

"Oh, it's easy," Thistle intoned, sauntering between her room and the kitchen so she could grab another mug of coffee. "I think you'll find that breaking the law is so much easier than following it."

Landon narrowed his eyes, his annoyance evident. "Thank you so much for your profound ... insight ... on the situation."

"Oh, someone is crabby." Thistle adopted a singsong voice sure to drive Landon round the witchy bend. "Do you need a hug?"

"Not from you," Landon grumbled, pulling back from the counter and focusing on me. "I'll take one from you, though."

He surprised me as he slipped his arms around my back and tugged me to him, burying his face in my freshly washed hair. He inhaled deeply and I remained still until he seemed to center himself a bit. When he pulled back his smile was in place, although it felt a bit forced.

"Better?"

Landon nodded as he straightened the part down the middle of my hair. "You always make things better."

"I'm totally going to puke," Thistle complained.

"And I'm totally going to make you eat it," Landon shot back.

Thistle and I exchanged an odd look, disgusted.

"What kind of threat is that?" I asked finally, confused. "You'll make her eat puke? That's kind of gross."

"Kind of?" Thistle cocked a confrontational eyebrow. "That's totally gross."

"You guys say you want to make each other eat dirt all of the time," Landon pointed out. "How is this different?"

"Because dirt is not vomit," I answered automatically, my stomach shifting. "And to think I was hungry before this conversation."

"You and me both," Thistle muttered.

"It's the same thing," Landon protested.

"Not even close."

Landon looked to Marcus for help. "Will you tell them it's the same thing?"

"I don't think they'll believe it." Marcus was almost always calm, and today was no different. "They're girls."

"Oh." Landon nodded, as if understanding suddenly slipped into place.

"What is that supposed to mean?" I asked. "Are you saying that we can't understand the vomit thing because we're girls?"

"Pretty much," Marcus replied, unruffled by the notion of a potential argument. "You can't understand because it's a guy thing. It's like us when you guys have your periods."

"Oh, gross." Landon's face twisted. "Don't try to help me. I'd rather be in the witchy doghouse than think about that."

I flicked Landon's ear. "You're on my list."

AMANDA M. LEE

"Gladly." Landon smacked a kiss to the corner of my mouth. "We need to make some decisions about what we're going to do."

"You found something outside," Marcus pointed out. "I saw it when you were out there with Agent Glenn. You bent to pick something up. I swear I thought you were going to show it to him, but then you changed your mind."

That was news to me. "You did?"

Landon nodded as he reached into his pocket, retrieving a scrap of fabric. It was bright white and fresh – it looked to be a boring cotton blend of some sort – but it clearly hadn't been outside for an extended period because it wasn't faded.

I touched the fabric, wrinkling my nose. "It's wet."

"It rained last night and there was dew on the ground when we went out there."

"And?"

Landon shrugged. "And I saw footprints in the area where the shovel landed. I know Noah saw them, too, although he made excuses and said I was seeing things."

"He seems mighty obsessed with the fact that you chose Bay over FBI domination," Marcus noted, making me realize he'd been listening at the back door even though he hadn't ventured outside to join us.

"Honestly? I would like to hate him for that, but all I can muster is pity," Landon admitted. "When I first joined the Bureau I felt the same way. I didn't have time for anything personal. Everything was about the job. Everything was about closing cases. That's all that mattered to me. Noah's attitude isn't exactly unheard of in law enforcement circles."

"What changed for you?" Marcus asked.

"Bay." Landon answered without hesitation. "From that first moment I saw her at the corn maze – the first corn maze – I felt … something. I'm not sure I can give a name to that initial emotion. It was probably lust, though."

"Oh, nice." Thistle wrinkled her nose. "That will make a lovely story to tell your children one day. 'Daddy took one look at Mommy and wanted to jump her bones.' Do you think they make a Hallmark card for that?"

Landon ignored the sarcasm. "What do you want me to say? I knew I wanted her the moment I saw her. Love wasn't part of that initially. That came later."

I pursed my lips, amused by his expression. "I think it came later for both of us." I grabbed his hand and gave it a reassuring squeeze. "It's okay."

"What did you feel when you first saw him?" Marcus asked, flicking his eyes to me. "I wasn't around regularly when all of that drama was going on. I was still trying to get up the courage to ask Thistle out."

"Yes, I remember that time fondly." I smirked at the memory. "Thistle kept buying animal feed even though we have no animals at The Overlook."

Thistle scorched me with a dark look. "Did you have to bring that up?"

"What happened to all of that feed?" I asked, legitimately curious. "You didn't throw it away, did you?"

"I donated it to a petting zoo in Traverse City." Thistle's smile was rueful. "I spent two hundred bucks on the stuff, so I didn't want to throw it out."

"I knew you didn't have animals, yet I never wondered for a second what you were doing with the feed," Marcus admitted. "How sappy is that?"

"Very," Landon answered. "I'm generally sappier, so I'll let it go. As for when we met, I'd have thought that Bay was terrified of me then. It's okay. She was supposed to be terrified of me."

I nodded sagely despite the fact that fear wasn't the most prominent emotion the day we met. I didn't want to cause a big scene. Thistle, of course, refused to let it go.

"She wasn't afraid of you." Thistle let loose with a derisive snort. "She said you were too hot to be a biker. She thought you were hanging around with them to up your street cred or something. She never believed you were as hardcore as the rest of them."

Landon shifted his eyes to me. "Is that true?"

"Of course not." The lie flew out of my mouth before I had a chance to consider whether or not fibbing was the best plan of action.

"She knew you were a big marshmallow from the start," Thistle added. "Of course, she probably didn't realize you were so dastardly as to punish her by withholding marshmallows at the time. That's might've changed her opinion of you had she known."

I worked hard to avert my gaze even though I felt Landon's eyes roaming over me. Finally I heaved a sigh and risked a glance in his direction. "I ... ."

Landon cut me off before I could think of something to say to ease the situation. "Were you frightened of me at all?"

I decided now was the time for honesty. "Frightened? No. I thought there was something odd about you. I thought you had the potential to be a pervert – and I was totally right. But I wasn't afraid of you. I've never been afraid of you. I'm sorry if you want me to say otherwise, but ... I believed in my heart you wouldn't hurt me, even from the beginning."

"Yeah? I never want to hurt you." Landon brushed his knuckles over my cheek. "I don't ever want you to be afraid of me. If you think I'm going to be upset because I'm not nearly as terrifying as I thought I was ... well ... I can't really find the energy to do that this morning."

"You shouldn't feel bad about that," Thistle said. "We grew up with Aunt Tillie. Nothing is terrifying once you've been in a truck with her while she's plowing snow."

"That's very true." Landon ran his hand over my back, taking on a thoughtful expression as he nursed his coffee. "Returning to the problem at hand, we are at a disadvantage because we don't have a lab and we can't question people on an official basis."

"That's never stopped me before," I argued. "I don't have the authority to question people, but I do it anyway."

"Yeah, but you can hide behind your job at The Whistler to do it," Landon countered. "You can't exactly do that now."

He was right. I knew he didn't mean it to be insulting, but it hurt all the same. "Right."

Landon was instantly contrite. "I'm sorry, sweetie. I shouldn't have said that." His face twisted as he slipped his arm around my waist. "We'll fix that, too. I promise you that. I just … we need to focus on Becky's murder first. That's our biggest priority."

"I know." I did my best to appear brave because I knew he needed that from me. "It's okay. If I never get my job back … well … it's hardly the end of the world. I can always find something else to do."

"That's not going to happen. You are getting your job back. I won't allow you to suffer for something you didn't do." Landon was adamant.

Thistle's expression was hard to read. When I locked gazes with her I lifted a shoulder and held my hands palms up. "What?"

"You're so full of crap sometimes," she replied, shaking her head. "What will you do if you don't get your job back?"

"I … ." I'd been wondering about that myself. I had no idea. "I'm sure I can find something," I hedged. "Maybe I'll open a store or something."

"Selling what?" Thistle's voice wasn't accusatory, but I still didn't like her tone. "You only know how to do one thing. You're not crafty. I guess you could do a fortuneteller shtick someplace because you can talk to ghosts, but it's not as if you can control when and where they show up. I seriously want to know what you'll do if you can't get your job back."

"I … don't know." I moved to step away from the counter, my heart rate increasing, but Landon stilled me with a hand on my hip.

"Leave her alone, Thistle," he barked. "She's been through enough, and I honestly cannot listen to you torture her … ."

Instead of backing down, Thistle squared her shoulders. "I'm not trying to torture her," she cut him off. "Believe it or not, I'm as angry about this situation as you are."

"I don't believe that's true," Landon gritted out. "You're not the cause of her unhappiness."

"Oh, geez." Thistle rolled her eyes. "You two are a great match because you both have martyr tendencies. Has anyone ever told you that?"

"You did just now," Landon replied. "What does that have to do with anything?"

"You're not responsible for this, Landon," Thistle shot back. "You're responsible for not calling when you should've called. Before this is all said and done, we'll make you pay for that, by the way. Bay was a whiny mess, and we had to pick up the pieces."

"Duly noted." A muscle worked in Landon's jaw. "I created this mess, though. You can't deny it."

"No, the bad guys created this mess," Thistle clarified. "You didn't attack Bay. You didn't hurt Bay. Er, well, you didn't hurt her physically. You know what I mean."

"I don't think you're making him feel better, Thistle," I said dryly.

"I know." Thistle rubbed her hands over her cheeks in an effort to refocus. "Landon, you didn't do this. Blaming yourself is counterproductive. We're witches. We believe in karma. You can't look back, so it's time to look forward."

"She's right." I ran my hand through Landon's silky hair, something occurring to me. "Wait a second … you won't have to cut your hair now that you're not going undercover again, are you?" I'd always found it odd that the federal government let him keep his hair that long when he wasn't on a specific investigation, but I didn't want to argue the point in case someone swooped in with a pair of scissors.

Landon chuckled as Thistle rolled her eyes.

"Is that really the thing to worry about right now?" Thistle complained.

"You once told me that you would have to make Marcus wear a wig if he ever cut his hair," I reminded her.

Marcus, ever unflappable, merely smiled. "That's good to know."

"I was joking." Thistle said the words, but they weren't very convincing.

"And I happen to like Landon's long hair and am not ready to see it go." I petted him as if he were a dog, resisting the urge to scratch behind his ears. "It's so pretty."

"The hair isn't going anywhere," Landon said. "I'm rather fond of it, too."

"I'm so relieved."

Landon poked my side. "I figure I will have to grow up and look my age eventually, but I'm not there yet. Besides, I think it makes me look terrifying."

"You're still not as terrifying as Aunt Tillie," Thistle argued.

"No one is that terrifying." Landon shifted on the stool. "I need to talk to Chief Terry to see what he has going. I'm not sure where else to look. I know you guys mentioned casting a locator spell to find Doug, but that worries me. How will we explain how we found him if we use magic?"

"You're worried that Noah will assume we're working with him if we discover his location," I mused.

"Pretty much," Landon agreed. "I don't want to give him more fuel if we can help it. Even if we had access to the lab, this scrap of fabric is common. We wouldn't be able to track it, which is why I didn't share it with Noah. He'd think we're desperate. But just because we can't use this doesn't mean we have nowhere to look."

"Where do we have to look next?" I asked, genuinely curious.

"I believe you stole a book when we visited the Bayside Bed and Breakfast," Landon reminded me. "It was in a police envelope. That must mean they gave it a special look for a reason. Perhaps we should do that, too."

"Oh." I felt like a complete and total idiot. "I forgot all about that book. I was going to look the day we got back, but that was when I lost my job."

"Which is perfectly acceptable … and you're getting your job back if I have to beat the living snot out of Brian Kelly," Landon said. "I think you should start with that book. I'll spend some time with Chief Terry so we can brainstorm. I think that's our best bet for starting the day."

"I would like to help, but I have work," Thistle said. "It's Halloween week. The town is bustling."

"That's fine." Landon crackled his knuckles. "In fact, to make things easier, I think Bay should examine the book at your store. That will keep her downtown – and out of trouble – while I'm talking to Chief Terry. We can compare notes again after that."

"The book is still at The Overlook," I reminded him. "I need to get it."

"Your mother put all of our stuff in my Explorer because she needed the room. Let's grab some breakfast over there and get going."

"You just want bacon," Thistle muttered.

Landon shrugged, unbothered. "You say that like it's a bad thing."

TWENTY-FIVE

"What is that?"

Thistle watched me open the police envelope and pull out a hardcover journal. The image on the front was of a fairy, and I had to swallow the uncouth urge to laugh because it reminded me of something a young girl rather than an adult would select.

"It's a diary," I replied, flipping the book over to look at the back before opening it.

"Get out of here." Clove shuffled closer and looked over my shoulder as I sat on the couch in the middle of Hypnotic. "Huh."

"Yup." I didn't know quite what to say about the journal either. "It's one of those journals you can buy at any bookstore … usually in the young adult section."

"Who keeps a diary as an adult?" Thistle asked, keeping one eye on the herbs she bagged while sparing regular glances for me. "Wasn't Becky a bit old for a journal?"

"I've never been the journal type, so I don't know," I said, flipping the book open. "Either way, this looks like a teenager's journal. All that's missing is a butterfly and little doodles that say 'Mrs. Justin Timberlake.'"

Thistle made a derisive sound in the back of her throat. "You're so old. No one thinks Justin Timberlake is hot now. They're all about the beaver."

"I … don't know what that means. Are you talking *Leave it to Beaver?*"

"Now you're even older in my head," Thistle shot back. "You've been spending way too much time with Aunt Tillie. She loves that show."

"Actually she much prefers *Bewitched*, but I get your meaning." I flipped a few entries in and scanned the writing. It was legible, but just barely.

"Anything good?" Clove asked after a few minutes.

"I'm not sure," I replied. "It's all … odd. She spends this entire entry talking about her sister and how much she hates the fact that their mother favors the sister and how everyone wishes she'd never been born so Rhonda could be the center of the Patterson world."

"If I had a diary I would totally complain about how much Aunt Tillie favors the two of you," Thistle pointed out. "I don't think that sounds unreasonable if it's really happening."

"It's not really happening in our case," I pointed out.

Thistle ignored me. "It's unfair. I hate being on that old woman's list."

"Yeah, but this is really juvenile," I said. "Like right here she says that the sister bought the mother an ice cream sundae from Dairy Queen and Becky goes on a three-page rant about how Rhonda is trying to steal their mother's affection and using ice cream to do it."

"Okay, that does seem like a gross freakout over nothing," Thistle conceded. "You said you didn't like her from the start. Perhaps she was mentally unbalanced."

"That's always a possibility." I flipped to another entry, secretly glad when shoppers forced Thistle and Clove to focus on their work so I could have a few private moments to peruse the diary. Before I realized what was happening, I'd finished the entire thing and closed it, resting it against my knees while I waited for the last customer to leave.

"That was kind of an odd rush," Clove said, wiping her hands on her jeans as she turned her attention to me. "Did you find anything else?"

"I found a lot of something else's but none of them make sense," I admitted. "She spends most of her time complaining about the mother and sister and how they don't get her ... how they keep telling her to get a real job, but she doesn't want a real job because selling meth is so much easier and she only has to work one day a week."

"Yes, well, values," Thistle said dryly. "You might want to consider the source before you cast aspersions on her."

"I was hardly casting aspersions."

"That's what it sounds like to me."

"Don't make me force-feed you dirt," I threatened, rolling my neck as I stared out the window. Landon had been inside the police station with Chief Terry for almost two hours now. I had to wonder what they were talking about. "I don't know what to think. I also don't understand why the police gave this journal back instead of taking it into evidence. She's very brazen when talking about the operation."

"Did she mention anything about the Doug guy?" Thistle asked.

"She did, but she wasn't very fond of him either," I replied. "She was clearly a very unhappy woman. Even though she went on these long boasts about the amount of money she was making and how little work she was putting in, it was easy to read through the lines. She was ridiculously jealous of the sister and thought that her mother favored Rhonda."

"And that upset her to the point where she was deranged?" Thistle asked, sitting next to me and snagging the journal. "That doesn't make much sense. There are days my mother prefers Clove to me, and I totally get it."

I'd been around for many of those days, and Thistle was remembering it a bit differently than me. That was neither here nor there, though. "At least you didn't lock yourself in a room and threaten to kill Clove in the bloodiest way imaginable when you were upset," I said. "Becky had several very ... um ... vivid daydreams about how she wanted to kill Rhonda."

"Do you think the sister knew?"

I had no idea. "We only saw the sister for a few minutes at the diner. Landon was going to question her, but thought better of it when we realized she had no idea her sister was dead."

"He didn't want to be the bearer of bad news?" Clove asked.

I shook my head. "He didn't want us to get in trouble for inserting ourselves in the investigation. If Davis showed up while we were questioning her – or if she let slip who told her – Landon could lose his job."

"I'm not so sure he cares about that any longer," Thistle noted, causing my stomach to roll.

"He cares about his job," I argued. "He takes a lot of pride in being a good agent and always getting to the bottom of a situation."

"I know he does, but he cares about you more, and he's very disillusioned right now," Thistle said. "Whether he wants to admit it or not, he might not have believed law enforcement was infallible but he always thought that people who took on the badge always wanted to do the right thing. His recent interaction with Davis and Agent Glenn has shown him exactly the opposite."

I wanted to argue, but I knew Thistle was correct. "He needs a win."

"Then we'll get him a win." Thistle was all business. "Other than proving that Becky What's-her-face was crazy, does that journal give you any insight into what they were doing or where Doug would've fled once he realized the cops were on to him?"

"That's the other part of the situation that I don't get," I admitted. "I can see Doug being upset because Landon fooled him and ruined his operation. I can see him wanting payback. I can even see him figuring out the basics of my relationship with Landon and going after me in retaliation. What I can't understand is how killing Becky and trying to frame me for her murder – a bad frame job at that – would possibly benefit him."

"It would've made more sense to kill you," Thistle said, her voice low.

"Don't say that!" Clove was scandalized. "That's not funny."

"I wasn't trying to be funny," Thistle countered. "The only reason

Doug would do what he did is to keep Landon distracted. Anyone who knows Landon can easily figure out that Bay is the way to get to him. Kill her and you cripple him."

"I guess I can't argue with that," Clove sniffed.

"Except if Doug killed me then Landon would only be off his game for a day or so before he swore bloody vengeance and went after him," I pointed out. "Perhaps Doug figured out Landon was undercover before we ran into each other at the corn maze. Maybe he already knew about our relationship and figured the best way to get to Landon was to put me in danger."

Thistle nodded, things coming together in her head. "If you died, then Landon would have nothing to lose. As it stands, you almost died, and that makes Landon manic. He doesn't want to be away from you. Landon won't risk you, so Doug has room to maneuver ... to do whatever it is he's trying to do."

"That's the real question, isn't it?" I gestured toward the diary on Thistle's lap. "That thing doesn't tell us anything except for the fact that Becky was unstable. It doesn't make a lot of sense for a guy moving as much product as Doug reportedly was to utilize a woman he knew was unbalanced."

"Unless there was something else in it for him," Clove finished. "So what?"

"I have no idea," I replied. "I think we'll need Chief Terry and Landon for that one. My only knowledge of drug trafficking comes from movies and television. I don't think that *Scarface* guy is going to show himself and explain things anytime soon."

"You're so old." Thistle rolled her eyes dramatically.

I ignored her, opening my mouth to say something derogatory. I didn't get the chance, because I recognized a slim figure walking across Main Street ... and she appeared to be headed in our direction. "Oh, crap!"

"What?" Thistle turned her head and stared at the woman. "Who is that?"

"Rhonda Patterson," I answered, clutching my hands together. "I don't suppose this could be a coincidence, right?"

"I sincerely doubt it." Thistle jumped to her feet, pressing the journal to her midriff. "We need to hide this. The sister might recognize it and know it was stolen."

That hadn't even occurred to me. Thistle was so much better in a crisis. "Where?"

"I … ."

Rhonda was almost to the door and Thistle knew she was out of time. For lack of anything better, she tugged out the V-neck on Clove's shirt and shoved the book inside. "Your boobs are huge. She won't notice a thing."

Clove's eyes widened. "Seriously? My boobs are square."

"Just don't let her squeeze them," Thistle ordered, hopping to her feet and edging Clove behind the couch with her hip.

"Welcome to our store!"

Rhonda was barely through the door before Clove greeted her with enough enthusiasm that I momentarily expected to find a Kardashian standing in front of a video camera. "I … okay." She looked confused. "I'm looking for Bay Winchester."

She obviously hadn't seen me yet, or at least paid attention to the woman sitting on the couch in the middle of the store. I hoped she had seen enough faces at the restaurant that she wouldn't recognize mine. That wasn't the case.

"You!" Rhonda tilted her head to the side as she looked me up and down. "You came to the diner with that hot guy – the one with the long hair who wouldn't stop falling all over himself to stick close to you. I remember, because I thought he was cute, the way he doted on you. You're Bay Winchester."

That seemed like a dangerous question to answer, but I really wasn't in a position to deny it. "I am."

"And you came to the restaurant the other day because … why?"

"Um … well … ." There was no acceptable answer to that question.

"You killed my sister." Rhonda's voice was firm. She wasn't close to tears and her anger caused the accusation to burn in the center of my chest.

"I didn't kill your sister," I countered.

"She was found dead at your home."

"That doesn't mean I killed her," I argued. "Listen, I understand you're upset. I don't blame you ... ."

"You don't blame me?" Rhonda cut me off, her voice growing louder. "That's certainly magnanimous of you. I'm so glad you don't blame me."

"No one needs the sarcasm," Thistle snapped. "It's the refuge of the weak."

Because Thistle essentially ate sarcasm for breakfast, lunch and dinner every day – and snacked on snark between meals – that was rich. Now wasn't the time to call her on that, though.

"I am not talking to you," Rhonda snapped. "Is your name Bay?"

"It could be," Thistle shot back, refusing to back down.

As if sensing that things were about to spiral out of control, Clove cleared her throat to get Rhonda's attention. She wisely remained where she was stood, arms crossed over her chest to hide the fact that she had square boobs, and forced a friendly smile. "I can't imagine what you're going through. That doesn't mean you have a right to attack Bay. She didn't kill your sister."

"Oh, really?" Rhonda tilted her head to the side. "Who should I blame? The state police said that my sister was killed at this woman's house. That she was found dead on the front walk and this woman was the only one there. Who else could it be?"

"Your sister was involved with some rough people," I interjected. "She was running meth with a group of people, including Doug Lockwood. The FBI was conducting an undercover operation, and arrested all but two of the people they were investigating the day she died."

"I ... um ... what does that have to do with Becky?"

Rhonda was either delusional or purposely obtuse. I wasn't sure which. "Becky was one of the two people who escaped arrest. Doug was the other. She was facing a long stint in prison when she ran."

Rhonda didn't look particularly surprised by the potential drug charges. That didn't mean she was ready to accept my word about anything. I guess I couldn't blame her. "So you think this Doug killed her? Why? Have the police told you anything?"

I shrugged. "I don't know that I can answer that. The police aren't sharing anything with me. Doug is still on the run. My boyfriend – the guy with me at the diner – was undercover with the group. I think there's a possibility Doug killed Becky on my property to warn Landon about going after him."

"Landon?" Rhonda's voice was barely a whisper. "My sister mentioned that name. She said ... I think she said ... maybe it was just wishful thinking, but she said that she was dating a guy named Landon."

I was fairly certain I didn't want to engage in a semantics argument with a murder victim's sister so I decided to let the bulk of that slide. "Landon was undercover. He gathered quite a bit of evidence against your sister. Doug was the mastermind."

"And Doug killed my sister?"

"I can't say that for sure," I admitted. "That's the working theory because he's missing, but we honestly don't know who killed your sister."

"According to the state police, you killed my sister," Rhonda pointed out.

"No offense, but why would I do that?"

"And how would she convince your sister – a woman she met once and only briefly – to come to our house in a different city?" Thistle challenged, her temper flaring. "Bay was attacked in her own home and woke to find your sister dead a few feet away. She's even more of a victim than your sister the meth dealer."

"And you don't find that convenient?" Rhonda challenged, ignoring Thistle's insulting tone. "Why would this Doug kill my sister and leave Bay alive?"

"He's a freaking sociopath," Thistle exploded. "Who knows why a sociopath does what he does. I can't answer that. All I can say is that my cousin didn't kill your sister. She had no reason to do it."

Rhonda wasn't ready to let it go. "Maybe she was jealous of Becky. Maybe she knew her boyfriend cared more about my sister."

"Oh, please." Thistle's face was so twisted it reminded me of the time she tried vegemite on a dare. "You said it yourself. Landon spent all his time worrying and watching Bay when they were in your restaurant. Do you honestly believe he cared about your sister? He already knew she was dead at that point."

Thistle's comment came off as cold and callous, but it was also effective.

"Don't talk about my sister that way," Rhonda gritted out. "She was a good person. She was simply … confused. She hadn't found her place in life yet."

"And now she never will," I pointed out. "It's not because of me, though. I had nothing to do with it. She got involved with the wrong people, and that came back to bite her. There's no other explanation for what happened, at least for you."

"But … ." Rhonda bit her lip. "The police said it was you. They said they were focused on you. You're saying someone else killed my sister."

"All I can say is that the police are wrong," I replied. "I'm truly sorry for your loss, but I didn't kill your sister."

"I think you should go," Clove said, her voice shaky.

Rhonda's eyebrows arched. "You're kicking me out? Your cousin is a murderer, but somehow I'm the bad element, huh?"

"Our cousin isn't a murderer." Thistle's voice took on a dangerous edge. "You're not welcome here. Nothing good can come from this interaction. You should definitely go."

"And what if I don't?"

"Then we'll call the police and have you removed," Thistle answered, not missing a beat. "I don't want to be a hardass – and that's the first time I ever said that and meant it – but you can't stay here."

Rhonda's gaze bounced from face to face. She finally heaved out a sigh. "Fine. But we're not done here. I'm going to talk to the police and make sure my sister's murder is avenged."

I never thought we were done – and when I put myself in her position I pictured myself uttering the same threat. "For what it's worth, I'm truly sorry for you and your mother," I called out.

"For what it's worth, you're a murderer and nothing you say means anything to me," Rhonda spat. "I'll see you pay for what you did to my sister."

"Okay, well, have a nice day." Clove faked a bright smile as another set of customers distractedly pushed past Rhonda and let loose with a series of excited exclamations when they saw the inside of the store.

"And please don't come again," Thistle added. "I think it's best for everyone."

"We'll just have to see about that." Rhonda turned on her heel and stalked out, pointing herself in the direction of the police station.

When Thistle turned her eyes to me, I was surprised to find them filled with mirth. "Well, that went well."

Apparently she bore witness to a different exchange. What were we supposed to do now?

TWENTY-SIX

I spent the rest of the day pacing Hypnotic, patience turning to frustration relatively quickly. I wasn't bothered by Rhonda's accusation as much as the fact that she didn't seem to have a problem believing I was a murderer when the evidence in Becky's death didn't seem to make much sense.

I didn't blame Rhonda for being upset. If something happened to Clove or Thistle I'd be all over the person I thought responsible. Of course, I would have a pint-sized mountain of terror in my back pocket – in the form of Aunt Tillie – when I launched my offensive.

Rhonda's reaction wasn't my most immediate problem. No, that award went to the fact that Landon had dropped me off at Hypnotic after breakfast, claiming he wouldn't be gone long. Now, hours later, Clove and Thistle were readying to close Hypnotic for the day and Landon still hadn't reappeared.

"You know you can go over there, right?" Thistle moved to my left and stared at the police station. "I'm sure they're simply busy and Landon figures you'll go over there when you're ready."

"He said to wait here for him. He's worried I'll be attacked again."

"It's not dark yet," Thistle pointed out. "You're only walking across the road."

She had a point. Still … . "I'll call him. The last thing I need is another meltdown after last night. He was not happy about the shovel incident."

"We're the only family in the world who can have a 'shovel incident' and no one thinks it's weird," Thistle said. "By the way, what was that shovel doing out there? It wasn't there earlier."

I shrugged. "It must belong to Aunt Tillie. She's been doing stuff that involves digging for more than a month now."

"And that doesn't concern you?" Thistle lifted a challenging eyebrow. "It's Aunt Tillie … and a shovel. What could she possibly be burying?"

"No one has gone missing as far as I can tell, so I'm not worried about her hiding a body or anything," I replied. "If Mrs. Little doesn't open her shop one day, well, then we'll have a long talk with Aunt Tillie about her shovel shenanigans."

"That would make a great book title," Clove said, giggling. "Everything is done in here. We can close up."

"We'll walk you across the road," Thistle offered. "Landon can't possibly find something to complain about if we do that. It's his fault for forgetting about you all day."

Landon could find almost anything to complain about when properly motivated, but I wasn't in the mood to debate the point. "Okay. Let's go."

The walk across Main Street was quiet, each of us lost in our own minds. Thistle and Clove didn't drop me at the door as I expected, instead following me inside. Chief Terry's secretary, a genuinely disagreeable woman who couldn't stand anyone in the Winchester family, wasn't at her desk, so I led the way through the back hallway that pointed toward Chief Terry's office. I heard the low murmur of voices right away, slowing only when I realized there was a third person in the office – and this one was female.

"I think you're full of it," Aunt Tillie barked, causing me to hold up my hand to still Thistle and Clove. We were well out of sight in the hallway and because the building was almost completely empty it wasn't difficult to make out the conversation. Aunt Tillie's voice has a tendency to carry, after all. "I'm not suggesting that we tell the state police we used a locator spell to find this guy. I'm simply saying that we can find him first and make up the facts to cover how we did it once we have him in custody."

"See, that's not generally the way law enforcement works," Landon countered. "We generally like to have facts and evidence in hand before we arrest someone."

"And that's why I hate 'The Man,'" Aunt Tillie fired back. "We know this guy did it."

"No, we don't," Chief Terry corrected, firm. "We think he did. We don't know anything. I will not risk Bay's life, her future, because we believe one thing when it could very well be someone else."

"Oh, whatever." Aunt Tillie was clearly annoyed. "Bay's life is already in danger whether you believe this guy is guilty or not. She could've been killed the other night."

"She wasn't, though." Landon's voice was so low I had trouble making it out. "Whoever attacked her – and we still don't know for sure that it was a man – wanted us to be distracted by what he or she set in motion that night. The attack on Bay was meant to pull my attention in a different direction."

"Bay said she was attacked by a man," Aunt Tillie pointed out. "I think she would know if a man or a woman grabbed her by the throat and slammed her head into a wall. We're just lucky whoever it was didn't crush her brain like a cantaloupe."

"You have such a lovely way with words," Landon muttered. "I believe that Bay was attacked by a man. I saw the bruises around her neck. Only a man would have hands big enough to leave those marks. That doesn't mean a woman wasn't there, too."

"So, we're agreed." Aunt Tillie sounded haughty. "This Doug guy is responsible. I can cast a locator spell and we'll have him in plenty of time to grab him, give him a good cavity search – which will fall under your purview, not mine – and then kill him and bury him behind the library. I don't see what the problem is."

"We're not doing any of that," Chief Terry snapped. "I don't understand why we even invited her here, Landon. She can't help us. All she's doing is forcing us further off the track."

"We have no tracks," Landon shot back. "We don't have anywhere to look. I spent the entire day here and we have nothing. No one has seen Doug. Not one sighting."

"Perhaps he ran," Chief Terry suggested. "Perhaps he attacked Bay in the manner he did because he wanted you focused on her to make sure he could make a clean getaway. He's obviously done that. He's gone."

"I would like to point out that you just agreed with me that he's guilty," Aunt Tillie interjected.

Chief Terry ignored her. "I don't like it any more than you do, Landon, but we have to consider it. We might very well never catch him."

"I can't accept that," Landon countered. "You know what that means as well as I do. That will ruin Bay's life, and I cannot live with that."

"Oh, please." I could practically see Aunt Tillie rolling her eyes. "Bay's life is hardly ruined. She's had a rough patch of it – that's for sure – but it's not ruined. She'll be perfectly fine now that she has her love monkey back."

"That's Mr. Love Monkey to you," Landon reminded her, although he didn't sound playful. "Davis and Noah are determined that she's guilty. They want to nail her so badly they can practically taste it. In Noah's case, that's a double win for him because it hurts me. Davis is merely trying to make his career. His refusal to look anywhere else is lazy, not personal. But that doesn't mean it won't hurt Bay just as badly."

"Landon is right, Tillie." Chief Terry sounded weary. "This could follow Bay forever. The innuendo alone could ruin her, although I don't think they'll allow it to get that far. At some point they're going to pull the trigger and arrest her."

"And then I'll make them pay," Aunt Tillie threatened.

"You might not be able to stop it," Landon said. "I might not be able to stop it. They could … take her … away from us."

"If you think I would allow that to happen then you don't know me at all," Aunt Tillie countered. "I will not let anyone split apart my family."

I pressed my lips together to keep from crying as Clove linked her arm with mine in a show of solidarity.

"I'm also determined to make sure it doesn't happen, but we need to move on this," Landon said. "We need to find Doug."

"Then let me cast the locator spell," Aunt Tillie pressed.

"But how will we explain how we found him?" Chief Terry countered. "We cannot come up with a feasible explanation for discovering him three states away."

"I say we find him and come up with convincing lies after the fact," Aunt Tillie argued. "You'd be surprised how easy it is to make people believe certain things. You can blame it on me and say I was the one who tipped you off. I'll testify to it in court and everything."

"Yeah, that is a terrifying prospect," Chief Terry said. "I'm not comfortable doing anything like that, so we've got to come up with a different scenario. Does anyone have any ideas that can help?"

Surprisingly, I found I had an idea. I separated from Clove and Thistle before they could mount an argument to stop me, and barely blinked as Landon and Chief Terry widened their eyes in stunned disbelief as I entered the office. "I have an idea."

"Where did you come from?" Chief Terry asked, flustered. "Were you listening?"

Aunt Tillie snorted. "Of course they were listening. I raised them. They've been in the hallway for the past five minutes."

"You knew?" Landon was furious as he stepped in my direction. "I didn't forget you Bay. We've simply been ... busy."

I fought to maintain my cool façade. "I heard. You have nothing, and you think they're going to come get me soon."

"Sweetie, I won't let them take you." Landon was serious, but I knew in my heart he wasn't omnipotent. He couldn't stop the inevitable if Davis decided to arrest me.

"You can't stop it," I said. "Our job is to make sure it doesn't happen."

"You said you had an idea," Thistle said, appearing in the doorway behind me. "What's your idea?"

"I've been looking around for Becky's ghost," I admitted, licking my lips. "I thought there was a chance she might show up because her death was so violent. I thought maybe that was the shadow I saw last night – although I obviously couldn't say that in front of Agent Glenn. I haven't seen her around, though, which means she's probably not hanging around as a ghost.

"I think we can all agree she was killed on the property – after I was knocked out, of course – so that means she probably visited the house with my attacker," I continued.

"You don't have to talk about that if you don't want to," Landon offered, grabbing my hand. "It's okay."

"I'm not afraid to talk about it. That's not really the point of what I'm saying. Becky has to know who attacked her. There's no way she doesn't know who did it. If we really want to find out who the culprit is, we need to ask her."

"Oh, ugh!" Clove slapped her hand to her forehead. "I can already tell where this is going, and I want to be the first to say that I think it's a bad idea. This always goes wrong for us."

"Oh, shut your hole," Aunt Tillie ordered, her eyes thoughtful as they locked with mine. "This is a great idea."

I balked. "You don't even know what the idea is yet."

"You want to conduct a séance," Aunt Tillie said, not missing a beat. "You want to ask Becky who killed her. I should've thought of it from the beginning, but I was distracted by other stuff."

"Yeah, speaking of that, we found your shovel behind the guesthouse last night," Thistle said. "What was it doing there?"

Aunt Tillie's eyes lit up. "Is that where I left it? Great. I couldn't remember."

"That wasn't really an answer," Thistle pointed out.

"When you ask me a question I want to answer you'll get an answer," Aunt Tillie supplied, her expression serious. "The full moon is tomorrow. We should have an easy time calling this woman's ghost to us tonight ... even if she doesn't want to come."

"Why wouldn't she want to come?" Landon asked, legitimately curious.

"Because she was there to kill me and ended up dead herself," I replied, holding up my hand when he began to shake his head. "Don't bother denying it. There's no sense. She thought she was there to kill me, but the killer set her up instead. I figured that out fairly quickly once I woke up with a clear head the following morning."

Landon clearly wasn't happy with the revelation, but he refused to give in to his baser urges and argue. "Do you think she'll talk to you?" He'd been present for a séance or two during his time with us. While he wasn't a fan of them – especially how theatrical Aunt Tillie got when she had an undead audience – from where he stood it was much safer to hold a séance than cast a locator spell.

"We can make her," Aunt Tillie said, tapping her index finger against her chin. "That's a good idea, Bay. We can definitely make this work."

"Thank you." I pressed the heel of my hand to my forehead, something else occurring to me. "We have one other problem, though."

"I'm almost afraid to ask," Chief Terry grumbled. "What's the problem?"

"Agent Glenn."

Landon worked his jaw as realization washed over him. "You think he's been watching the property, don't you?"

"I think there's a good chance he'll watch it tonight," I clarified. "We claimed to see something outside of the guesthouse last night. He doesn't believe us. He'll show up tonight to prove us wrong."

"That does sound like the little dung beetle," Landon muttered. "I'm not sure what we can do to keep him away. That's a lot of property to patrol."

"Don't worry about that," Chief Terry instructed, his expression thoughtful. "I'll take care of Davis and Glenn."

"How?"

"I'll invite them out for a drink under the guise of trying to get information," Chief Terry replied. "They won't be able to stop themselves from going because they believe they'll be able to trick me into talking. They'll be so proud of being smart enough to figure out my manipulation they won't recognize what I'm really trying to do … which is distract them."

He was probably right. Still … . "Won't that be a terrible night for you?"

Chief Terry shot me a fond smile. "It will be worth it."

"Well, that handles that problem," Landon said. "I guess that means we have the start of a plan."

"I wish we had a better plan," Chief Terry muttered.

He wasn't the only one, but we weren't in the position to overlook any plan at this point. There was no choice but to embrace it and see where the path led.

LANDON LED me to the Explorer as soon as we were done plotting. We would return to The Overlook for dinner before taking all of the laundry back to the guesthouse. Landon insisted we needed "quality time" after that. I was pretty sure that was code for canoodling on the couch – possibly naked – but there was no way I was going to argue.

"I'm sorry about all of this, Bay." He turned me away from the open door before I could climb inside and gave me a quick kiss. "I want to make all of the bad stuff go away, but I can't."

"Oh, you mean you're not the Goddess?" I smirked as I tapped the end of his nose. "It's okay. Everything will be okay. I have faith. You should, too."

"I'm supposed to be making you feel better," he reminded me.

"Yeah, well, I'm not particularly busy right now, so I don't mind picking up the extra load." I grinned as I leaned into him, resting my chin on his shoulder as I gave him a hug. "It really will be all right."

Maybe it was only because we had something to focus on for the evening, but I honestly believed that. The feeling didn't last long, though, only until my eyes landed on Brian Kelly as he shuffled in our direction.

"Oh, geez. I really do have the worst luck."

Landon jerked his head over his shoulder, instinctively pushing me behind him – as if to protect me in case someone should attack – but he let his shoulders drop when he realized who he was dealing with. "Well, I was saying not more than an hour ago that I really wanted to punch someone. I suppose he'll do."

Landon didn't lower his voice, so Brian had no problem hearing him. Instead of saying something snide, Brian merely lifted his hands in mock surrender.

"Don't shoot."

"I haven't ruled out shooting you," Landon muttered. "What are you doing here?"

"I came to discuss something with Bay."

"Yeah? Well, she doesn't want to discuss anything with you."

That wasn't entirely true, but I was mildly curious to see what Brian would do in the face of Landon's overt animosity.

"It won't take long," Brian said, cocking his head as his eyes flicked to me. The sun was almost down so the light was limited. "I have a proposition for you."

"Is this where you give me back my job because Chief Terry riled up the townspeople?" I asked.

"No, although I'd be lying if I said the outpouring of support in your favor didn't surprise me," Brian replied. "It's about the ... other thing."

"I don't know what you mean by that," I said. "What other thing?"

"You know ... the thing." Brian leaned closer and pointed at his crotch, causing me to stick my tongue between my lips to keep from laughing as I took a step back.

"Yeah, I don't want to know anything about that thing." I shook my head for emphasis, wrinkling my nose.

"If you try to show her that thing, I'll cut it off," Landon added. "Why are you even here?"

"Because I'm done," Brian replied, taking me by surprise with the way his shoulders slouched in total defeat. "I'm done with this town and I'm done with the newspaper. The people in town have made it abundantly clear that they will not advertise with The Whistler if Bay isn't editor and without advertising ... ."

"You can't keep the doors open," I finished.

"Exactly." Brian bobbed his head. "According to my grandfather's will, I don't have many options."

"You didn't have the option of firing me before I'd been convicted, but that didn't stop you," I pointed out.

"Yes, and Chief Terry has been very vocal about that." Brian made a disgusted face. "He actually hired his own lawyer to go over the will with me, point out my errors in judgment and the like. I seriously hate this town."

"And we seriously hate you," Landon said. "What is your offer?"

"I want to sell the newspaper to Bay," Brian replied without hesitation.

I swallowed hard as my knees almost gave way. "I don't have the money to buy the newspaper."

"Wait a second." Landon raised his hand. "How much do you want?"

"It doesn't matter," I hissed. "I don't have nearly enough money to buy it."

Landon ignored me. "How much?"

"I'll take twenty grand," Brian said, his voice even. "That's the bare minimum. Bay can have the newspaper free and clear for that."

Landon shifted his eyes to me, his expression unreadable. "Do you have that much?"

I shook my head. The asking price was a lot less than I expected, but it was still out of my reach. "I have fifteen grand, but that's it."

Landon rubbed his chin, his mind clearly working. Before I realized what was happening, he extended his hand and grabbed Brian's so they could shake on it. "Deal."

I widened my eyes, dumbfounded. "Wait a second … I just said I didn't have that much money."

Landon ignored my protest. "Have the paperwork drawn up. I want you out of that building by the first of the year. That gives you a little more than two months. I want that worked into the contract."

"Landon."

Landon slapped his hand over my mouth to silence me. "I will have an attorney go over the paperwork, so if you try anything funky be assured that I will go after you."

"I have no doubt," Brian said dryly, his eyes moving to me. "As for the other ... I'm assuming you need to handle that."

I shoved Landon's hand away and scorched him with a dirty look before turning my attention back to Brian. "I don't know what you're talking about."

"The green ... pimples," Brian gritted out. "They're on my junk and they appeared the day after I talked to you at the newspaper. Do you expect me to believe that's a coincidence?"

"Oh, well ... ." I rubbed my bottom lip with my thumb and pinned Landon with a look. "Aunt Tillie."

"She said she was going to start out easy and make things progressively worse." Landon's grin was so wide it clearly grated Brian. "It was probably smart of you not to drag things out further."

"You're enjoying this, aren't you?"

Landon shrugged. "I'm enjoying Bay getting what she deserves," he clarified. "We're not fixing the other thing until we have the contract validated with our attorneys, notarized and signed. Understand?"

"But ... it itches." Brian swiveled his hips to prove a point.

"Be thankful it hasn't fallen off," Landon shot back. "Get that contract to us ASAP. I don't want to see your face again until we have it."

"Fine." Brian's hateful gaze bounced between us. "Do you have any idea how much I dislike the two of you?"

"Probably a quarter of what we feel about you," Landon replied. "Get moving."

I waited until Brian was out of earshot before voicing my concerns. "I don't have the money."

"You have the money ... and the day is looking up. I can't wait for the séance tonight." He smacked a loud kiss against my lips before pulling back and giving me an odd look. "That is definitely a sentence I never thought I'd say."

Him and me both.

TWENTY-SEVEN

"So ... wait." Clove spooned a huge dollop of mashed potatoes onto her plate and pinned me with a doubtful look. "You're going to own The Whistler? How is that even possible?"

I was still trying to figure that out myself. "You'll have to ask Landon." I felt as if I was floating, a visitor in someone else's world. "I only have seventy-five percent of what Brian is asking, and I'm not sure I should purchase it at all given ... well, given a few other things."

Landon cocked an eyebrow as he mixed his corn and mashed potatoes. "What other things?"

"I ... nothing." I averted my gaze, causing Thistle to snort.

"Is this what you mentioned to us right before Landon returned from his assignment?" Clove asked. "It was during that diatribe when you were manic that he hadn't called by the third day."

If I could reach across eight people and pinch her without anyone noticing I totally would. Instead I feigned confusion. "I'm sure I have no idea what you mean."

"You're a really crappy liar," Thistle said.

I ignored her. "Can someone pass the bread?"

"You are a crappy liar," Aunt Tillie agreed, shaking her head. "I taught you much better than that. Don't you remember the time I told you to start crying when your mother accused you of stealing the tablecloth and turning it into a superhero cape? You pulled that off without the slightest hesitation, and your mother actually believed you were going through an existential crisis because you couldn't be Superman."

"I didn't believe that," Mom said, shaking her head. "I simply didn't like that tablecloth."

"I loved that tablecloth." Twila took on a far-off expression. "It had roosters and lemons on it. It was gorgeous."

"Roosters and lemons?" Landon was dubious. "I'm sorry I missed it. That doesn't change the fact that I know you're lying. I want to know what you're lying about. What are these 'other things' you're talking about?"

"It's nothing," I hedged, refusing to make eye contact.

"Oh, please." Aunt Tillie stabbed her hunk of meatloaf with a fork and lifted the entire slab to gnaw at it. "She's considering getting an apartment in Traverse City, because she doesn't want to stay in the guesthouse alone and she wants to be closer to you."

It was as if someone stuck a pin an Overlook-shaped balloon. After a sharp intake of breath everyone started talking at once.

"What? You can't do that!" Twila was beside herself. "We don't want the guesthouse empty."

"I don't think that's a good idea because you stay here for free," Marnie argued. "Why waste money if you don't have to?"

"I don't want you to move to Traverse City," Clove whined. "I hardly see you at all now that I moved. I think Thistle should move to Traverse City instead. We could use a break from one another."

"I told you before and I'll say it again, it's a terrible idea," Thistle said. "You'll be bored over there. And you don't cook. You'll go hungry."

I pressed the heel of my hand to my forehead as I leaned back in my chair. I stared at my plate, afraid to meet anyone's gaze. Then it dawned on me that the two people I expected to have the loudest reaction hadn't said a word.

I jerked my head, my gaze bouncing between Mom and Landon,

who were completely focused on each other as something unsaid passed between them.

"What's going on?" I asked.

"What? Nothing." Landon forced his attention to me. "You want to get your own apartment in Traverse City?"

"It's just something I'm considering," I replied, my cheeks burning. "This way we would be closer if you wanted to spend a few more nights together or something."

"Uh-huh." Landon's expression was impossible to gauge. "Did you ever consider moving in with me?"

I expected the question. I was hoping to be able to answer it without the rest of my family – and a few stray guests – acting as my audience. "Yes, but … I wasn't sure you would want that. I know men like their space and stuff. I didn't want you to think I was smothering you or anything."

Landon's expression remained immovable. "This was all before the most recent stuff, right?"

I nodded.

"How do you feel now?"

"Well, I feel like I want to live with you," I said, tripping over the words as I tried to find focus. "I also think this isn't the right time to talk about it."

"It isn't," Landon agreed, grabbing my hand. "I want to live with you, too."

"You do?" I couldn't hide my surprise – and relief. "Really?"

"What do you think?" Landon made a face and tapped my nose. "You drive me crazy with this stuff. Please tell me you were going to discuss this before throwing money out the window on a second place."

"I was … going to give it serious thought." I shot Aunt Tillie a warning glance. "It seems like a long time ago when we were talking about this."

"I don't doubt that, but no one is doing anything until we talk about a few things. And we can't do that until we find Doug and figure out who killed Becky," Landon said. "I swear to you that everything will be okay ... and I even have a plan ... so I want you to remain calm and focus on finding Doug and solving a murder over everything else."

"Okay." Wait ... . "You have a plan?"

"I knew I shouldn't have said that," Landon muttered, rolling his neck and glaring at the ceiling.

"What about The Whistler?" Clove pressed. "How will Bay buy it if she doesn't have enough money?"

"I have enough money to make up the difference."

I immediately started shaking my head. "I can't take your money."

"Well, you're going to," Landon said, refusing to allow me the time to mount an argument. "I'm willing to give it to you, but if you want to consider it a loan we'll talk conditions once everything is settled."

"A loan?" That sounded mildly better. "Will I have to pay you in bacon?"

Landon cracked a grin despite the serious situation. "Yes."

"I ... okay. Well, thank you. I like the idea of a loan."

"Good." Landon forked a huge mound of meatloaf into his mouth, and even though I couldn't hear through the hunk of food I was fairly sure he was mumbling something that suspiciously sounded like "freaking woman is going to drive me crazy" as he chewed.

Instead of lowering myself to the fight, I gripped his knee under the table. "I can't wait to start paying you in bacon."

Landon swallowed the food and leaned close enough so only I could hear him. "I'm going to make you wear a bacon bikini as part of the deal."

I stilled. "That doesn't sound sanitary."

"It's not real bacon. It just looks and smells like bacon."

"It smells like bacon?"

Landon nodded, excited. "It's scratch and sniff."

Hmm. That sounded interesting.

WE HEADED TOWARD the bluff right after dinner. Mom and my aunts stayed behind to take care of the guests, including to make sure they didn't wander out to the back of the property while we were engaged in a bit of mischief. Aunt Tillie was a wonder to every visitor, and sometimes they took it upon themselves to sneak around the property in an attempt to follow her. We wanted to make sure that didn't happen tonight.

Aunt Tillie immediately set about drawing lines on the ground with a can of spray paint, drawing my attention when I realized she was creating a modified pentagram. "Why are you painting a devil's snare?"

Landon followed my gaze, the question meaning nothing to him but my tone tipping him off that something was different about tonight's main event. "What's a devil's snare?"

"It's a trap," I replied. "It means she expects Becky's ghost to put up a fight."

"If you already know the answer, why did you ask the question?" Aunt Tillie challenged.

"Perhaps I merely want to be teacher's pet," I suggested. "Have you ever considered that?"

"Oh, I guess that makes you my pet chicken," Aunt Tillie replied. "Go cluck over there and help Clove light the candles."

I did as instructed, abandoning further conversation regarding the devil's snare. I knew why Aunt Tillie erected the trap. I wasn't generally keen on holding spirits against their will – it seemed a form of torture to me – but I couldn't argue with the necessity in this case.

"Okay, we're ready," Aunt Tillie said a few minutes later, giving the multitude of candles an approving look. "Let's bring this bitch back to Earth."

I flicked the ridge of Aunt Tillie's ear. "You can't call her names."

"Why not? She's dead. She can't do anything."

"It's tacky."

"Since when have I cared about that?" Aunt Tillie waved her hands, directing Thistle, Clove and me where to go. I cast a glance over my shoulder to offer Landon a reassuring smile and found him moving up behind me.

"What are you doing?"

"I'm going to be with you when you do this," Landon replied, moving his hands along the backs of my arms until his fingers linked with mine. "I want to feel it."

I widened my eyes. "Are you sure?"

"I'm sure."

I glanced at Aunt Tillie, who merely smiled.

"He won't hurt anything," Aunt Tillie said, taking her spot across the way so she faced me. "It might do him some good to feel. Just don't feel her up, Romeo. I don't want her distracted."

"I'll try to refrain," Landon said dryly. His heart thumped behind my head, the rate slightly elevated. "What happens now?"

"Shh." Aunt Tillie admonished him with a finger to her lips and pressed her eyes shut. "We call upon the power of the four corners," she intoned. "We're searching for one soul in a sea of the lost. Bring us Becky Patterson – that would be the Becky Patterson who liked to sell meth and write in a children's diary, by the way, just so there's no confusion because that's probably a common name. Bring us the dead."

Landon was quiet longer than I expected, but then he broke the silence with a whisper in my ear. "That was kind of anticlimactic. I expected chanting ... and rhyming ... and magic."

"Wait for it."

As if on cue, the candles flared brighter, the flames climbing dangerously high. The wind picked up, but it didn't affect the flames because they were bolstered by our bloodlines. Then the whispering started, drawing a white mist to the center of the pentagram, swirling faster and building to a crescendo that almost sounded like a scream.

Landon flinched behind me but never faltered. When the wind ceased and the screaming abated, a very angry spirit found herself trapped in the center of the pentagram.

"I am going to rip your throat out."

As far as opening lines go, I had to give her credit. It was fairly impressive. "Oh, well, um ... ." I wasn't sure what to say.

"We definitely need to work on your social skills," Aunt Tillie said, shaking her head. "It's tragic how bad you are at confrontation. You lived in a house with me for most of your life, for crying out loud. You need to learn to lay down the law."

"I think she does fine with confrontation," Landon countered, staring at the spot in the middle of the pentagram as if he could see what was trapped inside.

I studied his face for a long time, finally uttering the obvious question. "Can you see her?"

Landon nodded. "She's faint, but I see her."

I flicked my eyes to Aunt Tillie, dumbfounded. "Is that normal?"

Aunt Tillie shrugged, seemingly unbothered. "He's seen things before. I think he's always had the ability, but he's far too pragmatic to embrace the fantastical at times. Maybe your recent problems altered things. Maybe you're simply sharing your power with him and don't realize it."

That was an interesting thought. Of course, I had other things to worry about, especially given the fact that Becky seemed determined to test the boundaries on the devil's snare in an attempt to escape. "You can't get out," I called out. "You're not staying. We called you here to answer a few questions and then you'll go back."

Becky was haughty when she fixed me with a dark look. "And what if I don't want to answer your questions?"

"Maybe you don't have a choice," I shot back. "Maybe we'll make you answer the questions. How does that sound?"

"Like I should've killed you when I had the chance," Becky spat, her eyes firing to an evil red. Her anger was off the charts. I should've expected that. She was murderous before her traumatic death. The fact that she had been double-crossed merely made matters worse.

"I figured that was why you were there."

Landon tightened his grip on my hands, wrapping my arms around my middle – his fingers connected to mine – and keeping me close as he focused on the spirit. "I can't believe this."

"You and me both, honey."

I felt Landon's lips curve against my cheek before he focused on Becky. "When did you know?"

"That you were a Fed? Not until the day we ran into her at the corn maze," Becky replied, her anger obvious. "I was interested in you before that, but Doug warned me I might be making a mistake. He never trusted you. That day I knew he was right. I saw the way you looked at her and I knew."

Landon appeared unbothered by her words. "I figured. I wasn't expecting to see her. I couldn't stop myself from staring."

"It was the old lady who really sealed things," Becky said. "She acted strange – I mean really odd – and Doug and I both knew there was something more going on. We had a runner in the parking lot. Cyclone. I'm sure you remember him. Total idiot, but excellent driver. He followed the old lady and the blonde to Hemlock Cove."

"Stop calling me old," Aunt Tillie barked.

Becky ignored her. "It was easy to figure out what was going on once Cyclone hit town," she continued. "He asked the first person he saw about the blonde and heard an earful about witches ... and some hotel named from a movie ... and the blonde's FBI boyfriend."

"Why didn't you kill me?" Landon asked the question calmly, but it made my stomach clench. "Why go after Bay?"

"We needed you distracted," Becky replied. "It was obvious you were going to move on us. We simply didn't know when. Doug prepared everything so we could run that last day, take the product and money and leave everyone else to be arrested. The second we caught wind of the first arrest we were gone.

"We devised the plan the night we found out who you were," she continued. "We knew we would have to kill the girl. It was easy to find out where she lived. According to people in town, she spent most of her time alone while her boyfriend was away. People thought there was something strange about that.

"Our plan was to kill her as a message to you and then run," Becky said, grim. "Things didn't quite happen the way we'd planned."

"So ... what?" I asked, burrowing closer to Landon, thankful for his warmth. "You and Doug went to the guesthouse, hid inside and knocked me out when I came home. Then he turned on you?"

"I ... think so." For the first time Becky stumbled. "I'm not quite sure. Things just went black at one point. We were talking and then ... I wasn't there any longer. I was someplace else."

"I'm hoping you went to a bad place," Clove muttered.

"From where I'm standing, every place I've ever been is bad," Becky seethed. "Why have you people called me here? I didn't want to come back. I didn't want to see any of you. I'm guessing all of that crazy witch talk in town is true. That's the only thing that explains ... this."

"It's definitely true," I said. "We need to know where to find Doug. Do you have any idea where he is?"

"I obviously don't know Doug at all." Becky was bitter. I would've been, too. "Our plan was to kill you and cross the Canadian border while Landon was distracted and mourning. We were going to drive north right away and disappear in the terrain up there."

"Do you think Doug went without you?" Landon asked.

"I have no idea what Doug did," Becky snapped. "I don't care. I don't care about any of you!"

Her anger was palpable, but I couldn't help feeling a small tug of sympathy. "I read your diary." It was a stupid thing to say, but I wouldn't get another chance. "I saw how unhappy you were, bitter. You always seemed to blame someone else for your misfortune.

"It was always your mother's fault ... or your sister's fault ... or Doug's fault," I continued. "Why was nothing ever your fault?"

"Because I always did things the way I was supposed to do them."

"Except you didn't," I argued. "You always did the wrong thing and complained about someone calling you on it. When you juxtapose that with someone like Landon, who always tries to do the right thing and then beats himself up when the situation goes awry, I find it a bit obnoxious."

"That's easy for you to say, isn't it?" Becky sneered. "You've got your pretty boyfriend ... and your pretty house ... and your pretty life. Everything always goes right for you, doesn't it? Heck, I'll bet you're even a real blonde."

"She is," Landon confirmed, bobbing his head. "As for the rest, nobody's life is perfect. The key is picking up the pieces when your life shatters and finding a way to move on. That's what you refused to do."

"Now I'm getting philosophical advice from a Fed. How fun is that?"

Landon had clearly had enough of the snark. "If you don't have anything to share with us, this is a waste of time."

"I don't know what to tell you!" Becky bellowed. "I don't know what happened to me. My sister always told me to be careful of Doug. I never listened. I guess I should've at least once, huh? I probably wouldn't be here.

"I don't know where Doug is or what he has planned," she continued. "He didn't share anything with me. I can't help you."

"And even if you could, you wouldn't," I finished.

Becky bobbed her head. "Pretty much."

"I guess that's it, then," Thistle said, shaking her head. "We're no further along than we were this morning. We have no idea where to look."

"We could still cast the locator spell," I suggested. "In fact, I'm starting to think ... ." I trailed off at the sound of heavy footsteps approaching, shifting my eyes to the right and staring at the pathway.

"Who is that?" Thistle asked, squinting. "If it's my mother I'm going to run and hide. She keeps trying to coordinate things so we can have matching Halloween costumes. No one wants that."

She wasn't wrong. I was about to suggest a particularly embarrassing ensemble when a figure appeared at the edge of the clearing and took my breath away. It wasn't Twila. It wasn't Marcus or Sam, who remained at the inn to make sure no one escaped out the front door when Mom and my aunts weren't looking. In fact, it was the one person we didn't want catching us in the woods.

"What in the hell is going on here?" Noah asked, his face ashen. "Are you people ... doing witch stuff?"

"Uh-oh."

TWENTY-EIGHT

"Seriously, what in the hell is going on here?"

Noah looked like a man on the edge of sanity as he glanced around the clearing. His gaze didn't hover close to Becky – which told me he was unaware we'd summoned a departed soul – so that appeared to be our only bit of good news.

"Is this an orgy?"

Noah's question threw me for a loop. "Excuse me?"

"It has to be some sort of weird orgy," Noah said, his mind clearly busy as his gaze bounced between faces. "I mean … look at those two." He inclined his head in my direction and I realized Landon's fingers were still wrapped around mine. "They're clearly doing something funky."

Instead of reacting with threats and anger, Aunt Tillie merely blasted Noah with a look that would've shriveled the balls of most men, and made a clucking sound as she shook her head. "An orgy? Does this look like an orgy to you?"

"They're all over each other," Noah argued, pointing toward Landon and me. "He's feeling her up."

"He's not," Aunt Tillie shot back. "I ordered him not to do that."

"Like I would do it in front of you anyway," Landon muttered.

"Still, they're all over each other," Noah pressed. "I'm pretty sure that's against the law."

"You're an FBI agent," Thistle pointed out dryly. "Shouldn't you know what's against the law?"

Noah nodded without hesitation. "Yes, and what they're doing is against the law."

"We're on private property, you moron," Landon snapped. "Plus, we're not doing anything."

"You're ... touching her."

"I'm going to touch you with my fist," Landon muttered.

"At best you have them for public indecency," Aunt Tillie noted, adopting a pragmatic tone. "But this is private property, and we'd have to swear out a complaint. We might do that against Landon if he irritated us enough, but we would never do that to Bay. If you think what they're doing constitutes an orgy, well, you need to start watching better porn. I can get you a list if you're interested."

Noah scorched Aunt Tillie with a dour look. "You're trying to distract me. I know what you're doing."

"Oh, yeah? What are we doing?"

"I ... ." Noah broke off, glancing around the clearing with a great deal of trepidation. "You're doing something witchy," he said finally, running the idea through his head and then glomming onto it with enthusiasm. "You're doing something witchy!"

He was so excited that I had to bite the inside of my cheek to keep from laughing. Landon's chest rumbled behind me as he chuckled, amusement coursing through him.

"This is Hemlock Cove," Landon said, releasing his grip on my hands and stepping out from behind me. "Everyone does something witchy in Hemlock Cove."

"It's also almost Halloween," Clove pointed out. "If we didn't do something witchy before Halloween the tourists would not be happy."

"Yeah, but ... you're really doing something witchy." Noah glanced around, as if he expected to find confirmation among the candles. "What are you doing? Are you cursing someone?"

"If we were, we'd start out with you," Aunt Tillie replied calmly. "In

AMANDA M. LEE

fact, that's a fun idea. We should have an old-fashioned family game night and start it out by thinking up ways to curse you. The person who has the best idea wins a new car!" She bellowed the last bit as if she were Oprah, and danced around the circle, clearly enjoying herself.

"I'd suggest cursing him with boils on the butt, but he looks the type to already have those," Thistle said.

"Oh, that's gross." Clove wrinkled her nose, but kept her gaze focused on Noah. "Does that make it uncomfortable when you sit?"

"You know what's funny?" Thistle cackled. "When we were kids we used to call people 'zit face' as an insult."

"You stopped that when I started teaching you better insults," Aunt Tillie pointed out.

"Yes, but I'm talking when we were young and dumb," Thistle said. "If Agent Stick-Up-His-Butt has zits on his butt he is also a zit face. We're right back to being in fifth grade. My, how the world changes ... and yet stays the same."

"Yes, that's almost profound," Landon noted, shaking his head. "What are you even doing here, Noah? This is private property. You have no right to be wandering around."

"That's not true," Noah countered. "I can cross onto private property if I believe a crime is being committed."

"Oh, really?" Landon cocked a challenging eyebrow. "What crime do you think is being committed here?"

"He said he thought it was an orgy," Clove supplied.

"I'm not sure that's a crime," Thistle argued. "If we were doing it in the middle of Main Street, then maybe."

"We're not doing it at all," Landon pointed out. "I need to know what crime you think we were committing out here, Agent Glenn. It's going to be very important for the report I file tomorrow morning."

Noah balked, his jaw working. "You can't file a report. You have no standing on this case."

"That doesn't mean I can't file a report about my personal rights being trampled," Landon replied, his tone cold. "You just confirmed what I originally thought. I'm pretty sure you were warned to toe the line when it came to Bay. You know how I know that? Steve told me. Imagine how he'll react when I tell him you trespassed."

"Oh, yeah?" Noah's eyes flashed. "And what's going to happen when I tell him what you were doing?"

"What were we doing?" Landon challenged.

"You're ... standing in a circle," Noah replied.

"Quick, somebody call the Feds," Aunt Tillie said. "Five people are standing in a circle in the woods. It must be Armageddon. Wait ... the Feds are already here. We're saved."

Noah ignored her. "You also lit candles."

"So what?" Landon asked. "Hemlock Cove is a witch town and it's almost Halloween. I can't wait for you to explain to Steve that we were in a clearing with candles. That's not even the weirdest thing they've done out here this season."

"Yeah, at least everyone is dressed and there's no dancing or wine," Clove added.

Noah made an exasperated face. "You're trying to turn this around on me, but I know something funky is going on out here. I know it!"

Noah's meltdown was amusing, but his presence was troublesome. Chief Terry promised to handle Davis and Noah, yet there was no sign of him. If the two men separated, I could very well see Chief Terry staying with Davis because he was more dangerous. He would've called, though.

"Wait a second ... ."

Noah barreled forward as if he hadn't heard me. "You guys are probably conducting human sacrifices or something. Is that what happened to Becky Patterson? Were you going to sacrifice her and something went wrong?"

"That's the dumbest thing I've ever heard," Landon shot back, keeping his eyes averted from the center of the circle where Becky's spirit watched the interaction with unveiled interest. "Do you see anyone else here?"

"Then what are you doing?"

"I'm spending quality time with Bay," Landon replied, not missing a beat. "I believe that's that thing you find to be a waste of time."

"It is a waste of time."

"You're a waste of space," Landon seethed, clenching his fists at his side. "Now get off this property. You have no right being here."

Noah looked as if he were going to put up a fight, but instead turned and began to slink away. I stopped him by giving chase and calling out, forcing his attention back to me.

"Where is Chief Terry?"

"What?" Noah furrowed his brow. "How should I know where he is? It's not my turn to watch him."

The ball of worry sitting in the pit of my stomach shifted but didn't dissipate. "I thought he was supposed to be with you."

Landon flicked his eyes to me, his expression troubled. "What's wrong?"

"I ... don't know." I wasn't sure how to answer. I couldn't exactly explain a feeling, especially in front of Noah. "Did you see Chief Terry tonight?"

"I did," Noah confirmed, bobbing his head. "He was at the bar on the highway between Bellaire and Hemlock Cove. He invited us out. He wanted information, as if we'd share that with him."

He didn't really want information. He merely wanted to keep them busy. Still ... he would've called once Noah left, just to give us a heads up. "Where is he now?"

Noah shrugged. "He got crocked at the bar. Davis said he'd make sure he made it home. Then he suggested I come out here because you guys were probably up to something. It looks like he was right."

I shook my head as I pinned Landon with a worried gaze. "He doesn't get drunk. I can count on one hand the times he's had too much – especially in public. He wouldn't have risked it right now. I ..."

"It's okay." Landon's bland expression shifted and he tugged me closer so he could give me a hug. "I'm sure he's fine."

I didn't believe that. "We need to find him."

"Okay. We'll do that right now. I ... it's okay."

He sounded reassuring, but I didn't miss the catch in his voice. Part of him was worried, too. This wasn't like Chief Terry at all.

"**HE'S NOT** INSIDE."

Landon joined Aunt Tillie, Thistle, Clove and me as we rested against Chief Terry's vehicle in the local dive bar's parking lot. I couldn't help but wonder why he'd suggest this place to distract Davis and Noah, but then we didn't have many nearby options when it came to bars in Hemlock Cove.

"Did the bartender say anything?" Thistle asked.

"Only that Terry was here knocking back a few drinks with a state trooper and Noah," Landon replied, running his hand down the back of my head in a soothing motion. "He said that Terry seemed to be having a good time and was a little tipsy."

"Chief Terry doesn't get tipsy."

"You don't know that, Bay," Landon argued. "You're not with him every moment of every day."

"No, I'm not," I said, adopting a cold but pragmatic tone. "However, if you spent as much time with my family as he does – and you weren't getting sex out of the deal – wouldn't you find occasion to drink before this?"

Landon pinned me with an unreadable look. "Hell, I get the sex and I still need to drink. That doesn't mean that it's out of the ordinary for him to drink tonight. Maybe he just lost track of things. I seem to know a few Winchester women who have lost track of things a time or two."

He wasn't wrong. Still … . I shook my head, defiant. "Not tonight. He wouldn't have done it tonight. He was too worried."

"What was he worried about?" Noah asked, popping up on the other side of the vehicle. I almost forgot he insisted on following us. Aunt Tillie begged to curse him so his car smelled like rancid pickle farts, but Landon managed to hold her off because he didn't want Noah to have anything legitimate to complain to the boss about. That meant we couldn't do anything obvious to stop Noah from following.

"He was worried about Bay," Landon automatically answered, resting his hand on top of the cruiser's hood. It was cool to the touch when I placed my hand next to Landon's and pressed my eyes shut, as if willing a vision of Chief Terry to form in my head. "He loves Bay. She's like a daughter to him."

"We're all close with him," Thistle said, her expression dark. "He's always been extremely close with Bay, though."

"Did you have a sexual relationship?" Noah asked sagely. "That might explain why he's always so manic about you."

I didn't realize I was doing it until it was too late, but I lashed out and punched Noah with everything I had, jabbing his head back as he screeched and reached for his nose.

"What the ... ?"

"Bay!" Landon grabbed my arm and wrestled me backward, jerking me away from Noah before I could hit him a second time. "Don't! He's not worth it."

"She hit me," Noah yelled, cupping his nose. "She hit me in the face!"

"I didn't see a thing," Aunt Tillie countered, her demeanor calm.

"What?" Noah was on the verge of melting down. "She smashed her fist into my face!"

"No, she didn't," Thistle offered, shaking her head. "You accidentally ran into the side-view mirror when we were searching Chief Terry's vehicle. It was clumsy, but funny. I did my best not to laugh, because I didn't want to hurt your feelings."

"Ultimately she couldn't hold it in," Clove added. "I managed not to laugh, but just barely. I actually felt sorry for you when you smacked your head because I worried it might make you dumber."

Noah worked his jaw, dumbfounded, and then turned to Landon. "I'm going to file a report against her. She won't get away with this."

"What won't she get away with?" Landon asked blankly. "She didn't shove your head into the mirror."

Noah narrowed his eyes to dangerous slits. "This isn't over."

"I have no doubt." Landon watched him scurry across the parking lot, remaining silent until Noah slipped into his car and slammed the door. Then he turned on me with vehemence. "He could put you behind bars for that."

"You heard what he said," I protested, my eyes filling with tears.

"I did," Landon confirmed. "I wasn't going to let him get away with it. You shouldn't have hit him, though. That was my job."

Aunt Tillie snickered. "What he means to say is that he wanted to hit Agent Douchebag and you stole his thunder."

"That's not exactly what I meant," Landon clarified. "Bay ... you can't go around hitting people."

"I won't let him talk about Chief Terry like that."

"But ... ."

"No." I shook my head, firm. "Chief Terry did everything for us when we were kids. He got us a fairy house for Christmas one year, for crying out loud. He took us for walks and bought us ice cream. He was a saint."

"He really was a saint," Clove agreed. "We were rotten kids."

"I have no doubt about that." Landon looked resigned as he squeezed my shoulder. "Bay, you know as well as I do that Chief Terry is probably fine."

I didn't know that at all. "If he's fine, why isn't he answering his phone? Why did he leave his vehicle in the parking lot out here? Why did he let Noah sneak up on us even though he knew what we were doing?"

"I ... don't know," Landon admitted. "Maybe he forgot."

"Chief Terry doesn't forget," I argued. "He never forgets. Something has happened."

"What?"

"I don't know." I honestly didn't. I knew I needed to find Chief Terry more than anything, though. "We have got to find him ... and we have to do it quick." I couldn't shake the feeling that we were running on borrowed time.

Landon licked his lips, unsure. "What do you have in mind?"

I forced a smile because I thought it would make the answer go down smoother. "I'm glad you asked."

TWENTY-NINE

Landon knocked on Chief Terry's front door five times – increasing the volume each time – before casting me a sidelong look. "Do you want to show me some magic?"

I knew he was going for levity, but it hurt too much to fake a smile. It had been much easier to talk him into breaking and entering Chief Terry's home than it should've been under normal circumstances. "Move."

I shoved him out of the way, grabbing the handle and gritting out a quick spell to force open the door. The house was quiet. I didn't visit Chief Terry often at his home – almost never, actually – but it felt welcoming, homey even. It smelled like him. I could almost smell his aftershave even though it had clearly been hours since he slapped it on.

"He's not here."

"You don't know that," Landon countered, brushing past me and heading for the hallway. "He could be passed out in bed. He might not have heard us knocking."

The house, while comfortable and quaint, was empty. I could feel it. "He's not here. He hasn't been here since this morning."

I waited in the living room, my eyes drifting to a framed photograph on a shelf. Chief Terry sat in the middle of the frame, three small girls grouped around him. Two of the girls were blond, one brunette. The one sitting on his lap, the one with the biggest smile, had my eyes.

"You're right. He's not here." Landon looked grim as he joined me. We had dropped Aunt Tillie, Clove and Thistle back at the inn before heading to Chief Terry's house. Aunt Tillie claimed Chief Terry was fine and that he'd show up well before breakfast, but I read the worry on her face. She didn't believe it either.

"Is it Davis?" The question would've seemed absurd two hours ago. Trooper Davis was supposed to be a devoted public servant, after all. He was trying to climb the career ranks in the Michigan State Police. That's the assumption we'd been running on. Except … it didn't seem to fit the facts. It was starting to sink in that perhaps he merely wanted accolades so his fellow cops would never consider him as a bad guy.

"I don't know." Landon's voice was low, hollow. "I looked at his files when I found out he'd been assigned to the case. I remember thinking that he usually handled drug busts and not murders – so it was kind of odd that he was sent to your place – but I rationalized that he was given the case because Becky was part of a meth ring."

"Could he be involved?"

"He could."

"Do you think he's involved?"

"Bay, I don't know," Landon replied. "It would be easy to point a finger at him and say that he refused to look away from you because he was the one who set you up, but we don't know that. There are too many questions left unanswered."

"Like what?" I sat on the couch in front of the coffee table and snagged the frame so I could study the photograph. Chief Terry looked as happy in it as we did. I gave him the photograph as a birthday gift a very long time ago. He'd made a fuss when unwrapping it, as if it was the best gift he'd ever been given.

"If Davis is involved, that would explain how Doug and Becky were tipped off," Landon replied. "Becky didn't mention Davis, though. You would think she would've if he murdered her."

"You would think that if she was a rational person," I corrected. "She's not. She's more irrational than Aunt Tillie when someone steals her wine. That's assuming she knew Davis was a part of it. Maybe she thought Doug was the head of the operation."

"I guess that's possible." Landon sat next to me, his eyes drifting to the photograph. "Is that you?"

I nodded, tears flooding my eyes. "I gave it to him as a gift when I was eleven. He said it was the best thing he'd ever gotten, and then he took me for ice cream. I decided I didn't like my strawberry halfway through and he gave me his chocolate."

"Bay, we don't know anything has happened." Landon reached for me, but I slapped his hands away. I didn't want to be soothed. "He could be anywhere."

"No, he's in trouble. I know it. I feel it."

"Bay ... ."

"Shut up!" I exploded as I hopped to my feet, gripping the frame to my chest. Landon jolted at my volume, but remained calm otherwise. That made me feel worse. "I'm sorry." I pressed my eyes shut, hoping to stave off the tears. "That's not fair to you. It's just ... ."

"You love him," Landon finished, tilting his head to the side. "I know that. It's just ... we don't know that anything has happened to him. I don't have anyone to call to look for him. At most he's been missing two hours ... and we're never going to get everyone to agree that he's missing, because the last time he was seen was at a bar and he was apparently having a good time."

"That's not what happened."

"I know that, Bay. I don't know what to do, though. Even if we believe Davis is involved in this – and there are some holes in that theory, mind you – we still don't know where they are or what he has planned."

I sat in the quiet darkness for what felt like a long time. "If Davis is involved, how does he think he'll get away with taking Chief Terry and hurting him?" I asked. "Noah saw him with Chief Terry at the bar.

If Chief Terry turns up dead … ." I broke off on a strangled cry and Landon ignored my protests as he dragged me across the couch and pulled me tight against his chest.

"He's not dead. If Davis took him, there has to be a reason. He won't kill him."

Landon sounded certain, but I figured that was for my mental health more than anything else. "If he's involved, what's his end game?"

"I don't know." Landon pressed a kiss to my forehead. "Maybe he thinks we're on to him. That's all I can figure."

"We aren't, though. We had no suspicions regarding him until he disappeared with Chief Terry."

"No, but … we still don't know how this fits together," Landon reminded me. "We don't know if Davis is really involved. For all we know, Chief Terry really did get drunk and Davis took him to the police station."

That thought hadn't even occurred to me. "Maybe we should head there?"

Landon pulled his cell phone from his pocket instead of responding, tapping out a number and holding the phone to his hear as he gripped my hand. I listened as he questioned the individual who picked up on the other end, any hope I felt bubbling up waning quickly when he disconnected and shook his head.

"I called straight into dispatch," Landon explained. "They looked in his office to see if he slipped in when no one was paying attention. He's not there."

"Then he's in trouble."

Landon opened his mouth to argue before snapping it shut.

"He's in trouble," I repeated. "We need to find him."

"I learned a long time ago that arguing with you is a waste of time," Landon said. "You have good instincts. If you believe in your heart that Chief Terry is in trouble, then he's in trouble. How do you suggest we find him?"

I answered without a moment's hesitation. "The locator spell."

Landon cocked an eyebrow. "We're back to Doug? What if Doug isn't involved in this?"

"Doug is definitely involved in this, but I no longer think he's the mastermind," I replied. "I have no intention of conducting the spell to find Doug, though. I don't give a flying crap about Doug. I'm going to cast the spell to find Chief Terry. Whoever is with him when we find him had better watch out, because I'm not taking any prisoners. I won't let anyone hurt him."

Landon studied me for a few heartbeats before nodding. "I can see you've made up your mind. Okay. We'll do it. I hate to admit it, but ... well ... we're going to need help. You can't do this alone."

"Of course she can't." Aunt Tillie appeared in the doorway with a canvas bag and her shovel, practically taking my breath away when I saw the combat helmet and determined expression on her face. "She's going to need help. Why do you think I'm here?"

Landon shrugged. "I have no idea. I don't know what to make of any of this."

"I knew she would come to the same conclusion I did," Aunt Tillie said. "We need to cast a spell to find Terry. Lucky for you, I thought ahead. I have everything we need ... and reinforcements outside."

I leaned around Landon so I could look through the door, biting the inside of my cheek when I saw Thistle, Clove, Marcus, Sam, Mom, Marnie and Twila. "You brought everyone."

Aunt Tillie's smile was serene. "You're not the only one who loves him."

I knew that was true. Still ... . "We don't have time to waste."

"Then get off your butt," Aunt Tillie ordered. "We have a cop to save and drug dealers to bring down – which is exactly what happened on the last episode of *The Wire* I watched. I'm finally going to be the star of my own television show tonight."

That was a terrifying thought. "Let's do it."

AUNT TILLIE CONJURED the locator spell in the middle of Chief

Terry's living room, clutching the shovel close to her chest as the blue light flared to life and zipped out the front door.

We followed, Aunt Tillie climbing into the front seat of Landon's Explorer while Marcus and Thistle hopped in the back with me. Everyone else rode in Sam's vehicle, and he followed Landon closely as we drove out of town.

We'd been on the road only five minutes when I realized where we were heading. "And we're going to be right back where we started," I murmured.

Landon's eyes flicked to the rearview mirror and our gazes met in the reflection. "Did you say something?"

"We're going back to the corn maze," I replied. I didn't know how I knew, but I did. "This is where we started a year ago, too. Sure, it was a different corn maze, but we're right back at the beginning."

"At least our mothers aren't wearing tracksuits this time." Thistle rarely looked on the bright side of things, so I offered her a wan smile for the effort.

"Yeah, at least there's that."

My brain was in turmoil as I considered what we would be walking in to. Davis had to be involved. That didn't mean he was the only state trooper we might find ourselves up against, and whoever was out there was bound to be armed. Doug was also a factor. He was clearly involved the night Becky was killed. Whether that meant he intended to flee the area after the fact was anyone's guess. Whether he was still alive was another question. Perhaps Davis killed Doug and dumped his body someplace remote, hoping to use the man as a scapegoat should things go south.

That still didn't explain why Becky was killed in my yard, or why they did such a poor job of framing me for a crime I didn't commit. None of this made sense.

The blue light bobbed to the right as we crested the hill that looked over Barnaby Mill and headed toward the corn maze. I wasn't surprised when it hovered over the middle of the display. Chief Terry was here. Hopefully he was still alive. That's all that ultimately mattered.

Landon parked in the lot, casting a look over his shoulder and shaking his head as I joined him on the gravel. "There are no other vehicles here."

"Chief Terry is here," I argued. "The locator spell couldn't be bamboozled by a police officer and a drug dealer. That's not how it works."

"I'm not saying that," Landon cautioned. "I'm merely saying that this smells like a setup. Davis clearly has something up his sleeve."

"But ... how?" I protested. "How did he know we would be able to find him?"

"I'm not sure," Landon admitted, shaking his head. "Maybe he drugged Chief Terry, slipped something in his drink at the bar. Maybe whatever it was loosened his lips. Maybe Chief Terry told him about the witch stuff."

The thought hadn't even occurred to me. "No, I don't think that's it," I said after a beat. "Think about it. If someone told you that a year and a half ago, would you go to a corn maze in the middle of the night because you thought people would use magic to track you down?"

"No," Landon hedged. "I don't understand why we're here, though."

Something occurred to me. "Why were you here that day?"

"What day?"

"The day Aunt Tillie and I ran into you," I replied. "Why were you guys here that day?"

"I ... don't know what you're asking." Landon rubbed the back of his neck. "Becky had friends who worked here, and Doug said he liked corn mazes so ... ."

"So you really had no reason to be here," I finished. "That woman didn't really like Becky. No one did. She was hateful and mean to everyone around her. They needed a specific reason to be at this corn maze."

"What are you thinking?"

"I'm thinking that there's something here that they want," I replied. "Davis mentioned the corn maze in passing that one time. He said his uncle owned it."

"I … you're right." Landon licked his lips. "Holy crap! I totally forgot about that."

"Maybe they hid something in the maze," I suggested. "Maybe they didn't bring Chief Terry here because they were hoping we would follow. Maybe they brought Chief Terry here because they're grabbing something from the maze and they didn't want to leave him alone in case he decided to run."

"He might not be in any condition to run," Landon warned. "When we find him, you have to understand that … he might be hurt."

"If they've hurt him, I'll make them pay."

Something about my expression must've convinced Landon I was telling the truth, because he shuddered and grabbed my wrist. "We'll make them pay if they've hurt him. We still have to approach this logically. This is a big area to cover."

I flicked my eyes to the field before turning my full attention to Aunt Tillie. "I have an idea."

"Oh, geez," Landon muttered. "That's even more terrifying to hear coming out of your mouth than it is when Aunt Tillie says it."

"Isn't that the truth," Aunt Tillie muttered, rubbing her lower lip. "What do you have in mind?"

"Do you remember that time when we were kids and you convinced us to go mushroom hunting in the woods with you?" I asked. "You wanted morels for that sauce you liked. Mom said she would cook it, but you had to pick the mushrooms. You decided that sounded like too much work, so you cast a spell to illuminate the mushrooms and then took us on the search after dark so the mushrooms stood out."

Aunt Tillie snorted, taking on a whimsical expression. "You guys had a lot of fun that night. You thought I created a world just for you."

"We did." I enthusiastically bobbed my head. "We need light. We have a lot of people, but we need to cut off as many avenues of escape as possible. If they run we need witches in every direction to stop them. We'll have to split up. We won't get close enough to save Chief Terry as a group."

"I get what you're saying." Aunt Tillie glanced around, jerking her head back and forth. "I have just the thing."

Landon stared at her a moment, his face blank. "Why do I think this is going to be something I won't be able to explain if other law enforcement shows up?"

Aunt Tillie merely smiled. "Because I don't do anything small. Split everyone into groups. I'm coming with the two of you – don't bother arguing – but make sure everyone else has each side covered. We're about to teach some lowlifes a very rough lesson."

"Oh, well, at least I can't say you guys are ever boring," Landon muttered, striding toward the back of his vehicle. "I have two guns back here for Marcus and Sam. They might need them."

"They won't," Aunt Tillie said. "I have my shovel. Everything will be fine."

"And what's up with the shovel again?"

"You'll find out ... it's going to be glorious."

THIRTY

"Yup. I knew this was a terrible idea."

Landon rested his hands on his hips as the illuminated ghosts Aunt Tillie conjured flitted about the corn maze. She colored them with a rainbow in mind, a hundred different colored lights weaving through the stalks of the maze. The ghostly ball of light next to Landon happened to be purple and wore a solemn expression as it hovered nearby.

"I think it was a smart way to go," I countered. "If someone driving by sees them, they'll simply think it's a Halloween thing."

"I get that." Landon glared at the purple ghost as it floated closer to him. "But why is this one following me?"

"Maybe he likes you."

"It's a she," Aunt Tillie interjected, moving next to me. "I made her look like you. Can't you tell? She bats her eyelashes at him whenever he opens his mouth."

"Huh." Landon smirked as he tilted his head to the side and the apparition mimicked his actions. "She's kind of cute."

I thumped the side of his head to get his attention. "Stop hitting on the ghost."

Landon straightened. "I wasn't hitting on her."

"I'm much cuter."

"Of course you are." Landon kissed my cheek before turning to the serious situation waiting for us in the corn maze. "Odds are we have at least two armed people inside this maze. I'm armed, but ... if something happens run for safety first and run your mouths second. Do you understand?"

I automatically nodded even though I wasn't sure I could follow those instructions when it came down to it. There was no sense admitting it to Landon, because that would only lead to an argument.

Aunt Tillie refused to play, even for five minutes before we walked headlong into danger. "I'm going to run my mouth. I think you already know that. Lying about it would simply be a form of disrespect."

Landon lowered his gaze and pursed his lips. "I need to know Bay won't be hurt. I need to know that if something happens to me that you'll be there with her when she runs."

"Nothing is going to happen to you," I snapped. "I won't let it."

"I can't believe I'm saying this to you instead of Aunt Tillie, but you are not omnipotent," Landon shot back. "This is a dangerous situation, and it hasn't escaped my attention that I'm walking into this dangerous situation with my girlfriend and her great-aunt at my side. The only reason I'm doing this is that I can't figure out another way to do it, and I know you'd find a way out if I tied you up and locked you in the Explorer."

"If you try that I'll kick you in the nuts," I warned. "I was going to do it the day you came back. I won't hold back if you try to keep me out of this."

"I know that, but it's not why I want you with me," Landon said. "I need you with me because I can't do this alone. We're a team." He darted his eyes to Aunt Tillie. "All of us."

"Oh, you're a smooth talker." Aunt Tillie poked his side. "Marcus and Thistle are to the east. Marnie, Twila and Winnie are to the west. Clove and Sam are to the south. If someone runs, the ghosts will alert us to their locations. They're more than just flirty friends ... and the ones I put pumpkin heads on can scream if necessary."

Landon nodded and un-holstered his weapon. "Okay. I don't know what to expect in here. We can't leave Chief Terry. He's family, too, and as part of this family the only thing we can all agree on is that we don't leave a man … or witch … behind. So, let's go get him."

LANDON LED THE WAY, keeping his eyes focused forward as we treaded lightly through the maze. The walls were wide enough to allow us to walk three abreast, Aunt Tillie and me slightly behind Landon as he held his gun and carefully picked his way forward. By the time we got to the first fork in the pathway, an obvious question occurred to Landon and he fixed Aunt Tillie with a pointed look.

"Follow Bay."

"I said I was going first," Landon hissed.

"Not that Bay. I was talking about Ghost Bay."

As if on cue, the purple apparition floated through a wall and beckoned for Landon to follow. If I didn't know better, I'd think she was giving him a "come hither" look. "Why is she so slutty?" I asked in a normal voice before remembering where I was and lowering it. "I'm nowhere near that slutty."

"You are, but you don't see it," Aunt Tillie countered, gripping her shovel with both hands. "It's a little sad, but now isn't the time to talk about it."

"I'm not slutty."

"They say admitting it is the first step to recovery." Aunt Tillie patted my arm. "Of course, I doubt 'The Man' wants you to recover."

"You've got that right," Landon muttered. "Come on."

You might think following a purple ghost conjured by my eccentric great-aunt – a woman who was carrying a shovel to a potential gunfight – would be a nerve-wracking situation. You'd be right. However, I couldn't focus on how ludicrous the entire thing was because I could practically hear Chief Terry calling for me in my heart. He was all I could think about.

My mind brushed up against Chief Terry's. At first I thought it was my imagination. The second time I knew he was close … and alive. I

AMANDA M. LEE

couldn't read his mind or thoughts – and the experience was fleeting – but I felt him. I could barely contain my relief. "We're almost there."

"Not that I doubt you, but how do you know?" Landon asked.

"I feel him."

"Of course you do," Aunt Tillie said. "You're closest to him, after all. He's probably been thinking about you this entire time."

The thought both warmed and tortured me. "He'll be okay."

"Of course he will."

The sound of shuffling corn stalks caused Landon to lift a finger to his lips. We waited a moment … two … three … but nothing else moved. And then someone spoke.

"I know you're there. You might as well come out."

I recognized the voice right away. It was Trooper Davis.

"Stay here," Landon whispered. "I'll try to talk him down."

That was an absolutely terrible idea, and I grabbed his wrist, digging my fingernails into the soft flesh there to let him know I meant business. "I'm going with you."

"No, you're not."

"I am."

"No, you're not."

"Oh, geez." Aunt Tillie took me by surprise when she shoved between us. "Let me handle this."

"Wait!"

It was already too late. Aunt Tillie sauntered through the next opening, shovel in hand, and took a wide stance as she stared at something only she could see. Landon and I scrambled after her. Landon had his weapon pointed when he moved to Aunt Tillie's side.

I kept to the back a bit, taking in the scene and locking gazes with a dazed Chief Terry. He sat on the ground, his cheek bruised and his hands cuffed behind his back. The expression on his face when he saw me didn't reflect happiness.

"Are you crazy?"

Landon remained calm as he stared down Davis, who stood near the center of the small clearing. The figure to Davis' left wasn't who I expected to see.

"Rhonda?"

"Not who you were expecting, huh?" Rhonda shook her head as she scorched Davis with a dangerous look. "I can't believe you let this happen."

"And I can't believe you're blaming me," Davis shot back. "I didn't call and tip them off."

"You know what I can't believe?" Chief Terry bellowed, his eyes seemingly sharper now that he had something tangible to focus on. "I can't believe you brought her into the middle of something like this! What were you thinking?"

"I was thinking that I knew better than leaving her behind," Landon replied, his tone even. "I was thinking that she was going to fall apart if we didn't find you. There was no keeping her back."

"You've got that right," I muttered, narrowing my eyes at Rhonda. She didn't seem alarmed by the change in circumstances. "I guess I should've seen this coming, but … I'm still a little confused. I knew there was something off about your visit, but I never considered the fact that you weren't approaching me to talk about your sister as much as you were trying to find out if I knew what was going on out here."

"Yes, well, you're clearly not very bright," Rhonda said. "I figured that out when you checked into my mother's bed and breakfast under your own name the same night you visited the diner."

"Why do you even work at the diner if you're otherwise employed?"

"Because I know how to keep attention away from me," Rhonda replied, smoothing her hands over a dark hoodie that I couldn't help but recognize as mine. "My sister was the opposite. She told everyone who would listen what she was doing. That's why when I decided to take over the operation I knew enough to keep my old job."

"You took over the operation?" I continued asking questions as Landon and Davis stared one another down. They both had weapons pointed at each other.

"Someone had to," Rhonda explained. "You can't let the likes of

Becky and Doug have access to that much money when they have no idea what they're doing."

I rubbed my cheek, doing my best to ignore the purple ghost mimicking my actions to my right. "So Becky and Doug started – and I'm guessing they started small – and you and Davis here took over. How did that happen?"

"I listened to Doug and Becky talk about their operation and realized they were both idiots. They had no idea how big they could score if they did things right," Rhonda replied. "Of course, I couldn't let Becky know that I was her new boss. That wouldn't have gone over well."

"Yeah, I've got her diary." I bobbed my head in agreement. "She hated you. She thought you were manipulating your mother. I thought she was crazy – and she definitely wasn't what I would call sane – but maybe she wasn't as out there as I originally thought."

"No, she was flat out bonkers." Rhonda was extremely matter-of-fact. "She was uneducated, crass and watched far too much reality television. She wanted to be a Kardashian instead of the person who robbed the Kardashians blind. She never understood the strength in being the good one on the outside and only allowing the cracks to show inside. She always wanted to be the star of the show."

"Yeah, I'm starting to think you're flat out bonkers, too," I supplied. "Life is not a television show."

"No, but I've found that using television as a way to explain things to those not as intelligent as myself is far easier than taking the long route to answers," Rhonda said. "I'm all about cutting corners."

I could believe that. "So Doug and Becky started small, probably cooking themselves and selling to random customers," I mused. "Then they grew bigger, right?"

"Yes, and Becky's mouth grew bigger at the same time," Rhonda confirmed. "She liked to chat – and loudly – about how much money she was making. She didn't realize she was actually making peanuts. She was a terrible worker and never made much money. They weren't pulling in big money. I saw the potential. I simply didn't tell my sister what was going to happen, or that there was about to be a shift in the business model."

"And how do you fit in?" Landon asked Davis, remaining immobile.

"I was ahead of Rhonda in school," Davis replied. "We dated for a year before I graduated. We happened to run into each other at a function about a year ago. One thing led to another and we rekindled our romance ... and started talking."

"He jumped at the chance to take over the operation with me," Rhonda interjected. "I knew that he would. He never cared about being a police officer. He merely cared about the accolades."

"Uh-huh." Landon ran his tongue over his teeth. "You're not fooling anyone in the state police. They all say the same thing about you. You want the glory and don't want to expend the energy to earn it. By working with Rhonda you managed to arrest your competition, climb the ranks and rake in a bundle on the side. You were never going to climb as high as you wanted, but no one realized you shifted your expectations at a certain point. That was the best part of your cover. It's quite ingenious."

"Thank you." Davis was blasé. "What the heck is that thing?" He inclined his chin toward the purple ghost. "Did you bring a light show with you? By the way, how did you find us?"

"That's not important," Landon said evasively. "As for the ghosts ... um ... yes. It's a light show for The Overlook. We needed something to illuminate the area."

Chief Terry narrowed his eyes as he stared at the purple ghost leaning over his hunched form. "This one seems familiar."

"It's Bay," Aunt Tillie answered, speaking for the first time. She'd been so quiet I'd almost forgotten she was with us. "The fake her likes you as much as the real one does."

"That might make me feel better if the real one wasn't in the middle of this witch storm," Chief Terry shot back. "Get her out of here."

"She's fine." Aunt Tillie wrinkled her nose as she looked over

Rhonda's shoulder and into the darkness. "Aren't we missing a bad guy?"

"Doug," I confirmed, bobbing my head. "Where is he?"

"He fled after killing Becky," Rhonda replied. "He's the real bad guy here."

She was still hedging her bets. I could read that without hesitation. "No, Davis killed Becky," I said, things slipping into place. "He killed Doug, too. He just didn't leave Doug's body at the guesthouse. He killed Becky to serve as a distraction and then moved Doug's body so he'd make a convenient culprit if things fell apart.

"You said it yourself, Rhonda," I continued. "Doug and Becky weren't as smart as you and Trooper Davis here. You were the real team. Everyone else was expendable. You knew Landon was investigating the ring, and you knew long before we shared that uncomfortable interaction at the corn maze – a meeting I'm sure Becky and Doug got very chatty about.

"You hid all of the money and drugs before the raids – or at least as much as you could get your hands on," I continued. "Landon said the arresting officers didn't find nearly as much meth as they should have. That's because you guys took it.

"You grabbed it because Davis got wind of the arrests the night before, and you hid it out here," I said, glancing around. "I mean ... what better place, right? You could bury it out here and be fairly certain it would be safe until at least the first week in November.

"You lured Doug and Becky to my house," I said, licking my lips. "They still didn't know about Rhonda's part in all of this – which is exactly what she wanted. They thought they were going to kill me to send Landon a message. Davis knew that wouldn't work out well for him, though.

"He let Doug attack me so it would be Doug's prints on me should anything be lifted. Once I was out of it – and you made sure of that by drugging me and then faking the subsequent drug test. Then you killed Becky and Doug."

"That's pretty good." Davis said the words but his expression related anything but joy at me having figured it out.

"You took Doug's body with you when you left because you wanted to make sure you could always blame this on him," I said. "You also took my hoodie. No, I don't want it back. It's covered in skank cooties now. You didn't realize how many holes there'd be in your frame job, did you, Trooper Davis?"

"There were no holes," Davis protested.

"There were plenty of holes," Landon countered. "Bay was injured and you couldn't find anyone to agree with you that she was the guilty party. You wanted to arrest her that first day, but your boss said no because he didn't think your scenario made sense. Do you want to know how I know that? I called your boss and he told me. He wanted to give you a chance to figure things out on your own because he believed you were a good cop."

"Yes, well, that hardly matters now, does it?" Davis snapped. "We have quite the predicament here, ladies and gentleman. You know the truth, and we can't let you leave alive. You have to realize that."

"I understand that you think you can take us, but that doesn't explain why you went after Chief Terry," I pressed. "What does kidnapping him get you?"

"Time," Davis replied. "I knew Agent Michaels here would figure things out eventually. He's too devoted to you to let it go. When Davenport decided to invite us out for drinks, I knew something was up. I slipped a little something special in his drink when he wasn't looking, suggested to Agent Glenn that he was probably acting as a decoy because you all were up to something and then led the chief out to my car."

"The plan was to question him about what you knew, but the stories he told under the drug were so ... fantastical ... as to be ridiculous," Rhonda supplied. "You wouldn't believe the things he said. We definitely got the dosage wrong on that batch."

I risked a glance at Chief Terry and found him looking sheepish. "I can imagine what he said. Let me guess ... we're witches."

"How did you know that?" I thought Rhonda was about to burst out laughing. "I think he's starting to believe all of that Hemlock Cove hoopla."

"Yes, that's always a bad idea," I murmured. "What were you going to do to him once you got him out here?"

"Frame him with the drugs and run." Rhonda was blasé, which infuriated me. "We didn't need anyone to believe it for the long haul, but we did need them to believe it until we got across the border. I was going to leave your hoodie with him to focus the cops on you even harder while we escaped."

"Yes, well, that's no longer an option," Landon said. "You're going into custody with me."

"Hardly," Rhonda countered, snorting. "What makes you think we'd give ourselves over to you?"

"Yeah, we have two weapons to your one," Davis added.

Rhonda pulled a handgun from the waistband of her pants. "You might have three people, but we have two weapons and there's nothing you can do to beat us."

"That's assuming we came alone," I said, drawing Rhonda's steady gaze to me. "Do you think that's the case?"

Rhonda stared at me for a long time before nodding. "I do. I think you somehow figured out that we brought the chief here and you're determined to save him. You were with your boyfriend for obvious reasons, though I have no idea why you take your great-aunt out with you on date night."

"It's because I'm a joy to be around," Aunt Tillie said. "Bay isn't wrong about us not being alone. Of course, even if it was just the three of us we still have more power than you."

"Oh, really?" Rhonda cocked an eyebrow, amused. "How do you figure, old lady?"

"Well, for starters, the Winchesters travel as a tribe," Aunt Tillie said. "Everyone who loves Terry, who loves Bay, for that matter, is here with us."

"Where are they?" Rhonda glanced around the desolate area. "They don't appear to be running to your defense."

"No," Aunt Tillie agreed. "We needed them to cut off your avenue of escape when you run. We're ending this tonight."

Rhonda and Davis exchanged a brief look, something unsaid

passing between them. I could practically read the exchange. They didn't believe Aunt Tillie, yet they couldn't help being a bit nervous. Our sudden appearance in the corn maze couldn't be explained, and while colorful and seemingly harmless, the floating ghosts lent an eerie quality to the environment.

"You think we're going to run from you?" Rhonda asked finally. "Why would we do that?"

"Because you've underestimated us from the beginning and it's to your detriment," Aunt Tillie replied, gripping the handle of the shovel. I realized she was lifting it at the same moment Davis' movement registered in the corner of my eye. He was pointing his gun at Landon, preparing to fire.

"Landon!" I threw myself at him, knocking him to the side.

Davis' gun went off simultaneously, but things had shifted and it was as if we were stuck in a slow-motion movie moment. Aunt Tillie flung the shovel toward Rhonda and Davis as Chief Terry instinctively ducked. Landon covered my head to the best of his ability as he looked wildly about to see what was happening. That's when Aunt Tillie took control and screamed.

"Fortitudo!"

The ghosts, which had been mindlessly flittering about only seconds before, jerked to attention and swiveled in Davis and Rhonda's direction. Rhonda raised her eyes when she realized the ghosts were more than a mere light show.

"What the ... ?"

The shovel had disappeared in the night, never landing. It hovered over Rhonda and Davis' heads as the ghosts closed in, and the blade glinted in their light.

"Fortitudo!" Aunt Tillie bellowed a second time.

The shovel started spinning at the command, an unearthly wail keening as light sparked from both ends of the tool.

"What's going on?" Landon asked, blindly covering my head. "What is she doing?"

"Close your eyes," I ordered, burying my face in his neck. "The ghosts are about to handle the rest."

"But ... they're not real."

"It doesn't matter," I said. "Aunt Tillie's strength is real. That's what she's yelling ... in Latin, no less. Whatever she planned for that shovel was big, and now Davis and Rhonda are going to pay the price. Cover your eyes."

Instead of doing that, Landon tipped back my chin and pinned me with his gaze, the light blowing up to the point where it felt as if we were about to witness a nuclear detonation.

"I love you, Bay."

I smiled. "We're not going to die. I simply don't want you seeing stars when this is over. We'll have a lot of explaining to do."

"I still love you."

"I love you, too."

"Great. Everyone loves everyone," Aunt Tillie barked. "Now everyone needs to bow down to me. Oh, and cover your heads because a few things might start flying. Fortitudo!"

The light was blinding, the sound deafening. I lost sight of Chief Terry in the melee, but knew he was safe because I felt it in my heart. I pressed my eyes shut and rested my cheek on Landon's chest as he clung to me.

Then the world exploded, a hundred glowing ghosts attacking a screaming Davis and Rhonda. They never even got the chance to run.

Finally, it was done.

THIRTY-ONE

*C*leanup wasn't easy – to say the least. Landon piled everyone into Sam's vehicle the second the ghosts dissipated, giving me a swift kiss as I shifted with Aunt Tillie on my lap and uttering a brief goodbye before pounding his hand on top of the vehicle to gather Sam's attention before sending us on our way.

"What did he say?"

"You weren't here and if anyone asks, you were all at The Overlook the entire night. Do you understand?"

I nodded, confused, but Sam was already driving away before I could utter another question.

I paced the dining room until well after midnight. After I related what happened to those who missed the show in the middle of the maze, everyone said their goodnights and left me to continue my restless activity. They didn't seem worried about anything – least of all Aunt Tillie, who refused to own up to what she originally had planned for the shovel – and I could do nothing but panic as I waited for Landon to return.

Eventually I passed out on the couch in the family living quarters, my sleep uneasy. At some point I felt a body slide next to mine, an arm snake around my waist, and knew Landon had returned. I didn't rouse, though, instead falling deeper into slumber. I felt safe in the knowledge that he needed sleep and we were together. That was enough ... for now.

I woke in the same position the next morning, Landon snoring softly in my ear, and found Aunt Tillie staring at us.

"What?" I asked, keeping my voice low in an attempt to keep from disturbing Landon.

"You're in my spot."

"Yes, well, Landon is sleeping."

Aunt Tillie looked positively apoplectic. "You're in my spot and I need to make fun of the morning newscasters. That's what I always do at this time, and I don't like breaking my routine."

"Yes, but Landon is sleeping."

"Not anymore," Landon muttered, shifting so he could look over my shoulder. I couldn't see his expression, but I had a feeling I knew what I would glimpse there if I could. "You couldn't go one morning without making fun of the newscasters?"

"Apparently not," Aunt Tillie replied, shoving Landon's feet off the end of the couch so she could settle in. "Don't you have somewhere else to be?"

"You're so mean," I growled.

"That's rich coming from you after I saved the world as we know it last night," Aunt Tillie argued. "Speaking of that, what's going on with Davis and Rhonda? Are they getting the death penalty?"

"Michigan doesn't have the death penalty," Landon answered, rolling to a sitting position and bringing me along with him. "As for what they're saying ... when they regained consciousness – which took a long time, by the way – they had quite a bit to say. Davis' commander at the state police post arrived. Because they spouted a story that sounded like nonsense he didn't give it a lot of credence."

"If they keep telling the same story, though, will we get in trouble?"

"Not unless someone can prove you guys were out there," Landon replied. "Davis' commander couldn't stop laughing at the story. Steve and Noah showed up, too. For what it's worth, I had to do a little bit of creative storytelling to explain how I found Chief Terry at the corn maze. You might have to lie to cover that story, Bay."

If he thought I'd be upset about that, he was sadly mistaken. "What's the story?"

"We need to add Terry to that phone tracking app on your phone," Landon explained. "You know that one you use to track Aunt Tillie sometimes? I said you used that and I agreed to look for Terry myself because I thought you were overreacting."

"I can do that right now." I grabbed my phone from the coffee table and ignored the holes I felt Aunt Tillie's eyes burning into the side of my head.

"You track my phone?"

"Of course not," I lied. "Don't be ridiculous."

"Oh, whatever," Aunt Tillie muttered. "You're on my list."

Landon didn't bother hiding his grin as he slung an arm around my shoulders. "Rhonda and Davis are too busy pointing fingers at one another for anyone to call my story into question. Chief Terry backed me up. Steve isn't likely to believe an exploding shovel and fake ghosts saved the day."

"But ... what if he does believe it?"

"Then we'll cross that bridge when we come to it, sweetie." Landon pressed a kiss to my cheek. "It's going to be okay. Everyone is focused on Rhonda and Davis. No one is focused on you ... mostly because you've been officially cleared. In fact, Steve is insisting that Noah come to apologize in person now that you're not longer a person of interest in Becky Patterson's murder."

"That's really not necessary."

"That's what I said, but I think Steve wants to teach Noah a lesson in humility," Landon explained. "I kind of want to see how he'll handle it. He's supposed to be at the guesthouse around ten, so we can eat breakfast here before heading home."

"So ... that's it?"

Landon nodded. "That's it."

"It feels somehow anti-climactic," I admitted.

"Sweetie, we saved Terry's life last night with an exploding shovel and a bunch of fake ghosts. How can that be anti-climactic?"

That was a good question. "Two people are dead and no one cares. I don't care. They were horrible people."

"I still don't see the problem."

"The problem is that I have my life back and I have no idea what to do with it," I said. "I think part of me believed nothing would ever truly be okay again. Now, suddenly, everything is okay. What are we supposed to do?"

Landon's smile was sly. "I have a suggestion, if you're interested, of course."

"Even you can't do only that for the entire day."

Landon snorted. "Don't sell me short, but that's not what I was talking about. I have something else in mind."

"What?"

"I thought we could talk about moving in together."

His statement was so simple I was almost positive I didn't hear him correctly. "Right now?"

"Right now," Landon confirmed. "I don't want to wait any longer. I know what I want."

I swallowed hard. This was happening fast. "And you want me to move to Traverse City with you?"

Landon's headshake in the negative was like a dagger to the heart.

"Oh, you don't want to live with me."

"That's not what I said." Landon gathered my hand and stared at our interlocking fingers. "I want to move here with you."

My heart warmed at the admission – and the vulnerable expression on his face – and then I crashed back to reality. "You can't. You have to live in Traverse City."

"Not if I earned that promotion I told you about." Landon licked his lips. "I confirmed it with Steve last night ... although I guess it was technically more like early this morning. He gave me the promotion, which basically means I'm doing the same job for a little more money and special dispensation for our living arrangements."

"Really?" I thought I might cry. "You want to move here with me?"

"I want to be with you, Bay." Landon brought my hand to his mouth and kissed the knuckles. "I don't want to spend nights away from you. Not any longer. You're my match and I want to be matched with you as often as possible."

I pressed my lips together in a vain attempt to hold back the tears. "Do you want to move in to the guesthouse with me? We'll have to talk to Mom – you know, get permission – but I don't think she'll have a problem with it."

"She doesn't have a problem with it," Landon said. "I already talked to her about it. I told her I wanted to pay rent. We've agreed that the first few installments of that rent will be waved because I'm loaning you the rest of the money to buy The Whistler. And I can move in whenever I'm ready."

"I ... you already talked to her?" That explained the heavy look they shared the other day. I knew they were hiding something. "Why didn't she tell me?"

"Because I wanted to surprise you," Landon answered. "This whole thing was supposed to end with an elaborate surprise for you ... the undercover assignment, I mean. I wanted to surprise you with the promotion ... and the raise ... and the fact that we could live together. It didn't work out the way I expected, but I'm still hopeful you'll want to live with me."

"Do you honestly think I don't want that?"

"I think you've been through a lot," Landon replied. "I think that the guesthouse is going to seem crowded for a bit because my lease is up in a few weeks and Thistle won't be ready to move out for a few weeks after that."

Thistle. I couldn't help but wonder. "Does she know, too?"

"No. I thought about talking to her, but I knew she couldn't keep her mouth shut."

"I knew," Aunt Tillie said, drawing my attention to her. She looked smug.

"You did?"

"I heard Winnie talking to Twila and Marnie. Even though I heard only half the story I knew what was going on," Aunt Tillie explained.

"That's why I wanted you to slow your roll that day at the corn maze. I didn't want to tell you what he had planned, because I knew it would ruin everything."

"You knew?" Landon sounded surprised. "If you knew why I was working so hard undercover, why did you curse me?"

"Because you had it coming." Aunt Tillie wasn't ruffled by Landon's tone. "When you're undercover and you accidentally run into your girlfriend ... and you know she's upset ... you have to call her."

"I'd argue but I'm too tired." Landon pinched the bridge of his nose. "You still haven't answered my question. Do you want to live with me?"

"Are you kidding?" I threw my arms around his neck, smiling when I felt his lips brush against my forehead. "I've never wanted anything more."

"Good." Landon sucked in a steadying breath. "So, I was hoping we could get some breakfast – bacon would be good – and then head back to the guesthouse to spend the day alone. I bought one of those computer programs for interior design – the one you said Thistle and Marcus were using and you were all excited about. I thought we could decorate together."

"Seriously? That's like ... the perfect day. Can I try anything I want?"

"You can," Landon confirmed. "Or, more appropriately, we can. We just have to work around one piece of furniture."

"What piece?"

"The bookshelf I bought for you," Landon replied. "It's the one from the barn at the Barnaby place. I bought it the other day. It's due to be delivered this afternoon."

I slapped my hands to both sides of his face, giddiness overwhelming me. "How did things go from depressingly apocalyptic to perfect so fast?"

"It's called faith."

"It's called 'I'm going to puke' if you guys don't get out of here," Aunt Tillie interjected. "Good grief. I can only take so much."

I ignored her. "You've made everything perfect."

"Life isn't perfect, sweetie. As long as we're happy, though, that's all I care about. There are no happily ever afters, right? There's only the journey and the ultimate destination … and how you feel along the way. Are you happy?"

"Yes. Are you?"

"I've never been happier."

"Good." I smacked a loud kiss against his mouth. "I think this is going to be the best day ever."

"I think so, too. As long as there's bacon. We definitely need to add bacon to the mix."

I was too happy to lose my smile. "Consider it done."

Printed in Great Britain
by Amazon